The Tilted Cross

Titles in this Series

Henry Lawson: Selected Stories
Joseph Furphy: Rigby's Romance
Joseph Furphy: The Buln-Buln and the Brolga, and Other Stories
Catherine Helen Spence: Clara Morison

Cover photograph by kind permission of the *Advertiser*, Adelaide

HAL PORTER

The Tilted Cross

Introduction by

ADRIAN MITCHELL

Seal Australian Fiction
General Editor—Adrian Mitchell

RIGBY

Rigby Limited, Adelaide
Sydney, Melbourne, Brisbane, Perth
First published by Faber and Faber 1961
Published in Seal Books 1971

National Library of Australia Card Number & ISBN 0 85179 210 3
Printed in Hong Kong by Toppan Printing Co. (H.K.) Ltd

With loving gratitude to my sister and brother-in-law, Ida and Alan Rendell

INTRODUCTION

The Tilted Cross is Hal Porter's favourite among his works, a book that gave him a great deal of pleasure to write and more especially to research. "I loved the chore, and pored happily through books, prison records, Mayhew, disintegrating newspapers and pamphlets, memoirs and diaries in search of the period's most spot-on appropriate costumes, furnishings, slang, legal procedure, surgical technique, smells, background noises, vices, affectations, and so on." He found his characters in present-day Hobart and in the "still-Dickensian London underworld," and their names and idiom in records of the time. The setting of old Hobart Town was still available to him — *The Shades* was sealed off in 1950, *Cindermead* is a real house in Sandy Bay — and much of what Vaneleigh says is actually the recorded conversation of Thomas Griffith Wainewright, the endlessly fascinating forger-painter who might have murdered his sister-in-law because she had thick ankles, and whose career has caught the attention of a number of writers, Dickens, Bulwer-Lytton, Oscar Wilde, Havelock Ellis and Sacheverell Sitwell, to name a few. *The Tilted Cross*, then, is "a facsimile of reality" in intention; but despite its basis in historical fact, and despite Porter's claim to have no imagination, the novel takes on a life of its own, an imaginative vitality. The

Campbell Street chorus has all the roaring energy, the comic gusto, the bizarre and boisterous excess of, say, Smollett's low-life scenes, and if Hobart Town was not actually like this, we are led to accept for the moment that it might have been. The fusion is complete, the illusion achieved; Porter succeeds in transcending historical truth to imaginative plausibility.

But it is an odd sort of world that he creates (or re-creates, if we take him at his word). Paradoxically—and paradox is at the heart of this novel's achievement—the vitality comes from a peculiar deadness, a sort of life in limbo. A good deal of its energy is generated by inference and apposition. For example, the acid politeness of Sir Sydney and his household conceals violent passions whereas the stinking mob at the bottom end of Hobart Town display loyalties and sentimental affection, more generosity of spirit and therefore, oddly, more true civility than the cracked veneer of *Cindermead*. The various characters have the thinness of "types," they are distorted into caricatures inhabiting an unreal world, a world whose unreality is affirmed by the contrast with dimly recollected England. But so remote is the normality of Europe that the unreality and abnormality of Van Diemen's Land becomes, ironically, the new norm. Porter's ingenuity is to have contrived a situation that acknowledges the interplay of the seamy and steamy low-life with the elegancies of Regency society in a provincial outpost, to have captured their costumes and customs, their habits and mannerisms, and to have moulded all this about Wainewright/Vaneleigh, who stands enigmatic still, almost somnambulist, at the centre of the novel, abstracted and isolated from the whirling world of shadows and grotesques and brilliant surfaces that circles around him.

Judas Griffin Vaneleigh, convict no. 2325, and just given his ticket-of-leave, is a shabby gentleman who no longer commands respect in society, an artist who has once exhibited in the Royal Academy, an amateur philosopher who has lost the will to live, a broken, defeated man who knows he is dying, who acts as though he is dead since nothing within his immediate horizons interests him, whose involvement is with the dead, the past, and who survives only to be revenged upon the living. Given his physical and mental condition he is incapable of contributing much to the action. He is an inert seer, indifferent to what he prophesies because the future has no relevance, no interest. "Mr Vaneleigh, even he, like the rest of humanity, was a hunter who advanced backwards. He stumbled in the dead wind, the wind of days that have passed and will not return." He looks continually backwards, back over his life from his vantage point in death, or near death.

The action is slight and virtually independent of Vaneleigh, although his presence acts as a catalyst for the destruction. He is rather the focus of the novel's philosophical preoccupations; Queely is the focus of the novel's action. Queely dwells in the present, Vaneleigh on the past. The artist is concerned not with the physical but with the metaphysical. This division of interest is a potential weakness in the book, a weakness not altogether avoided but partly overcome by the novel's underlying theme, or more precisely the myth that supports it. It is appropriate for Vaneleigh to be divorced from the activity of the novel, to remain aloof from the vulgar pettiness, the small ambitions that inspire so much hatred and yield so much frustration. His aloofness is symptomatic of the crass world into which he finds himself released.

It has been suggested by some critics that the book is "a monstrous parody of Christian myth and morality," but such a reading is unsatisfactory because there is no point in the parody. Certainly the title is suggestive, and Queely is a kind of crucified Christ, especially as he is attended by thieves during the operation, and dying on Christmas Eve he croaks "I thirst." If he is a kind of Christ, he dies at Christmas, is not born. And twelve months previously Vaneleigh had been thrown out into the living world to get on with his dying. Heaven rejects the glorious ribaldry ascending from foul, loathsome, stinking Campbell Street —there it is a holiday, not a holy day. Vaneleigh specifically precludes it from the province of angels; angels belong elsewhere, this is a witches' coven, a moral sepulchre. Vaneleigh's Christian name is Judas, a cock crows appropriately, and Death on a pale horse gallops through the pages. Biblical allusions are scattered through the narrative, but only, it seems, to make a travesty of them. Porter makes his attitude perfectly clear:

> Sunday in Hobart Town bore its starveling resemblance to Sunday in the London which had exported to it the chimes of church bells along with the chimes of ankle-chains, the one to accompany and uplift duplicity, the other to accompany and weigh down obscenity. . . . The ugliness of nature was made, for an hour or two, very noisy with bells, and voices loudly and dolefully raised and strained to reach the ears of a Hebraic father incandescent as a blast furnace, and a son with snow-white woolly hair, brass feet and a two-edged sword in his mouth.

The point is not in the parody, the inverted Christian myth and morality, but in inversion itself.

Comparisons between London and Hobart Town recur throughout the novel, both in the narrative and the dialogue, and always the difference and distance from England is insisted on. From the very first sentence—"Van Diemen's Land, an ugly trinket suspended at the world's discredited rump, was freezing"—we are never allowed to forget that this is the antipodes, the other side of the world. Porter draws attention to the reversal of seasons, to the unfamiliar constellations, one of which provides the novel with both a title and an emblem. These are observed differences, actual, real as that classical impossibility, the black swan. But the antipodes projects more than unseasonable seasons; in this land of opposites, of botanical and zoological anomalies, human behaviour is capable of inversion or perversion too. Land and sky reject the English and their half-cultured urbanity because these things are alien, an urbanity securely established on a solid foundation of political brutality, crime, unemployment, and colonial corruption. This is historically true, and again proves actual the myth of antipodean reversal of values. It is a town of the dispossessed, a weed town grown perverse and obverse, where the West End, the Establishment residences, are southerly, and

Campbell Street—in London terms the East End—lies to the north.

What Porter does, then, is to show verifiable details of antipodeanism, and to extend the concept into the context of ideas and values. Not only are the compass directions changed about; so are the moral directions. Not only is the geographical landscape grotesque and disorderly, so is the moral landscape. Hobart Town is the moral and cultural antithesis of London, darkness to Europe's Enlightenment. In a thoroughly imaginative application of the myth, Porter convincingly represents this antipodean anti-world as the underworld, Hades, for the infernal regions best describe what colonial Hobart and the convict days were like. It is a realm of night, shades, death.

Porter has said that he culled his names from documents of the times, but there is an underlying principle that guides the selection. The most superior establishment is *Cindermead*, a mere alteration of real "Ashfield" but an appropriately dark and ominous name for the residence of the Knights. Rose is a kind of Queen of the Night, a Proserpine or Persephone. God of the underworld is Pluto, or alternatively Dis, which reversed provides us with Sir Sydney, an impotent potentate (the trick of reversed spelling also accounts for Nednil House). Teapot, we discover, is properly called Orfée. Queely's father is John Death Sheill, patron of *The Shades* taproom (consistently portrayed as hell-mouth): besides, Sheill is close to Sheol, Hebrew for Hell and a euphemism much approved by Tom Collins. If there is an underlying myth woven into the story, it is not so much Christian as the descent of Orpheus into the underworld, and if this is accepted the patterning of the novel emerges much more clearly. Orpheus is not the dominant interest, though, but the underworld itself, Hades and its "perverse, obverse" values.

Dis carried off his wife from the upper world, just as Sir Sydney brought Rose from England in his campaign for advancement (and much to her regret). He is mostly invisible, as is Sir Sydney. There is a change from the legend, however, for whereas Dis is an unfaithful husband, Lady

Rose Knight is the unfaithful wife. Orpheus, according to myth, returns to the living with Eurydice; and Teapot and Asnetha Sleep plan to return to England, to Brighton, Asnetha provided with a husband, also a cripple, called Dr Wake. Sir Sydney forces us to notice the obvious: "From Miss Sleep to Mrs Wake . . . I find a nice symbolism in the thought." Dr Wake is a figure contrived to supplement Orfée, and that is all the use he is, except that he is the surgeon who amputates Queely's leg, officiates over the ritual sacrifice that provides for lost Eurydice's return. Alternatively, he is the handsome prince who wakes the sleeping beauty—Asnetha suggests anaesthesia. And Asnetha is a monstrous caricature of Eurydice.

The allusions are as often playful as serious, yet clearly the dominant image is of the world of Hobart Town as the underworld, an extension into classical mythology of the ancient belief in the antipodes. Queely seems not to belong to this world; he is all golden beauty (until he opens his mouth), a veritable Apollo as Poli frequently testifies. His separateness is of course the means of integration: Orpheus was a follower of Dionysus, and the classical opposition is between Apollo and Dionysus. Still, it is unnecessary to force the classical connections. They are not the controlling feature of the novel, they merely provide Porter with a framework of allusions in which to explore, ironically and imaginatively, the idea of nature reversed. Poli's dance may be a dance of death, or it may be just another of the many brilliant grotesqueries in this weird, strange, charmingly sinister little town. The many images of reflection are suitable to a theme of inversion, of reversal, but they may also be accounted for quite simply as a means of emphasizing the hard superficial life of appearances at *Cindermead*. The repeated comment that Hobart Town is unseasonably and unreasonably cold, cold as the frozen wastes of hell, is at once a colourful meteorological observation and a further comment on the moral numbness of the protagonists. Van Diemen's Land is after all a suitable location, as well as a neatly punning name, for hell itself.

The antipodean theme invites almost irresistibly a satirical perspective, because it represents a topsy-turvy world, a complete inversion of normal (European) behaviour: the most celebrated example of such an adaptation is Samuel Butler's satirical novel, *Erewhon* (1872). Porter is alert to the ironic possibilities that his theme permits, but for the most part he allows them to remain implicit and prefers to exaggerate the abnormal into his comic eccentrics, his caricatures. Sheer excess of the specific itself becomes comic, the energetic piling up of precise details which is so characteristic a feature of Porter's style. (Nevertheless, it is interesting to notice Northrop Frye's prescription, in *The Anatomy of Criticism*, that satire is associated mythically with darkness, winter, dissolution, the defeat of the hero, and the return of chaos. It is unlikely that Porter would bother to read Frye, but he intuitively seizes on just these details to develop his central pattern of significance.)

Still, one comes back to the enigmatic figure of Judas Griffin Vaneleigh, with his cat twining itself about his ankles. Remote from the punctual world and aloof from the gallery of grotesques, Vaneleigh provides the norm in this abnormal world, and his dreaming and thoughts complement the synthetic world Porter weaves around him. Time, like the cat, coils and uncoils endlessly about itself until, with the closing of the door—and with the closing of hell-mouth door on Poli and Mr Sheill—"No human being moved on the slope of Campbell Street for that moment, that night, that summer, that year." The richness of *The Tilted Cross* is such that any one reading leads progressively on to another. It is an endlessly inviting book because endlessly fascinating.

University of Adelaide — ADRIAN MITCHELL
December, 1970

INTRODUCTORY NOTE

It will be obvious to informed readers that the character Judas Griffin Vaneleigh almost duplicates the infamous and inscrutable Thomas Griffiths Wainewright. Wainewright actually did what Vaneleigh does novelistically, in a similar manner and the same places: 49 Great Marlborough Street, Howland Street, 8 Campbell Street, Hobart Town. In the novel the dying Vaneleigh enters St. Mary's Hospital where Wainewright died of a cerebral aneurism on Sunday, 17th August 1847. This building still stands; the Rivulet still runs under the Palladio; even the remains of *The Shades*, sealed off in 1950 beneath the renovated Theatre, still exist.

Moreover, 99 per cent of the sentiments uttered by Vaneleigh, and the thoughts and actions attributed to him, are lifted directly from Wainewright.

Why not, then, simply call the character Thomas Griffiths Wainewright?

Because, just as Dickens, W. Carew Hazlitt, Bulwer-Lytton, Oscar Wilde and other fascinated writers on Wainewright drew conclusions lacking downright ratification, so I too have drawn one proofless conclusion. Albeit on instinct, I deliberately smudged one fact. The character, therefore, for all its detailed resemblance to Wainewright, crosses the line into fiction, and so—properly—bears the fictional name of Judas Griffin Vaneleigh.

H.P.

1

Van Diemen's Land, an ugly trinket suspended at the world's discredited rump, was freezing. From horizon to horizon stretched a tarpaulin of congealed vapour so tense that it had now and then split, and had rattled down a vicious litter of sleet like minced glass, that year, that winter, that day.

That year, that winter, that day, the terraces and cucumber frames and summer-house and stables and attic gables of *Cindermead* were also freezing. The pump had been frozen until ten o'clock; the peacocks skulked, and squawked imperial displeasure, in the barn; the gardener, as he hacked at metal clods, swore vilely as an earl. Elegance had no more been denied the icy scourgings and crystal grits from Organ-pipe Mountain than the gibbet staked in the heart of Hobart Town, than the gaols, the dolly-shops, the limekilns, the brickfield, the orphan school and the Jews' burial ground. At noon the sleeting had stopped.

Ladders and gallows and crucifixes of fused snow slanted up the precipices of Organ-pipe and the steeps of Knocklofty to the skylights of a firmament lacking angels to cosset anything or manna to sustain anyone. Land and sky alike seemed repelled by the English and the half-cultured urbanity they had securely established on a solid foundation of political brutality, crime, unemployment and colonial corruption.

On the mountain wall vast snow cameos pointed their profiles unseeingly east and west away from Hobart Town glued on the foothills below. It was a forty-year-old town smelling still of raw planks and sawdust and new guile.

Napping hammers and the rasp of trowels sounded among boulders like loaves rolled from above in derision of the hungry. It was a town of the dispossessed; half its creatures criminal, half its creatures lower class or lower middle class. It was the privy of London; it was indeed, a miniature and foundling London, a Johnny-come-lately London, turnkey-ridden and soldier-hounded, its barracks and prisons imprisoned between a height of stone and a depthless water. Nothing and no one attempted the barricades of Organ-pipe except convict escapees blotched, like leopards, with gaol-sores. No one returned over the crags except bushrangers, crazed from suppers of human flesh, and chattering a litany learned in a hinterland of horror. There was nowhere to go in Hobart Town except Hobart Town. Since it had been planted in perversity it had taken root and grown, a weed town, perverse and obverse.

There, therefore, in that place, West End, was southerly.

There, southerly, the lawns of *Cindermead*, inclining downwards below the upper-class and custard slush of Sandy Bay Road, rotted bluely beneath the intemperance of weather. The walnut trees and peach-orchard and lilacs were pick-pocketed leafless. The elm avenue was just old enough, and rooted just deeply in enough toward the frozen core of hell, to indicate without chance of being misunderstood the pointless falsity of its perspective. Intimating the grand manner of an hereditary wealth and aristocracy, though all-bones as Job's turkey, it led down barbaric and final slopes to nothing except the adzes of rock on the margin of The Estuary that was, that season, ice-coloured, ice-still, and icy as a penitentiary moat.

Yet Lady Knight, Rose, the once-reckless, hot-headed and exhilarating Rose Hartnell of Curzon Street, was bare of forty-year-old waxen shoulder and china bosom and statue arm. She had the saltless, unbuffeted and varnished look of the figure-head never at sea. Her figure-head face was pearl-powdered and decorously rouged, as though for a vice-regal, candle-lit eight at glaring three-thirtyish, that afternoon, that winter, that year.

It was a year in which women of her class hankered after, and wore with the insolent serenity of society madonnas, the cast-aside modes of harlots, of the mistresses of Louis Quinze, of Marie Stuart. It was a year of bodices whose gothic angles in Amy Robsart satin, goose-turd green, pointed downwards with reticent suggestiveness and defensive invitation from marble breasts to satin-swamped crutch. It was a year of Imbecile sleeves, of side-loops of hair oiled flat and riftless over the ears to shield their drums from words unfit for virgins.

Thus earless, in satin unusual for the hour, and marble *à la mode*, Rose Knight pinned between her breasts an agate too much like an eye. Unlidded and unblinking, this dead thing flashed more than her own half-lidded and half-drowsily blinking eyes. She was in the mindless and feminine stupor of dressing and decorating her flesh at an odd hour for an engagement that was, as yet, no more than and hardly even a storm in a washbasin.

Her husband, Sir Sydney, had arranged it for her with a malice so oblique that, though she was herself gifted in the expression and reading of directer malices, she was unable in this case, to translate his.

She was between lovers but not yet unhappily so. A month ago, her latest lover, a sentimental, gawky and twenty-year-old baronet, had returned to England after a year's prying in the colony. Her husband was aware of this, and was doubtless and less idly than she, appraising the few possibilities Hobart Town offered for a successor with an acceptable silver-mark. He could not be expecting her to use the visitor who was due at four and in whom, she knew, there was a serious imperfection of behaviour as well as of caste. She had never descended below a well-bred army captain. Discretion in the selection of a lover was the respect she paid her husband's position, ambitions and class, as adultery was the disrespect she gave his impotency. Even she herself, for herself, although at times coldly preferring an ungentlemanly man or another's husband, coldly selected and set about warmly enchanting only a gentleman and a bachelor. Sunk deep as it was beneath the chilly sands of fastidiousness, class and cynicism, her heart had never been a stumbling block to circumspection and charming hypocrisy. The wind of disillusion had twenty years ago sickled the wild and heady crop to stubble. She would not stoop to glean. She had been too mad for love when she married. Now too sanely, a housewife who had been gypped, she went shopping in prudence. The afternoon's approaching appointment was nothing to that purpose.

It did, however, promise more entertainment and less boredom than the maidservant's toothache, pock-pitted jaw and snuffling. Those had already encouraged Lady Knight nearly to the point of discarding an unusual and controlled tolerance for an affectation of vicious candour. She was, in short, just dressed in time. She left the maid in the dressing-room among the spillings of powder and sheddings of chamois dress-protectors and camisole. She advanced, she sailed, towards a fitter afternoon setting, to a conventional, sleek, pockless and ache-free fire. She was skilful enough not to let the bed that was beginning again to be her downy rack and nest of animal dreams arouse her to irritation. She swept through the large fashionable cell of bedroom. *Cindermead* was everywhere large: she crossed unnecessary spaces of floor polished by assigned convict servants, by junts bred in Lazarus Court and the rookeries surrounding Rat's Castle, by park-women, area-sneaks and the gamy molls of skittle-sharps. In those looking-glass surfaces, slippery as fate, urn-tables, rosewood armchairs, kingwood commodes and walnut tallboys were unmistakably reflected with apparent permanence. They were unmoving until moved. They mocked, in classics of wood and ormolu, her unclassical impermanence sweeping in the direction of flames, encounters, speech and living.

As she moved, she called to the woman she would have hated more and to the point of murder had not social need and diabolic patience damped down her feelings to no more than a game of thermal venom. The handle of a blade would have proved too cold for her falsely warm, moist palm. Calling, she used the voice enriched by the pretence of love that a woman uses to deny that she does not need the other woman she pretends to need: "Asnetha! Asnetha, honey!"

In such fashion women play with other women, those dangerous pets to be kissed lightly while waiting to be stabbed while kissing. Her Curzon Street voice, after four years of Van Diemen's Land, was lightly inlaid with Van Diemen's Land. Its original tones were partly lost in a complicated system of echoes. It was an expatriate and colonial voice, here sharper, there more muted, from its encirclement of grotesque landscape, newly-minted customs, and the parochial animosities and snobberies spawned between cold mountain and cold cove. It seemed a smoke-veined flame licking at winter as wanting to melt it to Venice, carnations and oranges: "As-ne-tha! Honey!"

So calling, still coddling half-drowsiness, she abstractedly tried out this or that pose of killing languor in front of a splendour of organized flame and a Vulliamy clock ticking her appointment nearer. Then, suddenly, body, face and emotion awakened.

She began listening to what she realized she had already heard: the noiselessness of Asnetha Sleep. Miss Asnetha Sleep, she thought, is lurking and waiting. Miss Sleep of Brighton, the cripple, keeps herself waiting, *again*, so that she keeps me waiting although I do not want to see her and she wants—she burns—to move like greased lightning to find out what I have been up to. She'll have whipped her page-boy again, oh, without doubt. A fool!—how I hate her! A cunning fool, a liar, a monster, a millstone, a spy, a danger! I'll be cruel to her as she is to that wretched, vile boy. She's lurking in the Chinese room. I wish she were back in England, in Brighton, in agony, in her coffin. . . .

Rose Knight's eyelids trembled in irritation against the deliberate silence that was persisted in although its source knew that the persistence was overheard and understood. Separated by rooms and corridors, both women breathed several deeper breaths in unison; at a precise moment their eyes glinted equally angrily. Then Asnetha Sleep called, most melodiously and throatily, "Dearest Rose, do I hear you? Are you calling me?", and jerked herself into motion and began to run, hobbling and dipping from side to side, more noisily than she need, on twisted hairy legs and crumpled feet, hidden below Bishop's Violet velvet.

She approached, circling like a drunken animal. Her abnormal muscles wheeled her erratically away to return her, flicket-a-flacket, really nearer until, dancing pig on the parquet, "Do I hear? You call. My love? I come! I come!" she rounded the Coromandel screen at the drawing-room doorway with her vixen's toenails and toe-jam and corn-lidded toes expensively concealed but indubitable to Rose Knight.

"Oh, oh!" cried the cripple, displaying by a wilder lurch that she was confounded by bare shoulders, satin and cosmetics at that hour. "I have been. In a positive kim-kam. I wondered in my solitude. I was aquiver. In my loneliness. Though cosy, cosy, cosy. And now, I see, I see."

She rolled her enormous magnificent eyes, closely set, but divided by a long, softish, spotted nose. It was a nose that seemed to touch life before the mind did, to hear before ears, to see before eyes. Those eyes of hers, usually seeing more than they saw, were balked, and saw only what they saw: boredom scarcely bothering to counterfeit politeness, calm a thin scum on irritation, placidity merely layered over dislike, the tissue skin pulsing on milk writhing to the boil.

Asnetha Sleep became arch.

"What *does* cousin Asney see?"

She wagged a freckled forefinger which alone on her right hand was ringless and truthfully bad-tempered although mimicking playfulness.

She mocked a paragraph from *The Lady's Magazine* in a high-pitched squealing, " 'It is twue that the wong-estab-wished custom of westwicting silk materiaws to the winter months and the half-season is now abowished!' " She laughed too richly at herself.

Rose Knight began a fake smile, but left it. Her colourless statue's eyes swam with *ennui*.

"Dear Asnetha," she said, observing with a superior Egyptian glance from her cheaper agate that the other wore a *common* brooch, diamonds and gold wrought in the form of a bird defending its nest from a serpent. "Dear Asnetha, do *sit*. You are a positive fidget, never still for an instant."

Her nose quivering at this chosen unkindness, Asnetha Sleep did not sit but lurched about portraying poor sweet brave Miss Sleep, wistful as iron, hen-hearted as a hangman. With her false ringlets of expensive blazing cheap russet, her padded breasts, her indiarubber stays, her clever colours, flaps of Mechlin lace and outline-blurring ribbons, she had once hoped for the sort of manner that wore an adjective . . . gay, giddy, flighty, kittenish. She had attempted to conceal by exaggeration her pain, her despair and envy, and the shame of being intelligent, awry and not inviting to fondle naked. She had found she was not either to be fondled in her maypole finery; even her ribbons repelled. To discourage pity she used too much scent. It encouraged scornful pity. She had too much money, and drank too much port wine. She had accomplished nothing except to turn sympathy into dislike, her own docility to delirium, and her own desires to perversions. She was always ready and decked for downfall and anguish hours ahead.

Conjecture could have put it like this: ravishment by tipsy knackerman or turnpike-keeper would have left her screeching for audience like a gin-palace trollop, and unravelling maudlinly on the cobbles in front of a plum-pudding stall; Rose Knight raped, even by dust-sifter or pig-poker, would have indolently rearranged, in silence and unseen, her swan-like plumage of flesh, and dropped a smile between her finger-printed breasts.

That day, however, they were merely two tricky women in a heated drawing-room on a bitter afternoon though it had kindly stopped sleeting at luncheon.

"Oh, oh, I *see*, I guess," Asnetha Sleep said, quietly as a mouse in a cheese, and hobbled near to touch wisely and jealously the other woman's satin, unsettling a fold to re-settle it, as one arranging the nightgown of a corpse, and with a prim expression.

"There is. A dinner at. Government House?"

There was no reply in words, for Rose Knight was sickening towards anger, but the chatterer shiftily pursued,

"This *toilette* will. Ravish H.E. and. Unsettle his lady. La, la, la!"

"There is no dinner," said Rose Knight, and pointedly became more upright, and, fingering her eye of agate, withdrew to the inner temple.

Asnetha Sleep stopped herself, just, and forbade herself ever, saying, "Secretive Rose!" Yet: "What are you about, *vache*?" her ribbons said with a fretful swaying and: "How cruel to one so devoted, deprived and . . . and crippled! Monstrous female!" her bird and serpent vulgarly flashed out, while she abandoned silliness and changed the subject so that what had gone in one of Rose Knight's unseen ears would not go out the other: "Cathleen will not. Be cold, today." She belched wine, but faintly as a nun. She giggled and lurched.

Hare-lip Cathleen, an assigned servant, Irish, convicted for stealing oysters, had worked at *Cindermead*. She had been intended as no more than a month's stopgap but her grunted and consonantless impertinence—for it could not have been mere bestial confusion and stupidity—had irked Rose Knight in three days to a distinguished rage in which she had had Cathleen sent, squalling and apparently vilifying, certainly frothing through her cloven lip, to the House of Correction. The Female Factory, swaddled in snow, stood on Knocklofty. It pleased them both to consider the aesthetic relief to *Cindermead* of Cathleen's chilblained feet no more slapping about within earshot but grinding the antarctic wind on the treadmill. Recollection of easement soothed Rose Knight, refreshed her so that she could bear to speak. She floated back, a brilliant eagle casting its shadow on the misshapen carcass; she spoke from aloft.

"Did you need to whip, today?" she said.

Asnetha Sleep's nose stirred minutely at its knob and went tulip-pink, but unhurriedly. Her eyes, however, quickly skidded sideways.

"I declare one beats. Him more than a carpet yet. He persists wicked."

Her nose abated. She whirled herself about to arrive at a balance facing the Coromandel screen. She limped towards it.

She cried out, in full voice, succulent as a fish-seller's, "Teapot! Teapot, treasure!"

She listened, her nose tracking the air.

"Teapot, are you alive? Answer!"

The air gave up, from rooms away, a jingle of little bells.

"He lives," she said to the screen. She increased her voice again: "Take off your. Bells. Wash your hands. Face. *Ears* behind. Come to Miss Sleepy. Drawing-room."

When she returned from the screen, Rose Knight, whose satin was getting hot, had moved from the fire. She was also warmed by the thought of no insolent Cathleen, and the outrageous gipsy appearance of her husband's cousin, and the rattle-brained performance she had given, and the beauty of her own fingers at which she was looking. They required no disguise of jewels.

She raised her idol-blind eyes to seem to look near Asnetha Sleep, and offered like a glass of raspberryade:

"One is dressed for no dinner. Sir Sydney. . . ." She used her husband's name as being that of a boring passer-by under the foggy planes of Berkeley Square long long ago, ". . . desires that I have a portrait done. The artist comes at four."

"Oh, oh!" Asnetha Sleep shook her ribbons and laces, and hitched at her velvet without conviction. "The dear love. *So* loves you! The thoughtful love! Mr Bock? The clever, clever? Lady F's Mr Bock?"

"Not Mr Bock."

Asnetha Sleep expected that Rose Knight would stop, and was prepared to commit follies.

But the figure-head continued, "The dear thoughtful love has found . . . oh, skilfully . . . a Mr Vaneleigh, a Judas Griffin Vaneleigh. . . ."

She permitted a centimetre of some sort of smile. Asnetha Sleep twitched. Amazingly, Rose Knight began again.

"Sir Sydney is positive, *quite*, that Mr Vaneleigh has studied under Mr Fuseli. Mr Vaneleigh . . . *he* assures me . . . has been hung at the Royal Academy, and must be as clever as pussy. He has painted Lord Byron."

Having allowed her cousin-in-law once again, for a hundredth time, to read in intonation but not in words, the implacability of her contempt for her husband, she paused. She lengthened the pause, and continued to lengthen it as if to *finis*. She stroked her own white elbows with her own white fingers while she stared through the western french windows in the direction of Sandy Bay Road.

There, visible between the sandstone gate-pillars, a frightful governess of a *parvenu's* offspring, and wearing a frightful Dunstable Cottage bonnet, slid about on one spot, a becalmed skater on the mud. Rose, Lady Knight, stared long enough at that person's genteel contretemps and increasing frightfulness so that she should be able to appear not to see Asnetha Sleep's nose betray Asnetha Sleep's thought—*what are you about now?*—and Asnetha Sleep's mouth becoming looser.

The nose moved, the mouth unstitched itself, Rose Knight appeared to be not able to see them. Sharp with satisfaction, she extinguished the governess, and said:

"Lord Byron or no Lord Byron, I'd have declared off . . ." a contemplated rebellion stiffened those words to threat, ". . . if . . ." the words became limper and suggestive of immoral policy, ". . . I had not encountered Mr Vaneleigh in London."

("Ah!")

The deformed body, attempting to still itself cunningly to a semblance of polite and placid interest, treacherously gave a tremendous jerk, and all its ribbons leapt.

"Rapture, my love! Coincidence and rapture!"

"Years ago," said Rose Knight, in surprise at saying.

"You knew him, my love! London! The past! An old admirer! Oh, oh, I see. . . ." She would have gushed on.

"I encountered," said Rose Knight. "I less than encountered. Years ago, I *saw* him in London."

Miss Sleep of Brighton who had known only a visitor's London, and from a bathchair, and had seen nothing that was dubious except the milkmaids in the Mall, controlled herself and waited. Reminiscence would be followed by cruelty, but she ached to hear of Rose's earlier London, of Rose flashing about in earlier London, of Rose and Mr Vaneleigh.

"Since, *dear* Asnetha, it was years ago, I was younger. I was gay. I'd not then considered the possibility of an existence without gaiety. I had not foreseen, nor, I think, had I known of, Van Diemen's Land. I'd not foreseen that I should need to take tea with the kind of people who . . ." She looked, but the governess of the-kind-of-people-who had escaped in filthy highlows in the direction of nagging, overwork and death. "I had not foreseen. I was not married."

And, that said, to her own astonishment she became unmarried and gayer.

"I saw him in Hickson's in Piccadilly."

Even Miss Sleep of Brighton knew that Hickson's, even in London, even in Rose Hartnell's day, was not a place for Rose to see in, even if Rose were as skittish as she used to be.

"Hickson's!"

Rose Knight really laughed; her voice was higher, careless, unsullied Curzon Street.

"Mama would have smacked my face. I badgered poor Tom Fitzhenry, who was always penning poetry and reading away at *London Magazine*. He was no great shakes but I could twist him. . . ."

She scratched the warm air with a long little finger.

"He hemmed and hawed, and hawed and hemmed. But he was a gone goose, honey. And white as curds with fright. To take *me* into *Hickson's*! Papa would have smacked *his* face! I was in a state of perfect ecstasy. I recall—Oh God, I wore a Crazy Jane hat!—that Hickson's had pastries from paradise, and the air cooled by showers of soda water. And such *persons*, all a-chatter: fribbles, Miss Nancies, and demi-reps in the most elegant modes. I felt loose, but since I wasn't, I felt shabby among all the spindly old beaux. And bucks who could have been wig-thieves or wherry-boys or sugar-bakers all tricked out like court cards in borrowed plumes, or stolen ones."

Smoke came back to her voice, trammelling its speed and adding dark weight to its light flames:

"Mr Lamb and Mr Vaneleigh were there together. Poor Tom pointed them out to me. Mr Vaneleigh was proud as Lucifer, and ate a macaroon."

The smoke, thickening into silence, flowed into her eyes, quenching their senseless phosphorescence and smudging a kittenish glaze. It was as though she knew some darkness of life and Mr Vaneleigh which it had not been possible to know, or which had not fallen, when the macaroon crumbs were hopping from his long, clever, sophisticated lips. Asnetha Sleep's thought, less patiently but less dangerously, hopelessly and murderously than Cathleen on the treadmill, trod its treadmill until the smoke blew off, the bubbles of eye became iridescently vacant with light, and there was a return to the pitch of Curzon Street:

"Mr Vaneleigh was as plump as a pheasant and prattled like poll-parrot. His hair was curled to distraction. I swear he had colour on the cheeks. Do I swear this? He *seemed* to have colour; he may have had. Then he stopped prattling, and looked at Mr Lamb with perfect sternness . . . such eyes! I heard him say, 'I do *not* scramble after the loaves and fishes.' In those days I was Rose *Hartnell.* Rose Hartnell did not scramble after, did not think of scrambling after. . . ."

She stopped. She stopped as a carriage stops from which one must descend, and descends, and puts one's foot square in the fish-guts. She stopped. She stroked her satin as stroking a gift of peahen. She looked at the bourgeois bird and serpent, and ceased to stroke the satin, and said like satin:

"But you do not ask me about Mr Lamb whose writings you adore. I've heard you saying to Sir Sydney that you adore Mr Lamb's writings."

"Oh, oh!" Some gestures of rings and fingers were made; no one would ever decipher them. "And Mr Lamb?"

"Mr Lamb? I remember he was there."

She said no more.

Asnetha Sleep, in the contrived and extending lapse which developed to cessation, felt her muscles about to betray her again by incontinently jerking her members about. She deftly span about twice to circumvent that. As she settled to asymmetrical equipoise, "Teapot, treasure!" she cried, for Teapot had appeared around, or it might have been from, the exotic landscape of the Coromandel screen.

"Modish Teapot! You *have* on. Your embroidered coat. Such colours. The golden *thread*. Your kinder than kind Miss Sleepy. So smooth a fit. Your hands? Washed?"

"I have on my new embroidered coat. I have washed my hands," said the impeccable and piercing voice of Teapot who was thirteen and a devil-black West Indian.

"Asnetha, honey," said Lady Knight, the blinding eagle with the blinding shadow wheeling down nearer. "Asnetha, honey, Mr Vaneleigh's eyes were as large as . . . upon my word, as large as yours. Perfect circles. Murderer's eyes. Grey too, I think to recall, though so *difficile* to tell in Hickson's and London."

The carcass below began to prickle with hatred.

"Whether a prettier grey than yours, I couldn't tell. But I think so. They were certainly more widely set and clearer in the white. Would you like to meet Mr Vaneleigh?"

At that moment the Vulliamy clock whirred like a grasshopper, and began to strike, and all the clocks, little and big, in all the rooms that were boxes for human beings to give purpose to with the enactment of human feelings, began tinkling and chiming and announcing a human hour. Asnetha Sleep, smiling and nodding and enacting fluttering frivolously, and balancing on her crooked props, was blotched with rage, and was yet able to say:

"I should like. It would be perfectly. Mr Vaneleigh! *Dear* Rose. To meet. Yes, yes, yes!"

Lady Knight yawned, or pretended to yawn,—she herself could not tell—and said, "Mr Vaneleigh is ticket-of-leave, Asnetha. Mr Vaneleigh *is* a murderer."

Asnetha Sleep could have bitten out her rebellious tongue which fervently shrilled, "I shall not. Meet him. I shall not. We Sleeps. . . ."

And though she could have bitten, for she knew Rose Knight would not have offered her the exciting diversion of meeting a murderer, she said again perversely, but in fuller tones to lend decoration to untruth, "I don't wish. To meet. I *shall* not."

As her body gave one of its internal kicks to make her stagger, Teapot was observed once more, like a new arrival.

He was pointing exaggeratedly, his finger too long, at the northern french windows.

"The foolish creature has come by the Estuary track and in the lower gate. He will be muddier than even murderers should be," said Lady Knight, and began to look magnificent, cleaving the heated and elegant tank of drawing-room air with her porcelain face.

Outside, in the commonplace and ill-bred iciness, were two men breathing steam like oxen or nags.

The women and the black boy heard one of the men uttering what seemed to be words in what appeared to be a weather-defying voice for it was loud and cockney enough to have to defy such weather:

"Queely'll find a tinkler and jerk it. You wait 'ere for Queely, Mr Vaneleigh."

2

Which of the two men who had blundered on to the side terrace, a wrong place for them to be, was crying out resolutely and resonantly, in words the two women could scarcely understand, they could not, although Teapot could, distinguish with certainty. The taller man's gestures, and the greater and denser clouds of steam billowing from his face, inclined them to mark him. The shorter man ejected scantier vapours. Moreover, the taller took the eye. He squatted to wipe the mud from the boots of the other with his bandana: the domestic genuflection of a dog, or a queer saint. The voice that had interrupted the women's petty drama was a voice patently cocksure that the ringing of a doorbell would abolish discomfort and cold, and suggested height and virility as well as the protective devotion of a slave or dutiful attendant.

And, indeed, the taller man, Queely Sheill, loud-mouthed and handsome as a god, though merely a mortal, twenty-two, and of classic symmetry, had been, for eight months, almost daily attendant on Mr Vaneleigh, the artist of No. 8 Campbell Street.

In that island, where the months that brought summer to England were vehicles that nightmarishly brought winter, in that town founded on and demoralized by mistrust, East End was north. The Ratcliff Highway of this northern East End was Campbell Street.

Campbell Street was accustomed to ruthlessness of behaviour and fact. It symbolically ascended from the Commissariat Stores and the Treasury on The Estuary's edge to a hill-top graveyard as abruptly and ironically as a human leaves a nurturing womb to ascend to an airiness of extinction. Left and right of the stony ascent were disposed the elements of a Christian civilization to which Nature allied itself with subtler cynicism.

Chapels and churches of tasteful design and beguiling purpose crowded in on the Penitentiary: artistic spires, witch-hat in shape, overlooked the artless flogging-post.

In cottages, cellars, area-basements, unlined attics, cheap coffee-houses and chop-houses, a moderate humanity was jammed cheek by cheek with an immoderate. They snored and whined and beshrewed on the doorsteps of each other's ears. They guzzled and fornicated or starved and coveted without mincing the matter: the rope-maker with the gallers-good, shepherd with woolly-bird-stealer, prude and ponce, cheatee and cheat.

The shifty and politic wind of the age stirred them, clouds without rain, here and there and nowhere. Under a sun bleak as a whale's eye, their natures ripened to decay as perceptibly as melons under an equatorial planet.

Hobart Town Rivulet leaked out, pure, from Knocklofty. As it descended it sponged up the town's muck and the Criminal Hospital's offal and, turbid with them, choked at Campbell Street under the bridge called Palladio. Opposite the Palladio and the Criminal Hospital stood Queen's Playhouse and its underground tap-room *The Shades*.

At the Palladio parapet, on a Christmas Eve, Queely Sheill met Mr Vaneleigh.

It was hot twilight, footpad hour, and it stank. It stank of the slaughter-house and its turbulent mane of blowflies; it stank of the Rivulet and its throbbing nap of maggots. The muzzled gruffness of blowflies and cockchafers was the tamest note in a festival of uproar: in the celebration of Christmas, morality, that troublesome fruit from Eden, had been hurled away.

From the Criminal Hospital came the sound of a fiddler fiddling on his fiddle to accompany the hullabaloo of the dying, to dissipate the stink of gangrene, and to scratch lines across the handwriting of the heavens.

From *Fox Inn*, *Rumbling Bridge*, *Black Snake Inn*, *The Grasshopper*, *The Brown Bear*, *Whaler's Return*, *The Man on the Wheel* and *Help me through the World*, from every gin-crib, rum-shack and grog-shop in Hobart Town gushed the bawlings and whinnyings, the obscenities vile to the point of innocence, the punctilious blasphemies, of tin-men and their gap-toothed doxies, of spit-curled ostlers and sweaty cocottes, of gin-crazed fan-makers and spewing chawbacons.

From Nature, eternally at her lewd balance sheet, could have come nothing but a smirk of approval. From heaven came nothing but what its ears had tasted and rejected: the echoes of a glory of ribaldry.

Already, night not yet down, the reeking necessaries overflowed, the fingers of bug-hunters were at the fobs of the dead-drunk, the hand of the randy sawyer fumbled the bonnet-maker's gape, the gristle of the cooper gardened in the long eye of the backyard slut.

To the wailing cat-gut of the elbow-jiggers and the screams of doll-commons, at some arbitrary hour, Christ would be imagined infant again, and bells would ring bats and starlings from their towers into the mosquito-spiced and earsplitting night.

Solitary in the twilight, Mr Vaneleigh leaned on the Palladio parapet.

Moths and cockchafers seemed to be pelted out of the pounding air at the whale-oil street-lamp which lit his concealment within himself—and with himself, because all eyes were elsewhere. His secrecy made him deaf. No increase or abatement of caterwauling aroused him to the comment of even a flicker. He seemed not to see or breathe. It was as though, in directing his pupils towards the rats furrowing the Rivulet's junket of maggots and putrescence, he saw not them but the fog-gauzed sheen and swans of Regent's Canal, as though Campbell Street rose through a Regent's Park lit by the gas-lamps of George IV to the stylish hump of Primrose Hill.

Although his eyes stared forward and had led him forward

by the side of many streams and over many bridges to that Palladio, that trench of stink and those rats, the eyes of memory circled over the past. Mr Vaneleigh, even he, like the rest of humanity, was a hunter who advanced backwards. He stumbled in the dead wind, the wind of days that have passed and will not return.

Suddenly, with Anglo-Saxon abruptness and resolution, the uncircumcised began to jolt and jar from their church-bells the advertisement of the birth of Jesus Christ.

On the opposite side of Campbell Street from Mr Vaneleigh, who remained immobile under the addition of struck metal, a young man appeared.

He emerged from the cellar Bedlam of *The Shades*. He shook himself; he capered about a little; he beat at his pea-coat as though it were tainted, and gulped the dirty twilight as gulping with hisses of relish a sweeter air. As he thus renovated himself, he caught sight of the blue-coated form bowed on the parapet. He stood and stared at it for some minutes during which he detected not even the signs of breathing. A regard for the privacy of others was gradually put aside: the contrast of the other's attitude to the activity he had just renounced was so striking that in the bowed-over immobility he imagined a nameless anguish, a peering into the sockets of suicide. He waited with a doubting reticence until the waiting became unbearable to him and, perhaps, as dangerous to the other as deliberate and inhuman delay can be.

Were one responsible for every next move in life, and aware of the responsibility, there are corners one would never turn, rooms or roads one would never cross. One turns, one crosses, and accident defrauds one for ever of a greater ecstasy or a greater affliction.

No experience had taught or would ever teach the young man prudence, offhandedness or the delights of inhumanity. One turns. One crosses. Queely Sheill began loudly to sing, adding his voice to the widespread sound of bells and bawdiness. Singing thus to inform the other of his approach, he crossed Campbell Street.

When he saw that the blue material of the coat imperceptibly moved to the rhythm of breathing, and a calm breathing, the maidenly indecision that had kept him staring across long enough for the other to die or attempt death or be sick into the Rivulet turned to anxiety. His noisy arrival had not startled the form's breathing. He blinked and flushed with his trepidation. That back-turning lethargy, indiscreet at that felon's hour, in that felon's street, dismayed him.

"Sir," he said. "Sir, are you—are you wretched?"

He had hoped to speak softly but the question broke like a hound from a kennel, theatrical as barking in tone, and hectoring in its diffidence. An under-note of cockney indulgence alone properly revealed an intention to be nothing except sympathetic.

Mr Vaneleigh displayed by no movement that he had heard. It was not a voice for him to move at, even in impatience. His privacy desired no visitor and required none, least of all one bred near Crutched Friars, to assist the drunken storm that had followed Christ's birthday to a frontier town at the fringe of polar ice-fields.

Queely Sheill's purpose had, however, acquired the tense aspect of an abscess. It positively shone with strain. He trusted his insight which forbade him to retreat from a deliberately offensive inattention. The explosion of a "Go away!" would have satisfied him that he had intruded: he would happily have gone away. He did not possess the insecure pride that would have him flouncing off on its own behalf and the pretence of being hurt by the rejection of a kindness. Knowing also that remorse for what one has not fully done is the deepest and most abiding remorse, he spoke again. He desired to make less noise, to use a voice like ointment, to shield the unblemished light of his honest apprehension by the hand of restraint, but his second question was again noisy:

"Ain't you un'appy, sir? Ain't you wretched?"

Mr Vaneleigh could do no less than abandon the rats and the swans, the present and the past, the maggots and the water-lilies, and straighten up in his poor dandy's abraded blue coat and white topper, and turn to face the future.

Mr Vaneleigh was short, almost as light in build as a

coachman. His face beneath the tilted-back topper, was pale and had a contrived blankness as though to veil by refined control the sardonic muscles and bones. His left eyebrow had lifted itself as urbanely as it once had used to lift when he had toiled up the heart-breaking staircase of Somerset House to yet another art exhibition. It was a signal of ironic and tactful abstraction, of a wariness of mind, of remoteness.

Each of the two men had his perfected and differing wisdom. They flagrantly counted each other under the lamp-post.

The taller man with his avidly searching blue eyes was disconcerted: he sought less, and observed more, distress, and distress of a new kind, than his simplicity had selflessly forgotten to bargain for. The short man used his grey eyes, wide-open and wide-apart as a cat's, with an analysing indifference that was the lees, the steady and glowing lees, of a bygone mockery and a contemptuous wit.

While the men regarded each other, at Mr Vaneleigh's feet a shape of shade undulated and unfolded itself into a cat; it also regarded the intruder with a ceremonial incuriosity.

Then, for there is the etiquette without which even indifference skirts vulgarity, Mr Vaneleigh spoke. One cannot, anyway, go on staring for ever at a handsome waxwork that stares back winkingly. He spoke softly and with a formal vagueness in which there was the tint of a cultivated mischief: you've compelled me to talk so I'll *talk*. His remarks seemed to be addressed to some noble and subtle shape behind Queely Sheill, some miniature of a gentleman, some exquisite mind which his mind and eyes sustained themselves on.

"Wretched? Now *that's* a settler, a perfect staggerer!" he said in an effeminate, wilful, *salon* voice. "Let us say that I was, until recently, in a situation of desolate wretchedness too heavy for pity—a super-wretched situation."

He was not lying perhaps, yet it was as easy as lying for him to lisp on with the tinge of mockery that suggested lying.

"Let us say that I am, at this moment, conscious of so little of personal wretchedness that it's no bigger than one's oldest finger. You see me, my slender-loined gallant, merely idly busied."

He contemplated cessation, farewell, departure: no one who knew anything of anything could find conversation with a magnificent brute, in a singular location, in any way stimulating. But, with an unruffled thought of revenge towards the agent of recall, he continued:

"My feelings are too deep for the fathom-lines of uninformed minds. They are hardly come-at-able: they are not hot in my mind. Oh, once they constantly were; we had feverish sensibilities to all around us. That was in another world. I correct myself—in other *worlds*. Not in this one."

A lackadaisical gesture indicated the broiling twilight and its bestial plots of increasing turmoil.

"There *may* be, this night, a grand *levée* of the powers of heaven—oh, heart-quelling, with angelic guards winding through the air from earth to heaven. But not in this quarter. A witches' gala rather! A brown shroud of dust! Vices rolling round in giddy wheel! A moral sepulchre! I speak, you observe impetulantly."

He imperceptibly nodded his head in farewell.

"Come, cat, I've hit off my tale now."

The delicate discrimination of his lisp had turned the sharper edge of words towards the listener, accusing him of blunder, of outrage, of climbing orang-outang-like a shuttered and private tower. Twilight cat, winding its soft hobbles of jealousy around and around Mr Vaneleigh's ankles, added to his restraint of manner.

But Queely Sheill, who had climbed carelessly to save, had seen through the shutters more than he had thought to see, and was not to be knocked or cajoled down. He had waited for the attempt to crucify with silver pins to be over. He moved, for he had been very still, and said:

"You must forgive, sir. From hover there you seemed as hif you was in pain. . . ."

He forced himself to speak less loudly.

"Sir, sir, hif you please, the *happearance* of your back distressed Queely. . . ."

The other lightly and listlessly touched his moustache, certifying by it the mouth's presence, as though as unsure of it as of what it should say to the pea-coated, perhaps crazed,

Adonis. God knows, he thought, what visionary and chaotic philosopher confronts me; God knows what sorts of monkey tricks. Yet his mouth, when it gave forth, showed no relenting:

"You've an informal habit of mind. I do not know whether your freedom of manner can be considered innocence or—impudence."

He paused, giving Queely Sheill time to raise his fist. No fist was raised; no move was made; the bells began to reduce their rowdiness. With an air of signing a letter, "You are . . . I imagine you'll not misconstrue my meaning . . . of obtuse apprehension. Good evening," he said. It was a gingerbread and cautious scorn.

To Mr Vaneleigh's dismay, and before he could depart, the tall man struck himself on the forehead, and shouted out, "Queely didn't go for to do no 'arm. . . ."

He was clinging still at the tower-shutter, noisy and stubborn, his jewelled eyes fearless and outrageous.

"And Christmas too!" he cried, "Christmas, sir!"

"This", said Mr Vaneleigh, still softly but less decorously, "creates a *very* fine cut-throat sort of effect! I need no ear-cracking celebration to remind me . . . I am unable to distrust my own memory."

The cat, forewarned of the next move by its own assessment of tone, briskly unwound the hobbles. Mr Vaneleigh turned, languidly but decisively. His interchanges, which had intended nothing more than cool rebuttal, had tricked him too far from a remote attitude, and pointed therefore to the finality of absolute withdrawal. The cat's tail insultingly uplifted to show its little dark anus, and the blue coat-back turned to him and in retreat from the lamplight, aroused Queely Sheill to cry out in shock:

"Queely *hassures* you no 'arm . . . not hany. I ain't no dark 'orse. Queely's the kindest thing in nature. A *good* boy, sir. No 'arm, no 'arm. 'Twas 'uman feeling."

The cat ran ahead, and Mr Vaneleigh, in retreat, following it and gingerly paddling the dust, did not turn to face again the desperate impoliteness. Yet, without turning, he called over his shoulder, clearly and ruminatively enough to betray a pedant's interest in his own statement, levelly enough to reveal disinterest in another's hearing it:

"Eschew human feeling. Sympathy buys shame; it will buy you infamy. . . ."

"*No!*"

It was the clamour of one wringing the hands of his heart. It had the air, the desolation and loudness of *Stop thief!* It struck at useless heaven.

"No 'arm comes of 'uman feeling, no matter what; not of proper 'uman feeling!" Queely Sheill moved after the other.

Mr Vaneleigh stopped mincing off. When he turned, as he did, his eyebrow had flicked itself higher. His face was embellished with the smile of the well-bred man who has reluctantly bitten on sow-thistle and found its juice wry but denies wryness.

"It's a million of pities," he said, "but I learnt these things so long ago."

The cat, callously angry, throned itself within the circle of its own tail and watched Queely Sheill come yet nearer to its master's smile and begin shouting:

"Sir, you're a gemman. You can't go to believe what you said. You can*not* believe so. I'll not let a gemman believe so. That is a wickedness to all the 'umans in the world. You mock yourself. You mock Queely's feeling."

It was grotesque to hear heroics ranted in a voice that could scarcely find enough words to express them. Mr Vaneleigh's countenance kept its mannered and grievous expression, which being read by Queely Sheill, roused up, salt on fire, a clearer flame than either needed:

"You can see Queely's no gemman."

His voice vibrated strongly; it rattled down the screens of politeness, safety, mendacity and platitude to reach and attack the miseries of all men through the one man:

"I'm the son of a cackling cove. Sheill the actor's the dad."

Since the actor's son had paused, startled and interested to hear of an actual figure's birth into a conversation about the faceless and formless, Mr Vaneleigh shrugged, and spoke as one at a wine-table:

"We feel we may hold you excused. Virgil was the issue of

a baker, Demosthenes of a smith. Socrates . . . this hits my fancy stronger . . . was the son of an old *accoucheur*—I should say *accoucheuse*. You're aware, of course, that in more modern times Pope's father kept a cheap warehouse where he sold Irish shirting."

"Not *haware*. Queely's hignorant. 'E can write, but 'e's hignorant. The dad keeps *The Shades* too. Oh, the dad's foxier nor a fox."

"A place we have heard of . . . and hear . . . *The Shades*."

Mr Vaneleigh's expression was untranslatably thorough-bred in its disparagement.

"Birds of all feather, beasts of all bristle."

Both men listened to the boorish din from the other side of Campbell Street.

"Mops and mows and chatterings of apes," said Mr Vaneleigh.

"I just been hand left the dad over there."

His voice, dealing with a human being, was reduced in volume. It was less on behalf of his own flesh and blood that this diminution occurred than that an abstraction required from Queely Sheill more heat in explanation than a human did.

" 'E's drunker nor a fiddler's bitch, the old slush-bucket. Roaring and reeling and cunt-struck. Buying grog for every ligby and ganymede and gutter-blood from Jericho to June. But 'e's 'appy. Hapes and birds and beasts whatever, they're all '*appy*. They mean no 'arm."

"Such nice, pleasant, good-for-nothing people," said Mr Vaneleigh. He and the cat continued impassive enough, and did not touch their moustaches, but their fragility showed.

Queely Sheill, sensing an embarrassment, hacked on the air with small hopeful gestures in hopeless essay to outline a gospel too large for illustration.

"Oh, sir, do not *mis-ap-pre-'end*. Mouth almighty! Queely jabbers too much but 'as no contempt of 'is dad nor no one. I tends 'im and shall till the cow comes 'ome. But no contempt of 'im. Don't mis-ap-pre-'end, I pray."

His eyes demanded some answer, some comment not even approval. Mr Vaneleigh made none. He watched the cat scratching arcs on the air at low-flying cockchafers. From this he knew that the cat knew that he was finding entertainment.

" 'E irks, and plays fast and loose, and 'its Queely. But 'e 'as Queely's tending. I would die rather than not tend. *That* is my 'uman feeling."

Mr Vaneleigh wore a look as if he were not listening to or thinking of the transcendent sentimentality of his companion, but his shadowed mouth unbitterly seemed to emit a ritual triteness:

"Highly-to-be-commended example of a devoted son. . . ."

There was nothing else possible to emit, or worth emitting, to anyone, at that time and place, among all those whizzing and temporary insects.

Crumbled as the remark was, Queely Sheill heard it.

"Don't know about devoted . . . 'tis something I gives no mind to. Queely does what 'is 'eart tells 'im must be done."

"Ah!" Mr Vaneleigh, with neutral eyes and retired thought, languidly matching flawless against flawless—as he had years ago intaglio against intaglio—and idiosyncrasy against idiosyncrasy, at last lisped out:

"I've not the vanity to affect a fancy, much less an imagination, but we *consider* you possess an insolent confidence: you rely on the inscrutable dispensation of whoever —or whatever—guides your heart."

"Queely thinks 'e tells his 'eart what 'is heart tells 'im."

Queely Sheill smiled, for he had said something he had neither said nor given thought to before. Then he shuffled in the vile and velvet dust and dusk. Then he clapped his hands together. Then he shouted:

"*You* 'ave a 'eart, sir. It 'ides. It 'as been scratched. It 'as been spat on."

Smiles of all enchanting sorts freely continued to occupy and adorn his face, smiles wise and proud, smiles childlike and humble, smiles that had fought with Mr Vaneleigh for the right to appear, smiles ingenuously cunning and unfalteringly certain of their cause.

"Queely *sees*, and you mustn't deny . . . that'd only be talk from mouths, not 'earts. You ain't cold has cucumbers. I sees your 'eart."

Immediately after that he begged to be temporarily excused.

"Queely must make long tea," he said, and turned his back on Mr Vaneleigh, and unbuttoned.

"Come, Julius Caesar!" he shouted. "Out, Jack-in-the-box!" and began peeing, but with great care, playing the stream to write on the dust his name and an interknotted paraph. Back still turned, as he finished peeing and buttoning, he said:

"Told you I could write. Told you I sees that poor 'eart. Sees as you're a good gemman. Queely knows."

His name behind him, he was facing Mr Vaneleigh again.

Mr Vaneleigh, who had been thinking, could have said "Tosh!" Mr Vaneleigh and his cat could have said nothing. Mr Vaneleigh said:

"I observe that the restraints which the rules of polished society and tight breeches have placed on the oppression of the passions are not yours. *Your* mind is cleared from warps and prejudices. But, whatever it is you conceive to've divined, your pride and smiles are hardly justified. You have not plucked out the heart of my mystery."

Mr Vaneleigh lifted his large white hand as though it held a goblet.

"Have you ever", he said, "drunk an infernal cordial over the surface of which you see a flame pass as it nears your lips?"

Queely Sheill and the cat made no move, no noise. Mr Vaneleigh drank his invisible potion.

"My heart," he said, "—my fate—was a subject of trifling importance—it was judged mortal."

His intention to continue speaking veered. He was surprised to find it changing its shape to a desire to continue speaking. He faltered at his own foolishness. Unhallowed familiarities were magicking him into a puddle-stirrer—and his own puddle! The information he had been on the point of displaying to a fantastic stranger was not worth the giving. It seemed already a ragged legend, a dishonoured and ordinary flag too shabby to run up promiscuously on a sandstone bridge over a reeking brook on a humid Christmas Eve to a man who could have been mad or a murderer.

Moreover, there was another truth, another flag of immaculate white, and untattered hem: he knew that he was dying. But that was a truth too powerful to cause harm or, at the most, any more than a sorrow so harmless and so useless that it could be consoled. Only the dead are inconsolable.

Mr Vaneleigh, having faltered into thought and analysis, shrugged his shoulders at himself. This man, he thought, is heart-thawing . . . or tongue-thawing. He seems to have for me the power of the rattlesnake over its prey. He waits obstinately as a cat. Let me not repay his earnest fervour with a notice of my inexorably-nearing death. Death is, after all, no more than retirement from business. He thinks he wants what he thinks is news of my life. His meek imbecility implores it.

Mr Vaneleigh began to run up his dirty pennant.

"No," he said, "you've not plucked out the heart of my mystery. On that I can make my oath."

He walked to the parapet, and leaned with some grace against it. He picked a cockchafer from his lapel, and threw it towards the cat which was outraged.

"To begin is a great exertion: many things have contributed to break and daunt my once elastic spirits. But *not* my in-dwelling, never-dying flame. Whatever dark fears come across me, that flame's unabated constancy will drive away the black vapours of the brain."

He paused.

"You've called me gentleman . . ." he began.

Once again he faltered. He grew restless within; his soul trotted about affectedly in that low street of that squalid outpost. With an expense of will he recaptured it. He raised his eyebrow. He went on, laurel-giver on dais, handing out heatlessly and punctiliously wreaths of what seemed to him someone else's lies:

"I have a sentence getting cold—*gentleman?* Was that it? You've called me gentleman, eh? But I am scarcely twenty-four hours free. Freed from the Penitentiary on that crest of rock behind you; freed from the Criminal Hospital at your very elbow—you smell it? you hear the reel of pain the fiddler tortures from the strings?—freed from the faraway hulks at Portsmouth—long ago, long long ago and only yesterday!"

Queely Sheill was heard to whisper; his exquisitely carved lips puffed out, "Poor, poor 'eart! Poor darling 'eart!" but otherwise he did not move.

"I haven't the most distant notion," said Mr Vaneleigh, and his tone was minutely sharpened, though his posture remained nonchalant, "and can positively assure you that I do not care—not a farthing rush!—whether or no your splendid proportions have been outraged by donning the yellow dress. Say nothing! I don't care to know. I'll not let you answer on that. But you'll have seen that yellow in this street on uncountable occasions, worn by a thousand erring sons of Mr Anybody and God-knows-whom. A colour and costume to warm and elevate the fancy and stimulate the exertions! How forcefully the black print of FELON sets off the yellow! Canary, is it? To a nicety! Oh, eye-cutting! This body has worn it, and these eyes have seen."

The twilight had thickened and continued perceivably to thicken its bombast to opacity. So, too—wheeling far-flung about the two men, and the cat, and the lamp in its hurricane of demented wings, and the lamp-post ringed at its foot with a piled annulus of stunned and hashed insects—the texture of celebration thickened with harsher noise, with the brutalities of beasts growling deep, with raw screamings, with a grinding as though the zodiac had jarred on Organ-pipe and grated its constellations there.

The speaker, whatever he spoke, however lenitively, kept the fine edge of impersonality on his sentences.

"These eyes have seen the murderer's busts in the bread-room of Newgate—a joint-loosening array of masonry! The glare of those blind orbs left one in no doubt whatever that hope was close, very close, to the box's bottom. Yes, these eyes have seen those eyes.

"This mind—oh, 'twas a tasteful mind with an uncorresponding purse!—recalls itself torturing itself to a mad jealousy of those who cried jellied eels and pickled tripe in Ivy Lane and Rose Street. They called *outside* the walls. They could sleep in their own bed-chamber and their own bed, no matter if 'twere a hard old flock-bed. I lay behind the walls, my potencies abated, on sour Newgate straw. Huddled with a bricklayer and a sweep! Oh, we were quartered among the comets of the season; we had rooms in the temple of the darlings of *The Pocket Newgate Calendar*. And yet, and yet —what a hard-hearted muck-worm I was! how lacking in proper gratitude!—I felt my neighbours' distinction to be an indignity to myself. I'd have left instanter.

"Envy, jealousy, what-you-will—it was a standing dish. Good lack-a-daisy! I have struggled from nightmares overrun with stray phosphoric curs, to nightmares of jealousy as I heard the hackneys cantering in Paternoster Row. I was jealous of the jarveys, of the very horses themselves as they passed Amen Corner to canter down Ludgate Hill. *Then*, in that world, I *was* wretched. Therein was a fascinating agony. I recall it. I recall that there was pain, but must not pilfer an attitude: I can't feel that pain now. What use to recall the pain of learning that the art of sinking is much easier than that of rising? For the *first* time in nine years I am *free*."

The cat, having bored itself by a surfeit of calculated cruelty to injured moths and beetles, pretended to become civilized and adoring, and stropped its body on Mr Vaneleigh's pantaloons. He lifted it to the coping, and began stroking it.

"You *observe* that I am free. It has been presumed by nutshell minds, by windy inconsistent minds, by various so-and-so's, that, pretty generally, the gaol has made me fire-new, that their corn-cutting and small-tooth-comb work has left me matchless in moral condition. *Imprisonment* was the best caustic to eat away the rotten part; *freedom* is . . . what? One is free to listen to the rats in the ooze under this arch, to overhear exiled humanity—you hear? you hear?—gulping and drowning in the dead black waters, to see the staringly obvious mountain, the town that is the birthplace of no one, the tides that are permitted to take me nowhere. One is free to fondle a cat born and bred in a gaoler's scullery! One is free to spend Christmas Eve watching the pretty son of an actor write his name. . . .

"Gentleman! You have called me so. I was a wardsman in that hospital there, the scrubbing-man for a God-deserted multitude, the servant of the revolting and the sordid, the slop-boy of the blasphemous and filthy."

Mr Vaneleigh's revelations were delivered as though by a man who had chosen to live under his breath. No note of rancour contorted his face or the lisping music of his voice. Had he been using another language one would have suspected him of reciting pastoral elegies. Raving, grimaces and gestures would have disquieted Queely Sheill less. The control, the varnish, the conscious and restrained recital of self-pity and finicky disgust scored the pulp of his tenderness deeply.

"I have carried," Mr Vaneleigh was whispering, "pails enough of the dung of felons to build a muckheap high as Knocklofty. I've poured away enough porringers of blood cupped from the veins of highwaymen and rapers to flood the Rivulet until it washed over the Palladio. Blood!"

Queely Sheill clapped his hands over his face to conceal a treacherous exhibition of feeling.

"I have learned to regard the flayed and bloody back as no more than a shaving cut, a fatal downpour from three hundred strokes of the cat as no more than chin-blood."

"Queely 'ates blood," came distorted from behind hands.

Mr Vaneleigh, having unwittingly upset his audience, decided to draw to a close. Under his fondling finger-tips the cat continued to simulate sleep.

"Blood *is* courage-blasting," said Mr Vaneleigh. "You perceive now the appositeness of my metaphor of infernal cordial? I drank. There came a darkness over everything like a sweep from the weighty wing of some unknown power. Oh, night at noon!"

Queely Sheill's eyes were still hidden behind his fingers: he could not see that Mr Vaneleigh's expression had the suggestion of an exhausted relief, an *Ain't-that-good-eh?* satisfaction.

It was latest twilight, night enough. The soup of heat was

cooling. It stank, or seemed to stink, less. Nostrils hunting upon the entangled odours of gloom had a chance of springing a whiff of a sun-charred exiled rose or the meagre aroma of the stale and wizened planets above Organ-pipe. Unpredictably, and for an unpredictable brevity of time, the grog-shops, blotting with outspilt ruddiness the dark of the town, were merely grumbling in their scalded and ruptured throats.

Mr Vaneleigh's well-chosen last words had darkened to invisibility. They had soaked away, as Queely Sheill's urine had into the mob's dust, into blacker sands better not watered or walked.

Mr Vaneleigh felt like feeling for a snuff-box, he had the air of one about to do so, to take a pinch of exactly so many grains, and cry quits to a coarse exchange of confidences. He chose some words as he might have chosen snuff:

"Whatever rotten planks compose my flooring, ingratitude has no place there: I thank you for your ears and your . . ." He hesitated. He selected, ". . . your sensibility."

Queely Sheill took his hands from his face, and the hands of the lamp-light nervously shuddering at the bombardment of moths, returned to it.

"Never a tear," said Queely Sheill, "never a tear. Not a one on the skin. Queely won't go to weep, you see. 'E 'as fought the tears hoff. Oh, but when 'e's in 'is crib 'e'll sob and carry-on. 'E knows tears are not worth a bean but 'e'll carry-on."

His voice, patiently disentangling itself from skeins of emotion to undertake lucidity of statement, had declined to mildness. His custom of sensitivity or insight told him he must kiss the wound from which insight had egged him to rip the bandage.

"Your poor 'eart, sir. You must do what you will with me, tell me farewell or skedaddle or what-all. Oh, I *knew*, sir. The back of you said wretched . . . Queely halways knows."

The cat, aware of absolute decision on the way, firmly stood up and leapt to the ground, and began to lean at many grateful and importunate gentle angles against Mr Vaneleigh's legs.

"Ah!" said Mr Vaneleigh, unable to resist himself. "The world is tired, my heart is tired. *I* am tired and . . ." his voice blurred for the first time ". . . and not well."

He began to move.

"Cat and I lodge just past the Playhouse. On the corner. Number eight."

It was perhaps an invitation to walk to the door. Queely Sheill thought so, started towards him, and walked beside him.

" 'Tis not", said Mr Vaneleigh, "a walk-inviting night. The stars here have no names I remember as fashionable."

He stumbled. Queely Sheill's hand moved.

"Do not touch me," said Mr Vaneleigh. "I am not yet dead. There has been too much touching during too many years."

As they crossed Campbell Street, "I am Vaneleigh," he said.

The Shades, like a world's mouth gaping to show the rum-swollen tongue and dripping molars and song-raked purple gullet, belched thunderingly, once. Immediately, as though gulping back its own drunken horror, the mouth shut.

In that relative quietness, Mr Vaneleigh with undeniable weariness spoke another arrangement of words which might have meant something to Queely Sheill:

"I am Judas Griffin Vaneleigh."

The words meant nothing to Queely Sheill.

They meant, at that moment, scarcely more to the man who uttered them. It had been a name on a prison record: No. 2325: Vaneleigh, Judas Griffin. It had appeared on none of his paintings, drawings or essays. It was a name for gossips, and muckrakers not yet born.

He had jettisoned that name years ago, as he had serenity and hatred and trust and charity. He had jettisoned contempt, the last phial on the shelf and the one from which draughts can, to the end, restore the failed spirit.

An elegant defiant husk whose wit and anguish were alike mummified, whose wine of life was almost drawn, he was untouchable, scandalous, and dying though not yet ready to be dead.

He was an almost empty plate from which time had gobbled the juicier delicacies and gnawed at the bones.

Those bones—delicate, polished, hard as daggers—alone remained, a danger to the fingers of inquisitive vulgar minds.

3

"Queely'll find a tinkler and jerk it. You wait 'ere for Queely, Mr Vaneleigh," shouted Queely Sheill.

"Quick, black boy," said Lady Knight. "Tap on the window. Tap, fool! Open the window!"

"Teapot, treasure, tap," cried Asnetha Sleep, and as she whirled in a disturbance of ribbons, cried once more, "Tap, quick. With black. Hand." She hurled herself violently towards and on to an ottoman where she began picking with over-jewelled fingers at her tags and hangings.

"Quick," said Teapot, running across the room, his lengthy flat feet flapping in prunella boots. "I must tap on the window. I must open the window."

No trace of Teapot's exotic darkness dyed his voice that could, imagination suggested, have oozed forth like molasses or vibrated like a humming-bird. It kept to the strict, fearless and piercing level of an immoral Eton-grimy schoolboy's presenting a flawlessly accented denial. It was an engine of diction no cataclysm could make waver. It did not imply that he was—as he was—old enough in years and delusions to have already considered himself prodigious and rare, and a number of his most private thoughts a discreditable mystery.

Queely Sheill was moving away to seek a doorbell when Teapot began smacking on a pane of the french windows with his palm of anonymous mauvish colour. On that rectangular flatness of flesh, of hide, Mr Vaneleigh saw too clearly and with repugnance the criss-cross hieroglyph of lines, the plan of a tomb.

Common-sense slipped its leash. Not only passing time,

but more—the long drag of an ill-considered short cut—had brought him shuffling nearer to a physical death than he had yet been. From a face starched, blanched and contracted after the wading through tangible neaps of glaciated air, he stared beyond Teapot's incandescent, foolish and meaningless grin framed in the muslin curtains fringed with blue bobbles. A transport of powerlessness overcame Mr Vaneleigh; there was an unholy abdication of will.

Here, he thought, I abandon the sordid contrivances of man for the inexplicable and bewildering attractions of death. Here is to be the inconsequential end to a sullied journey, on the wrong day, a hole in my sock and in my mind, and catless. Let it be so! That shame is life's pet is death's most characteristic allurement. I shall die on this gravelled terrace. That child, that black, is the idea of night and death transmuted to matter. He will batter through the glass with that palm on which is the message I did not yet want to read. He will touch me and. . . .

But Teapot, his grin open for seeming ever, at last flung apart the windows, and Rose Knight, too composed, slid too ceremoniously into the frame, an insincere and lavish portrait, already executed and too new of colour. Queely Sheill, recalled by Teapot's slapping, appeared behind the artist and breathed steam on his topper. He was another portrait which she allowed herself to observe with the upper part of a glance. Her heart flushed and opened, and she heard a rosy voice call to her. The colder hand of her mind slammed the doors and stilled the cry, and her lady's legitimate partial glance slipped to its duty and Mr Vaneleigh without exposing that it had admitted Queely Sheill as far as a door needing to be closed.

Cold airs, and the activity of getting Mr Vaneleigh to *Cindermead* over the low and slimy ridges, had coloured Queely Sheill to a greater beauty or, rather, had pointed up his most eye-catching qualities. His youth and vigour, weather-burnished, shone more romantically behind the shorter man who had dragged himself by suffering steps to stand, dingy and bitten to the bone, like a starving vagrant about to beg toad-in-a-hole.

Weather, however, is gothic. Weather can mar, debilitate and even destroy, but is escapable. Inconstancy and its own senselessness sabotage it; the social vigours of civilization deny it. Civilization, for better or worse, is inescapable; Mr Vaneleigh's hat was swept off, and his bow was made with a skill, a timing and propriety that Rose Knight instantly endorsed as too fluent and, at the same time, too offhand to be a lackey's.

Twenty years had passed since she had last seen Mr Vaneleigh. This second view of him informed her that his eyes, at least, were unforgettable. She had been near enough to see their colour, and had slyly observed them long enough to be aware of their probing intensity. Otherwise the creature had dwindled, had aged, was a little stooped and no longer curled his long dark-brown hair. But the hair of his manner seemed still curled.

"Mr Vaneleigh," she said, "you are promptness itself for so vile a day. Sir Sydney this morning doubted if the weather would let you come."

She indicated entrance, for all was as it should be, murderer or no, and the next moment had come.

"My portfolio, if you please," said Mr Vaneleigh over his shoulder to Queely Sheill and, receiving it, walked his few paces as straightened-up and dominant as Beau Brummel, and entered the drawing-room. He passed Teapot and there was no underhand odour of mortality. The notion of collapse began to fade as the conservatory warmth, and the efforts and force of his social will, began to revitalize him.

"I imagine," said Rose Knight, "—and I'm *quite* in distress—that you've come by the more provoking and shorter track. It takes longer."

"It takes long," he said, "and's certainly provoking. 'Twas not a lucky hit."

"You must need to recruit your strength," she said, uncaringly, as to a sister-in-law.

The white marble of the Belgian chimney-piece was altar enough for his need. Its god visibly and with fluid modesty wrestled itself within it. Like all gods it was not to be caressed without hurt; like all gods it was invoked only in need; like all gods it was made by man.

Since she had indicated the room with a gesture and with eyes which questioned the suitability of the room for his purpose and, at the same moment, showed her determination that it was ideal, he was able to tack about professionally, and establish himself centrally, and let his body sponge up the fire's medicine. He was able to say . . . oh, charming and blank! . . . "Is this the chosen room?"

She inclined her head.

"Very good. *Very*. Its height, I take it, is about fourteen feet six inches. Excellent. Those french windows! . . . the luminosity, you know. I am quite luminosity-mad."

He put his portfolio, definitely, also with care, on a sofa-table.

With an effort that did not show and an ease that did not reveal its employment, he arranged to not see Asnetha Sleep for he gathered that she was to be not seen although she rustled gaudily and could not not be seen.

"I'd *thought* this room." Rose Knight was flattered enough, even though he was merely a gifted curiosity to her, and her husband's unwanted donation to her entertainment. Or a spiteful whim.

Asnetha Sleep's leg flashed out in its velvet shroud as he moved. He stepped over it. He narrowed his eyes in pretended and congratulatory examination of Rose Knight's choice:

"This room . . . ah, ultra-absolute! I vow't could nowhere be bettered. That disposition of windows! Stimulating as soda-water!"

My God, Vaneleigh, he thought, you're thorough-going, you're high-flying! The lady is pure rock: you're in danger of tasting the grass beyond the nose of your steed! That fire has unhinged you!

Yet he could not cut his charm at *soda-water*.

"And," he finished, "what so brings out a similar quality in my subject . . . it's inspiring and will bear repetition! . . . the *luminosity*, the radiant luminosity!"

That was as far as he was prepared to go in formal

gallantry and specious charm. From the lively, he thought, we must now ascend to the sincere.

He had adroitly moved about and possessed the room, not too much to make enthusiasm eccentric and decision boorish, not too little to disclose his deep indifference to anything except his crayon transfiguring an uncertain and scented mortal to the certainty of a scent-stripped immortal. To force a next move he laid down his beaver gloves by the portfolio.

A dead point occurred. It was a dead point in the relations of that group, and of a few moments' duration only. In it they paused like children who do not know they are growing older or that the sun will set. Disposed, apparently carelessly, within sight of each other, the quintette made a tell-tale design. Each of them so perfectly understood, and so perfectly paid a merely objective deference to, their parts that carelessness found them exactly in character. It needs a mere moment for fate to sprinkle the invisible seeds of cataclysm.

At the window he had been told to open, and not yet told to close, Teapot, with his man's fingers blackly curled over the porcelain handle, waited for an order, a rebuke or an edulcorated suggestion. He could have been waiting the whip. He was the eternal and corrupted page-boy who appeared not to have the ability to indulge an uncertainty. Nor were certainties his to indulge. His grin, at that dead point, was quarter-ajar, was ready to squeeze shut or open far too wide enough to display nothingness.

Mr Vaneleigh had yet to untie his portfolio and take up a crayon. He held his impatient artistic hands to the fire to dry poverty from them.

Rose Knight, having thought too late of a fan to promote by contrast the loveliness of her hands, stopped thinking of a fan. For no reason, or because seductive women in portraits did, she relaxed her left hand between her breasts where it felt the agate eye. The eye was cool as withdrawal. It had no responsibilities to seeking or ignoring, to sleeping or simmering in sleeplessness, to denying tears entrance, or squinting with desire. Its touch at the heart of her palm stilled her to a posture of gracious ladyhood.

Outside, in the unmistakable afternoon where no warmth

could veil, emasculate or falsely embellish him, stood Queely Sheill and his visible breath. Unconcerned with the notion that he would wait, he waited. The idea that he need not wait in that spot, exposed as a garden deity and more neatly clothed than a scarecrow, had not yet come to him. He could have chucked the little black under the chin or into the air—there seemed little else to do. He waited: the classic groom too handsome not to be ravished and thrown away.

Asnetha Sleep, her deformities arranged in a hope of concealment, sat insecurely bolt erect in expensive bedragglement for, without movement, her adornments had flagged, had relapsed to litter. To Mr Vaneleigh, who did not wish to meet her, she could be nothing until he was presented to her. She knew Rose Knight would not present him. In crying out "I shall not meet him" she had dropped a chance for humiliation to be jumped at by Rose Knight. Asnetha Sleep had more money than her cousin's wife and more advantages than a poor relation in her intelligence, affectations, artful dodges and deformity, yet poor relation was what Rose Knight contrived to make her appear. From within her casings she watched Queely Sheill. He seemed to her a servant. She knew what could be done with the bodies of servants. What could not be done with the well-proportioned body of a murderer's servant?

Rose, Lady Knight, hostess, lifted her hand from the eye of agate, and began smoothly to do what she alone of those five people was empowered to do. Unless there had happened some injury to natural order—an earthquake, the appearance of an archangel or the late King William—no one else could, with decorum, order the next move.

She spoke, and what seemed a solicitude was a future stirring in its sleep:

"Your man, Mr Vaneleigh. . . . ?"

"He will wait," said the artist, at the tapes of his portfolio. He untied them. Then, explanation being felt necessary, he added:

"He's not my man. Months ago he offered his services to me—it was *not* a solicitation for *paid* employment. He continues to offer them, to *grant* them. His eccentricity is to offer services *sans* obligation. He is, I fear, his heart's dupe. Truth to say, he's a strange medley. Those gloves I wear are his gift."

Mr Vaneleigh wearied of that. Queely Sheill had emotions the reverse of most men's: they relished committing themselves. He was a portfolio-carrier, a gloves-giver, he took short-cuts, he. . . .

"He will wait."

"He will surely be cold, Mr Vaneleigh." A less handsome man could have frozen to death under her nose.

His locks are golden, thought Asnetha Sleep, her nose moving at the sight of the pale hair that Queely Sheill, his cap off, now harrowed his fingers through.

"Black boy," said Lady Knight weakening to a weakness, "listen to me. Take the man to the little Chinese room where there is a fire. Ask Romney to give him ale and bread-and-cheese. Close the windows as you go."

"I am to take the man to the little Chinese room. I am to tell Romney ale and bread-and-cheese. I am to close the windows." The over-cultivated monotone was pitched to that last height before breaking and foundering towards the tones of masculinity.

Teapot went outside, and closed the windows.

Mr Vaneleigh chose among his pencils and crayons.

The women found themselves compelled to sham not watching the black boy talk to and lead the man from the terrace towards the back of the house.

As he disappeared, Rose Knight's satin moved, flowed, slithered—a sleepy viper on a tree of fruit.

Asnetha Sleep gathered that, at last, the time for her to be formally disregarded had arrived. She pressed herself up from the ottoman, and violently plunged forward and wheeled around, her rings blinking as her arms flailed like wings to steady her. She was about to be bolder, to be striking, to babble from the midst of her hangings drenched in aromatic vinegars something that would leave Rose Knight nothing to do before discarding her but introduce the little murderer who had so obviously once been a gentleman though an artist.

Rose Knight was too gifted not to be quicker. As the cripple completed the pirouette that would find her placed for speech, Rose Knight swooped on gleaming pinions:

"Asnetha, my love, since you are about to desert me so selfishly, do, I implore, send Romney in. Marsala, Mr Vaneleigh?"

He wished to start drawing; considered that, if anything, brandy; but bowed his head to marsala.

"And macaroons?"

He nodded macaroons. Asnetha Sleep had a reckless spasm of malice in appreciation of malice.

"Send Romney in with marsala and macaroons. And two glasses, Asnetha, honey."

Since macaroons were an admission, more even than two glasses and not three or one, of the sharp stone imbedded in Rose Knight's peach-like behaviour, Asnetha Sleep trusted herself to no more than a sudden pealing forth of "Macaroons! I fly to ring. For Romney and. Macaroons!" and, circling and dipping, she was gone from the room. The uneven tattoo of her soles was tapped on remoter and remoter floor-boards until her voice, dulcified by distance, and upping and downing like a gull bewildered by indoors, was heard:

"Teapot, treasure! Teapot, treasure! Where art thou?"

"She knows where he is," said Lady Knight, as tame as poisoned cream, to no person. Then, "Shall I be in this chair, Mr Vaneleigh? On the ottoman? The sofa?"

Ten minutes passed before the marsala arrived.

Mr Vaneleigh was seeking still, his crayon poised and anxious, for the subtler outline of spirit which just underlay the surface of flesh arranged on the sofa before him, when Teapot and the salver appeared around the screen.

Lady Knight's voice was not kind:

"Why are you butler, black boy? Where is Romney?"

"Where is Romney, ma'am? He is in his pantry ma'am."

Teapot's grin, white and blind and unhappy, settled on his face like something that need not have been there but had nowhere else to go.

"Did Romney bid you bring the salver? Don't grin, don't grin, child."

The grin went out.

"Miss Sleepy bade me bring the tray. I'm not to grin."

"Miss *Sleep* bade you bring the *salver*."

"Miss Sleep bade me bring the salver."

"Put the salver on this table."

"I'm to put the salver on the table."

"Nearer to me. Really, you're a fool. At my elbow."

"Nearer to ma'am's elbow. I am a fool."

His burden given up, he hung his hands by his sides, and the overgrown black fingers, lined on the inside with a nameless other colour, flinched secretly to discard the irritation of chilled silver.

Desiring instant dismissal, headlong escape, he did not watch her pour the wine with heightened style, but eyed the screen around which he saw himself racing to find out what Miss Sleep was doing.

"Mr Vaneleigh. . . ." Rose Knight had finished pouring. He took a glass.

"And", she said, handing the dish, with an overacted flatness which verged on an arch cunning noticeable and surprising to him, "a macaroon." Then, seeing that Teapot craved to go away, "Black boy, you may have one macaroon . . . no, let it be two. Eat them by the fender."

"I may have one macaroon. No! I may. . . ."

"Stop that. Talk no more," she said. "To the fender. Eat quietly, and try not to spill."

Teapot and his macaroons moved to the end of the fender where, because he did not like to be seen eating, even by people who did not look at him, he turned his back. His buttocks were wincing with fury.

She sipped.

She said, "How very very strange that this should be: the *last* time I saw you, Mr Vaneleigh, you were eating a macaroon."

She looked at him fully before lowering her lids.

Although he could be surprised, he had no intention of showing surprise, and possessed the skill to uphold that intention. Nor had he the intention of showing interest. Yet his hand did put down the macaroon he had not bitten, and his left eyebrow, as of its own volition, minutely arched itself.

She sipped again, pacifically giving him her lowered lids and their barricade of lashes.

"It was in London. Years ago . . . twenty years? You were with Mr Lamb, Charles Lamb, in Hickson's *pâtisserie*."

Whatever shadow she was attempting to incarnate, it was a foregone and half-forgotten self he had not wished to be confronted with, startled or disgusted by. He preferred to have up his own ghosts at his own order. With perplexing charm he said:

"I am *quite* afraid—I am indeed—it must have been an only occasion. I seem to recall that Hickson's was, with us, in the worst odour. Of course, little vanities and weaknesses freckle the gravest minds. Even the gravest."

She would not be rebuked by anyone or a poised ex-convict. She raised her lashes, and released an unadorned glance empty as a glass knife.

"I was there many times," she lied. "*Darling* Piccadilly!"

Then she continued truthfully but with no change of tone that would index her lie as one, "It would have been twenty years. Such a crush! I was near enough to hear you speak to Mr Lamb. One thing you said I've not forgotten."

Her last sentence was flavoured with regret—most tranquil and succulent of all emotions. It warned him that what he had said was what she might once have wished to say herself. My God, he thought, she's caught me at some moment of mawkish do-me-good insipidity! But, whatever wildfire and brilliant noise he had made in a silver past, he no longer cared. This fugitive encounter, from a time when he had his own footman William, and his own establishment at 49 Great Marlborough Street in the house once Sarah Siddons's, was not to be allowed to irritate him unless more response than the trite and seemly were required from him. Subduing a thought in irritation's direction, he said:

"I cannot at all remember what sentiment worth your remembrance I can have expressed." He could not forbear to add urbanely, "In such a place."

"You said that you did not scramble after the loaves and fishes."

He did not falter, neither did he flare. He delayed comment on the young Judas Griffin Vaneleigh, of *London Magazine*, essayist and art critic, though affecting not to delay by closely and unnecessarily watching himself put down his glass of marsala most unnecessarily very slowly. More than very slowly, the notion minted and paid out coin by coin, he said:

"*That* snake reminds me too much of a large eel! I think now, Lady Knight, that any belief I had then could only have been provisional."

Immediately this total struck him as plated. It was an idea as enclosed and useless as a rotten egg. He had, with premeditated spuriousness, denied himself.

"Lady Knight," he said, "I've just heard myself tell a lie. Some of my younger beliefs were auto-adulation, were running *mad*. But I did *not scramble*; 'twas hateful to me *then*. Is *now*. Works of mine that, formerly, would have brought loaves and fishes but which had no value in *my eyes*, I have given to the burning. How else could I, in honesty, have continued my self-imposed task of trying to restore the public scale of taste to a fitter equilibrium?" His eyes did not diminish or intensify their essence but his voice softened, "I should commit the portrait of you to the burning did it embarrass my conscience. This, even if I should lose a benefactor thereby."

The macaroon he had put down remained unbitten, he had merely and dispassionately kissed the rim of his wine-glass. He took up a crayon. It was obvious to her that even a murderer she had been indifferent to meeting could be a bore, and also that he was finished with one sort of good behaviour. Before he could direct her, she assumed the posture chosen for the portrait. This did not prevent him from saying:

"I do trust, Lady Knight, that—for the sake of a portrait that should please us *both*—you'll not find it too irksome to look this way, directly at my left shoulder. . . ."

As she turned her transparently pale and almost phosphorescent eyes in the artist's direction she said to Teapot's bowed and embroidered back, "You may go, black boy. Go quietly."

"I may go. I must go quietly," gabbled Teapot from a high confusion of mental sin. Soundlessly he went.

Mr Vaneleigh saw that the whites of her eyes were a pink of the same tone as the pallid blue iris and the cosmetic pink of her cheeks. The shallows-feigning glaze on the eyeballs obscured a depth he must let give up its leviathans if his crayon were to do revelation. The stiffened satin, the stare of agate, the mock-meek hair meant nothing. He had, as well, in times gone, drawn too many perfect breasts. Those before him, too, told nothing. The eyes, and the outlines attempting to control hidden outlines and absorbing them in the effort, were what he and his crayon sought. If what was sought turned out to be a lie, that was what he and his pencil would find and manufacture into a truth.

Imprisoned to munch macaroons in the drawing-room Teapot had endured disquiet through an eternity: it is to the prisoner, the sleepless and nomad that the hours and life are long. Disquiet became an ordeal of suspicion and jealousy. There was the archway he could not flee through until bidden, there were the screen, the wall, and the walls beyond, through which he could not see or hear, and through which it was imperative he should see and hear.

Another sense, an extra instinct whose rousing-up he could not foresee or control in its comings and goings, had informed him of that necessity to escape. The instinct had been ingrafted within him from his father's loins and mother's womb. It had been educated by their fluttering fingertips and musky embraces in a Brighton mansion near a sunless sloshing sea and a beach of pebbles like ossified potatoes. That inheritance had suddenly, as he carried the salver to the drawing-room, begun to expose to him that *Cindermead* for him, that afternoon, was riddled with nameless information.

Instinct, the memory that is still unsullied by civilization, retains its ability to lead the consciousness directly towards the essential, the primitive centre of the forest. Apprehensions had vexed Teapot on his way to the drawing-room; in its heated trap there had appeared omens.

In the furtive agitation he had felt all about him were warnings. The flames of the fire had significantly though subtly changed outline, and their speed and direction of movement. The figures on the screen had turned their pin-prick eyes suggestively elsewhere. From the two macaroons fragments had fallen on the hearth in a prophetic pattern he had peered to translate into knowledge of a definite shape.

What takes place among dark trees does not whole-heartedly concern adults; hints of ornamental carnality, mysterious screams or the implications of disgusting whispers satisfy passers-by sullied by sophistry and carrying Self like a lamp. Children, more avid, fearless and bestial, carry no lamp, are themselves lamps. Teapot had suffered carking premonitions until released for his dash towards the centre of the forest.

Outside the drawing-room, he began to run tiptoe, to hurtle noiselessly through the corridors, through the boles and underbrush, towards the Chinese room and the hidden centre. When he was near enough to the closed door to hear the voices within the room he stopped, he concealed his disproportionate hands in his armpits, his mouth fell open, he listened.

Lust is generally gifted in using all the resources of guile. Lust does not bother itself with more than a minimum of time-wasting wiliness when a difference in station has already disposed the quarry to a useful servility. Platitude, inanity and gossip will serve.

Asnetha Sleep had discovered from Queely Sheill who his father was. The young man stood by his interrupted bread-and-cheese, and answered questions, and listened.

To keep on talking, however long, foolishly and affectedly on the subject of a father, however odd, to a son, however unusual, gave, she thought, force to her careless impersonation of guilelessness. She had done that. Of the young man's body she had, at least, the ear. Secure in that, her sentences no longer fractured themselves. Unaware that she fished wrongly in the wrong section of the waters with a bait that, to Queely Sheill, stank, she rattled on, continuing her impersonation of the chatterbox lady with no purpose except magnanimity.

"I declare," she was saying to Teapot's ears also, with what he recognized as more than usual false dottiness, "I declare I shall *really* be in the pathetics if, *now*, you don't tell me of Mr Vaneleigh. So striking! So *clever!* We ladies of Hobart Town cannot keep our minds from him. His *heavenly* skill!" She rolled her eyes. "You must be consumedly proud of your master."

" 'E is not," said Queely Sheill, "my master!"

"Of course! Of course! La, la, la, I heard Mr Vaneleigh say so himself to Lady Knight. He unmistakably said you were not his servant."

"Truth, that. Queely's no one's servant."

"Then, that being so, how much prouder you must be! How *very* much prouder of your *friend's* skill and fame."

She was surprised when his face ran forbidding.

" 'E is not," said Queely Sheill, "my friend. 'Ow could 'e *hever* be? Mr Vaneleigh is a gemman."

His sternness, though merely relative, startled her to a sense of peril. He had laughed about his father. He frowned handsomely about Mr Vaneleigh. Peril in the offing stimulated her discretion and mollified her antics.

"Indeed!" She clasped her hands together quite sensibly. She was interested. "You produce here a diverting mystery for me. He is not your friend, and yet you trudge the miles from Hobart Town by his side! You wait for him! You are not his man, and you carry for him!"

" 'E is a sick gemman."

"That would scarcely forbid him being your friend."

"Ho, *no*! But Queely's Mr Vaneleigh's friend. Suppose 'e hasks me to go a mile, well, Queely'll go two."

"Mystery on mystery!"

The relationship, in which she had lost interest, was a man's puzzle. It began to ruffle her. She would drop it. But Queely Sheill kept on.

"No mystery. Queely's 'is *friend*, that's all."

"And he not yours!" Pique began to show.

"I don't hask no payment for being a friend. Mr Vaneleigh don't 'ave to fret hisself with that. Queely's Mr Vaneleigh's friend."

Asnetha Sleep was nonplussed. Golden hair, with his winning profile, and his vile and engaging accent, seemed to flick at her and her desire with his abrupt nobilities. She abandoned flim-flam. She flicked back, and with heavier hand than she intended or the situation demanded.

"Friendship is the proper return for friendship. I observe you scorning to accept this. Perhaps 'tis no fault of your Mr Vaneleigh. *You* are proud. Proud!"

Outside, at the change of tone, which he had himself often quailed under, Teapot's face loosened a shade from sullenness, and his head bent itself farther forward.

"Not Queely. *Never* Queely." He laughed at the thought of what she meant by pride.

Inventing insolence and a contempt in his brevities and coarse laughter, she flushed. She swayed on her chair.

"I see!" she cried nastily. Teapot squeezed his fists deeper into his armpits. "Oh, I see you! You are charity." *Charity* sounded like *incest*.

Here's a high flight starting, thought Queely Sheill, here's pepper! He raised his voice to explain patiently:

"Hit is no charity, ma'am. I hassure you. Hit's what Queely cannot 'elp. Nor does 'e try to. I must give myself where I'm needed. *Hif* 'e's *proper* needed, Queely's there."

She was aroused. She curbed her voice so that it flowed from her lips like a bitter honey:

"This . . . this Queel-y is cute. And vain! Cute and vain! Oh, a pretty fellow and a charitable dog! The clever Mr Vaneleigh has, then, *needed* you! Has *thrown* himself on your charity . . . oh, la, la, la, forgive me! . . . has thrown himself on your *benevolence*."

"Not thrown!" His tone borrowed from hers, but a stronger honey, and sweeter than bitter. "Not 'im. 'E's a gemman. 'E 'ardly knows Queely's in hexistence. 'E don't even call me by name—hafter seven or eight months. A friend don't need no name. A friend don't need no calling after. Ho, they've spat on 'is 'eart, and will not again. I'll bet a 'orse to a 'en on that. 'E's too proud to let 'em spit again. 'They 'ave scouted me,' 'e says to Queely. 'They 'ave scouted me and I'll be revenged.' "

Queely Sheill accompanied his quotation with a baroque gesture filched from his father.

Asnetha Sleep began to laugh. It was an ejection of sounds as crippled as she, and as disordered as her clothing. It tended to hysteria.

"You are indeed an actor's son!" She jerked out the words. "Actor's son . . . an actor. . . ." She placed her hands with their jewel-thickened fingers over her mouth as Queely Sheill moved nearer.

"Ma'am," he said, "Mr Vaneleigh, 'e's too gentle, 'e's gentle as a sparrer. 'E's too weary for revenge and what-all *hor* any such wickedness. 'E says revenge to *say* it to me, but not to mean it. Queely knows."

His placidity enraged her. She snatched her hands away from her mouth. Her legs jolted about. She ignored their feckless activity, and clapped her hands, clashing the rings together in an exaggeration and travesty of applause:

"You see! You hear! I applaud your chivalry to a murderer!"

Teapot could have skipped into a waltz as he heard this malignity, but his dead parents' fingertips on his temples and the nerves inside his elbows flickered *Wait*!

"Wait!" said the far-off ceiling and the lisping fires and the grooved skirting-boards and the enkindled air, "Wait!"

"*How* I applaud your perception of a murderer's need!"

She ceased clapping, and her weighted hands dropped dead down into the velvet mess of her fleshless and pitiful lap.

"Very kind you are, ma'am," said Queely Sheill, breathing rather heavily with restraint among the flimsy *Chimoiserie*. The restraint was too hard bought to be more than momentary. Immediately afterwards he shouted:

"Murderer or no murderer, Queely takes no 'eed, Queely don't ask. I ain't no one to judge. The same old snow or what-all falls down on the good ones and the bad ones."

He walked away from her to the other side of the table, and once again shouted:

"I don't *hask* so I don't know. I can't know hif what they all say in *The Shades* about Mr Vaneleigh. . . ."

He dropped that. Then, she could not see why, and nor did he know why, he sat down.

Although parts of her still trembled and her hands still glowed from clapping, she felt extraordinarily refreshed, almost stimulated to dropping her pursuit.

"How exceedingly provoking of you to shout so!" she said with an insulting return of her first manner. She parodied herself, utterly aware that she was doing so but not able to guess what next response this female chicanery would inflame forth:

"Oh, la, la, *la*, tiresome *creature*! Noisy creature. And yet you do not say what your friends in *The Shades* know of your Mr Vaneleigh."

His face changed. Its expression became at once cunning and male. He rose with care, and minute muscles beneath the skin of his cheeks and jaw quaked equally on both sides of his face. Risen to his height, he picked a small piece of cheese from the platter and put it in his mouth. As he chewed, he said:

"I 'aven't said what, because it don't matter what. And you, ma'am, 'ave not said what I knows you want to say."

Queely Sheill had learnt from his own life by being forced to watch himself live it. His desire to comfort others, at whatever cost to himself, was a defiance flung fearlessly in the face of a warier and selfish humanity. It was a defiance flung, with severity, in his own face, that had had its moments of contemplating blindness, of turning its eyes from the sight of the desperate taker to the profitable giver.

He expected, from the crippled woman who had suffered an ecstatic shock, evasion and mendacities.

"What I wish to say?" she said. Her face had become stern and haggard. "You know what *I* wish to say?"

"Queely knows."

"You must then do me the honour of acquainting me with what I wish to say. I'm unaware of any such wish."

"I shouldn't say to ladies."

He had no incurable modesties; he had plunged naked too often into the burning abodes of too many lives. The crackling, charred and hurtling rafters gave him no fear. Nevertheless, his breeding had given him, and experience had not taken away from him, some gentilities.

"Ah! What I wish to say is not fit for you, for a man, to say!"

"*Queely* shouldn't say it. That's *hall.* 'Tis not for 'im to say."

"Pride! I foretold you proud." She had already forgotten that he had already laughed at what she had already said.

He laughed. He took another piece of cheese and held it up.

" 'Tis not for me to say, but I'll say."

He put the cheese between his lips which edged it in to his teeth. He chewed.

"You want Queely," he said. He swallowed.

"Monster!" cried Asnetha Sleep tangling her rings and speckless fingernails among the ribbons at her false breasts. "You are a perfect monster. I shall scream."

In her agitation she made vowel-like sounds. She lurched from her chair, and clung to its back, uncertain if she were terrified or elated.

"You won't go screaming. And Queely's no monster. 'E's a good boy. I seen what you want in your eyes and what-all. 'Ot as pepper and . . ." He crossed his eyes. "See? Heasy to tell. All ladies the same."

Lopsided, uneasily tethered by her claws, she began to whisper a number of times, "Vanity! Outrageous vanity!"

Teapot, unable to hear, was terrified.

"Queely's no gemman, ma'am." He imitated her, delighted at himself in imitation, "Owh, a pretty fell-oh . . . 'e's a pretty fellow is Queely."

"Conceit masked as charity! Vanity offering . . . offering love like . . . oh, like a pet monkey."

Queely Sheill flushed.

It was no more in his nature to be virtuous by revulsion than it was to be made greedy by attraction. A happy Venus and a contented leper found him indifferent. He condoned his employment in the service of others only when those others wore the peculiar talisman of failure that he was somehow able to distinguish among haphazard baubles. But his condonement did not have a pacific character, and he would not be misunderstood. He sprang from his chair and fell to his knees. In this attitude, simply borrowed from plays, and most absurd, but seeming necessary and correct to him in life, he gazed anxiously at Asnetha Sleep who clung to the chair-back. He began to speak:

"*Not* love, ma'am. I've gone on marrer-bones to say it. I offers no love to no one, I don't. Never you mind about saying pet monkeys. Queely don't love *no one*. Not 'is dad. Who's 'is dad? It's no good only loving them that loves you. It's no good loving them that don't love you. Mr Vaneleigh! So Queely don't love 'is dad or Mr Vaneleigh or no one. Queely's for them who *wants* Queely. Everyone who wants, I give them what they want of me. *Hif* their 'earts are wretched and put-upon. But not *love*. What is love? The love they all say, or in books and what-all, is what they call something else. You keep your ogles hon *that* and you won't get pinked in the peeper. Love ain't what they make up to say. Queely'll take some turns in Bushy Park with you, ma'am. You can use 'im. But love! Ho *no*!"

He had talked his anxiety of being misunderstood down. His innocent and experienced eyes shone with a holy pleasure, and he blew his nose. It was agony for him to mangle out explanations, but his skill had just surprised and appeased him. It had never dawned on him, and never would, that his emotion was a seductive liar and a treacherous counsellor.

There was a space of silence, of what resembled mutual appeasement. Asnetha Sleep did not pretend to herself that she had understood anything more than that the young man's body was hers for the planning. In that she felt competent. The remainder of golden-hair's thoughts had, for her, run about like fowls in a rainstorm. She had a feeling she should have been in her Byron brown velvet.

Queely Sheill, having looked at what he had blown into

his handkerchief, remained kneeling, either because it did not matter or he had forgotten.

Teapot was shuddering impressively in the corridor. The whites of his eyes showed. In a sort of epilepsy of jealousy and fear that might have made noise, he clawed and clenched at his shapely black throat to prevent that. His ears had translated adult lunacy of expression into enough for his small intelligence to understand. He could not understand silence. His instinct which had led his ears had also presented him with erotic incredibilities. Silence terrified. He escaped it. More silently than silence he tiptoed to his own absurd and comfortable room, and locked the door, and found that he had brought with him and his agony nothing except a silence he dared not break with outcry.

Asnetha Sleep broke the silence in the Chinese room.

"There was," she said, ". . . there is, I assure you, no need to be on your knees."

She said no more.

She rocked herself into motion, whirled, hobbled to the door.

As she disappeared, Queely Sheill got up, brushed his knees with his hands, and sat to the ale and food he had been interrupted at. Presently he had finished. He poked the fire, he sat in a chair beside it to await Mr Vaneleigh, and fell into a doze.

It is difficult to escape being the sort of person another thinks one is. One suffers censure not for one's million careful avoidances but one's two careless collisions, not because one lives like a saint but because one looks like a rogue, not because one violates one's own conscience but because one trusts in the consciences of others.

Time had passed in the drawing-room where Rose Knight's increasing boredom had driven Judas Griffin Vaneleigh to apply the piece of bread he used as an eraser to this or that line, and his crayon to replacing them with lines that were boredom-netting. Time had passed in Asnetha Sleep's bedroom where she and her Welsh maid wrestled her into her Byron brown velvet. Time had passed in Teapot's bedroom where the black boy had searched his drawers and caskets for a lesser treasure than the one he held in his hand and did not wish to use as bribe for Queely Sheill. Time passed in Van Diemen's Land, and on the whole earth which is not aware that time is on it, or man who makes time. Time passed in the Chinese room, and Queely Sheill slept on.

It is difficult to escape being, even in sleep when one is no one, the sort of person another thinks one is.

Teapot entered the room, and closed the door. He stood watching Queely Sheill.

Those with fair skins and fair hair seem, when their pale eyelids are down in sleep, to be more shell-less, nuder and more innocent than the darker sleepers. Thus Queely Sheill. Teapot, knowing from eavesdropping that this abated and softly purring form was noisy, a monster, a murderer, wicked and his enemy, was abashed to terror to find this unnatural conjunction, as of the malevolent dead and the meek living, in one shape. It was in terror that he moved towards the sleeper, mutely as a danger from his own dreams, and began to stroke one of Queely Sheill's hands with its decoration of gilt hairs and its pink knuckles.

As Queely Sheill came from sleep, Teapot concealed his terror, and illustrated his feverish desire to placate, by the widest smile he could arrange. As Queely Sheill digested the smile and Teapot with it, the black boy put a long finger across his purple lips and his teeth to enjoin the silence Queely Sheill had not arrived at breaking. Teapot's eyes, despite their darkness, iris and pupil melted into one, and difficult to read, nevertheless implored the continuance of silence with a fervour no finger could have.

Queely Sheill, fully awake, smiled and nodded, placing himself trustfully at Teapot's disposal.

Teapot took up, between his two black hands which were cold and silky, the white hand he had already stroked. He stroked and fondled it again, with a gentle urgency, with the imploring diffidence of one who stroked the devil on the back.

Throughout this, his eyes, in the most ultimate depths of which Queely Sheill discerned dark lights glowing like rubies, made a long quest into the other's blue eyes, those naked and uncompromising fields. Not once, as his eyes demanded and his moving hands pleaded, did Teapot blink. It was pity that terror, and the exercise of holding it in check, held also in check Teapot's instincts. He was bravely and frantically trying to invoke what he had no need to.

Then, as Queely Sheill was on the point of making some move, some trustworthy gesture, in deference to his visitor's still mystifying but ardent and important performance, Teapot ceased manual supplication. It was as though those placatory strokings and the quest of his eyes had not proved fruitful, as though the interlocking explorations, and the unexpressed implication in the silence and the disclosures that lay beyond the avoidance of speech, had not proved a point.

Without unlocking his gaze he retreated a few steps. From his new position he began a pantomime.

He hobbled soundlessly about. He stumbled and lurched. He whirled in a circle with his arms outstretched. He plucked at the bosom of his embroidered coat as at fripperies, and curled his fingers. He sidled, dragging one foot. This elaborate and shameless impersonation of the crippled woman over, the black boy pointed at Queely Sheill, and shook his head a number of times.

Queely Sheill got up, and was about to speak, but Teapot flashed his finger to his lips, and looked at the door, and shook his head again so much in an anguish, that the man said nothing. He smiled and put out his hand towards the boy.

Teapot, eyeing the door, quickly drew from his pocket a gold chain on which were strung seven gold coins. A fever to be gone had come over him. He darted to the man and, taking his hand, placed the chain in it, and closed down the pale fingers on the gift, the offering, the bribe. He ran to the door, opened it, and was gone before Queely Sheill could say anything or "No!"

"No!" said Queely Sheill to the chain, the guineas, the closed door, to the Chinese wallpaper.

"Poor 'eart," he said, "poor little black 'eart," and he

swung the chain, and thought, That's a leveller! That's a cracker! Queely don't want the lady nor the gold! That's a doubler in the bellows! Queely must think.

At this point clocks everywhere in the house uttered and persisted uttering some hour.

Asnetha Sleep's voice called, "Teapot, treasure! Where *art* thou? Teapot! Teapot!"

Cindermead displayed all sorts of voices at varying distances. A door slammed. Unseen footsteps walked in and out of Queely Sheill's life as he dangled the chain, and could think of nothing to do. He heard a carriage drive up on gravel, and the hoofbeats and wheels pass from gravel on to brick and to cessation.

There was a tap at the door. As the door opened, Queely Sheill closed his fingers over the chain, and put his hand in a pocket.

"Please, sir," said Teapot in piercing and immaculate voice, "I am to bring you to Mr Vaneleigh in the front porch. Ma'am says it is six o'clock. I am a fool."

Queely Sheill, about to speak, saw Asnetha Sleep in the corridor behind Teapot, and said nothing, and kept his hand around the coins lest they should rattle.

Asnetha Sleep looked at Queely Sheill, and her long earrings glittered and shook. Queely Sheill looked at Teapot. Teapot looked at no one.

"Lead on, Teapot. My treasure. On little. Black feet," cried Asnetha Sleep again snapping sentences in two.

As Teapot led, his feet flapping, as Queely Sheill walked after him, Asnetha Sleep, reeking of another scent and too much, followed them both, hobbling, and dragging a foot as though imitating Teapot imitating her.

Judas Griffin Vaneleigh who progressed slowly and Queely Sheill who kept in step were caught by the rising moon as they walked over the bridge of Sandy Bay Stream and began to climb Barracks Hill, but it was not until they reached its crest that Queely Sheill stopped shouting the songs he had shouted since leaving *Cindermead*, and both men halted. Mr Vaneleigh was panting heavily.

The sky, itself clear of untidier and more formless elements resembling dirty rag-mops, contained an object immoderately clear-edged and lucid; the rag-mop clouds had been dragged back over Organ-pipe so that it was easy and practically unavoidable to indulge the unwholesome pleasure of staring the moon in the eye.

Neither of the two men loved what most men loved; the chilling intoxication of mystery. They loved, on the one hand, more than most men; on the other hand they loved less. Mystery was the least of their loves. They were unable to deceive themselves, or put their faith in the absurd, or cry aloud for miracles.

Queely Sheill had therefore sung as he reined his pace little by little to the slackening but patient shuffle of the artist. To sing was no better, wiser, crueller or kinder than to keep silence or suffer in imagination while Mr Vaneleigh suffered. Another's pain, in any case, is unimaginable, as one's own departed pain is unrecallable.

On the hilltop, Mr Vaneleigh leant against the barracks' wall to discourage exhaustion, and garner strength for further suffering and fresh exhaustion.

Behind lay *Cindermead* and its imported luxuries and furies and triflings. Before lay Hobart Town.

"It has," said Mr Vaneleigh, "a square, hard, clumsy look even though set on hollows and uprisings like—like a sort of land-breakers, inactive waves. Split me! it has the very atmosphere of a spa stuck down for outcasts to take the waters of fear. And see how the moon . . ." He broke off.

Queely Sheill waited, and became tired of the boiling and rattling of frogs.

"Tell Queely," he said.

Mr Vaneleigh was blank. Tell whom what?

"The moon it was," said Queely Sheill. "You was at 'See 'ow the moon. . . .' "

"The moon . . . that moon, that *same* moon!" Mr Vaneleigh raised his hand and pointed.

"Oh, don't sir! Don't point at the moon!" Queely Sheill was disturbed. "Forgive, pray, but hit's *bad* to point at the moon."

"One moonlight night," said Judas Griffin Vaneleigh, "we had dined well at my apartments in Great Marlborough Street. A group of us, no matter whom. *One* was Macready the actor; your father will have heard of—perhaps known, perhaps acted with—him. Did we eat partridge-flavoured veal and ham pie? It was my favourite. In a red dish. A whimsy, the red dish. Matters not. We'd have dined *well.* Oh, I was certainly an amiable creature in those days. Every action of my life emanated from a wish to *please.*

"After dining we took a turn in the nearby streets. I and Macready. And the others. But *Macready.* The *actor*! I was in high gig: it was my declared opinion that modesty and humility were starving qualities; I had adopted the invincible spirit of bounce, and it had brought me distinction. To be Peter Pastoral and dote on dogs in a turnip-field . . . *not* for *me*! To lie on my pomona-green morocco *chaise longue* and eye my delicious, melting love-painting by Fuseli, *that* was an ecstasy sharper than scourges! I wanted, I and my . . . my *friends* wanted more macaroni and champagne, less boxing and bull beef. You see us?"

"Queely sees you hin the moonlight."

"Tell-tale moonlight! You see a once-serene state, broken now like a vessel of clay. You see an unanswerable truth; hypochondriasis on a horrid hill-top. You see what the moon I must not point at sees; the abodes of the miserable who never truly lived, whose countenances are negative and whose sensibilities are all wiry and frittered! Imbecile and indurated grovellers! Blind-brained! A ragged regiment of beggars in velvet rags!"

His voice, in tone, did not match his meanings. From against the barracks' wall he denigrated quietly; his objectivity was almost as gentle as gesticulations of compassion.

"Odds bobs! lo! 'tis no heart-cooling moon, and has led me into warm digression. You see us? I repeat. We have dined. We have wined. The moon . . . ah, a bottle of champagne for the eyes! . . . sheds unspeakable splendours as we stroll through Carnaby Market to Silver Street. Our cameo breast-pins flash; I touch my nose with my atturgal-scented handkerchief . . . where *was* I? Silver Street in the moonlight.

Then on, slapdashing through Golden Square, to Regent's Quadrant, startling the moon and the patrol and ourselves with our wit-fights. There was *no* gagging-bill in that company. We exhilarated each other to display our attainments to each other, to be boisterous in self-praise. 'Twas all high-thoughts-creating! Such adepts we were in diagnostics! The moon—rat me else!—was as elegant above the Quadrant as my gilt French lamp. *Both* those globes could have been painted with flowers and butterflies! Alas, I'd not yet paid for *my* globe, *nor* for the veal in the pie. I'd not paid the grocer, the baker, the coal-dealer! But I had my best *loons* on, and coursed at a spanking pace through the harmonious entanglements of a happy life. Everything by fits, and nothing long! I changed about—not with the phases of the moon, but the minutes on the clock—one revolving hour found me artist, critic, poet, essayist . . . and buffoon! I could *laugh*! I had not a crowd of bitters behind me in those days, or on that moonlight night . . . Let that night pass from my chatter, as it has from immediacy. Let it pass! Let the years pass!

"Art is grown old and imbecile a second time—it is even so. Is nature now also worn out? Has the knight of the cloven foot smudged the ineffaceable prints of his all-grasping fingers on the moon's globe? And the phoenix of this age, is it no more, fevered with self-curativeness, to burst from its crazy shell? The altars are ready but where are the gods? And why should I, anonymous, flinch? What's to come will come, what's done's done!

"Let moons pass, and the veal cutlets *en papilotte* be eaten, and the sauternes be drunk! Let butcher and wine-merchant go unpaid! Oh, the wines *are* downed and the bills *are* given the go-by! *Easy! And* easy—oh, *how* easy, to dive into the murky dungeons from the high-heaven-piercing tower!

"I sat in my Newgate cell. The jury that condemned me were *not* august presences or the instruments of gods. The judge was a mortal and acid lord. I boggle at the thought of describing my keepers. *Or* my companions. *Pu-gh!* Pah! None of us would have distilled into frankincense and spikenard! We stank like carrion. We enticed therefore those who are nourished on carrion. The sight-seeing tour of Newgate's guests is an invention that takes well with reputation's blowflies. So, while I waited the ship, the—what do they name it?—the *floating academy* that would jettison me at this world's end for ever, I was quizzed by the *beau monde* and the respectable. In their Sunday cravats and flowery bonnets they came endlessly in staring and giggling streams to gratify the most debased curiosity. Reputation's blowflies! Flashy witlings, affected coquettes, gilt chimney-sweeps, oh, any *lady* within the boundary of gentility, chuckle-headed papas with boiled-gooseberry eyes, chalk-and-charcoal-faced misses common as air, the broad-bottomed and nutshell-brained, the half-dipped and pre-judiced, the sow ladies and the gentlemen swine!

"Did I speak before of friends, of a friend, of Macready my guest? He had walked on the garlands of my Brussels carpet, and ransacked with his eyes the agreeable chaos of my possessions . . . the paper-nautili, the humming-birds in spirits, the enamelled watchcases, bronzes, prints, and books in Roger Payne's bindings. Now he walked the flagstones of my new lodging-house so exquisitely situated on Ludgate Hill under the shadow of hell and St. Paul's. He and his attendant spirits reached my cell. They were vastly gay: the miseries of those who *have* been found out elevate the spirits of those who have *not*. He lifted the eyehole of my cell-door. Behind him were Dickens and Cattermole and Hablôt Brown; as his eyes ransacked *me*, I heard them imploring him to make haste for there were less tedious offerings to come; some women to be whipped at Bridewell, a dinner with Dickens at Doughty Street. I felt him recognize me, and sensed that he began to tingle *dreadfully* at the dark gulf that lay betwixt us. 'My God!' he cried, 'there's Vaneleigh!' Under this pretence of *horror*, he left me for ever. Indeed, why not? He had his whippings and dinings to go on to. There was nothing left of the Judas Griffin Vaneleigh he had caroused with except the mould-marked rind. Of the moon we had roared at together in Golden Square there was not even the rind."

During the months Queely Sheill had known and kept his

eye on Mr Vaneleigh there had not been many occasions on which they had spent much time together. Queely Sheill had carried the artist's portfolio several times to places within easy distance of Campbell Street, always to the houses of people of a certain class. He knew that the artist, although poor to the point of starvation, and weakening physically towards some collapse, had refused commissions. Ill-health had partly caused these refusals of bread-and-butter; more often an artistic pernicketiness or snobbery, or a social snobbery, or some stubborn nicety too delicate to be expressed in anything more than an indicting shrug, had been the motive. When the artist had accepted Sir Sydney Knight's commission, Queely Sheill had offered to hire a hackney. "I'll not have straw about my ankles," Mr Vaneleigh had said, and had talked involvedly of straw on the skirt-hems of women who used hackneys, as though lack of morals rather than lack of their own carriages had excited them, even in Hobart Town, to deliberate public exposure and outlandishness. Queely Sheill decoded this attack. It said to him that beaver gloves could be accepted as a gift, unpaid porterage as a quirk, but that paid-for lifts in a hackney were alms, and not to be taken.

Misgivings had accompanied Queely Sheill on the walk to *Cindermead;* misgivings stayed with him on the return journey, but fewer, for no hour of arrival dictated their speed. He was delighted to find Mr Vaneleigh dallying of his own accord, since he would be unlikely to dally at another's instance or entreaty. A motherly wisdom informed Queely Sheill that the legs of Mr Vaneleigh's memory as they frisked through the streets and rooms of other years left his physical legs to recoup themselves more freely and for longer.

Moreover, Mr Vaneleigh's recitals of doings in a world in which there were the strongest contrasts had, for Queely Sheill, a fascination and a quality of high drama that, like a child, he would listen to until the moon was the sun. That world of blackest black and whitest white, of fame and infamy, of delights he could not understand and degradations he could not see the reason for or find degrading, had a sensuous element for him. Mr Vaneleigh's faded voice, rococo style and impassivity of delivery, in no way purged this element, rather they intensified it for the faithful and watchful listener.

He would never understand that the events and emotions recounted and so intoxicating to him had come to have nothing for Mr Vaneleigh but an aesthetic value. They had become diversions for his memory, nouns of experience requiring the adjectives of meditation, paradoxes giving an abstract satisfaction but setting off no emotion.

Mr Vaneleigh's monologue over, Queely Sheill, wishing him to rest longer, anxious politely to repay confession with confession, and with puzzles of his own that needed airing, took from his pocket the chain threading the coins, and dangled it in the moonlight.

"Teapot give it me."

"I have not," said Mr Vaneleigh who had been about to move on, "the *remotest* notion of whom or what you speak."

"Little black Teapot give it Queely."

Mr Vaneleigh was still not able to have other than the *most* distant notion.

"The black at *Cindermead.* The coat gold and *hall* colours."

"Oh," said Mr Vaneleigh who did not consider wondering why the chain had been given, and did not care.

"Poor little black 'eart. 'E's jealous of Queely, jealous of me *hand* 'oppy-go-quick. Ho sir, it's not for gemman to com-pre'end. The little black's found what me and old Conky's going to do. *Bust* me!" said Queely Sheill, and he swung the chain round and round and round. "Bust me hif Queely *knows* 'ow Teapot knows. But black ones halways knows. They know what gemman don't know, and books don't know. 'E thinks I'll take old Conky away from whatever she's been about with 'im. Queely! Ho, *no!* I'll catch 'er fleas for 'er, but no more, no more than that. That's all old Conky needs. Pretty fell-oh, eh!"

He stamped his feet on the rocky road, swung the chain a last time, and returned it to his pocket. But Mr Vaneleigh remained in the shadow of the barracks' wall and, for the first time since he had met Queely Sheill, asked him a direct question.

"What does the cripple need from you?"

Queely Sheill was astounded. He had told his truths often and not been surprised to be asked to repeat them. But that the artist, who never asked, should ask, unbalanced his control.

"She wants me to . . . She wants Queely to lay 'er."

"Oh," said Mr Vaneleigh and came out of shadow and moved on to the road and faced the descent into Hobart Town.

But Queely Sheill had lost his head. Looking directly ahead over the roofs diminished and flinching under the moon, and the countless chimneys sending up their smokes and sometimes a spray of sparks, he whispered:

"Why did you murder?"

"Ah, ha!" said Mr Vaneleigh, and the two men stood, eyes ahead, above their dirty little world, and the mountain stood above them on the left, and the salt-pale waters of the Estuary lay below them on the right, and the moon was before them.

"You've listened *and* learned! You've learned several things from your long-nosed cripple. One learns much from ladies. Or from women."

His voice became softer.

"Even from wives. A wife of strong will—rabbit me, she can teach what one should *not* learn! I must take you about more in what goes for the *ton* here. *Cognoscenti* bakers' boys and their women! Van Anybody the dancing master, and his wife from a tripe-counter! A hundred bread-and-butter-faced chits with their light kid gloves darkened by the action of animal warmth! *They* will teach you. They will dress worthless trash for you with a rich sauce."

Queely Sheill lifted his chin a little, and shouted above the roofs:

"Queely said 'e didn't care *hif* you murdered."

"You needed not to sue for me. Let them unshirt me and reshirt me as they will."

"I don't judge no one. Friend *hor* foe. I shouldn't 'ave *hasked*."

"Since you judge no one, why not ask? Yea or nay can make no difference to your judgement. I've known *one* judge to whom one nay was indisputably yea. You do not judge. *Bien!* You'll not judge me then if I say to you what I think I once said to another whose imprudence equals yours. A dashing recollection! What *did* I say? Ah! I said, 'I murdered my sister-in-law because she had thick ankles.' "

He moved off immediately. He began to descend the slope, towards the moon, towards the east, towards Campbell Street. His shadow jerked along behind him. Queely Sheill remained where he had been left.

Mr Vaneleigh had dragged himself and his shadow some little way when shouts of laughter came from the direction of the hill-top. Although the laughter was solitary, and unmistakably that of one who laughs at himself, its flagrant and sonorous portions were not trimmed to spare the ears of those who could have no interest in them or their echoings and re-echoings from the mountain and the mountain-gullies. It was, in all, a proclamation so sudden and resounding that the kangaroos finically pilfering on the outskirts of Hobart Town might well have dropped their stealings, asses their fodder and goats their random gobbets. Evening stew might well have spilt from the bowls of red-coats at table in the barracks, black pudding or Yarmouth bloater might well have caught in the gullets of startled picklocks, stable-boys, disbanded marines, dog-breakers, hurdlers or rake-and-ladder-makers' broods. To the meal of air the unemployed were privately, and with distaste, sipping in the lee of waterfront warehouses it might well have been a sauce they had forgotten how to make and wished to make—but bitter withal, bitter and unfattening.

Then Queely Sheill ran, drumming down the hill-streets and bringing the fragments of his laughter with him, to catch Mr Vaneleigh up. At Mr Vaneleigh's side (Mr Vaneleigh had not slackened his slowness or turned his head) he diminished his stride and ejected the last rashers of laughter.

"Queely," he said, "needs a larruping. 'E's a tahsome creetchah. 'E's a noiseh creetchah."

His mimicry of Asnetha Sleep brought on more laughter

which he found difficult to regulate. At last he arranged himself at docility and, as though sobered by the possession of an extra eye, began to walk with dignity. After a while he decided to let words from their fold watchfully lest with the tame ones should escape those that might run amuck:

"You must forgive them for saying because they don't know what they say. You must forgive Queely for hasking because hit don't matter what *'e* believes. Though I didn't reely *believe*. The little birds and what-all don't fret habout tomorrow nor shall I. *They* don't know what they say."

"I regret," said Mr Vaneleigh with great care and some effort, "that my fixed limits of time are filled with these present most . . . most *unintentional* ailings. Otherwise I could speak amply. Let this suffice. Neither the sun nor man permits themselves to be gazed at fixedly. One must view the first through darkened glass, the second through eyes darkened with love or . . . what you will . . . pity, jealousy, ignorance, scandal . . . what a blind world this is. . . !"

Mr Vaneleigh trudged on.

He trudged on, carefully balancing the inadequate jar of impulse and strength he had replenished on the summit of Barracks Hill. For a long time, occupied with his body's machinery, he did not speak. He began to draw deeper breaths, to pant.

"Cat . . ." he said, still adamant in resolve to let no physical distress strike him down to final wordlessness in streets of chuckling gutters and greasy stones, "is . . . waiting . . . and I've . . . earned . . . loaves and . . . fishes . . . and milk. . . ."

His hair hung over his ears, his hat-brim shadowed the enigma of his stranger's eyes, his moustache and its shadow drowned his stranger's mouth, but Queely Sheill knew, though he did not know why or why he knew, that Judas Griffin Vaneleigh was the smiling and pain-enduring stranger, the stranger smiling and dying at the same time.

4

In a front room of Playhouse Cottage, Queely Sheill was mending theatrical costumes. The intensity of solicitude and love that he was granting a papier mâché breastplate and its rim of glass emeralds was sharper than any he could give himself or any other animal.

Man, to save himself being slivered to rubbish by nature, needs his undestroyable secrecy. Except in concealment without sentiment it is impossible to be lonely. Mere physical absence does not serve because the mind's highway is overrun by summary hordes which can neither be run down by time nor run out of memory. Sleep changes only the climate. In the caricatured weather of dream, the dead mother lawlessly appears, the discarded lover repulsive as a sick monkey, or the primrose child-friend who has long been a bearded bore. Once must watch the reluctant self enacting a part in spurious distresses or flavourless delights. Only in an unpenial occupation can man savour that rarest food, loneliness. Carnality and communication and death are the dubious and ceaseless gifts of the earth. Man seeks solitude and emancipation in doing what the earth abhors, the creation of what cannot procreate: beauty without blood, the statue that cannot conceive, the painted summer not to lose a leaf or loose an adder, the cathedral that outlives the garlic-riddled prayer, the armour more indestructible than its tenant.

Unblooded swords of tin, masks of false devils and plumes of fictitious heroes, surrounded Queely Sheill's peace and abided his attention. The repelling fascinations and obligatory philanthropies of the world, the world itself and its burden of desires, had contracted to a gem of glass. It was world enough. Sunset overtook it, but, for a while, nothing more; no clock could be heard shooting its darts at the hide of timelessness. Presently, Queely Sheill lit a lamp to light his world.

As a flame baits a cockchafer, so his solitude and his lamp seemed to bait someone from the twilight, and the cobbles birthmarked with spittle, and the smell of organs from the bellies of quadrupeds stewing for the bellies of bipeds.

His repast of loneliness was over. He heard the back door of the cottage being opened so slowly and with so few and such minute attendant noises that he recognized the entrance of the friend who lived with him and his father. Next, came an interval of progress along the corridor, mothlike flutterings and misgivings, sheepish reticences of advance and, finally, after an eternity, the shallowest of breathings which signalled a halt, out of sight, outside the open door of the room in which he was working.

"Come on in, Poli," said Queely Sheill.

"Is it *you*, Apollo, my love?"

It was a threadlike voice; relief and disbelief together haunted it. It gained a little strength as it continued, and the delicate sound of a hat being removed accompanied it:

"If it *be*, then I am quite *safely* returned. Oh, if you had been some *other*, an *unknown* with a *pistol*. . . ."

Abashed, piecemeal, a long rectangular face with absolutely vermilion cheekbones, insinuated itself at one corner, under the lintel. From beneath a baldness on which lines of black hair were pasted by bear's grease, two large jet eyes mistrustingly probed the cloaks and plumes and tiaras, and finally directed a liquid gaze at Queely Sheill.

"Shall I," said the face in a less uncertain but still deathbed whisper, "be *asked* to enter? Or am I *too tired*? Shall I be asked to *sit*? A *chair* will do."

"Queely 'as said, 'Come in!' Queely repeats hisself, 'Come in, Poli!' "

Diffidently and tenderly, Polidorio Smith, the actor, brought the rest of his lean body underneath the lintel.

Bowed over, for he was seven feet high and did not trust ceilings even without his hat which he held before him, he advanced minutely, soundlessly on semi-tiptoe, elbows in. At the sight of three chairs he quivered with indecision.

"These," he whispered, "are the *chairs*, one of which you have *not* asked me to sit *upon*. . . ?"

"Queely'd like you to sit on a chair."

Polidorio Smith deliberated, attempting a shrewd choice to outwit his enemy inanimate nature. Objects, without life for others, took on a wilful sentience in contact with his timidity. Handles fell from doors. Keys snapped off. Cups sprang, like frogs, from saucers. Gratings opened in footpaths. Knives and razors sliced him. Animate creatures also recognized him: seagulls shat on him alone in a mob; dogs had hysterics of mock fury; rams usually unbelligerent as slugs butted through brush fences at his innocent passing by.

On some indefinable superstition, he chose a chair. He placed his hat on another.

"I *commend* myself to *God*," he said, and sat. He pressed knees and feet side by side together. He narrowed his narrowness. He held his long boneless hands at his chest so that they swung there timorously and pawlike. He invoked weightlessness, and waited to be hurled to the floor.

His large semi-circular ears seemed cupped like palms to hear what he was going to say next for he had a reason for coming to Queely Sheill's room, and had forgotten it. Queely Sheill knew this; otherwise Polidorio Smith would not have come to disturb him.

He knew also that he would have to await revelation; except on the stage, in the dark or in his cups, the actor could reach no destination without sidling through the labyrinth of inconsequential stumbling-blocks his pusillanimity and skittishness threw up before each attempted pace forward.

"You was wanting to tell something, eh, Poli?"

Queely Sheill gambled directness solemnly but without hope that it would shorten the intricate and addling adventure his visitor had begun in apprehensive good faith. Directness might, indeed, sidetrack the actor and lengthen his meander.

Polidorio Smith veiled his eyes.

"You have," he whispered coyly, "the delicacy of an oyster. You are the *soul*, the *perfection* of delicacy. To say *Poli* is perfect *delicacy*."

He unpeeled his eyes. He said with mild peevishness:

"The generality say Polly. Titled *ladies* have done *so*. People one does not *know* have dared. *Vagabonds*. Wire-walkers. Hebrews and *usurers*. Pretty *Dick* called me so. . . ."

His face arranged its folds in another pattern which displayed that a matter of lively importance had come to mind, though not the matter he lay distrustfully in wait for.

"*Audacious!*" he squeaked. "I apply to your *emotions*, Apollo, for a loving *sympathy*. I *implore* it. I have been *rifled*!" And, thrusting forward his humble and houndlike face beyond his swinging paws, "You perceive a *difference*? A notable difference that shocks the *sense* and offends the eye?"

"A difference? Queely's not saying; 'e's not saying 'e sees what *shocks*."

"*Charitable* Apollo! I *repeat:* the delicacy of a *winkle*. But I *insist* on truth. Let us, even in *friendship*, condone neither falsehood nor *pretence*!"

One hand sprang to life and flourished itself like a tragedian's. The chair creaked. Polidorio Smith froze.

"My *God*," he whispered, "if it be in Your august *power* . . . ." The chair remained substantial.

"Speak, Apollo!" he breathed.

"Queely's 'ad no shock but is hinclined to see too much rouge."

"I *know*!" Polidorio Smith became sadder, "I *knew*! Apollo you have eyes like a *wasp*. I declare I was so *ashamed* of myself. I kept *on* at myself. 'Enough, *enough*!' I begged. 'Stop it at *once*!' But I took *no notice*. I couldn't bear to *look* at myself. Do *you* yourself, Apollo, though *blooming*, feel the *need*? A *little* colour?"

Queely Sheill was laughing. He shook his head.

"What *teeth* you have! And such a *pretty* tongue, pink as *ham*!"

He became more animated in manner, but using his surfaces only, as though constraint of his larger structures were keeping the chair whole.

"I was *reviled* in public places. Vulgar epithets were *shouted. Kitchen* latin, my love. But, one must confess, in *alleys* only. No one *threw* hard objects."

"You was rifled, Poli?"

Queely Sheill continued happily patient: the stream always reached the shore.

"I *knew* you would observe the difference instantly with your bee-like eyes, even with a little *rouge* to deflect glances from *loss*. One is *certain* no one spat at one *either*, although one can never be *certain*."

"You was rifled, Poli? Tell me, I pray."

"You look like a *daffodil*, but drier. I can *barely* touch 'em. Eek! wet as handkerchiefs, the wet horrids."

"Yes, Poli, wet."

"I recall it all, *all*. Yes. Pretty Dick was *sitting* on your *knee*. After the play last night. In *The Shades*. Pretty Dick was sitting on your knee. He will *frisk* poor Apollo, I thought. I *hurried* across to you, and. . . ."

" 'E was on *your* knee, you old poofter."

"*Was* he?"

Polidorio Smith, for the first time, allowed his fantastic, wrinkle-folded, gentle face a fragmentary grateful smile at a memory of himself. A blackened tooth sat centre of the tawny ones. He tittered.

"*How* exceedingly provoking for me! How *kind* of me! It comes to me that I was *singing* to him. I was *drunk* as a *mouse*!" He tittered again.

Queely Sheill laughed loudly.

"The Dutch 'ave taken 'Olland!" he said. "Drunk, Poli? Poli, you was Martin-drunk. Mouth almighty, you come over gabbling like a bubbly-jock to warn me to watch *my* pocket . . . as *hif* Queely didn't know Pretty Dick was a stook-buzzer and 'ad been a canary. You warned me habout Pretty Dick. Next minute he was hon *your* knee!"

Polidorio Smith had listened carefully. With interest, he saw all. It fascinated him. He nodded.

"Pretty Dick, Pretty *Polly*! Pretty Dick, *Pretty* Polly! He *called* me Pretty Polly." The blackened tooth shyly appeared. "He was *full* of admiration for my singing. 'A thrush!' he said, 'a veritable *thrush*!' He *whispered* to me. He *assured* me he had *nowhere* to sleep. The *pavement*. *Under* the Palladio. Whisper, whisper. Under *wharves*. I brought him *home*. I am as *indulgent* as *horses*."

"Queely '*eard* you. Like a 'undred Hirish Pats."

"I can-*not* pretend . . ." said Polidorio Smith thinly and with a dignity of vagueness and perplexity, for he was finding himself with every sentence further from the enigmatic motive of his visit. "I cannot *pretend* to be insensible to the fact that I possess *all* the *vices* incident to human *nature*. I have had from *infancy* an *inclination* towards yobs. I think *many* with my mama's Latin blood share this inclination with your *humble*. Oh, *delicious* inclination, like apricots! But so many, so *treacherous*, so grasping! I knew the dangers of sharing my *privacy* with pretty Pretty Dick: one is, alack, no *longer* innocent."

He sighed. He clasped his hands.

"Once my *tempter* was *upstairs* . . . our tiptoeing did not arouse my Apollo? . . . I said, 'You must *forgive* your song-bird, but the complicated excitement to *me*, consequent from *your presence*, has so stimulated my functions that I must *descend* to the necessary? It was *prevarication*, Apollo, my love, but not intended to operate to anyone's *disadvantage*. So *much* tiptoeing hither and *thither*, like a *thrush*! I pretended to *use* the necessary but hid my *money* and *watch* there."

"Fox-drunk! You was *fox*-drunk, Poli."

The actor modestly lowered his lids. Then he revealed again his large tarry eyes.

"Pretty Dick was in *bed*. Oh, naked as an *egg* and more *pimples* than a cowcumber. A smell of *socks*, my love, and anti-rheumatic *red flannel*. I undressed *myself*. I snuffed the candle and *locked* the door. Today, I have *sworn* never to drink rum again. *Why* has your humble *sworn*? I forgot to *remove* the key and hide it in my right *boot*. From infancy, from the womb, this has been my wise custom . . . heed it,

Apollo, and *always* the *right* boot . . . when sharing *folly* with *strangers*. I said my prayers, and *fell* asleep. I now *perceive* the folly of *disinterested* Christianity. 'Slumber unhappy mortal,' I said to him. 'Your *pimples* are prettily disposed but I am tired and your diddle is too small!' In the morning . . . the key *in* the door favouring flight . . . the wicked *creature* had *flighted*, had *flown*, pimples and socks and carroty hair and *all*. I was *rifled*! A *Christian* was rifled!"

" 'E had frisked the *privy*?"

"No, *no*, my love. He had *sheered off* with my pictorial *bible* and my *curls*."

He lifted his hands to touch his temples and raddled cheeks.

"My beau-catchers! All those *miles* from Tavistock Street! And none to be *got* in Hobart Town. Gentlemen's patent *wigs*, *yes*. I've walked a *thousand* miles today. *Seeking*. Taunted. *Spat* at by all. Pelted with *tiles*. It was like the *tea-room* at the London *Opera*."

His eyes began to gleam with tears.

"Poli," said Queely Sheill. "I considers you make a better visage without 'em."

In the lamplight the thick discs of paint glistened more outrageously on the wrinkle-fluted cheeks which had otherwise paled with pleasure. Once again the veined eyelids concealed the eyes with a shyness.

"A *better*! Oh, diddle, diddle, dumpkins! Oh, diddle, *diddle*, dumpkins! A . . . a . . . *younger*?" It was a bleat for verification of a hope.

"A younger . . . hat least *Queely* thinks so," said Queely Sheill.

"I forgive, I *forgive*!" squealed Polidorio Smith, agitated with delight, and recklessly disregarding the chirruping chair.

"You must *halways* forgive," said Queely Sheill.

"You speak *truth*, Apollo. I *forgive* him without private *censure*. I'm not, as *you know well*, Apollo, my love, a *fiery hot* subject. I'm not of a *disposition* to judge too harshly the *wickedness* of another which may well be the result of some *calamity* . . . eh?"

Queely Sheill nodded and smiled as at a child who has at last learned its prayers.

"I forgive him the *curls*. I *had* forgiven him the pictorial *bible*, the *pimples* and the *leetle* peter. To think that I was *driven* to a state of *distraction*! To *walking* the streets! In the dumps! I now forgive—*quite* without private censure—the curls, the ugly *ugly* curls. So *ageing*! When we *encounter*, be it *where* it may, among whom I *care* not, I shall *bow* to him. Yes. Bow in *this* manner. . . ."

He bent his striped head and narrowed his eyes with an essay at coldness of manner but his sad eyes could flash no metallic rebuke.

". . . but I positively *decline* to let him *snore* like a *star-fish* in my bed, even if *starving*, or sit on my knee like a cat. . . ."

He ceased abruptly. He drew in his breath. His eyes rolled ceiling-wards.

"Cat!" He shuddered. "Your humble should not *speak* of them. I shall *swoon*."

He shuddered again. His fingers interlaced themselves into a large knot.

"Oh, *oh*!" he said, and suddenly leaned forward, electric-ally charged, serious and fearful. "I *recall*!"

Portentously, in deeper accents, thrilling with the re-captured purpose of his mission, he spoke:

"A *cat*," he shook his head with distaste, "a *see—ay—tee* spoke to me on the Palladio."

Queely Sheill was no more than a little surprised.

"Tell Queely," he said, "kindly tell what the cat said hon the Palladio?"

"You *ridicule* me, you *ridiculous* creature! You are pleased to be *facetious* at my expense. Artful Apollo! You *know* a see-ay-tee cannot speak. Mi-a-ow, mi-a-ow, and so forth, but no *more*. You must not *laugh*, Apollo, or I shall not *tell* you of the gentleman who *approached* me on the Palladio. You look so *clean*, Apollo my love." He paused. "You must *ask* me *whom*."

"Who was the gemman?"

"I declare I don't know. I could have *fallen* down because

of his reptile, all *fur*, and moving *about*. And a *tail* all fur! It made no *noise* . . . eek! But I shall take *courage* and not *indulge* myself. I shall not *prose* about the *reptile*."

"Did the gemman say anything, Poli?"

"I feel *confident* he did, for he was so *small* and *quite* a dowdy. Not at *all* in the *first bloom*. Confidentially, I suspect his *hat* of concealing a scarcity of *hair*. Unfortunate *fellow*, I thought, for he seemed labouring under a nervous *fever*; *poor old man*, he is about to beg or commend me on my *acting*. An *uncultured* soul, I thought, but *frantic* about my acting."

Thereupon, Polidorio Smith skilfully and swiftly disentangled his fingers, and began to make graceful gestures which his eyes slid lovingly after . . . they were his Sir Andrew Aguecheek gestures.

" '*I was*,' " he murmured, " '*adored once*, *too*.' "

"Poli, dear Poli," shouted Queely Sheill. "For God's sake, what did 'e say? What did the gemman *say*?"

The actor loosely entwined his fingers again on his lap.

"He told me I knew *you*."

Polidorio Smith pouted.

"You must not *shout*," he said. "It makes me *untidy*. I recall that *he* spoke *graciously*. Naturally, I was *instantly* in a *fear*. He *speaks* like a *gentleman*, thus and thus, I thought. His *moustachios* are false *additions*, I thought. He is no *gentleman*, I thought. He has a look of the *French*. I could not *move* for *terror*."

"Silly Poli, 'twere Queely's Mr Vaneleigh and 'is puss-cat. . . ."

Polidorio Smith squealed.

"I beg you not to mention that *reptile*," he said faintly, eyes closing. He woke up. He scratched under his armpit. His brow twined its wrinkles anxiously together as he scratched.

"Ah!" he said. "Lice *again*. I'll not sleep with mischievous *vagabonds* any *more*."

"I 'ave told Mr Vaneleigh of the dad and of you." Queely Sheill, still patient, still patiently awaited the actor's news.

"You *spoke* of your old *friend* to this *gentleman*! Ah, he could *not* resist your *blandishments*: he *hastened* to The Playhouse. He has *seen* me on the stage! I sensed it, sensed it, *sensed* it! A *respectable* gentleman. Orderly. *Charming*. Of unspotted *character* despite his reptile. Perhaps not *his*—a mere *passer-by* of a reptile. I conceived him cultured *at first glance*. His manner of *address* could not be *bettered*! 'It would do me *honour*, I should be *perfectly delighted*, dear sir,' I said, 'to give Mis-ter Queely Sheill *the note*. Delighted!' We were *enchanted* by each other. We *bowed*, reluctant to *part*. We parted. Bye-bye, *youthful* admirer! Bye-bye!"

Polidorio Smith waved a hand in farewell. Then he eyed Queely Sheill with reproach.

"Unfeeling *dog*," he said, "you have not *thanked* me, not a *tittle*. Can *this* be jealousy, the *green* of eye, *can* it? That is *not* your manner; that is not *my* Apollo. 'Oh, miserable world, as I do live by food,' I have been *rifled* of curls, molested by *reptiles*, unthanked by Apollos. . . ."

"The note, Poli!"

"You are *shouting* at your old *friend*."

"Poli, where is the note?"

"Which *note*, my love?"

"The note from the gemman."

"It don't, I hope contain bad *news*. I should *die* to be the innocent bearer of. . . ."

"Poli, you 'ave not *given* Queely 'is note."

"Oh! This is a surprising *impulse* in me. I must have had a *jealousy* of your *dowdy*. But *momentary* and *conquerable*. Diddle, diddle, dumpkins, where have I *put* it?"

Polidorio Smith sat horrified, self-disgraced and wretched.

Queely Sheill came to him. He stroked the bald head.

"Don't be hafraid," he said. "Hif you've lost it, I'll forgive you. But Queely'll look in pockets first; *'e'll* frisk you."

The note was in the first pocket. Polidorio Smith who had sat, an image of anxiety, revealed his cinder-dark tooth with relief.

"Relief!" he breathed. "I *feel* relief! I feel *exhaustion*! I've *suffered* too much this day! My *cup* overflows! I'll make *tea*, and *drink* it!"

Queely Sheill was refolding the notes, for the one enclosed another, by the lamp; Polidorio Smith was bending his length floorwards to pick up the chair that his rising had knocked over, when a vigorous and deep-toned baying began outside:

"Ho, varlets! Within there, ho!"

To this enriched sound the front door was torn open. The front door was slammed.

"Down, parcels!" the voice continued, as richly as chocolate. "Away, hat!"

There was a breeze of rum and sweat. In a sky-blue cloak that was opulent, dirty and unsuitable, John Death Sheill, actor, father, fat man, balanced swaying at the doorway. Polidorio Smith pursed his mouth.

"Queely, fruit of my loins and light of my declining years, your fawther has returned from the Scotch Pie House!"

That, rendered in a voice of a thousand dramatic modulations and plum-dark intonations, had the ring of a tragic denunciation though it came from within a face as round as a pudding, and active with sensual and simple happinesses. John Death Sheill was a globe: a careless and astonished eye seemed to find him equal in height and width and thickness. Not any of these dimensions had been bequeathed to his son who far outdid the short fatty in height and slenderness and harmonious grandeur of proportion. The father had, however, handed on to his son the blue of his eyes, and his fairness of hair. The older man's hair, which hung well down over the braided collar of his cloak, was marbled with the grey of years or dirt. Many dimples or part-dimples moved in his fiery cheeks and about the ends of his dark mouth full of little yellow teeth.

"I have returned from the Scotch Pie House with...." The sentence was sonorously begun; the pause was a meaning one; the climax was of drumlike tone, a booming: "... with whawt, Duchess?"

"I hear a voice," said Polidorio Smith, and searched the ceiling not far above his upturned eyes.

"With whawt, my Duchess, my Polly, my civet-cat? Speak!"

"*Pray*," it was a squeak only, "*pray* do *not*, you vulgar *mass*, *speak* of that reptile or I shall *swoon* to the oil-cloth."

"With whawt?" The room seemed to vibrate.

"Tell 'im, Poli, or we'll 'ave 'eadaches."

"With *cats* . . . no, no, no . . . with see-ay-tee pies . . . with *pies*, *pies*, *pies*." Polidorio Smith drew together his ragged streamers of thought, and became admonishing, "It is *unfair* in you, Deathie, when you are fully *aware* how repugnant *flesh* foods are to me. I seek the *aspiring* vegetable *only*. *Not* the vegetable that *hides* in the *ground* . . . the potato, the *turnip*, the whatever-it-is. But the aspiring . . . the *celery*, the cabbage, the. . . ."

"You are *sober*," thundered the fat man. He lowered his thunder to velvet, "I should scorn, nawsty Duchess, to be as sober as you appear to be. Sobriety does you disservice. It blankets *your* awbilities. It pee-inches your vee-oice. It is unwomanly in you."

Polidorio Smith stamped his foot. A helmet fell from its peg.

"Eek! You *see*? You observe. All was *peace*. Now a *shower* of *hats*. Of *abuse*. Apollo, my love, save me from this *pod*, this pot-guts who say he's your *father*."

"Silence, sliver!" hissed John Death Sheill from the midst of dimplings. "Silence! And sit!"

He whirled away from the doorway. He was heard bumping, and heard groping, and cursing, and clashing, and striking lucifers.

"*Save* me!" said Polidorio Smith, teetering about, his hands flapping. "I must *fly*. I must *swim* away like a *nightingale*. I must *not sit*. Deathie will be my *death*." He began to giggle. "That is humour, that is *comedy*! Deathie—death! Death—Deathie! Or is it poesy?"

"Queely thinks you'd do fairer to sit."

"Not in that *chair*! It will *ruin* my voice!"

"Sit on the dress-basket, Poli."

"*Sit!* Sit on the dress-basket, you candle-mould!"

John Death Sheill had taken off his cloak to reveal his spherical bulk in magenta swallow-tails of exaggerated cut, and his broad hams straining his nankeen tights. He carried a tray of four brimming rummers which he placed on the work-table. He took one rummer for himself, another he extended towards Polidorio Smith.

"Drink, Duchess! Toss it down! You'll not then wawnt for countenance, my elf." His voice lowered itself to a purring level of enticement, " 'Twill bring colour to those haggard cheeks."

"I have *forsworn* rum," said Polidorio Smith taking the glass and sniffing its surface. "I don't *like* rum. I do *not*, indeed, like *any* strong waters."

"You dote on rum, Poli. Hit's a physic," said Queely Sheill.

"Do I *dote*? Oh, diddle, diddle, *dumpkins*, I dote!"

Polidorio Smith drank, gulping *one*, *two*, *three*. The glass was empty.

"Queely, my heir, remove the empty vessel from the relaxing grip of those demon fingers. Restore to them a full vessel."

Father and son winked at each other, blue eye to blue eye.

"Come, Duchess," boomed John Death Sheill, "*both* hands in use! Gravity hath oft, ere this, snatched a goblet to . . . haw! she drinks! Whawt power! Whawt speed!"

"I *do* like rum," said a voice already energized to vibrancy. "I can't *deny* it, Deathie. Indeed, I am *convinced* of liking it. I *cannot*, for my life, *conceive* why you should consider me as not being *partial*. I find myself *wondering*, however, *is* this Jamaica Pineapple Rum?"

Queely Sheill removed the drained tumbler from the outstretched hand, and replaced in it a third filled one.

"I *imagined* it to be the Pineapple," said Polidorio Smith, setting his lips to the third as fervently as if it were a first. He lifted his lips when the rummer was half-emptied. "I imagine it *still*. It has been, since *infancy*, my *absolute* favourite. I *drank* it from my mother's *breast*. I *wept* for more. *More!*" He emptied the glass, wound both hands about it in his lap and raised his voice. "Ah, since the *cradle*! *Magical* beverage! It makes your humble *shorter*. It imparts the effect of *delicacy*, of *grace*. It gives *speed* . . . oh, feet of *fire*! It gives *lucidity*. It *encourages* song. *Gentlemen*, it may surprise you to know that, since *infancy*, I have possessed a *peculiar proneness* for rum and *melody*. I, sirs, have sung in the Coal Hole, the Two O'clock Club . . . oh, much admired, much, *much*! Deathie, you'll have *observed* that I have *shaved* my *curls*."

" 'E looks younger without Newgate knockers." Queely spoke with meaning.

"Duchess, I congratulate you. The years have dropped away. You are youth itself."

"*Deathie*, you're a flattering *wretch*!"

"I swear it, no flattery!"

"Deathie, there is a strong branch of *evidence* that you have *drained* my *rummer*!"

"Forgive an old friend. 'Twas in an absent-minded moment. Come, Duchess! To the kitchen for pies."

"And *rum*."

"For pies and rum, Duchess. Let us leave my temperate son who is a good boy."

Polidorio Smith rose with lightness, assurance and grace. With curled fingers he held up the skirts of his coat on either side. He danced from the room, humming lightly. In the corridor he began a plaintive song. Plaintively singing, lightly lightly dancing, cowardice and perplexity sluiced away, he went to the kitchen.

John Death Sheill, mournfully, fixedly and sipping like a rural dean, regarded his son.

Presently, "Tell me," said Queely Sheill. "I knows what the skinny dad's up to, but tell Queely."

He picked up a glassless quizzing-glass through which he regarded the fat actor.

"My temperate son who's a good boy," repeated the father. "He *is* a good boy?"

"Halways."

"You have your mother's voice, her very accents. Your mother waws aw good female, Queely." He sighed profoundly.

"And 'er son's a good boy. Go and eat."

"I knew it, for I have beaten goodness into you. For your

mother's sake. Aw good wife. Aw good mother." His voice fluctuated tragically. He sighed three times.

Queely Sheill put down the quizzing glass.

"Go to Poli before you start aweeping. Quick, or 'e'll break things."

"Do you love your fawther?"

"Queely won't answer such questions. I've set the fire and laid the table and what-all. Lope and brush, or you'll 'ave Poli chopping fingers off."

"Your mother's exact tones. . . ."

Queely Sheill came to his father. He placed his hands on the thick, sloping shoulders. He bent to kiss the parti-coloured hair. He smiled down at the large fleshy face with its quiescent dimples.

"I told you a 'undred 'hundred times: I don't worry habout the dad's poultry. I don't fret. If 'is dad's 'appy, Queely's 'appy. Get your pies from the parlour and go to Poli."

"Aw good boy," said John Death Sheill.

There was a wail from the kitchen. Other wails followed and approached quickly, and Polidorio Smith appeared at the door. His eyes were wide with a sort of shock; he flung out his hands in appeal:

"Apollo, I am *worthless*. I am not *fit*. I'd a *note* for you; someone *entrusted* me. *Worthless!* Faithless! 'Tis lost, lost, *lost*. . . !"

"Queely 'as it, Poli. You was very kind and took a lot of trouble. Go and eat pies, both of you. Go *hon*!"

No longer mindlessly and blissfully lost, to himself and the others, on the heavenly and pathless plains of an uninhabited land, Queely Sheill continued to work at the breastplate. He was again in the world of paths and bypaths. As he worked, and whistled softly, his thought watched his thoughts follow the footprints his nature drove them to follow: Polidorio Smith, painted like Punch, hesitantly scouring the world for curls; John Death Sheill, his cloak swinging into every tavern between the Scotch Pie House and the cottage; Mr Vaneleigh appearing, dapper and shabby, to confront Polidorio Smith with the notes:

Mr Queely Sheill,
Queen's Playhouse.
I have received a letter from Lady Knight appointing tomorrow (Saturday) at 3 *for what I hope will be the final sitting for her portrait. I shall leave Campbell St. at* 2. *The enclosure was also brought by her man.* *J.G.V.*

The enclosure bore no signature. The handwriting was interlaced, fragile, decorated and unfaltering:

Tonight, at 9 *o'clock, a lady will place three candles in the farthermost window* (*west*) *of* Cindermead. *This window, which will be open, is most safely attained by entering the wall door farthest from the drive gates in Sandy Bay Road.*

In the kitchen the two actors ate and drank and bantered and sang. Queely Sheill kept an ear to them. The fat man was performing with relish and the thin one participating with relish in their daily evening ceremony. The mysteries of this ceremony, on the surface barbaric, were to a degree subtle. Rum and noise, flattery and hectoring, had to be in medicinally correct proportions to produce in Polidorio Smith enough fearlessness and memory and voice for him to amuse that night's audience.

Queely Sheill's thought moved into the future towards *Cindermead* and Asnetha Sleep. It saw a path, straight, though unfamiliar, but without danger. His thought turned to another path, straight though familiar, and promising no more danger than maudlin remorse. Queely Sheill knew, whenever his father spoke of his dead wife, that the night's womb was already infested. Therein nestled some woman his father had chosen or some trollop he had not yet picked up in *The Shades*, and with whom he would lie, and quarrel, and then leave his son to placate.

In his pathless solitude the wayfarer had not needed to whistle, for there was no scented and flower-weighted undergrowth behind which the dangers of being joyful or giving joy could conceal themselves. But, equivocal dangers, in the world of paths, cocked their ornamental ears to an equivocal whistling which could not foretell if it were a sweetness to lure forth, or a melody to hide the fear that they might spring forth, retracting as they sprang the downy covers from their talons.

In this fashion Queely Sheill whistled, and a wind began to move peevishly out of its sleeping, and night came closer to Van Diemen's Land and Hobart Town.

5

Across the last and iceberg-cluttered ocean, night came closer yet to Van Diemen's Land and Hobart Town with the positiveness of predetermination and a purpose to spy.

Foretold by the explicable creeping local shadow of Organpipe, night seemed not to be the world's own explicable simple shadow causing lucifers and Congreve matches to be struck.

Chandeliers and candelabra, the fat-lamps and whale-oil flares were lit so that eyes could still see abhorred pretty faces or beloved pock-strewn faces, or faces pregnant with the sins the body had not deigned to commit, faces worn vacant by a surfeit of sins committed, faces adorned by the peace of stealing liberties from others. Night was felt to come like a face itself.

First, came the shadow of some infinite body drawing nearer and nearer to kneel at the skylight of space, to lean forward and nearer until the great face occupied all, pressing close, straining to understand with its dark and uncomprehending eyes. Thus it seemed: to feel itself watched by a mindless image of itself is the world's vanity and a stupidity of the male. A woman makes no guard and no god, either from the stained clay of night or the stainless metal of day. Woman makes within her body creatures to whom, in magnanimous agony, she grants the power to destroy themselves. Man makes, like a deluded boy, what he will destroy; or destroys himself in philosophy—that withdrawal from the immediate obligations of living.

Hobart Town was man's. It was the Englishman's miniature of London from which no home-recalling and cherished detail had been left out except the batswing gas-lamps, the toshers who searched the sewers of London, and the six railway stations from which the lines rayed out and carried the top-hatted and bonneted London cattle to stare at the cattle. All else was to be found in Hobart Town: Adelaide velvet and the yellow dress marked *Felon*; tilburies and treadmills; the butler's sleeping-closet and the penitentiary dormitory; Schools for Young Ladies in French, velvet-painting, wax-fruit and crystallization, and the Women's Factory whose bastards were required to bear the unequivocal marks of vaccination. The colonists brought bellropes and the gallows; the gallows night-cap and Capuchin hoods of taffeta; leg-irons and chinchilla muffs; Flogging Tommies and backs to flog. In sweat-stiff shirts, stinking boots and urine-splashed buckskin breeches they hunted with infinite care and to extinction, the naked people who had built no chapel, no gaol, brewery, snuff-shop or brothel.

It was through that town Queely Sheill set out to walk to *Cindermead*. It was through a wind, wide-eyed awake at eight o'clock, that bandied the smell of Roman Catholic fish suppers from Friday chimney to chimney and was as uneasy as a mind playing with premonitions.

Above were the constellations that did not know their names: Whale, Hare, Scorpion, Dog, Crow, Wolf and Phoenix. In that zoo lay discarded The Cup, the empty cup, The Crown that fitted no head, The Cross tilted to fall.

Beneath them, Queely Sheill entered the wind. Leaving Playhouse Cottage he walked past the Playhouse, under the inquiet trees next-door, to cross the Palladio towards Mr Vaneleigh's lodging-house. The Palladio lamp on the other side of Campbell Street lit the porter shutting the gates of the Criminal Hospital. Queely Sheill heard the bolts, the metallic decisiveness, the key.

Above that organized and professional din he heard a sound he knew he could never make himself. It too had a professional note as though the pain that inspired the scream which was rising and falling with exquisite regularity were a pain of such perfection and power that nothing but the most finished expression would do it justice. The Rivulet threaded its amateur gurgling through the flawless screaming in the manner of the idly scribbled vein of disregard that winds through the world's perpetual pain.

"Poor soul, poor soul, poor soul," he said, and took off his cap.

At the corner he looked up to Mr Vaneleigh's window but no candles showed. Over the walls shadows of nothing ran heartlessly as water so that the stone seemed about to dissolve; the flame of the street lamp, lightly punched at by the air, could throw merely the liquid images of its graceful smoke and its own withdrawals and dodgings.

Leaving the ephemeral husk of the artist's room to disintegrate, to fuse with the wind and slide away like melted years, he turned towards the south and *Cindermead*.

He had crossed the Rivulet by the Palladio; on his right, across the narrow stream, lay the Criminal Hospital and its unfaltering but rhythmically designed screaming. From the new angle, that exposition of agony was heard to be accompanied by many voices cursing in impure and irregular pattern, and several crude voices attempting in harsh song to snarl the faultless signal of agony. From the hospital incinerator a nauseating smoke was taken by the wind, a vile lively awning lit from beneath and flushed with a flush like a fine mesh of blood.

Sweat appeared on Queely Sheill's forehead, his halo of hair wavered, he began to run, saying as he ran, "Sleep hor die, poor soul. I prays for you: sleep hor die."

Behind his back the screaming stopped. Behind his back a hospital wardsman threw more fuel of refuse on the fire, except for some larger pieces which he heaved over the wall so that they bounced down the low sandstone cliff on which the hospital was built, and splashed into the Rivulet. The screaming, now disorganized and grating, began again, but Queely Sheill was out of earshot, and the sweat had dried on his forehead.

He hastened with long strides through streets Polidorio Smith had ducked into short-cut alleys from, indiscreet with terror, taking tiny frightened steps towards the bazaar near

Cheapside House in search of lovelocks among the jelly-glasses, spittoons, pickle stands, feet baths and lemonade cans.

He passed the Scotch Pie House John Death Sheill had loudly swaggered to, grog-shop by grog-shop, and back from, in his magnificent dirty cloak, grog-shop by grog-shop.

He reached the cross-roads at the heart of Hobart Town. On one corner was the gaol built to lodge the new criminals of the new world; the Campbell Street Penitentiary was for those who wore the ball-and-chain from the old world. On the right rose Barracks Hill from whose eminence the military barracks, the lobster-box, overlooked and suggested protection to the town's well-planned centre . . . gaol opposite courthouse, courthouse opposite cathedral, cathedral opposite gibbet, the gibbet opposite the gaol. Behind the courthouse was Government House and its bare elms through whose branches duelling without heart in the wind, shone the lighted windows of a dignified, decorous and mild stand-in for a governor undignified, indecorous and stubborn who had been recalled lest he further embarrass the stubborn, indecorous and undignified scandalmongers. Someone there sadly and badly played on a harp.

He skirted the cathedral burial-ground and passed on to skirt Barracks Hill at its base. He put on his cap and began to walk more quickly; it would seem he did not care to have the simplicity of his mission too closely observed by the hissing dead, the growling red-coats, curtsying women, the watchman, or the starving who tumbled about silly-eyed in the rubbish heaps at the town's rim.

Queely Sheill had, however, no consciousness of eyes that might spy, mouths that might blab or ears that might eavesdrop. He had no consciousness of the great face peering down; he imagined nothing of night, but knew it darker and more imprudent than day. Night was night.

So, to him, carnality was carnality. It had no extra value for him since his beauty had never let it fall into irritating disuse. The importunities of others for what he came to esteem less, and to consider objectively, had early taught him that great pleasure is as troublesome as great pain. He had acquired the ability to sidestep involvement in corrupting betrayals with *fiancées* of other men, with wives, with actresses old as his mother and betraying their age, with Polidorio Smith attempting to betray his father in the same way as his father's women had attempted to betray him. It was easy to be desired. It was self-delusion to desire in return to a flagrant desire sprung by his straight nose and shapely form. He felt he knew when the wine and bread of his body could not be denied.

He reached *Cindermead*, and passed the drive gates where the wind tormented the lantern flames, and reached the smaller gate, and went through the garden, and came to the window where drawn-back curtains let three lit candles be seen. The window was shut.

Within the room he was able to see Asnetha Sleep seated on the bed, her fingers interfitted so that her two hands made a jewel-cobbled orb in her lap. Perhaps she prayed, perhaps she strove with relinquished modesties, perhaps she enclosed between her palms a future she was frightened to release. She was outrageously dressed. There was no need to sit on the bed.

Removing his cap, Queely Sheill brought his face near the glass. The night, which had given him birth into light with his hair surging and his eyes seeking indication of a next move, abandoned him there unobserved for long enough to examine the shape in red, the gaudy doll on whom the fire-light imitated the fire in movement.

She saw him. Instantly her eyes expressed some emotion he could not translate since it was a message to herself of what she must do, and be watched doing from behind the pane, before she could reach the window. She broke the orb, she flattened her hands on the bed to thrust herself upright, she listed once left, once right, she span in the candlelight and firelight like an experimental pillar of flame, sleeves fluttering as arms softly lashed the light. She could then hobble to the window and, in two journeys, moved the candles from the sill to her *bonheur-du-jour*. She floundered back to the window and opened its valves. He smelt the wine on her breath and the scent on her silks. She wheeled, she made a run for, and sat on the bed, and manufactured again the orb from which the bluebird or weasel of future had gone to freedom. As Queely Sheill stepped through the window and closed it:

"Yes, close it," she said. "Close it, and draw the curtains."

That done they were safe from the wind and the constellations, from Toucan, Peacock, Chameleon and Mouse.

"I needed", she said in her most social manner, "to close the windows. The tiresome wind kept blowing the candles out." Her eyes seemed closer together than ever.

That was a saddish picture to him, saying, "Yes, ma'am," and standing with his back to the curtains and night and mountain and the road back to Campbell Street. He looked at her trying to keep candles alight, and drinking anxious wine, and she looked at him, and he, wiser than she though a man, and more foolish than she because a man, as day is more foolish in its wisdom than night, saw that she was in some sort of funk.

"You mustn't fear," he said. He put his cap on a chair.

"I've many fears," she said, wine giving her lie a feeling of truth to her. "Oh, not this house, not my cousin and his wife. They are at Government House. Even were they home this room is privacy and safety. Besides, they are upstairs people."

"Teapot?" he said.

Her nose slyly moved but she said nothing.

"Hif Teapot comes tap-a-tap-a-tap at the door, Queely's baked."

She was not sober enough to wonder why.

"Teapot", she found herself saying in some trance of tea-and-chit-chat, and nearly telling the truth, "used often to call out in nightmares when he was a smaller child. Rarely, now he's older. I've given him several glasses of port wine. He'll not have nightmares and . . . come tapping. La! 'Tis not the people of the house I've fears for. Give me some wine," she said. "The salver is by the candles."

He poured a glass, and brought it to her, and having given it, remained nearer her.

"You will drink with me?"

"Hunless you hinsist, I don't take wine. Queely throws 'imself about hunder wine, and makes more noise than creatures."

She drained the glass.

"I have fears for what is happening. I'm tipsy, and that is *why*. I was tipsy when I wrote the note I was able to give to the groom. I'm tipsy because being a cripple and, at the same time a Scarlet Woman. . . ." She looked from side to side at her red sleeves and made a stray warped movement with her lips. ". . . being a *cripple* compels me to a directness which females are safer without in matters of—in *these* matters. This is the *first time* in Hobart Town. I have my fastidiousnesses. 'Tis not, however, *the* first time. In the last hour, however, the thought of *your* directness, your *honesty*, awoke my fears." Sober she would not have said so much and would have said no more. She raised her voice, "It suddenly alarmed me that it was the honesty of a lunatic or a murderer . . . and you *are* a murderer's friend."

He shrugged. He shrugged off her remarks as those of an irresponsible, and genteely scratched in his groin, but said with gravity:

"I'll go 'ome. What-*hever* Mr Vaneleigh's done, and Queely believes 'e 'asn't, Queely wouldn't 'arm a midge. Hif my 'and done something I'd just as soon chop it off. Should you think I'm a murderer *hor* a lunatic, I'll go. 'Ave no *fears*; you don't think so."

"La, la, la! Perhaps, I've no fears now."

At that her body canted, her legs jerked about, her ringlets sprang elastically up and down.

"You see! You see!" she cried. "I am no beauty despite my fastidiousness."

" 'Ave no fear."

"I am twisted, ludicrous, a grotesque figure from a country fair! I have only money!"

She flourished bitterness, was exhilarated by the flourishing, and near tears. She sipped her glass and licked up the heel-tap with a long, strong, pallid tongue.

"Money's honly money."

"Indeed? You see, you see, you see I am too honest. Oh,

one thought of several discreeter ways to fee you . . ." Two tears, both of self-pity, one from each eye, ran down each side of her nose, joined at the tip, and fell on her bodice. "Oh and *oh*, I am. Beyond discretion. You must. Immediate. Ly go. The window."

He came nearer, and took the wineglass from her. He put it on the floor. He took hold of her fingers.

"Now," he said, "Queely'll take your rings."

She did not snatch away her hands, but her mouth opened with a moan, and her nose stirred with terror. He removed several rings of which she was able to add up the values. As he kept on stripping her freckled fingers:

"I don't want your money. Hor your rings. Hor anything. Queely's hundressing you. 'E's got no time to waste. You be calm. You won't need no rings for Queely and 'is Jack-in-the-box."

When her hands were bare, he picked up the wineglass and, neatly as a housewife, put it and the handful of rings on the salver.

"See!" he said, "Queely's hoff with 'is coat." He hung it on a chair. He blew out one candle.

Returning to her, he sat on the floor at her feet and, looking into her close-set eyes and not once lowering his to see what his skilful tender hands were doing, began to remove her strangely designed and distorted boots from her repulsive feet. Her legs resisted.

"Quiet, now. Qui-et, *qui-et*," he said. He bent his head and kissed her hands with a fair number of lightish pouting kisses, now and then licking her knuckles with the tip of his tongue. "Quiet till I gets off the trotter-cases. Oh-*ho*, warm little trotters!"

He fondled the misshapen and limp bulbs of feet with firm and affectionate courtesy.

She was able to say, "Such warm hands yours!"

"Halways, halways warm!" He smacked a kiss on one of her thumbs. "Now, hoff with *Queely's* trotter-cases. I can't absquatulate with-*hout* trotter-cases."

As he arranged his boots, tidy husband, side by side near the bed, she began to tremble.

"You must 'ave hanother wine."

"No," she said. "No more. I am drunken already."

He moved swiftly in his socks; he filled a glass; he blew out another candle; he put the wine in her hand. As she drank he began on the buttons of her bodice beneath which lay secrets less terrible than those of her lower body but terrible enough. While the bodice was being unbuttoned, and the camisole ribbons loosened, Asnetha Sleep sipped and trembled but, suddenly, the glass emptied, and the last ribbon untied, she moved his hands away and crossed her arms. It is the immodest whom fate compels to have discoverable modesties.

"No," she said. "No. I shall undo the stays. They are not easy . . . they are not *usual.* Take the wineglass, if you please. And snuff the last candle."

It was a retreat from unaesthetic display of the trappings of nakedness rather than a flight from nakedness itself.

Firelight lit the two animals at their preparations; the woman tweaking and plucking at the mail of coiled wire and tapes and squeaking indiarubber elastics, her shadow signalling on ceiling and hangings, and wrestling with furniture and shadows of furniture, and tangling with and wrestling with the active shadow of Queely Sheill stepping from his trousers and folding his trousers and hanging his trousers, and stepping from his tattered drawers in front of the fire, and lifting his shirt-tail to warm his backside, so that a liaison of shadows, of gigantic gestures, had already taken place before she had completed her labours, and the contrivance that bound her upper body into a semblance of femininity and to idol rigidity and safety was loosened. Then Queely Sheill lowered his shirt-tail, and came over. He lifted her and laid her on the bed and, lying beside her, sought with his hands beneath the muddle to appease and fondle the ridged flesh and the flattened breasts imprinted with a basketry of criss-crossings.

They were less the fondlings of a lover than the blessing caresses of a healer, but they were also the patient conversations of a lover soothing a bruised mind by soothing the bruised body that had bruised the mind. Presently the mind was tamed, and the body was tamed. In its safe captivity, the body permitted itself the freedom of joy and began to quicken, to kindle towards fury and extravagance and annihilation.

"I love you . . ." said she who had been Asnetha Sleep, "I love you . . . Now . . . Now . . . I love you."

Queely Sheill said nothing.

His hand had taken its course under the scarlet skirt, along the bony legs to the last buttons and the way for his body to follow.

He was aware that, already lost and distorted in the firelight, their faces had also, like their bodies, sold sanity for turbulence. There was to be the interlocked affront and striving and battle of flesh. With eyes closed, mouths agape and askew, brows plaited in tameless agony of expression, the deathmask-in-life of consummation, they were to destroy what had infuriated them.

He would not answer that this was love nor admit or deny to her that she knew what she was saying. Lust betrays itself in action but is betrayed by its own fulfilment. For him it was a crucifixion hedged with tears, it was mortality preserving itself in the forgetfulness that is too instantly mortal, it was a perfect imitation of life. Whatever the act meant to her, its terms were different for him; his violence and frenzy were not those of the one who hungers but of the one who is sacrificed.

Teapot awoke to his body's report that it was about to vomit the wine Asnetha Sleep had made Teapot put in it. He was able to get out of bed quickly and safely because the little night-lamp was still on. He ran to the night-stool and lifted its mother-of-pearl-inlaid lid, and was sick. In a few moments that was over. He got the handkerchief from beneath his pillow, and wiped his eyes and mouth, and blew his nose. That done, he heard the wind that had not bothered to sleep, and was moving fussily about outside with the importance of a messenger laden with communications. He saw that the lamp-flame was motionless, a stubby finger held upright against unseen lips.

The lamp was a persisting left-over from a childhood he

had quitted for the later childhood which was soon to be quitted. Much of the furniture in Teapot's *Cindermead* bedroom resembled the lamp in being left-over. It had been bought for his room in the Brighton mansion of the Sleeps; it was undersized for the Teapot of Van Diemen's Land, who had grown longer during the months of sailing-ship seasickness, and fatter in the cage of *Cindermead*. The furnishings were lacquered and gilded and orientally inlaid to set off his West Indian exoticism. It was miniature Brighton Pavilion stuff constructed for a Teapot, newly orphaned, seven years old and as engaging as a marmoset. It ridiculed his size and needs at thirteen.

Similarly, the gilded restrictions and lacquered furtivenesses of upper-class English modes of living were too small to accommodate what heredity had given him in colour, class and instinct. Among the costive elegancies and mannered palaver he was able to act immaculately what he had been taught. He did not pick his nose in the drawing-room or tell the truth at the wrong time. Although unintelligent and black as a stove he was a perfect little gentleman; he recognized the usefulness of the gestures he had been taught for they could conceal what he knew. What had been bred in him flourished on in the hoodwinking shade.

He had known that the wine was being too freely supplied but could neither guess why nor remain awake to find out. Wine and sleep had been vomited away.

Awake, he could have bamboozled himself, and gone to sleep again. But the lamp held up its insinuating digit which the air of his room, though suggestively swirling about, did not dare to lessen the importance of by disturbing. The "Hush! Hush! Hush!" of the wind outside, and the wings of the Chinese cranes painted on the porcelain door-fittings, specified the manner in which and the direction he should go. He put on his slippers. "Hush! Hush! Hush!" the wind said. He took off his slippers. Over his night-shirt he put on the wrapper that matched his dragon-embroidered night-cap. He opened the door, and closed it behind him softly as plush.

In the corridor, offshoots of the wind slid about the floor

with serpentine cold agility and sibilance. They looped themselves about Teapot's ankles; the tug of their movement in the direction of Asnetha Sleep's room he did not deny. The floor seemed to his bare soles as chilled and resilient as the surface of a river; as he felt along the panelling it pulsated with calamity; his head began to ache. He felt some tormented sneak behind his forehead and eyes increase its agony of staring into the darkness his eyes could not break. His hand touched the curtains quivering with their own weight, awareness and portent at the entrance to the turning towards Asnetha Sleep's room. He passed between them as from a lesser dream to a greater, as from a tributary stream into a greater, and reached the door.

In that part of the house the wind was more to be heard. It had the sound of immense bodies sliding their bare surfaces across and back across the tiles of the roof; vast and fluid hairless arms and legs entwined themselves about the chimneys, and instantly unwound; now the bellies, now the hams, now the buttocks, lightly bumped their cushions on the walls.

From within the room itself he heard no sound defined enough to fit actions he knew of; neither experience nor instinct freshened his hearing to take in anything except gradations of sound so secret and subdued that the activity of his own loneliness inflating itself to jealousy far outdinned them. He imagined no more than a muffled dance of half-crazed partners retreating and advancing without feet, their mouths sealed down and their eyes cut long and glinting.

He sat, back to the wall near the door, to wind his feet in the skirts of his wrapper. The pain in his head began to melt into globules, to diminish into what were like tears that linked themselves and ran into the cistern of his heart.

To scratch on the door he knew was locked, to tap, to pound and scream out, "Miss Sleepy, I am sick. I have chundered in the night-stool. Whip me, whip me!" were sounds and a plea he could not make. His hands could not curl themselves to knock; his voice could not uncurl itself to cry out. He imagined, crouched like a beggar in timelessness, the little whip biting his bareness deliciously, and the hand with all its cool rings fondling him erotically into a stupor like sleep. It was in that other world and under its positive assurance of bliss that Teapot fell asleep.

He was aroused suddenly, after seconds or hours, by a feeling that another quality had been admitted into the scheme, that some curtain had been swung apart and, before dropping together again, had revealed lightness, emptiness and deception.

It was, indeed, what Teapot had not heard; Queely Sheill departing by the window and into the wind and its useless freedom and undemanding restlessness.

Teapot recognized departure by the sound of Asnetha Sleep's stockinged heels thudding backwards and forwards with the freedom of a woman alone, with no one to stand still for or not bump into. A murmuring could be heard. It was also the murmuring of someone alone, of one who addressed no one: it was praying or blessing or the babble of a scheme. There were no other sounds except the wind wringing its hands with disappointment. Teapot rose up.

As he returned, the floor, the heavy curtain, the tributary floor, the panelling cold and smooth, disdained him. He ground his teeth. The handle of his door resisted him.

Inside his room, he wished to scream, to fall down and kick, to break the lamp globe and gash his cheeks.

He opened a drawer, and groped among objects that no longer fascinated him . . . musical toys, and small caskets a younger Teapot had crammed with a rubbish of gleanings and beggings and stealings. To have picked up a shell ever, to have begged a deck of old playing cards, to have stolen a top on the other side of oceans, and centuries ago, was tomfoolery and for his contempt. He was older than toys.

He found the little dirk he sought, and paced the room seeking whom he could slice and probe. There was no one but himself. In front of the looking-glass he pricked himself on the throat. He observed that he was less angry with himself than with the man he had given his chain to. He threw down the weapon. He climbed into his bed where he lay breathing with so violent an anger through his teeth that presently a little foam appeared on his lips, and he fell asleep with those lips still withdrawn, and remaining withdrawn while he slept.

Queely Sheill hurried in the direction of Campbell Street and *The Shades*, and Asnetha Sleep's scent came with him towards John Death Sheill who would be treating too many hangers-on, and dipping his sticky fingers between the buttons of breast-tight bodices, and towards Polidorio Smith who would be singing, and keeping an eye on the pot-boy and the takings.

Cocks, because of the wind, or the influence of some upstart cock too young or too old to restrain a whim, were crowing to each other and each other's echoes. So far did arrogance and answering arrogance spread that the remotest crowing was thin enough to have come from beyond the mountain, from beyond Van Diemen's Land, from some cock of snow on an iceberg turret far beyond the thought of civilization, in a waste without hens or life or light or anything except the bird and its icy throat and empty answer. It was a sound as empty, as lonely and futile as the screaming that had garnished the air wiping by and over the Criminal Hospital.

It was not the screaming that, refined by distance and his bedroom walls, had aroused Judas Griffin Vaneleigh. He had, indeed, fallen half-asleep to its song and could not have known if the song had reached an end. It was a song he had heard often in Van Diemen's Land.

It was not the wind flinging against his panes the sound of drunken footsteps among the ruts, and drunken singing from *The Shades*, that had tormented him awake. Those were sounds possessing no key to the casket of his memories; for too many years he had been enclosed with and closer to worse noises, and had yet effortlessly sunk beneath the surface, and drowned his senses, and slept.

But the crowing of the cocks, circle beyond circle, roundabout intersecting roundabout endlessly, had called him from half-asleep to recollection, and recollection as unpleasing as the news of one's own death. Near and far, the birds called and answered—far and farther and farther. One cock, so distant an outrider, and an outcast beyond the remotest circuit of cries, had most damaged his wish for forgetfulness. It seemed the very crowing he had heard in his last second of freedom, the wind blowing it across the years as though it had never ceased and never would.

Go to! he thought, go to, and let me drown!

He did not hide his ears beneath the pillow. He heard the wind, the singing, the stumbling in the ruts, the world of crowings, and, beyond all, the outcast.

Oh, go to! he thought, you are a naughty invisible and an unpunctual mystery! You do not cry in the punctual world. You cry from cavernous depths. Or are you the weathercock of the infernal smithy that blazes like diamonds, and where are shoed the hoofs of the Four Horsemen? You do not cry from the world I died in, you do not cry from under a shower of spicy rains or from a barnyard in the midst of a dark blue scenery broken into a hundred little hills studded with elmy farms, villas, parks, churches and plantations of firs. But you recall that world to me. Whether you wail from a mysterious den or a ferment of intolerable lustres, you recall that world. Nine years. . . ! Oh, dead self, I'll none of you!

Lying on his darkened bed he pressed the palms of his hands upon his eyeballs; he whispered, "The dead are not safe."

The dead are not safe, he thought. 'Tis the course of nature that life springs from death. Even this life from that death, this shameful life from that shameful death.

Nine years, he thought, nine years: one imagined eternity longer. Nine years. The green, green month of June. The roses. The park trees dusty. I see the one I used to be . . . crazy nerves! all the faults of recklessness! Six years of French safety; six weeks only of English.

I see the one I used to be . . . no, I see *myself*.

The June night itself, it alone, shall hide me from Bow Street eyes whenever I walk. The plane-trees of Fitzroy Square shall add their shade. The women in their shawls go by, and I am a shadow strolling the shadows of the trees. The shadows embolden me. And who can shave with a night-time glance my French beard? The shadow of my beard emboldens me. I walk on, enjoying solitude with the consciousness of neighbourhood. From the little farm by the brick-kiln in Tottenham Court Road the cock crows. I am still free. I can walk back into the shadows.

With none—oh, with *none*—of the uncertainty and hesitation of terror, I walk on. I am in Howland Street. I stand beneath the street-lamp. I open my snuff-case precisely. I stand beneath the street-lamp, the magnifier: I take precisely two seven-eighths of Paris. What sound is that? What shadow falls? *Whose* shadow? A tap on my arm. A *smart* tap; it needs not tumble me down on the flags and break me all to bits. But it does. It is Bow Street, reeking with the nauseous fumes of tobacco and porter, who taps. Daniel Forrester, the runner. He is to speak.

Let him not speak!

He speaks:

"Ah, Mr Vaneleigh, how do you do? Who would have thought of seeing you here?"

Whatever other words are to be said by others, those words are death. As I die, I hear the cock crowing from Tottenham Court Road. I hear it now.

6

The wind, after occupying itself all night with the smoke, fetors and noises of Hobart Town, withdrew.

The English trees no longer querulously clattered thin bud-pimpled switches; the gigantic ferns in the mountain gullies and unexplored valleys stopped brandishing their primitive plumes; native trees with their perpetual morocco leaves shimmered and glittered less.

When the sun had entirely appeared, and the medical students were freed from Greek History and Homer, there was enough sunshine to give the effect of more. The street-corner chiropodist cried "Corns to pick!" earlier, and with summer confidence; the ringing pleas of the knife-grinder, the rat-catcher and the chimney-sweep suggested such warmth and prosperity that batches of the workless and the hungry outside the Hiring Depôt took on the light-hearted appearance of an audience gathering at the doors of a pantomime. The loungers in shepherds' coats outside the lush-cribs were happy enough to drink air for a time, to puff out the exquisite blue smoke of reeking Sydney tobacco and negrohead, to spit and lie and blaspheme with sparkle, to trowel wax from their ears with the ends of lucifers as though the time of the year had already arrived for clearly hearing each other's obscene ambitions for the rice-straw-bonneted females being bounced past in britzskas and phaetons on the way to the circulating library.

At *Cindermead*, the gardener scythed in the orchard. The peacocks moved about in a manner foreign and niggardly, but now and then concealed the meanness of their profiles by backing them with the quivering discs of their outfanned tails.

At a quarter to two, Queely Sheill leant on the Palladio parapet, one eye on Mr Vaneleigh's lodging-house. Otherwise he eyed the Rivulet which, like all waters, seemed less noisy by day. The ear was tricked to obtuseness by the eye which fished the bediamonded sludge and among the sun-spangled collops of hospital refuse. How almost voicelessly, abated with repulsion, the water curled around the putrescent portions imbedded in the banks! He wondered if behind the hospital wall the screaming voicelessly persisted still; if the unguessable agony had multiplied at its root to an intensity from which the wires of the voice had snapped, leaving the mouth, still open and labouring and split at its corners, with nothing to release but silence. Or had his prayer of "Sleep hor die, poor soul" been answered by opium or death? It was inconceivable that the agony itself could have withdrawn or transferred itself like a stray pet to the cradle of another body.

At two o'clock the front door of the lodging-house was opened, and Mr Vaneleigh appeared. Queely Sheill hurried across to him, and offered to carry the portfolio to *Cindermead.* His manner of offering gave no hint that he had watched and waited to offer, or that the artist had been precise in his note as to his hour of departure. They were both at a certain place on the stroke of a certain hour, and Mr Vaneleigh was delicately surprised but, he said, grateful, for he had not slept well—cocks had crowed, all the cocks in the world. Mr Vaneleigh looked sick enough and bowed enough to be in bed, at least to travel by any other way than on his own feet. Queely Sheill dared not offer pick-a-back or hackney. Like mourners arriving at a graveyard the two men departed from Campbell Street. Mr Vaneleigh was usually, when in movement, so occupied with the maintenance of movement, and so miserly with his breath, that there was little conversation. He had no need to say anything to Queely Sheill to stress that, that day, a diversion of his physical resources would be abhorrent if not impossible. So, slowly, more slowly than ever before, they passed through Hobart Town and up the incline of Barracks Hill.

Queely Sheill who had not sung or whistled as he usually did to decorate the speechless and toiling progress of the little, foppish and threadbare artist, had been occupied with a conundrum. Discriminations of behaviour he was unable to evaluate needed, he felt, Mr Vaneleigh's comment, Mr Vaneleigh's advice.

In the cosmos of John Death Sheill, *The Shades* and Polidorio Smith, hypocrisies were fewer, of a different hue, and differently distributed than in the cosmos Mr Vaneleigh had once inhabited and of which he still retained many habits. Queely Sheill had no hypocrisies, and would have shouted at God had he found it necessary. Nevertheless, he granted the mercy of his silence to those whom he considered were in need of that silence and that mercy. Asnetha Sleep's demands on his intentional gullibility had set him the problem in ethics. Since he had met her in Mr Vaneleigh's territory, and while under his shield, and had in a moment of outburst to Mr Vaneleigh, already revealed intention towards her, he had decided it was fitting to reveal more. He had no idea how people of Mr Vaneleigh's and *Cindermead's* class spoke among themselves; the theatre, and the people he lived with, gave him no pattern. He was afraid that lack of information should, by some freak of incident or conversation, leave Mr Vaneleigh under an embarrassment or, worse, completely flummoxed and fully humiliated.

On the top of Barracks Hill, he waited until Mr Vaneleigh, seated on a milestone, had regained breath and was less pale. He meantime watched a convict ship draw into harbour, and drop anchor. He watched a soldier dragging a roller around and around the barrack grounds. Presently, Mr Vaneleigh having lifted his head—for he had been sitting elbows on knees and head in hands—Queely Sheill began to select words:

"Sir," he said. "Queely's brains 'ave been trudging round and round *hand* round like the lobster hin there with the hadjutant's gig. Wonder what 'e done to be punished. . . ? I knows what I done, *hand* thinks you should know too. Was with Old Conky last night. In Old Conky's bed."

Mr Vaneleigh had drawn out a handkerchief for some practical purpose but on this information he touched it to his moustache, perhaps to conceal a flicker of disgust or incredulity. Above this hidden evidence of feeling he fixed Queely Sheill with an unsolvable expression.

"Old Conky?" he said. "The lady with the nose, and the grimaces of an Italian mountebank?"

"She '*as* a big conk," said Queely Sheill. "Thought as you should know. Hin *case*."

"I need hardly," Mr Vaneleigh flicked at some insect, or imperfection in the air, with his handkerchief. "I need hardly express my perfect confidence in the success of your—your magnanimity. I'd be surprised, did I not know that you suffer from no cold-blooded prejudices. I've heard you forcefully expressing belief in the humanities, and am sure you've not sinned merely to pamper delinquencies."

Although Mr Vaneleigh's lisp was more pronounced than Queely Sheill had heard it, he did not miss a touch of dislike in the blurred accents.

"Not *sinned*. Queely nor Conky 'aven't sinned. I stripped 'er and laid 'er, but not nasty. *Not sinned*."

"I said *not sinned*. I perceive you'd prefer—now what?—let's be precise!—*not performed!*"

"Queely 'opes you don't mind 'im telling."

"Mind? She can have made no addition to her social consequence—but why should *I* mind? And you've made none to the safety of your skin."

"Safety of . . . I don't ap-pre-'end, sir. I *hassures* you that . . . ."

"The woman calls me murderer?"

"Oh, sir, that is but. . . ."

"The woman then calls me murderer."

He began to fold his handkerchief so that its holes were hidden within the less-worn fabric.

"I should be *thanking* you for the knowledge that your—bedroom companion has spread her slanders before the grave had closed at once on my indifference and my forgiveness. I'd meant to thank you ere this."

"She meant no 'arm."

"I said I was indifferent. *And* forgiving! But—slander no *harm*? 'Tis the grating of the swords. I meet with no intellectual relief from this conviction of yours. I can *not* believe that anything can so have reversed the course of nature that harm is not now consequent upon slander. Whetting her teeth with horrid delight, she called me murderer. Oh, the stream runs, the gutter runs, the sewer runs: what might she be now calling you? In her mind *or* elsewhere?"

Mr Vaneleigh put away his handkerchief. He seemed to have finished, but drew a breath, and spoke on, "I saw you from my window today. You stood on the Palladio and looked in the water."

"Yes."

"What did you see there? What were you looking at?"

"I was waiting. I saw the muck. But I wasn't thinking of the water hor the muck."

"But you saw. Water from the mountain there, water from the pure rock and the pure snow. Pure until it enters Hobart Town. At the Palladio what? A sewer. *Muck!*"

"Queely told you of Conky because *not* of wanting you to know about beds and what-all but so you'd come to no . . . no *hawkwardness* with the quality."

"It is not I who'll come to awkwardness. I've sufferings enough—past, present and in prospect—'tis not from *that* direction, now or in the future, they'll come to me. That class can arrange no more sufferings for me. But you! 'Tis no part of my duty to pronounce on your behaviour—have we not all a nature of mingled metal, silver and lead! There's a gulf between humans and animals: I've always thought it to be narrower than many suppose. I'll not pronounce then on your behaviour, but I do say that you should recollect your perilous situation—for 'tis perilous as I see it. I seem to recall, on my first encounter with you, saying something of the same sort, that pity will beget you infamy. I pitied my wife, and am infamy itself . . . an unhanged murderer! You'll suffer, as I did, not because you erred, but because you trusted. Let the water come from the snow, let you be as pure as that water . . . You catch my meaning?"

"You mustn't fret hover Queely. Them who're frightened of nettles don't piss in meadows. I ain't frightened."

Mr Vaneleigh stood. He indicated the descent towards the bridge over Sandy Bay Stream and the road to *Cindermead.* As they moved off and down, he said:

"I do not *fret.* But I should be much damaged in a sense of gratitude if I did not say: I find it a lack in myself that the tenderness of nature cannot be perfectly subdued by the utmost degree of human resolution."

Queely Sheill was shocked, stimulated and honoured, as if a sacred dog had chosen him to sing to; Mr Vaneleigh's face faded emotionless and as indolent as the labour of maintaining seemly movement downhill would allow. It was enough beyond belief to Queely Sheill that Mr Vaneleigh had lifted a head over the rim of his nest of lethargy to pronounce qualms about his porter's safety, and opinions of danger. That he had also made a confession, however aslant, of a regard, however muted, for the cockney, was so infinitely beyond belief that Queely Sheill said:

"Tell Queely again."

Mr Vaneleigh said no more. He was to say no more on the subject, then or ever. He walked towards *Cindermead* with the expression of a man who preferred, in silence, to suspect himself of having said absolutely nothing.

Queely Sheill did not, then or ever, ask again.

At *Cindermead*, Lady Knight was once more pinning the eye of agate at the bosom of the green satin dress. Government House the night before had been boring to exhaustion; her eyes ached; the afternoon's portrait-sitting promised nothing but further boredom; Mr Vaneleigh's charm, conversation and skill, even if at their peaks, would leave her unmoved. During the morning she had considered sending the groom to call off the artist, had written a note and, her hand on the bell, had decided that the sooner over the better. She was in dangerous mood, and her maid in terror.

Asnetha Sleep, who had spent the morning pressing blackheads from her nose and chin, sat in her bath-chair in the garden close to some jonquils and early daffodils. An elaborate afternoon gown enclosed her; her newest parasol of fringed taffeta with whalebone ribs, and ivory point and handle, was held above her bonnet and curls. Over her knees and about her shoulders hung fringed shawls. She wore no rings, and had arranged her hands, and continued to re-arrange them, conspicuously and in postures of petrified negligence, to recommend their ringlessness to Queely Sheill's secret notice. She had been unable to resist wearing her largest and most involved ear-rings.

Teapot also wore ear-rings. His ears had been pierced when he was five; he often wore his own plain circles of gold wire. But, since he had been troublesome all morning, Asnetha Sleep had lent him her amethyst ear-rings wrought like bunches of grapes. They had not completely soothed him. Appearing taller and thinner and straight-backed in a turban, he wheeled her here and there, and there and here, to her directions, as she sought a suitable place to be surprised in. She thought of a shorter nose even if black-headed, and sprays of blossom above. The one already blossoming tree on the estate was too far from where Queely Sheill might see her . . . languid, decorative and joyful. Teapot's attempts, at her command, to herd the peacocks near the bath-chair, had failed. She fidgeted, and kept on being doubtful if the chair were in the most romantic setting. Teapot sulked, and stood straight-backed. That straight-backed posture and manner, and no turban yet on, had been there since early morning.

Before breakfast, he had tapped at her door and, permitted entrance, had entered and stood erect to say with a threatening clarity:

"I have been beastly sick."

"La, la, *la*! Uncouth Teapot! You have not. Said, 'Good morning!' Teapot." She had had a box of ringlets on the bed.

"I have not said, 'Good morning!' I have been beastly sick."

"When sick? Where? Poor, poor Teapot! Tell, Miss Sleepy." She had held up and quizzed some ringlets.

"I was sick . . . I was sick just now. It was dark sick. Like blood. Oh, horror!"

She had been startled, and had stopped trying to decide

whether or not to add two extra ringlets to each side-bunch. She had dangled them in agitation, saying:

"Blood! Teapot, treasure! Come here!"

He had not moved. He had been *too* upright. She had narrowed her eyes; she had raised her voice.

"Liar! *Blood!* Untruthful monster! Come *here*!"

"I am to come there," he had said, callous and unmoving.

Then he had said, sharpening his precision of tone with accusation:

"I said *like* blood. In the night-stool. Pooh, pooh!—it smelt like wine. It *was* wine."

Her nose had flickered several times quickly; she had been about to scream at him when her maid had come with breakfast. As the woman poured her chocolate, Asnetha Sleep said in an unwrinkled tone:

"Megan, Teapot has. Been sick. Senna. A big cup. He will want. No breakfast."

"I want breakfast."

"Senna! If you have. Just been. Sick."

"I want breakfast."

She had thrown a handful of ringlets on the spot on the floor where Queely Sheill's boots had stood, shiny as a gentleman's with Warren's Black Japan. She had screeched:

"Pick those. Up, Megan! Give him breakfast! Take him, Megan! He's a monster!"

As Megan had edged out to wait in the corridor, Teapot had been about to dig in his heels and Asnetha Sleep about to become louder. Sir Sydney had been heard at the end of the corridor, a light voice. Neither Teapot nor his mistress had wished to present their domestic difference to Sir Sydney's Saturday ear, particularly after a night at Government House. Teapot had left with Megan. Asnetha Sleep had reeled from her bed to the breakfast table near her lover's window.

All morning Teapot had hung about intending to notify menace by his manner. He had rolled his eyes brainlessly in corners, had gritted his flawless teeth, and scratched wolfishly at her locked door behind which she and Megan had tried to come to conclusions about an afternoon *toilette*. Sir Sydney's presence had shielded Asnetha Sleep from more tempestuous attacks by her West Indian; she had not been caught alone. By luncheon, Teapot had waned to merely sulky, to hopelessness and to fear of what the afternoon was to be shaped into, for Asnetha Sleep, he wretchedly knew, was shaping it. If he were to be of the design it would not be as himself, a coddled and inviting animal of flesh, but as an extra fan, a necklace, a reticule trimmed with coral and containing nothing. He would be made wear his bracelet of bells.

Although Asnetha Sleep could never reveal her possession of Queely Sheill who was beyond caste, it was not possible for her not to display the effects of her satisfaction. She was so inspirited by easy victory, and the nature as well as the appearance and ability of her conquest, that she forgot to disbelieve that she had inflamed Queely Sheill. It did not appear to her that an experienced innocent with a quirk had been invited to feed a hungry body on a windy night in a house whose front door he would never be asked to enter, but that she, gracious lady, rich, intelligent and merry, had yielded to an ardent importunity because of a romantic heart. She saw herself in sprigged muslin on a swing hung from a blossoming pear tree.

She wore Venetian red. She sent Teapot indoors for a vinaigrette. She opened and shut the parasol. She replaced her hands, whenever they relaxed, into rigid arrangements of relaxation as in statues. She tried cajoling the peacocks. She did not once look directly at the drive gateway through which must come the man who would discover her accidentally, frail and irresistible.

It was Sir Sydney who surprised her.

He had been heard being waspish in the stables, the coach-house and the orchard: the stinging softness of his rebukes, denunciations and criticisms was always followed by acceleration and increase—the scythe stone more loudly and quickly honed; well-buckets clattered; brooms at cobwebs, and hoes at mossed bricks, more energetically expressed their purpose.

He came upon her as she pinned two moulted peacock feathers on Teapot's turban.

Sir Sydney was one who did not enjoy his world because he did not see it. He was the embittered child with an excess of imagination. The child with imagination does not see distinctly what is in front its nose. To see one's surroundings and enjoy them, one requires a more complex constitution, and senses no longer innocent. He was of the simple constitution that mistakes ambition for achievement; he was innocent in condoning his wife's adulteries—more innocent he would have less wisely strangled her, less innocent more wisely have divorced her.

"Has Mr Vaneleigh arrived yet?" he said.

"Mr Vaneleigh. . . ? There, Teapot, my treasure, you look like a maharajah! . . . Mr *Vaneleigh*? Oh, the artist! I declare, my love, I'd *quite* forgotten he was coming. I do not know, cousin."

"Indeed, Mr Vaneleigh, the artist. Is there another Mr Vaneleigh."

"La, la, one is so *stupid*! I don't know if he has arrived."

He would not leave it at that.

"But you have been on or about the drive since luncheon. Surely. . . ?"

"I have not been watching," she said so pettishly that he thought he knew she had.

"Oh!" That meant disbelief.

She said, and with some stiffness, "I think—I may be at fault—but I *think* that, last time, Mr Vaneleigh took the Estuary Road. I *seem* to recall Rose saying so. La, I'm *convinced* she said so."

"Very well." His disbelief was not to be quenched: "The Estuary Road in a hackney? Good God, woman, the wheels would be off."

"I doubt if he affords hackneys. Mr Vaneleigh seems to walk."

She attempted to erase her former revealing pettishness and said, too clearly, "Shall I send Teapot to see? They may be here."

"They?" he said.

Her nose moved. She twirled her parasol in a tantrum with herself.

"Teapot, treasure," she said. "You are. Not to grind. Your teeth."

"I am not", said Teapot, "to grind my teeth," and he ground them again, though in the diddling fashion of a smaller animal than he had been being.

"They?" Sir Sydney had not been sidestepped or side-tracked.

"*They?* Oh, Mr Vaneleigh and his friend, his servant . . . I'm not sure which."

"It's of no moment. But to walk . . . and by the Estuary Road!"

He wore an unusual costume when, on Saturdays, he nagged and nosed his way about the grounds and outhouses of *Cindermead*—a mohair frock-coat and Clarence boots. He smacked his ash-plant in a most masculine style on the side of one boot.

"You've seen, of course, what he has done? The first stage of the portrait?"

"No, Sydney. Mr Vaneleigh still has the work in his *porte-feuille*. Rose says he promises to complete the work today. She hopes so. She perfervidly hopes so."

"Why, pray?" He rat-a-tat-tatted more feverishly on the boot. "Why this hoping?"

"The tedium, perhaps. I'm not certain, Sydney."

"Has Rose mentioned tedium?" He tapped gently, more slowly, more slowly.

"Directly, *no*, Sydney. But I sense that the restraint in one posture for a couple of hours encourages tedium."

"Indeed!" That had the exultant sound of "I had hoped so!"

Encouraged a little, she rotated her parasol very, very slowly and said, "I feel too that, in some way, Mr Vaneleigh about the house is boring to Rose. I cannot say. *I've* not met him."

There fell a silence in which Teapot was heard to stop grinding his teeth. Sir Sydney, distinguished-looking in a recessive way, suddenly became quite distinguished in a definite way. He swung the ash-plant, hitting at and missing a beetle on a jonquil.

"You must have *your* portrait done. He's a very sound man. Charming too. The Inspector-General of Hospitals, the Surgeon-in-Charge, the Deputy Purveyor all recommend him highly."

Sir Sydney's patronage was economical: it occupied his wife with a suitable boredom, followed a fashion followed by men useful to him, and was a cultural altruism.

"Should you *like* a portrait done?"

"Oh, la, la, *la*! Oh, yes, dear Sydney."

Immediately, she amended her enthusiasm.

"Not—of course—*completely* from vanity. La!"

That got rid of a madness to have her nose hanging on a wall.

"But to *grasp* an opportunity. *Teapot!* stop rattling bells on black wrist! Rose informs me that the unfortunate creature has painted . . . was it Lord Byron? At least that he has been hung in London . . . the Royal Academy? Somerset House? We rustics are never positively positive!"

Surfeit of imagination had brewed subtlety of an inferior sort in Sir Sydney's nature. Education having accustomed him to hypocrisy, he did not understand spoken words because he was in pursuit of purposes behind them. He denied words an unsullied meaning. Years of uneasy adjustments had left him no consoling verities.

"His undoubted skill should not influence your decision. I should not have ordered him were he not skilful. Are you yourself, Asnetha, happy at the thought of a portrait? By Mr Vaneleigh? Or whomever?"

He was giving her the chance to refuse a record of her imperfections, but refusal would have enraged him, and he expected none. He had already made his decision.

She had elation about Queely Sheill to keep hidden in her acceptance:

"Sydney, I've *said* I shall be pleased to grasp the opportunity. Your assurance of his ability is sacred to me. What is his fee? Oh, certainly a portrait. By Mr Vaneleigh or whomever. A murderer or whomever. *Certainly.*"

"I shall speak to him today. Murderer or whomever! Really, Asnetha, you've an odd turn."

"Oh, Rose tells me that Mr Vaneleigh is one. A positive fillip to sitting. What is his *fee*, Sydney?"

"You are a fool, and Rose is in error. I'll speak to her on it. I shall inform her that Mr Vaneleigh was transported for a *forgery*. And a forgery on his *own* expectations of fortune."

It was satisfying for him to be able to be right and righteous. His dignity increased.

"Does Rose think—do *you*?—that I should go to the extreme of large-heartedness, and introduce a murderer into a household of females? I shall pay his fee. My *pleasure*."

Teapot's bells rang as he pointed and said, "The man!"

Queely Sheill and Mr Vaneleigh were half-way up the drive.

Sir Sydney, standing between them and the bath-chair, obscured her view, and so hid her that she could have been anyone and maybe a toothless grandmother taking the air.

"Mr Vaneleigh, sir!" called Sir Sydney, beckoning, advancing a little and making play with his ash-plant.

Mr Vaneleigh was seen to touch his cravat, to give his posture attention, to slip an expression of alertness on his pallid and weary countenance, to approach and, at the right moment, at the right distance, to remove his abraded white topper and make his bow.

Queely Sheill remained standing where he had been left, in full view of Sir Sydney's disregard and Teapot's hatred. Sir Sydney and Mr Vaneleigh completely hid the cockney from her. By the time she had propelled her chair into the bulb-bed Queely Sheill's back was turned to her.

"Teapot, treasure," she cried musically. Teapot was pretending to be watching peacocks. She would have screamed like a barge-woman had the others not been there. As they started strolling towards her, the subject of a portrait commission most obviously being discussed, she was musical again:

"Teapot, treasure! The naughty chair has positively *bolted*. Come, help me!" She was femininity itself.

"I am to come and help you," said Teapot lackadaisically, and he threw a pebble at a peacock and, as slowly as he dared under Sir Sydney's eye, lifted his feet one after the other and, the feathers in his turban shaking and his bells jangling, as slowly as possible dragged the machine and Asnetha Sleep from the bulb-bed.

"Let us, Asney, go in with Mr Vaneleigh," said Sir Sydney, lightly as a toxic insect, "and tell Lady Knight that he can spare us time for your portrait. She will be perfectly enchanted."

Asnetha Sleep's legs lashed about a little. When those had become dormant again they all moved off, and Queely Sheill who had not been interested in them knew they had gone and thought himself alone. Upstairs, from her dressing-room window, Lady Knight saw him. She would have said that, in spite of finding herself quickened by the sight of him on Mr Vaneleigh's first visit, she had forgotten him. It seemed not so. The young man who stood below she remembered, but not as a once-seen, immediately-forgotten object. She remembered him, to her surprise, as one remembers an object carried about in one's purse for days. An extra weight is perceptible; the fingertips brush accidentally along the outlines and thus, at random, learn them; one idly feels and idly understands its texture. It is an object whose full value, quality and use do not strike one until it is brought to daylight and all the senses, either by need, in disaster, or casually.

Casually presented to her, Queely Sheill's physical beauty had further effect. She was able also to examine it unseen, and without distraction.

One does not expect to see such beauty un-selfconscious. Human beauty falters at itself, and makes itself a dignity; it attitudinizes; it seeks to round itself out with a perfection of expected gestures. It falls in love with itself; it cannot prevent itself staring into its own pores in a looking-glass; it must always be slipping sidelong glances in those other looking-glasses, the faces passing by dazzled. Queely Sheill's beauty caused him to do none of those things.

Mr Vaneleigh's admission of a sort of affection had exhilarated him. During the artist's absence he could display that exhilaration. He did it by pacing about whispering to himself, arguing with himself, gesticulating to himself as he made points; his problem, seeming more easily solvable in happiness, was the problem of how to return to Teapot his chain and his peace of mind.

Ugly people, mouthing and gesticulating to themselves in misery and bitterness, are repellent to or scorned by the observer. Their flaws of flesh are seen to betoken evil or lunacy. Beautiful people are seen as prophets with power to illuminate, or royalties playing an important game. One withdraws.

She, Rose Knight, her black and tangled humours blacker in contrast to the colourless and unravelled harmony she was witnessing, withdrew from the window. *Cockney* churl, she thought, cockney *churl*, and snatched at her satin skirt, and left the room, and descended the stairs, and crossed the shining floors, and arrived in the drawing-room by one door as Asnetha Sleep was wheeled around the Coromandel screen, her voice at its most silver-toned chiming:

"No farther, Teapot, I implore! Hold, hold, with black hands, my treasure, or we shall run down the canterbury."

She was laughing with great accuracy and melodiousness.

Rose Knight put an instant stop to that. Rigid at the other door, she flung her words directly as daggers:

"Your parasol! How dare you? In the house with an open parasol!"

Before Asnetha Sleep, the open parasol held across her knees, could say, and truthfully, that she had forgotten, Sir Sydney, entering with Mr Vaneleigh, said:

"That is superstition."

That is, said the voice in the depths below the glazed surface, that is stupid, scatter-brained, absurd, *peasant* superstition.

His glistening voice continued, "You might also rebuke Teapot for his feathers."

"Good evening, Mr Vaneleigh."

She and her satin and a smile brilliant as ice sailed towards them. The Vulliamy struck three.

"Punctual creature!" she said.

Then, "I should certainly rebuke the black boy for wearing peacock feathers in the house, were Mr Vaneleigh not here to be bored by my fantastics."

"You would *not* rebuke him, of course, for the feathers are Asnetha's doing."

Her husband knew that she would like to sweep from the room.

"Then I should rebuke Asnetha. But," and she smiled very brilliantly again, "*so* gently, as woman to woman. And *en famille*."

She would go no further than that in public reflection on her husband.

"But, Rose dear. So elegant. The feathers are. So fitting with. The turban." Asnetha Sleep, having gone so far in audacity, went further. "Mr Vaneleigh must. Tell us. Do you consider the feathers. . . ?"

"I'm certain Mr Vaneleigh", said Sir Sydney gently, "has no belief in this nonsense of parasols and feathers."

Mr Vaneleigh, who had been examining the nap of his hat with an intentness which suggested that it had grown there since he left Campbell Street, said, "I have known people who'll not point at the moon." He returned to the nap.

"Nor shall I point," said Rose Knight. And, "I am *quite* ready, Mr Vaneleigh."

"Alas! I have left my portfolio outside. I shall. . . ." Mr Vaneleigh was suave, though haggard.

"The black boy will get it," said Rose Knight. "The man with the portfolio is on the drive."

"Teapot, treasure. So quick. So good. Run, Teapot, on black. Feet."

Teapot said nothing. He made no move to go. His eyes rolled about. They were terrified of not finding a lie to tell.

"How do you know the man is on the drive?" said Sir Sydney. "Are you certain?"

"I am certain," said Rose Knight. "Hurry off, black boy. We are waiting. Mr Vaneleigh is waiting."

Teapot grabbed at his belly, and the little bells rang.

"Oh, ah! Oh, ah!" he grunted. "I am sick. I am going to chunder."

It was a well-chosen lie.

"Run," squealed Asnetha Sleep, melody forgotten. "To your room. Run! Run!"

"I am to run," said Teapot, and was heard running and jingling in the passage.

As Mr Vaneleigh was himself about to leave, Sir Sydney said, "No, Mr Vaneleigh. Remain here. *My* pleasure. I'll see your fellow for you, *and* see that he's off the drive."

He put his head back around the screen, "Asnetha, you must tell Rose your surprise. Joys should be shared."

As though unwittingly, she whirled the parasol, as doubling the delight of maddening Rose Knight safely, Mr Vaneleigh there.

"I declare. My love," she said, "that Sydney. Is a perfect positive love. Mr Vaneleigh has. Been persuaded by. The *dear*. Man to paint my portrait."

"The loaves and fishes, Mr Vaneleigh?"

She raised an eyebrow. So did he.

"Those one must have," he said. "But I'd deny myself them rather than. . . ."

Rose Knight did not want to hear that again. She interrupted, "I *know*, Mr Vaneleigh. *There*, Asnetha, Mr Vaneleigh means . . . I am sure . . . that he'll find your portrait a more stimulating task than mine. Your face has more . . . more character, more life, more *movement*, more striking features. You are so fortunate in your *eyes*. And it is, of course, a younger face. Wine, Mr Vaneleigh? *Your* face is quite pale. Shall I ring for wine?"

"Neither wine, thank you, nor macaroons."

It was very nearly not done with charm. It did not divert her from the cripple.

"My *husband's* cousin disapproves of Hickson's—as you do. I am certain she has never been there."

"I am. A Brighton rustic, Mr Vaneleigh," Asnetha Sleep said, stopping herself from closing the parasol which, opened, was becoming a nuisance. "The Chain Pier. You know. The gossiping, the raffling. Bracing winds. You see me so?"

"I deny rustic for you, Miss Sleep. 'Tis not possible."

He spoke as though they were still in England; as though the cock crowing from Tottenham Court Road had not been heard in Howland Street accompanying the salutation of the Bow Street runner.

"I envy you your Brighton. When I lose all relish for artificial existence, I can trifle away the summer hours at anchorage in a clover field near the green salt sea."

Sir Sydney appeared with the portfolio.

"I've sent your . . . I've sent the young man to the coach-house," he said. "We have another cockney there. They can talk about Newgate or us. In the meantime, Asnetha, we must leave Mr Vaneleigh to be finished with Rose so that he can sooner sharpen his pencil for you. I shall be your chair-man. Hold up your parasol so that it does not catch the screen. Come!"

As Rose Knight sat to Mr Vaneleigh that afternoon she was, at first and for long enough, silent. She was in rash thought. Passions span and then dissolved their webs on the moulding of her face. Instantly other films were elsewhere spun and as instantly unravelled. Much less than skin-deep, those variations, constantly and subtly variable, were in-appreciable except by the artist's eye.

My God, he thought, his crayon pursuing delicacies of shade and light, what incoherencies and chasms of emotion! what-ill-disposed and sick-hearted angers are at work in that alabaster!

A deadly rage, a rejuvenating wantonness, and an avidity for revenge smudged and weakened the lines of her face minutely, but enough to leave her looking wearier and lan-guidly cunning. She tempted herself not to speak, but Mr Vaneleigh was flagging, and she had been silently immobile for over an hour that seemed ever. She spoke:

"Mr Vaneleigh, you've exhibited, Sir Sydney tells me, at the Royal Academy?"

"I had once a quizzing glass, a Tomkisson pianoforte, a Damascus sabre, and a pet robin called Bobbie."

"I do not perfectly take you. . . ." She had forgotten how tiresome he was, and wished she had kept her mouth shut.

"*Bric-à-brac* of the past. I *used* to exhibit. I *used* to have."

"Your Bobbie has flown maybe. But not your Academy reputation. Sir Sydney speaks highly. And ladies of my acquaintance who've sat to you. You are perfectly famous."

Mr Vaneleigh was too tired; his lisp was as noticeable as his disdain:

"Nose-led, well-meaning daughters of nose-led, well-meaning England. They speak as highly of my fame as of my infamy."

She defended without pitch, "Of your *fame*, Mr Vaneleigh."

"Oh, in the London days I possessed gifts, a talent."

"You are too modest. You still possess talent."

"I *possessed* a talent; it now possesses me." He worked on.

"You've your talent, and. . . ." She was reaching a point. ". . . your kind friend. Many are without talent or friend."

"Friend?" His crayon touched the corners of her sketched eyes and drew more years there.

"You told me he was not your servant."

"Oh, he! He would be *everybody's* friend. He's young, lusty and full of sap, and has an ardour for excellence: he hastens about with all possible expedition on behalf of this ardour."

"He seems, shall I say, almost your disciple."

This, *this*, he thought, is the fretful unease one is so wearisomely accustomed to in beautiful women. He rested his crayon. I do not feel well, he thought, but said:

"That is mere *seeming* and is, perhaps, my fault, not his. I *allow* him to carry for me. But disciple, no! Whatever instruction I could give him could take him no further than I have gone."

He shrugged, indicating the impropriety of his journey so far.

"I could only instruct him, as disciple, to be like the famished beggars who sit with their whispers of 'I am starving'. *I* shan't live *long* enough to starve. He needs no instruction from *me* on how to be betrayed by himself or others."

He is, she thought, worse than Government House.

She said, more briskly, "Is he an unemployed?"

"He is employed by his father who leases Queen's Playhouse. I lodge near the Playhouse. He lives in the little Playhouse Cottage. This proximity", said Mr Vaneleigh with an old snobbery, "led to our accidental encounter."

She had hardly been able not to show interest; she touched the eye of agate.

"An actor?" she said.

"*He* is incapable of acting. His father, nevertheless, seems to be one. I have this from the young man—we ticket-of-leave men are forbidden the theatre, gaming or billiards."

His grey eyes, too steady, were as depthless as nothing.

"He is *incapable* of acting. That is his imperfection. Perhaps this is hyper-criticism, and I don't wish to degrade simplicity into inanity—or undervalue the sanction of his honesty, but he is too honest to be gratified by praise and too stubborn for discretion. He has a heart compact and united enough to contrive happiness, but not head enough to avoid the consequences of happiness. Too *natural* yet arbitrary! He has a *sublime* vision of a dissolving world!"

She had heard every tired word but he had talked her down, and she remained silent. She saw Queely Sheill, enriched by tedious analysis, pace the gravel, and heard his soles make a sound beneath her dressing-room window (and she alone,) that she fervently wished was being made by the same soles but thinned by walking through Edmonstone's Heraldry.

Mr Vaneleigh erased a line or two of imperfect nicety, and replaced them with truer lines and less flattering ones. He looked ghastly, as though he had been drinking all night. The drawing was almost finished.

Meanwhile, Sir Sydney wheeled his cousin, Miss Sleep of Brighton, all over the world, and it could have been next week, and it was hardly warm enough to be out without rings. Sir Sydney's ability to find imperfection, which he expected and went straight to, infected the manner in which he pushed the bath-chair. The wheels for him had the extra element of skill which eyes and soles lacked in testing the smoothness of paths. Asnetha Sleep's body was what so usefully and immediately picked up the wheel's signal and translated it into sound.

"Oh, *oh!*"

"There—just *there?*" said Sir Sydney bringing the chair back to test a bump. "There? Or is it *here*, Asnetha?" That was the sixteenth or millionth bump.

"Oh, *here*!" she cried. "Sydney I am *quite* in a kim-kam. You will *kill* me."

"Opposite the laburnum," he said. "Opposite the laburnum, on the *east* side. Have you that in your skull with the others?" he said to the gardener who tested the paths with them.

She would have called off, fainted, thrown aside her shawls and hideously staggered indoors days, weeks, months ago, if the hope of seeing Queely Sheill had not fortified her.

The paths finished with, and the gardener having returned to his scythe with which he, stimulated to efficiency by humiliation and anger, cut down hundreds of Sir Sydney Knights, the examination continued. His Saturday tours were, when the weather did not make fault-finding a misery to him, always thorough. That Saturday he would have found the needle in the haystack.

Dressed like an empress, and wheeled about like an infant which sees only the places its nursemaid wishes to see, Asnetha Sleep visited every place where Sir Sydney went to find botchery . . . garden beds ill-dug, vines untied, flimsy growths uncherished, dung-heaps not domed enough, a nail too many, a flake of paint missing. Mad with irritation and occasionally executing her muscles' erratic demand for a convulsive jig among her shawls, she sat through the tormenting of servants. The upper servants had been too rigorously examined before hiring, were too well-trained and too constantly harried not to make certain that all was what they considered ship-shape and flawless. The assigned servants, with the treadmill, the triangle, the Hiring Depôt and beggary just outside the gates of *Cindermead*, had never been given, and tried not to give themselves, the chance to develop any imperfections.

To them, one by one, free or assigned, Sir Sydney softly, softly, pointed out the hair-line fault they had not seen. They watched it open softly, softly to a crevasse without bottom into which they could be hurled to invisibility. Sir Sydney was exercising the muscles of his malice on lesser incidents and lesser mortals for he had seen the banners of recalcitrance fluttering above his wife's head.

Asnetha Sleep attempted, from time to time, to be amusing for the sake of amusing herself as much as for amusing her cousin. Preoccupied, or pretending preoccupation, he misread or pretended to misread her efforts into silence.

It was almost too late when, near the coach-house, she heard Queely Sheill and the groom laughing. She had been lolling. She took notice of her stays, and sat as upright as she could.

"Oh, *la*, la, la! I've been nearly *asleep*, Sydney. Oh, you're to examine the coach-house now!"

But he had his back to the coach-house. He was looking up at a chimney of the house. The smoke was smoke impure and of the wrong shape and revealed to him a domestic machination.

"I've already seen the coach-house," he said.

She trilled, girlishly.

"I should like to see it," she said, and could have said nothing sillier than that truth.

"See the coach-house?" He abandoned the smoke, and returned to the back of the bath-chair.

She had committed herself to idiocy, and was forced to continue idiotically, "Yeth, Couthin Atheny would *dote*."

It was an old cousinly nonsense that had always been successful.

"My dear Asnetha," he said, "you've seen the coach-house, outside and inside, hundreds . . . well, many times."

She perceived that it was time to begin a headache.

"Is it *quite* clean?" she said. "I find I no longer want to go. I declare I've a sudden headache."

"You've your vinaigrette. But I'll take you inside."

"No!" she said, and sharply. "Leave me. Here the fresh. Air will."

He began to wheel her towards the house.

"Stop!" she screeched. "You jolt. Me and all. The afternoon. A monster!"

"I shall certainly leave you," he said, and took his hand

from the chair, and tap-tapped with his ash-plant as he moved off. But too late!

Teapot appeared, and stood like a witchdoctor pronouncing a spell, and called icily as a young prefect, "Ma'am, says five o'clock. Mr Vaneleigh is leaving. I am to hurry."

"I must tell his fellow," said Sir Sydney, and walked to the coach-house, and entered it.

"Teapot, treasure, come!" she cried, crazily rearranging her shawls. He heard her. He moved slowly from the door towards her . . . one pace, two paces, three paces.

"Run, run!" She was quite a-flutter.

Teapot gave a grin, turned and ran into the house.

She heard Sir Sydney directing Queely Sheill from the coach-house to the drive. It was by the door of another wall. She did not see him, even his pea-jacketed back, nor he the ringless hands she had worn for him. She was beating them passionately on the arms of the bath-chair, and tears of temper were bounding down her nose, when Sir Sydney reappeared. He picked up the parasol she had pushed away.

"Come," he said. "I *shall* show you the coach-house . . . Ferris has done the most *ingenious* trick with. . . . Pray, what is wrong?"

"My head, my head," she moaned. And before he could ask, "And I've. Pins and needles. In my hands. Pins. Needles."

"You've a chill," said Sir Sydney and, though he did not intend saying it, "Rose will be enchanted."

He wheeled her into the house, and was about to call for her maid or Teapot, when he noticed the parasol still open across her knees. He pushed the chair quickly towards the drawing-room and, with a fine and shocking curve, around the Coromandel screen.

Rose Knight saw them in the chimney-piece looking-glass: the reversal of their countenances, right for left and left for right, hyperbolized their expressions. Asnetha Sleep's was weighted and mottled with undigested spleens. The flesh of her face seemed to drag downwards, unhealthily dewlapped, with cantankerous fatigue. Now and then her eyelids fluttered minutely, quickly, and with a kind of saucy fear.

Sir Sydney's expression was that of a man ready and heart-burning to attack. His face, seen unfamiliarly in the glass, had the neatness of its breeding, its *distingué* balance, marred by pique and lopsided by the slanting antagonism of his mouth that was sweetly enough cut to ooze syrup rather than stinging scent. He gave his wife time, his lips moving spitefully with impatience, to give him an advantage in attack by attacking him first. But she continued to look at her portrait which she had propped against the clock, and to wait. It made a winning picture—the graceful and handsome woman examining her portrait, the good-looking husband and the sick sweet woman in her bath-chair struck still with admiration at the doorway of a tastefully furnished drawing-room. Sir Sydney moved. He wheeled the chair farther into the room.

"You admire yourself," he said.

Rose Knight looked at his image in the looking-glass. Her voice was softer, cooler, more provoking than his.

"I admire the artist's skill."

"Fiddlesticks!" He went nearer the portrait. "Or shall I say, dear Rose, that I find it difficult to believe that you do not admire yourself."

"I admire Mr Vaneleigh's skill."

"Perhaps, *perhaps*, I err. Pray, forgive me. You *can* scarcely be admiring this representation of yourself. You are admiring the skill with which Mr Vaneleigh has made you look older."

He strolled, oh, with ease and dignity, and placid, to the french window to spy on whatever immodesty the sunset was committing. She turned away from the drawing and the looking-glass. With back still towards him, she said:

"It is not he who has done that. I have spent no more than five hours in the same house as your murderer."

Asnetha Sleep who had just removed her bonnet and the four ringlets secured to its lining, two each side, which she had not been able, at the last moment, to begrudge herself, stroked the things like pets, and indiscreetly said:

"*Forger*, my love. Mr Vaneleigh is. No more than. . . ."

She stopped. Rose Knight's eyes had paled, and she had

brought those eyes several swift steps nearer to the bath-chair, so near that the cripple could smell satin slyly settling itself to carved solidity. She was cut off from Sir Sydney by the statue and its white lethal gaze. She heard him saying from the refuge of sunset:

"Yes, Rose, forger. What need for lies about a man who. . . ."

"You dare! You dare again to flaunt an open parasol in the house!"

"Rose, my *love*!" Asnetha Sleep tried to sound as if she were not on the point of gibbering with astonishment. "I am perfectly mortif. Ied. I assure. You."

"You are not mortified. You are brazen. Deliberate in insult. And your hideous black creature with peacock feathers, he too, I suppose is. . ."

"Peacock feathers!" said Sir Sydney, still on the outskirts of the jungle. "Peacock feathers! Open parasols! For neither needs Asnetha abase herself. Godless superstitions! It's absurd, it's monstrous, to require denials, protestations of innocence or apologies of any sort because of a senseless quiddity of yours. *And*, that Vaneleigh fellow was a forger *on his own expectations*."

Rose Knight remained a second after that still as an icon, and Asnetha Sleep sat hunched below its varnished surface.

"This," breathed Rose Knight, "is not to be tolerated."

She went, in a torrent and fury of satin, and on cruel stalking soles, swiftly to the fireplace. From there she could face them both, her posture that of a keel driving forward to ride them down, and not to be stopped by anything.

"No!" she said, "*none* of it is to be tolerated."

She began to raise her voice.

"Since I must be drawn by convicts—and the distinction between murder and forgery is not one I should be placed in a position to contemplate—but since I *must*, 'tis surely not before a convict that you should humiliate yourselves. And strain yourselves to humiliate me; to behave before the creature as if I were no more than an idiot servant or a vicar, as though my opinion had no value."

"Parasols! Peacocks! Murderers!" He flicked his fingers and produced, "Hysteria! Hysteria is not an opinion."

She lifted the back of her skirt a little to warm her legs, but her voice was plated still and venomous:

"Nor do I wish him here again in this house. Be warned!"

Oh, she meant it; he, that man who took her about as a wife. And she, that raree-show, Miss Sleep of Brighton who did not bathe enough, and tippled sherry wine and port. Be warned!

"For all his sly whispers and—skill. He is not to come to this house again."

"Your decision is tardy. Asnetha is sitting for him next Saturday."

"Not in this house." She was whispering.

"You suggest where? The barn? The summer-house?" He laughed to signify amusement. He stopped laughing. "I say again: your decision is tardy. Mr Vaneleigh will do his work in this house."

You would not be warned, her face said. Having said that, it arranged a smile like a bracelet of ivory and glass.

"Work?" she said. "Your Mr Vaneleigh will need to. Has he—can a mere human really possess—so much skill, so much courage?"

"Oh, oh, oh! Teapot! Treasure!" cried Asnetha Sleep, crushing her bonnet and its four brown tails. "I am a cripple. Cruelty! Sydney! Teapot! *Cousin* Sydney!"

"Control yourself, Asnetha," said Sir Sydney quite as loudly as a human being. Then, as mild as someone addressing the dead, "Mr Vaneleigh, my dear Rose, is obviously skilled and courageous. He had the skill and courage to portray your age."

She reached for the drawing, and looked into it. She looked at her face in the glass.

"This portrait is a lie," she said. "It has become one. I am already older than this. I am someone else. I shall never be this again. 'Tis the likeness of a woman who is no longer living."

He saw, too late, what she was about to do, and, although too far off and smug, skidded across the parquet at her. She had already torn the drawing into two, into four. He grabbed at her as she let the pieces fall and, accidentally, pulled away her bodice. The agate fell. One breast stared at him with its fawn eye. It was marble, and she quietened to marble, and said like marble:

"I am not for you. I am not for impotent men."

He struck her in the face.

She immediately placed her hands over the breast and, quickly, but not hurriedly, left the room.

Asnetha Sleep, whose hand had leapt to her cheekbone as though she had been hit, started a whimpering laugh. Then she applied her hands to the wheels, and with difficulty backed her chair from the room, and sailed dangerously along the corridor, wailing, "Teapot! Teapot, treasure!"

Teapot appeared at his door. Behind the swiftly advancing craziness he saw the parasol rolling on the floor, and the dead animal of the bonnet asprawl. In terror, he slammed and locked his door. As she began to drum on it and nudge her chair against it, Queely Sheill began to knock on the french window behind which Sir Sydney was taking snuff, and wondering about brandy.

When Sir Sydney had opened the window, "Oh, sir, pray, sir, a gig," said Queely Sheill who had run hard, and with blazing eyes and burning face had never looked so handsome. "*Please*, sir, to borrow a chaise or what-all for Mr Vaneleigh. 'E's fallen smack on the road."

While Sir Sydney's groom was putting a horse in the gig, Queely Sheill ran back to the artist whom he had left propped against the sort of tree Mr Vaneleigh knew was un-European although he felt himself also where trees could be nothing but European.

I am, he thought, cut up into a thousand littlenesses; I am at once here and everywhere.

"Mr Vaneleigh," said Queely Sheill, panting and anxiety-ridden and a god. "Sir, Mr Vaneleigh, Queely's got a gig. 'Twill come. 'E give me a flask of brandy, Sir What-all. Come, suck haway."

Judas Griffin Vaneleigh drank.

" 'Ow are you? '*Ow* are you?" said Queely Sheill.

"I am nothing," said Judas Griffin Vaneleigh, a man of respectable appearance, brought up, charged at Mansion House, London, Saturday, June 10, 1837, with having used a power of attorney for the sale and transfer of stock with intent to defraud the Governor and Company of the Bank of England.

"I am nothing."

Nothing, he thought, a thousand littlenesses. I crouch bowed to the very dust of Van Diemen's Land with Death appropinquating more and more with every circle he describes. And yet I sit, after a tolerable dinner at George's Coffee House, and hold up a *petit verre d'eau de vie de Dantzic* to the waxen candle; I watch with scient eye the number of aureate particles—some swimming, some sinking quiveringly, through the oily and luscious liquor, as if informed with life—and gleaming, like golden fish in the Whang-ho . . . swimming . . . sinking. . . .

'I am nothing,' I said, 'I have been an independent gentleman, and had considerable property. . . .'

"Come, sir, suck haway, once more," said Queely Sheill with the flask, "The gig should be 'ere soon."

"The sun is quite set?" said Judas Griffin Vaneleigh.

"But a *nice* hevening," said Queely Sheill, his eyes pleading with the roadway in the direction of *Cindermead.*

'I have been an independent gentleman!' . . . Good morning, good *morning*, I must *fly!* I am almost too late: engaged to meet some *prime coves* of the fancy at twelve, Tippy, my tulip; positively a *mill* promises. Then to the Fives Court. *Must* be at the Royal Institution by half-past two. Take my twentieth peep at Haydon's picture in my way back. Letters to Belzoni till five. Dinner *chez moi* with the little philosopher and the doctor at six. Don our azure hose for the Lady Cerulea Lazuli's *Conversazione*, at half-past nine. Opera—applaud Milanie. Sup with the Corinthians in St. James's Square at two Sunday morning. Good-bye. Hope to see you at church tomorrow if up in time. Or meet ye at Sir Joseph's at night. Good-bye. . . .

Come away! I am a man of straw, of stone, of *any*-thing. I

wander about in great distress seeking everywhere for what I cannot find. I walk in Campbell Street, past *The Shades*, past Queen's Playhouse . . . I walk, repelled by the noisy rebels in the gallery, out from Sadler's Wells with my clothes covered with fragments of gnawed gingerbread, and rendered unwearable by the steams of gin and quids and aniseed. . . .

"Queely thinks that gig won't be long."

'Have you been here long?' the judge says at Mansion House. 'I see you are described in the warrant as an artist.' The judge is a mortal and acid lord. . . .

'I am nothing. I am no artist. I belong to no trade or profession, and have been in France these six or seven years. I arrived here about six weeks ago.'

Exhausted in mind, chilled with cold and hunger I awake —*he*, Judas Griffin Vaneleigh, awakes to enact anew that most pitiable of all characters, the poor gentleman. How can he—how can *I* bow down my stately masculine head before unstately hump-backed giglots scrimply arrayed in two guineas' worth of trumpery British muslin or a scrap of Spitalfields silk at seven and fourpence a yard? How else than by bowing, by writing lists of pretty books for sofas and sofa-tables, shall I pay for the truss of fine blanched lettuce, a good dig of Stilton and a slice of ham. . . ?

I walk the vapoury dews of morn. Oh, endless streets! The gas is waning fast, so are the patrol and watchmen. With creaks, rumbles, *gee-whut's*, and the smell of matting and cabbages, the market carts come from the villages to Covent Garden. . . .

I walk. I am in Howland Street beneath the street-lamp. I open my snuff-case precisely. I take precisely two seven-eighths of Paris.

'I have been in France these six or seven years. I arrived here about six weeks ago.'

The cock crows.

Daniel Forrester of Bow Street crows out tobacco and porter, 'Ah, Mr Vaneleigh, how do you do? Who would have thought of seeing you here?'

'What are you?' says Mansion House next day.

'I am nothing.'

'I see,' says Mansion House, 'you are described in the warrant as an artist.'

'I am no artist. I am nothing.'

'Prisoner, do you wish to ask any questions?'

'None at all. I am not yet steady in my head. I was arrested but yesterday. I am nothing.'

'The charge is a serious one; do you wish for time?'

'I am nothing . . . nothing . . . nothing.'

"The gig!" cried Queely Sheill. "*Ho, dear* Mr Vaneleigh, I should like to weep. The gig! Suck haway a suck for the gig."

"Help me to stand," said Mr Vaneleigh, and London and Great Marlborough Street and Somerset House and Newgate and Howland Street and Mansion House rose with him as Queely Sheill helped him, and were brushed away by Queely Sheill's hands as he brushed twigs and broken leaves from Mr Vaneleigh's coat.

"Queely'll 'old you. 'Ave no fears."

"Do not hold me, I pray," said Mr Vaneleigh whose tongue struggled to eject those blunted and mossy words. His left arm and hand swung, numbed for ever.

"My hat," said Mr Vaneleigh, "if you please, my hat, before the gig arrives."

Queely Sheill waved his cap, and the gig bowled nearer, and Judas Griffin Vaneleigh stood beneath the tree and thought, 'Tis not my chaise, and not my stallion Contributor of Barbary sire and Arabian dam, with white reins judgmatically arranged, that comes. 'Tis a horse and gig from nowhere on its way to nowhere; 'twill stop; 'twill pick up Judas Griffin Vaneleigh; 'twill pick up nothing.

Queely Sheill came back to the shabby fop simulating erectness beneath the tree, and with ostentatious flourish the vehicle stopped.

7

Sunday in Hobart Town bore its starveling resemblance to Sunday in the London which had exported to it the chimes of church bells along with the chimes of ankle-chains, the one to accompany and uplift duplicity, the other to accompany and weigh down obscenity. The quality, the army, the professions and the trades sang hymns, prayed and were preached at; the criminals were permitted no opportunity not to yowl hymns, grunt the syllables of prayers, and be preached at. The ugliness of nature was made, for an hour or two, very noisy with bells, and voices loudly and dolefully raised and strained to reach the ears of a Hebraic father incandescent as a blast furnace, and a son with snow-white woolly hair, brass feet and a two-edged sword in his mouth. The father had four beasts speckled with eyes, seven lamps and a book with seven seals on its backside.

The ladies and gentlemen, the red-coats, the lawyers and doctors and their wives and children, the glaziers and twine-makers and drapers and corn-porters and hay-dealers and tanners and their wives and children, had early prepared themselves to sing and mumble to that legendary father and son by an unravelling of curl-papers, a combing of side-whiskers, and a lacing into whale-bone stays. Some feet were washed; cravats were tied; there was everywhere a putting-on of horsehair petticoats, Polish mantles, Hall's patent elastic boots, musquash boas and steel jewellery.

While masters and mistresses and convicts prayed for the Queen and each other, well-buckets were being raised and lowered, pump-handles were jerked up and down, slugs were washed from cabbages, potatoes were peeled, and, presently, the smells of roasting mutton and sirloin, and the fetor of cabbage boiling in iron saucepans, warned servants to lay out the Copeland dinner service. In curricle, britzska, tilbury and phaeton, the church-goers came home, and grace was said, and they ate. It was afternoon.

At *Cindermead*, Sir Sydney Knight had gone to church alone, and had returned alone, and eaten alone, his whiskers fragrant with a new pomade.

The *Cindermead* dishes were being washed as furtively as murderer's bloody hands when Rose Knight came downstairs magnificently dressed for outdoors. She had left her maid sobbing, and thinking of suicide.

The house Rose Knight descended to was being run more perfectly than it usually perfectly was: no servant would have dared the most microscopic carelessness for danger lay everywhere and in everything: a smear on silver, a petal fallen from an epergne, a crumb on a table, a hair on a floor.

Lady Knight's voice was too clear, too high.

"Miss Sleep," they whispered, soft-footed as camels and with eyes like dogs', "Miss Sleep is keeping to her bed, m'lady."

Without striking them, Rose Knight went directly to the cripple's room. Since leaving the drawing-room the day before, she had neither seen nor spoken to anyone except the servants.

At the cripple's door Rose Knight did not forget to forget to knock, as though the door were a servant's. From the door, which she had closed abruptly and with noise, she eyed and addressed Asnetha Sleep, who huddled beneath the bedclothes feigning sleep.

"You are not asleep," said Rose Knight. "You will be positively befuddled with port wine, but you will not be asleep."

Asnetha Sleep, feeling movelessness and silence not a convincing representation of sleep, made one of the small curvilinear moves and two of the moaning sounds people pretending to sleep think people make when sleeping.

Rose Knight advanced, and pulled the bedclothes down.

Asnetha Sleep—a wretched performance—simulated waking up, and looked hideous, and smelt of wine.

"Ah, Rose. My love. What's the time? I am. At the portals of. Death."

"You are at the portals of drunkenness."

"I am. Sick a. Little port. . . ."

"You have decided to *affect* sickness."

Asnetha Sleep tried to straighten her night-cap and its rosettes. She tried to fade paler; she wished she had on fewer and less ornate rings. She made her hands shake.

"I swear," she said in a trembling voice, her night-cap still awry, "to you. Positively that I. Can scarcely lift my. Poor head."

"There is little reason for you to lift it. After yesterday, oh, little reason at all."

"Naughty, *naughty*, Rose. So provoking. Still not. Surely? Angry from yesterday."

"Still disgusted, still utterly disgusted, from yesterday."

"Forgive, Rose dear. Forgetfulness. A migraine. Jolted about the grounds. Forgive."

"I do not forgive."

And, indeed, Lady Knight *née* Rose Hartnell did not ever forgive.

"Had I a weakness to forgiving, I could not forgive what was unforgivable."

Asnetha Sleep moaned; she pressed her fingertips to her temples.

"I implore you. Rose, my. Vinaigrette. My head! My temples!"

Rose Knight did not move from where she stood rigid by the bed.

"You are an imperfect liar, but a perfect fool. You were not asleep; you affect a migraine; you reek of wine like a jockey. I know Miss Sleep."

Asnetha Sleep lit. Her fingertips left her temples. Her voice twanged, despite the lopsided rosettes.

"You are unkind," she said, regretting she had no stays to stiffen her body as much as her words.

"I'm not a charity visitor," said Rose Knight, highly,

more clearly. "I intend nothing but unkindness. I've not come to your—your noisome room to be kind, or to pretend kindness. Kindness has been ill-served in this house. 'Tis a virtue to be mocked. Why should I persist in it?"

Asnetha Sleep's nose stiffened, its skin tightened.

"Because," she said in her modulated voice, her assured voice; and her beautiful eyes glinted very near each other, 'I am your guest."

"You are frivolous; you are antic! You are no guest of mine."

Asnetha Sleep put her hands over her ears.

"Stop your ears then," said Rose Knight. "Oh, stop them if the truth embarrasses them. You are still no guest of mine. You are your cousin's guest."

"Then I am your husband's guest."

"A man who is not a man is host to a woman who is . . ." Rose Knight shuddered minutely. "Imperfect blood to imperfect blood."

"Leave this room, Rose. Leave me."

But Rose Knight did not leave. She toyed with the gauntlet of a glove.

" 'Tis not I who'll be leaving this room."

"Oh, oh! Say what you want to, speak wildly on. You are a wicked woman, Rose."

"I *want*," Rose Knight became dulcet. "I *want* to say nothing to you. I never wanted to have to say anything. When I married *him* it was not to have conversations with the Sleeps, not to be overrun by Sleeps and their crazes. Their whim-whams and blacks."

"You take cruel, cruel advantage of a cripple. 'Tis monstrous! Abominably wicked! 'Tis the depth of viciousness to attack one who lacks every advantage. Oh, leave me!"

Asnetha Sleep was becoming shrill but she was still controlled, feeling that deformity forbade home-thrusts by the other.

Rose Knight laughed very sweetly, and spoke sweetly and quickly.

"Lacks every advantage! I've cause for laughter! *You* have *always*, from your cradle, been treated with every conceivable indulgence. You have sickened me by constant reference to this very fact. You possess an ample fortune; your expectations are more than ample. God knows what estates you have in your upstart Brighton, what annuities, what investments! You have your ill-bred jewels, more trinkets than a Hindu. You have your deluded audiences: '*Dear* Asney, so *sweet* of nature, so *brave*, so long-suffering. . . !' You lack nothing—since rumour also gives you wit and intellect—except a lady's manners, and the consciousness of what is due to the mistress of a house."

Rose Knight lifted her chin a little, and looked towards nothing. There she seemed to see an aspersion not seen before. As softly as her husband she said:

"And, of course, you lack a husband! So, then, do I. But I didn't seek what I successfully have not got."

She began to raise her voice, to become high and clear once more.

"You have spent a fruitless and feckless year in pursuit of the husband you came here to buy."

"You are. Wicked and. More than I thought. Not for a husband. No, not."

Asnetha Sleep beat her hands on the bed, a helpless and incomplete sound.

"You lie! Why did you come to this place where half the population are in cells, and breaking rocks, or assigned as servants, and breaking Rockingham? You came for the Opera, the spas, the castles and ruins?"

"I shall. Not listen." Her limbs jostled each other.

"You need not. You've listened enough. I am going. You may return to your sleeping or tippling. I am taking your black creature to drive the gig. Where is the creature?"

Asnetha Sleep did not answer.

"Where is the creature? Where is your parish-boy?"

The crippled woman pulled the bedclothes over her head with the gestures of a czarina, and Rose Knight swiftly and noiselessly left the room.

Teapot's fear of Lady Knight did not vanish at her commanding him to do what he loved doing, and could do well: he was gifted with horses. His fear, however, took second place to his excitement and, in doing so, acquired the nature of a double-fold misgiving. To his original fear of a woman who despised him as a curiosity, and was repelled by him as himself, was added a mistrust of her motive in selecting him rather than Ferris, the groom. He knew her dislike was eternal: no charm or sacrifice on his part, and no miracle, would diminish its intensity. He could not guess how it could take place, but imagined that she intended nothing but discomfort and downfall in ordering him, which she had never done before, to do what gave him the greatest pleasure in his world.

Rose Knight caused trouble by insisting on having Black Boy harnessed instead of one of the other horses nearer at hand.

"A black boy will drive a Black Boy," she said icily, delighting Teapot whom she intended to discomfit.

Black Boy was brought from the paddock; the groom had put him in the gig and was holding his head, and they were on the point of climbing into the gig, when Sir Sydney arrived.

He gestured at the groom.

"Go away, Ferris," he said. "I shall hold."

When the nails of Ferris's boots had clacked on the bricks far enough away, Sir Sydney spoke. She had been watching him with pale eyes, and a smile that did not part her lips, and was merely a faint buckling of the skin about her mouth.

"Rose," he said, "this is contrary to my expectation. I thought you were unwell. I explained your absence from church so. Sir Charles was most. . ."

"Climb in, black boy," she said.

"Moreover," said Sir Sydney, soft-tongued as ever, and his aromatic whiskers black as a wagoner's smock, "Asnetha needs Teapot."

She climbed into the gig.

"Start, black boy!"

Teapot reached for the whip. Sir Sydney's voice hindered him with his great parti-coloured hand outstretched.

"A *moment*, Teapot. Lady Knight wants you to go to Miss Sleep. Get down and go to her. The groom will drive Lady Knight."

Sir Sydney foresaw that this would ruin the drive; wilfulness would lose its value for her with his interference and countermanding; she would leave the gig, and return to the house, and break a cracked dish.

"Ferris!" he called, "Ferris, come here!"

The man came running like a newly shod pony.

"Ferris, we've decided to use another horse. Bella, perhaps, or Pale Lady. Hurry down, Teapot, you keep us all waiting. Quickly, boy!"

Teapot had already stood up; he moved to descend.

She took his arm, and pushed him down again into the seat. She leant across him for the whip.

"Take your reins, fool," she said.

With a superb gesture, refusing to be blackmailed by the groom's and Teapot's presences, refusing to be blackmailed by her husband's ardour to present the front of a happy and gracious family to his influential friends and Government House, refusing to be blackmailed by the social untruths told to excuse her absence from a Government House church party, refusing to be blackmailed by years of a breeding that would find her behaviour, thus in front of a servant, degrading—and scandal-starting, she lashed at her husband with the whip and caught him across the face. He let go the horse's head, and stepped back.

The groom was not well enough practised in masking emotion; he drew a breath that was almost a word. His expression, usually rustic and blunted, became savage, reflecting savagery, and horrified, reflecting horror, so that a brutal and fleeting replica of an expression at one and the same time mingling the master's and the mistress's expressions concealed any he himself might have been startled into disclosing.

She had, throughout, said no word to her husband.

"Start, black boy," said Lady Knight.

Shock did not impair Teapot's skill. In a stylish curve the gig left the yard, and swung up the slope into the drive, and out of the drive into Sandy Bay Road, and turned north in the direction of Hobart Town.

On the right, at the foot of the cleared and half-cleared

slopes, lay the Estuary, its surface of flat scallopings, like the scales of some miles-long reptile skin, spread and stretched taut; on the left stood Organ-pipe, so high that no scream or prayer could tear the bluish-white tegument of the sky which seemed nearer though it seemed also to rest on the wall-top of the mountain.

Between that wall blotched with freaks of snow and freakish vegetation, and those imperceptibly creeping scales of water, and that blank lid of whitish-blue skin, the glittering gig span along. The horse, black as the horse released from the breaking of the third seal of the legendary book with seven seals on its backside, fled towards Hobart Town, up the hill topped by the barracks, and down the hill into Hobart Town.

Composed as a petrifaction, straight-backed as the Virgin Mary and, like her, looking neither left nor right nor behind, the woman monosyllabically directed her black driver to turn certain corners and to take certain streets. She did not bow to those who bowed or lifted their hats to her. Presently, they were passing beneath the loftiness of the waterfront warehouses of Salamanca Place, they passed the Commissariat Stores and came to the Treasury. There was no one to bow and no one not to bow to; the people who were about were no one.

"Left!" said Lady Knight to Teapot, and the black boy turned Black Boy into Campbell Street. They passed over the Palladio where skeletons in tatters spat into the ooze.

"Stop!" said Lady Knight, and Teapot made the hooves of jet and the iridescent spinning of wheels stop near Queen's Playhouse, in front of Playhouse Cottage.

To travel ensures physical arrival somewhere . . . at a chosen destination, at an accident, at an unknown place, at the edge of a cliff, at the end of a life. The mind and the soul and the emotions are compelled to take whatever journey the body they activate does, but their nature permits them as well to take bypaths from the track their body cannot desert, to climb ecstasy while the body dumbly descends a slope, to run for cover while the body sits on display like an effigy, feverishly to rake and sift the hours while the flesh lolls with gloves and slumbering hands.

As the gig stood, and Rose Knight examined the setting of her destination in factual dimension, she gave an inward glance at the array of complex and subtle lies that anger and desire and a madness for revenge had driven her to set up in readiness like an array of stimulating cordials. On that final survey, on the very point of offering them, they seemed to her to be as inviting, as intoxicating and as unrejectable as when she had cold-heartedly distilled them the night before. No young man, even if cad and cockney, could find them anything but irresistible.

"Wait, black boy," she said and descended from the gig and, holding her skirts clear of whatever poisoned the surface of Campbell Street, walked to the cottage which, from Mr Vaneleigh's description and the name *Playhouse Cottage* carved above the door, she knew was her destination.

Behind her, bolt upright in the gig, and no longer in a rapture of driving, Teapot stared directly ahead but observed her also, and became once again uneasy with misgivings.

She knocked at the door.

From within the cottage, and following so directly upon her knock that it informed her the knock had been heard, came the crash of something dropped.

"Lord, what noise is *that*?" cried a slip of voice.

Something else was said, petulant in tone, but not loud enough for words to be distinguished. There was then silence. The silence grew longer, grew so long that she knocked again. A voice came from nearby:

"I *see* you, madam . . . I see you *clearly*, and your *stylish bonnet*. Who *are* you?"

It was a voice of wandering and wavering uncertainty, a voice tenuous as a grasshopper's. Polidorio Smith's lank face, white as turnip, and with wide-open molten eyes, peered out between the curtains of the front window.

"Is this," she said, raising and directing her voice to pierce the panes, "Mr Sheill's cottage?"

In the gig, Teapot closed his mouth, and his eyes swung

right and left several times with alarm. The man! He wondered if ma'am had heard about the chain. He watched from the corner of his eye, and listened.

"I am *inclined* to *trust*," said Polidorio Smith, holding the curtains, through which his head protruded, underneath his chin. "One *moment*, madam."

But he continued his steady gazing for minutes longer, his face retreating by infinitesimal degrees backward into the obscurity of the room. The curtains fell together. After another interval the door began slowly to open; the tallest man Teapot had ever seen emerged and, with intense slow care, closed the door. He turned then to look down on Rose Knight. As she was about to speak he raised a forbidding grimy hand.

"You *see* me, madam, you *see* your humble not at the *peak*, though I have *this moment* combed it. Ah, Sunday! Your *knock*, so *sudden*, startled the dye from my *hand*. I fear there's a *basin less* in the universe. You have, madam, *lighted* on me at a *moment* when *hair* is my occupation. *However*, your Witchoura is *twice* as ravishing as *anything* you could name. It invited my *trust*. People of the *first fashion* are wearing them. Though *not*," said Polidorio Smith hurriedly, "with an *atom*, I assure you, of your manner. *Ah, quel joli manteau!* Come, madam, *unfold* your tale!"

She had bargained for unimaginable tawdriness, for peculiarity and coarseness, but not for this spindle-shanks hop-pole with its pleated face and idiot chatter. Having come so far, she stuck to her guns:

"This," she said over-precisely and a little more loudly, as one talking to a Chinaman, "is Mr Sheill's cottage?"

"I *implore* you, madam! Softly as a *spider*, madam, I pray! Mr Sheill . . . I give you this *in confidence*, and trust your *Witchoura* . . . Mr Sheill is drunk as David's *sow*, *drunk*, and in an unbuttoned stupor. 'Tis *not* a sight for Witchouras. Your humble *dares* not drink, *positively* dares not, not even a *half-thimble* of rum. It affects, as you *doubtless* know, the *colour* of the hair. And what is life without *hair*? *His* is grey. Rum, of *course*. You will, madam, not *betray* his shameful *failing* nor my traitorous *confidences*?"

"I may be in error. I may be at the wrong house. The Mr Sheill I ask for is certainly not grey of hair."

"Madam," Polidorio Smith became dignified, "it is *grey* as roast *mutton*. The original tint is *here* and *there* perceivable, a *sort* of gold, a hair or two or *three* of gold. Alas, the mutton is *fast* overtaking the *gold*. But the *son*, Apollo, is still *radiantly* gold. He drinks no *rum*. Oh, diddle, et cetera, *dumpkins*! I've not yet given my *name* . . . 'twill be one you'll have remarked *often* on the *lips* of the *world*. You will have come to *compliment*. . . ." He bowed and made a leg. ". . . your *servant*, Polidorio Smith."

"I should like," said Lady Knight, "I should like, Mr Smith, to speak with the son, the young Mr Sheill."

"Young!" Polidorio Smith uplifted his eyes towards heaven. "Youth *itself! Apollo!* An *agile* and gifted boy but perfectly *brainless*. My good *woman*, had you but *asked! Had* you but *indicated!* But I am your *servant*. I shall *get* him for you. He will come *bounding* like a *primrose*. But a *door* or two away! He has taken some *porter* and oysters to a sick see-ay-tee . . . to a sick *gentleman* who *lives* with a see-ay-tee. I shall not, I *dare* not, ask you in, for Deathie would certainly start from his *stupor* and *roar* like *elephants*."

"I shall wait for a little while," said Lady Knight, "in the gig."

"You are very *clever*," said Polidorio Smith, and walked with her to the gig, and handed her in. He saw Teapot.

"Well, I *declare!* A yobbie *noir!*" he squeaked, and he smiled past Lady Knight, so winning and long-lasting a smile in which sat the darkened tooth, that Teapot grinned back.

"*Delicious!*" said Polidorio Smith to Lady Knight. "It *lives!* It *moves!* Does it *speak*?"

"*Ebony* yobbie," said Polidorio Smith across Lady Knight to Teapot, "You must *forgive* my wet *hair*. Never at its *peak* of a Sunday. Sunday's a *soothing* day, is it not? You are fortunate in your *teeth*. Bye-bye!"

Hunching his head between his shoulders, he abruptly and secretively left them, and, looking surreptitiously from side to side, and sometimes over his shoulder, ran on small tip-toe steps past the Playhouse to the corner house where the door stood open. He peered within, he dallied, he gained courage enough to begin calling up the narrow stairway.

"Apollo, my love! Apollo! Apollo! Apollo!"

Not until he had called a number of times, and his voice had increased in volume, did a door off the landing open. Queely Sheill came to the top of the stairs.

"Poli, what *his* it? Why are you blinking your winkers like that? Come hup to Queely."

"I dare *not*," whispered the actor. "I am in a *terror*."

"No one'll 'arm you. You can't come in Mr Vaneleigh's room, but you can come 'ere and tell me what you want."

"The reptile!—miaow! miaow!—the reptile!"

" 'E's hin the room, and the door's shut."

"I shall go. I shall not *give* you the *message*. *Always* messages. I am a *flunkey*. I have run *like an ant* for you . . . old friends do not *mind* running like ants for old friends. . ."

He began to pant exaggeratedly, and coughed several death-bed coughs of great faintness, and stooped below the lintel, and lowered himself to sit on the foot of the stairs.

"I *shall* go. Ingratitude has *killed* runners and ants ere this. I see, oh, I see, I have nursed a *snake* in my *grass*. . ."

Queely Sheill came down the stairs.

" 'Ave no fear, Poli. The—the reptile his shut in. 'Tis sitting on Mr Vaneleigh's bed."

"Eek! I shall *swoon*. On—the—bed!" Polidorio Smith did almost faint: in that picture lay for him a terror not to be contemplated.

"Poli," said Queely Sheill, "your 'air is a treat. So black. I hadmires the black. Hit becomes you."

"You *think* so?" He struck playfully at Queely Sheill's legs beside him. "*Artful* chimpanzee! *Flatterer*, you *cannot* think so! Although the black boy agrees with you. 'You will forgive a *stranger* and *passer-by*,' he said to me. 'I cannot resist *speaking*. Your *hair! Black* as *coal! Lustrous* as ebony! Finer than *gossamer!* Words fail me.' Observant and *pretty* black boy!"

"Teapot!" said Queely Sheill.

"What *is* gossamer?" said Polidorio Smith. "Let there be no talk of *teapots* while black boys tell me of gossamer. He is *with* his *mama*. *Can* it be his mama? How can one *tell*?"

"You can tell Queely, *hand* quick. Mr Vaneleigh's waiting. A lady and a black boy—where?"

"They are in a *gig* of *superior* elegance. A horse, I *think*. A black boy, *certainly*—and comely as apricots. A lady? How can one *tell mamas* and *ladies*? Ah, yes, a *lady*—for her Witchoura is a *perfect dream*. She *wants* you. 'I *want* the artful wretch *instantly*,' she said. 'I am *resolved* at all *hazards!*' She stamped her little *foot*. ' 'Tis a matter of *life* and *death*,' she said. Tears fell. She wrung her *hands* white as *onions*. 'Tell my *lover*,' she said. Then, 'My little *boy* is *quite* deaf,' she said softly. 'He can *hear* nothing.' "

"She limps, the lady?"

Queely Sheill, with Mr Vaneleigh sick upstairs, awkward visitors without, and Polidorio Smith seated on the stairs, had already decided on his first allegiance. Patiently he waited for Polidorio Smith's rigmarole to finish, and a solution for the satisfaction of the others to appear.

"Limps! My *dear* Apollo! One *cannot* limp in a gig! Even *ladies*. Even yobbie *noirs*. He has more *teeth* than a *fairy*. You must come. You will ravish the lady. To ravish is to *amuse*, Apollo, to *exhilarate*, to start the *tinkle* of laughter. I shall sing to the *boy*. Since *infancy* I . . ."

"Queely can't come."

"You *must*, Apollo, my love, slip *outdoors* then, and *tell* them so. Since *infancy*, I continue, I have had a *dream* of yobbie *noirs*."

"Dear Poli, listen to me. I'll not come houtside, 'tis better so. I must go back to poor Mr Vaneleigh. Hand, you hold nancy, you mustn't go to make a mustard-pot hof Teapot. Queely says so."

"I am *confused* with *teapots*, I am *vastly* confused."

Polidorio Smith, attempting to do what he could, attempting to absorb lest he forget, *was* confused.

"Teapot is the little black's *name*. 'E's *called* Teapot."

"How *clever!* Teapot! Teapot! *Teapot!* One must *remember*. I should like to be called *Cup*. . . ."

"*Listen* to Queely. I won't come hout. I'll write a note for Old Conky—for the lady."

"A *note*, Apollo, my love! You are *cunning* as a teapot." He giggled. "Witchoura will be *mad* as a wet *hen*."

Queely Sheill ran upstairs to beg paper and pen from Mr Vaneleigh.

"Teapot," sang Polidorio Smith quietly. "Teapot *black*, Teapot *noir*, Teapot *apricot*, *Teapot* apricot. . . ."

He was still singing to the open door and the afternoon when Queely Sheill came downstairs with a folded blue paper.

"Dear Poli, listen. 'Tis the lady's note on a sugar-loaf paper. Listen, Poli: tell 'er that I'll be obliged hif she will hexcuse. Queely's Mr Vaneleigh's today . . . must go back and wash Mr Vaneleigh's poor feet. Hup you get, Poli. 'Old it *hin* your 'and, and say I begs to be hexcused."

Polidorio Smith arose slowly, left the house slowly, and returned very slowly up Campbell Street, the note held at arm's length before him. He dared not let it from his sight for an instant. Downcast at his failure to be returning without Queely Sheill, he was more downcast, and to the brink of melancholy and of horror, by the scene he knew he should describe to the occupants of the gig.

Rose Knight was about to order Teapot to drive away when Polidorio Smith came from the open door. He advanced minutely towards the gig. She waited, impassive, curious, repelled and irritated.

"Madam," said Polidorio Smith, "I *swear* to you, to you *both*—and the horse, though *scarcely* necessary—that I can do *no more* than *this*!"

He waggled the note.

"I implored Mr Queely Sheill on my *knees*. *Bended*. Sharp and *painful*. Bare boards. A house of *penury* and *suffering*."

Tears entered his eyes, and several dripped down.

"You will *forgive* this self-indulgence. 'Tis a tear for my suffering *friend*, a *brilliant* artist, *refined*, with whom I sat *all night*. The hours *endless*, you know; the candles *constantly* replenished, and not *wax*. Such *agonies*, such exhalations of *anguish*, the *streaming* brow, the angel of death *hovering* like a duck, the see-ay-tee *mocking* him from the bed-post, its *wicked blue eyes* agleam like *rubies*. I am naturally *exhausted*, my hair positively *damp*. Today, therefore, it is Apollo who sits for a *few moments* in the death-chamber of my *lifelong* friend. He is in a *delirium*. 'Agnes! Agnes, my *wife*,' he cries, 'Come to me!' She cannot come. She has gone *before*. She harps at the pearly *gates*. And all the little ones, eight or *nine*—one cannot *recall*—all gone before, *harping* at the pearly gates. Gone before—no sadder words! Graves *everywhere*. The room *filled* with lockets—their golden, *golden* curls. Apollo *begs* to be excused . . . he must stay with my dying friend until my *hair* dries out."

Lady Knight said to the madman trembling at the drain-edge:

"I am sorry to hear that Mr Vaneleigh is sick. Is he *really* so *desperately* sick—your Mr Vaneleigh?"

"Madam, I *know* no *Vaneleigh*. How futile then, and *unavailing*, to *question* your devoted! I must go *indoors*—my hair is *aching*. A golden-haired person has given me this *billet-doux*—people are *constantly* doing so. The golden-haired person begs to be *excused*."

He handed up the note.

"Good evening, madam," he said, and once again bowed as in a drama. The black strips of hair, dried-out a little, slipped about on the bare skull.

He suddenly opened a smile of great eagerness about the central darker tooth.

"You will be *astonished* and *ravished*, boy, to know that I know your *name*. As *mine* is, 'tis the subject of *universal* conversation. Good evening—" He paused archly. "Good *evening—Kettle*! Are you *astonished*? I *see* you are! Bye-bye!" said Polidorio Smith, and ducked his head, and ran for the cottage.

Teapot, hands over mouth, wriggled with laughter.

"Quiet, fool! Oh, quiet," said Rose Knight, and opened the blue paper.

Rose Knight and Teapot, in spite of their experience of the affectations of Asnetha Sleep, had been amazed at Polidorio Smith, she more than he. To her his eccentricity was lunacy; it was more, she felt, than her foolhardiness warranted. That it was a lunacy she could be contemptuous of assured her of its harmlessness. It was not conceivable that such a feather-brained something could possess feelings or thoughts.

Teapot had been entranced by the height, the vivacities and the sounds of the strange visitor whose smile had been a marvel to him. It hinted of a foolish gentleness of love, of a love without rancour, a love whose demands would be little ones and inconsequential. Teapot, from his own experience of being a toy, would have found nothing freakish or improper in having the ageing actor as a toy . . . the one who was a man had never been anything else but a timid child, the one who was a child had been too early and too long used as a mock and midget man. They could have spun their tops, and climbed trees together, and for ever, happily.

Rose Knight needed to read the note on the piece of sugar-loaf wrapping once only:

Q.S. begs to inform Miss Sleep that he cannot desert from Mr V. at time of writting but thursday will be happy to oblidge as before if Mr V. don't need Q.S. and will come to window at nine so no more for now and Mr V. very poorly.

With a cry she threw the note out of the gig. Her face had gone dark and brutish.

"Drive, black boy!" she said, then, immediately, "*No*, idiot! I have dropped my note. Climb down. Get it."

She had travelled for forty years to arrive too late at void; to arrive, under the impulse of revenge and lust, one neither stronger than the other, in a narrow street, near the waterfront of a convict town at the world's icy margin. She had reached the brink of a precipice over which she could not leap. In her rashness she had hurtled nearer to salvation and a saviour than she knew. With him she might have committed mischief still, yet no more evil. He denied, she was to return from the rim of the abyss to commit evil on evil.

She was in the driving-seat when Teapot climbed up with the note. It had fallen open. She had already, after reading it, folded it with someone else's fingers for it was someone else's note. Once again she folded it, and her fingers were calamity, and the note's concealment in the palm of her glove was catastrophe, and she was already a murderess.

She lifted the whip and struck the horse. It started wildly, and wildly she began to drive.

She had driven little for some years but an old art had not grown enfeebled, nor had an old wantonness been subdued.

At first she drove merely wildly, watching the roads but not where the roads led. Time and again they petered out on the northern selvedge of the Hobart Town she scarcely knew; time and again, and just in time, with an arm of ivory and iron, she reined the horse upright to its hind-legs so that the fore-hoofs curved up, curled up like coarse hooks from the cracked and knobbed ground, to strike and hammer and tear at the outskirt air.

Here and there, she startled up, from hollows or from behind boulder or stump or fallen trunk, threadbare and gaping lovers, clodhopper and kitchen drab, destitute paper-stainer and out-of-work seamstress, from where they mollified semi-starvation with semi-love on the lichen. Now and again, long-haired ragamuffin children with bony faces and eyes of glass sprang barking from the rocky corrugations or scuttled to the tip-tops of rubbish peaks to crow and gesticulate at the gesticulating horse and the tilted gig.

She was repeatedly lost, repeatedly confronted and turned back by the hideous flange of her world—the slaughter-yard with its crow's-nest heaps of rib-bones, skulls and horns, the navy-yard rock-fenced on its headland of roadless rock, by scrublands, by quarries, by outrider burial grounds, and—always and finally—by the Estuary and its scale-coated depths, and the steeper foothills buttressing the base of Organ-pipe.

She was forced to turn inland, to race through and leave the foothills with their flour mills, lime-kilns, malt-houses, brick-fields, sheep-folds and windmills, to restrict her insanity, and balance it by an increase of speed, to return to the streets, the macadam roads, the picket fences and overlooking windows.

Black Boy was already slippery with sweat and lathered with foam. She struck him again and again, and galloped the streets, and became more solitary in her power as Teapot hung desperately on, elated with terror, while Sunday-walkers and their children huddled at fences, and discreeter carriages pulled aside in an exclamatory fashion.

One drives as insanely to nowhere, or heaven or purgatory, as one crawls inch by inch on ascetic knee-caps. One reaches the present at the same moment, whether one ceaselessly runs, or lies night and day in one bed in one room.

She had learned her alphabet and how to plait her hair, she had learned to dance, and bow her head, and charm, to clean her teeth and cut her toe-nails and turn a phrase, to clip the curls in her armpits, and smile over a fan, to value an opinion and mistrust a judgement and assess an emotion, to arrive at being nothing except a vain, malevolent and beautiful woman driving showily as a fashionable actress or a duke's drunken mistress up and down the humpback streets of Hobart Town.

She had arrived at solitariness. It is the solitary man or woman who has the vision of a criminal. This vision includes calculation, the obsession to rearrange ingredients to serve self.

Rose Knight had been less solitary and less criminal before she had read Queely Sheill's note. She had intended merely to break her own rules, and the rules of her class, and to betray her husband. When she had walked from the dining-room with the mark of Sir Sydney's hand on her face she had begun moving towards the door of Playhouse Cottage. She had never let herself seriously consider betrayal before . . . her lust affairs, conducted as secretly and efficiently as her corn-cutting, were not betrayals to her nor, indeed, to Sir Sydney. There were, at best, betrayals only of her husband's betrayal. The partners were, no matter their height, weight and age, invariably gentlemen who did not dare the satisfaction of indiscretion, of a long tongue, a false step or a false move. They were of acceptable standard. Betrayal at last wildly and revengefully contemplated and set about, only an accident of timing, because of a flinty and spiteful impatience, had tripped up her plan to seduce Queely Sheill.

As she lashed Black Boy up hill and down dale of Hobart Town's startled streets, she was, in some sort, doing with that flamboyant and perilous display what she had purposed doing by an *affaire* with Queely Sheill: humiliating her husband in seceding from her own tenets and mutinously violating his. But flashing whip, rearing horse, and hoofs clattering out sparks were sapless substitutes and—unless she ran down and mutilated some greasy and rose-pink butcher's podgy Sunday child or drove headlong with exhausted Teapot into the Estuary—would cause no more than an evanescent rash of gossip, harmless whatever Sir Sydney might imagine.

She had returned from the brink into different country, different climate and a different year. She was solitary, she was criminal, she was calculating.

When she had killed no one, and was bored with mouths opening to yell at her, and her wrists and arms had begun to ache, and she had plotted an opening gambit in the new and different game, she drove towards *Cindermead.*

The groom had heard the gig crossing the planking of Sandy Bay Bridge, had sworn filthily, and had spat with trepidation, had combed his hair and washed his hands, and was waiting at the coach-house when the gig arrived.

A subordinate must have, or must enact having, a thinner intelligence. That fact, or acting of fact, is more sensitive to flattery and prompter to take offence. Subordinates at *Cindermead* received no flattery, and had forgotten that they had ever had an offendable nature.

What mark on the groom's mind the sound and sight of the lash across her husband's cheek had made did not concern Lady Knight. Nor was any mark visible in his attitude.

He took the horse's head as usual, and stood, as usual, with his eyes lowered. The lids were lowered also, that day, to hide whatever gleam his eyes might have taken from his extra knowledge of her, but he was ready to leap, to skip deferentially at her order, ready to perform anything to illustrate that he did not have that knowledge, to intimate that he had been blind and deaf as the whip-thong struck the baronet. His position was hazardous; the tongue that might say too much occupied the same body as the eyes that had seen too much. When the gig had driven off, Sir Sydney had said nothing, had walked soberly and firmly away with scented whiskers and the birth-pangs of a black eye.

The groom, his hands smelling of Windsor soap, attempted to appear as though he were a close-tongued and faithful servant. That he was indeed so went for nothing: employers required often of their employees the possession of niceties, idiosyncracies or vices, to the master's tastes or to their advantage, over and above the stock abilities and virtues they engaged and paid wages for.

"Into the house, black boy," said Lady Knight.

As Teapot stepped from the gig he stumbled—fear, and a tenseness of muscle consequent, almost undid him on the horizontal and unlurching bricks.

"To your room, fool. Lie down," said Lady Knight, and she watched the West Indian walk with decreasing stiffness towards the house.

To the groom there was no possible doubt, from her dismissal of the black, and from her posture, and from the clear, finalizing look with which she watched Teapot enter the house, that the field was being cleared, and that something was to be said.

When she turned towards him, the groom was very, very busy with his cracked, clean hands. The indigo tattoo of a crucifix on his right arm was empty still. It was a relic of soldiery and a tattooist next door to a cigar-shop brothel in Blue Anchor Yard. The theft of two pencil cases and a coral necklace had qualified him for Van Diemen's Land. Good behaviour on the hulks, the convict ship and in the Penitentiary, and a knowledge of horses, had qualified him for *Cindermead*.

"Stop fiddling, Ferris," said Lady Knight taking the galling blue paper from the palm of her glove, "and listen to me."

"M'lady. . . ."

Had his ears been able to flap a signal of preparedness

they would have. His small yellowish eyes, foxy and sensual, strained with assiduity.

"This paper is for Miss Sleep. I wish you to give it to her."

"Yuz, m'lady."

That was simple.

" 'Tis to be given her privately."

"Yuz, m'lady."

That was still simple.

"By privately, Ferris, I mean that it is to be given her in such a way, at such a time, and in such a place, that neither I nor Sir Sydney sees the giving. I want you to understand—to *positively* understand—that neither Sir Sydney *nor I* witnesses the giving."

"Yuz, m'lady."

Simple still, but the ground was getting boggy.

"Now listen most attentively. I really cannot vouch for your skin should there be a blunder." Ferris protruded his eyes as much as he could. "In giving this—this correspondence to her, you are to say it was given you by—by a man with yellow hair. Have you listened?"

"Oh, yuz, m'lady!"

"Repeat your orders."

"To be given private, m'lady. No one to see, not even m'lady. And from a man of yellow 'air."

"Quite. You are further to say that it was given you by—that the man was another *servant*, a servant of an artist who has been here."

"Yuz, m'lady, and pardon, m'lady, but I know 'im with the yellow 'air. Calls 'imself Queely."

"I could not know, Ferris. But since you seem to have had the fortune of meeting him, you'll find no trouble in description. You've known him long?"

"Met 'im yesterday, m'lady. Sir Sydney brought 'im 'ere yesterday, m'lady."

"That will be the man."

She seemed to look at him more closely, through the pale curving jellies of her eyes. Lady Paula Pry, she was, her.

"You must tell me, Ferris, when and where you were given Miss Sleep's note. How you met the bearer."

The groom blinked. Lady Paula Pry, what's she about?

"You were not needed this afternoon, Ferris. The black boy drove the gig. Miss Sleep and Sir Sydney were resting. You were free."

"Yuz, m'lady."

"I gave you a permission to take a stroll."

"Oh! Oh, *yuz*, m'lady."

"You took the air along Sandy Bay Road."

"Yuz, m'lady."

The groom moved, and the muscles of his forearm stirred the indigo crucifix as though it too remembered Blue Anchor Yard, and St. Ann Street and Orchard Street and the soldiers' prostitutes and the songs and lies. Ferris remembered how to lie:

"I took the hair, m'lady, and met 'im in the road. Met 'im by chance. 'E give me the paper."

She dropped it on the floor of the gig.

" 'Tis getting late, Ferris. You'll find an opportunity today?"

"Yuz, m'lady."

She left the coach-house.

That the groom would get the note to Asnetha Sleep, perfectly act out the fabrication of meeting Queely Sheill on Sandy Bay Road, and keep his mouth shut long enough, Rose Knight did not contemplate questioning. Whatever he was thinking of Asnetha Sleep, she did not care. Whether he read the note or not, she did not care. When she had struck her husband in his presence she had shown how little she cared what he thought of her. Since she no longer herself, and for the first time, cared what she thought of herself in relations with servants, it did not matter what he thought. No servant had an opinion worth expressing or hearing.

And Ferris, whom they had hitherto considered truthful, was, she had discovered, a liar.

Mr Vaneleigh, his feet washed, his shaving over, his slops emptied, his room brushed and straightened, was again in the bed Queely Sheill had re-made. The cat's bowl was filled with milk. Queely Sheill had brought oysters, porter, bread and candles. The food, and the hospital medicine were at hand. Queely Sheill lit two candles, closed the window to keep out the noxious night airs and unhealthy exudations of trees, drew the curtains, and closed the door as he left.

Mr Vaneleigh had bought from the penny box outside the second-hand book shop a copy of *London Magazine* ten years old. It contained a gaiety of his *The Essence of Opera.* He took a pinch of snuff. He looked at what he had long ago written: *The Essence of Opera,* Imogène et Almanzor. . . .

When Queely Sheill arrived at the cottage he was surprised at its quietness; by that hour of night on Sunday it was usually noisy.

He opened the door. A candle guttered on the parlour table; a broken basin lay on a dark stain on the floor. There was the fume of burned stew, negrohead and spilled rum. Down the passage, light seemed to flutter from the open door of his father's bedroom, to flutter in flakes as though wind rummaged vaguely in smoke and flame, to wax and wane like a large and weary blinking.

Then came the sleepy and sonorous voice of John Death Sheill, a voice at its most consciously and artfully rounded, drunkenly rich and bloomed over with contentment, and waxing and waning in a rhythm parallel to the cloudy surges of candle-light.

"Dawnce, Duchess," intoned John Death Sheill, "Dawnce, Duchess, dawnce and dawnce! Awh, dawnce, my goddess of rum, awh, dawnce! Dawnce, *de*vine being, dawnce!"

Queely Sheill went to the doorway.

By the light of four candles Polidorio Smith was dancing in the centre of the small room to his half-drunken, half-dreaming audience.

John Death Sheill sat on the bed, his back to the wall, his globular face tilted back. He was swaddled in a dressing-gown of crimson stuff; he was a vast fruit ripened to the moment of slipping from the vine it had dragged earthwards. His bulk, his burden of heavy folds of crimson, his curves and impassivity, seemed alone to weigh the room down, for all else seemed fragile and fluid, defenceless against annihilation.

Beside that crimson mound lay a sleeping woman, slender, infinitely slight and delicate. Her dark torn petticoat, a vesture of shadows itself, revealed her unexpanded breasts and the pallor of her limbs to the continual caresses of sliding and writhing shadows. She seemed to breathe gently and, as when John Death Sheill had intoned, to the rhythm of the shadows. Her pretty face with its lips gaping was childlike, its weary sullenness a thing of air, she lay like the light-blotched shade of a leafy branch, a breath too many would have diluted her to a patch of vapour, to semi-transparency, to disappearance.

A scarecrow harpmaker on the other side of the room had arranged his dingy and friable angularities on a chair in the exalted posture of one who harps on a crag; beaked and gimcrack, he plucked with long skinny fingers on the unseen wires of air; and the supple shadows shuffled and slipped over his brittleness, and through his transparent bones, and the diaphanous white hair that hung over the wafers of his temples and cheekbones.

As though thrown into the corner near the harpmaker, Pretty Dick lolled on the floor, a doll of feathers, sodden in the sediment of shadows, washed and worn to melting and rotting by the currents of muddier light there in the depths, and the cross-currents of muddier shadows. His flaccid legs were curled away from the tranced orbit of the dancer's feet.

With reserved stateliness and straitened gestures, the ostrich plumes of a theatrical headdress pouring like smoke from forehead and skull, Polidorio Smith danced. Grave and grotesque, in a melancholy whirlpool, he revolved and undulated in his dance, and his brother shadows, and shadows of shadows, danced about him, beyond him, and on the ceiling above him, the disposition and waving and wavering of the four leaves of candle flame causing brother to infringe on brother, brother to stain and digest brother, brother to eclipse brother, one frieze of wraiths to bow and swoop and drag across and through the others, others shedding others like membranes of gauze.

Polidorio Smith's face, mobile and sage with a thousand perpetually shifting degrees of sadnesses, revealed that the dance and the dancer, the eyes that watched, and the walls that enclosed, and the sleep that the woman vaporously slept, were ephemeral and nothing and gone. His arms rising to the plumes and the restless ceiling were tangling together, and disentangling and tangling again, the foggy skeins of years gone, and of years to come and go. He and the mingling shadows, said he and the mingling shadows, were useless spectres; the audience and the walls would go, and the leaves would fall from the candles. No arithmetic of music diverted his movements from serenity or caged their truth; the invisible harp-tune of the tatterdemalion skeleton did not pervert their simplicity. He danced the beauty of human sadness, of the weariness of knowledge, of the sorrow of existence, of the calm stupefaction in bemused and tarnished wisdom.

He picked at the shadows with his long livid fingernails; the shadows picked and pecked from him and his audience the half-squalid seconds, the worn-out minutes, the torn-up dreams, the bugs of memory. In the sour crevices of the walls and floors and door-posts, and in the seams of their shabbiness, and the herbage of their unwashed bodies, the bugs and lice of fact were at rest, as they themselves for a minute space were at rest on the unwashed body of the earth.

With whom he danced, other than himself and shadows, the dancer could not know . . . he may have danced with planets lost beyond reckoning, with pasts yet to come, with the eternity he was and was of.

For whom he danced he could not know . . . four animals watched: harpmaker, actor, actor's son and pickpocket. But they watched him less than they watched the dream they called the present, and which wound them in its peace, and which appeared permanent, and was already gone and would never come again. He may have danced unknowingly for Time itself, to lengthen its divisions and drown its roar with feather-soft reticences; or for Life, to halt its accumulations of ever-blackening blood; or for Death, the one illustrious and living god, who grants all and wishes to die, and is yet the one undying, the one eternity.

Unavailing as tears, tears of tallow wound and faltered down the candles, building tears on tears that in their turn fled into tears, and the dancer began to slacken, to flag, to revolve like a fatigued and ludicrous actor needing a tumbler of rum; and the bugs and lice began to stir; and the cadaverous harpmaker decisively finally jangled the wires of air and snatched back his fingers to rest; and John Death Sheill bent over and began to lick one of the delicate breasts; and Pretty Dick stretched out his little muscular legs; and the woman pushed the sucker lips and blazing face away from her body; and Queely Sheill said:

"Queely's haway to 'is crib for 'e's tired."

"Queely!" they all said—and "Apollo, my tulip!" and "My son! My noble son!" and "Queely! Queely! Queely!"

"Come, boy, and buss your sire ere you depawt," said John Death Sheill. "And, Richard the Pretty, pour the Duchess aw beaker, pour Hester aw beaker, pour for us all, except my godly child."

"What of 'Ester Kitchener?" said Queely Sheill. "She must go 'ome to 'er mam."

Hester Kitchener, who had taken her gown from where it hung on a nail to shawl her shoulders and breasts from Queely Sheill, said in a voice as delicate as she, as sweet and weary as she:

"I'll go to mam. I ain't forgot mam. I fell to sleep while the Duchess jigged."

"Come, buss your sire, my heir, and to thy couch. She has slumbered while the Duchess dawnced. I have been deprived of her enchawntment. You must all begone. Hester and I will pawtake of another goblet and then she'll desert me, fly away like aw pretty little bird. Buss me, boy, and begone!"

"Diddle, diddle dee," said Polidorio Smith. "I shall *sing*! *Shall* you hear me sing, Pretty Dee?"

"Put on your gown, 'Ester. I'll walk you to your mam's."

She laughed, and all her fragilities and unexpanded graces quivered with the vibrations of her crystal bitterness.

"Dear Queely, I know the streets. I'll put on my gown, and drink a drink, and go." And she smiled her child's petulant smile. "But you're the tired one, and I shall walk you to *your* bed . . ." She was being saucy. She got up from the bed.

John Death Sheill began to cry.

"Aw jealous son . . ." he was understood to say. "Aw jealous boy . . . his jealous mother's jealous boy. . . ."

Queely Sheill sat on the bed beside his father, and Hester Kitchener concealed her worn and torn petticoats and barenesses in the gown, and Polidorio Smith buttoned it up the back, and Pretty Dick handed rums around, and the harpmaker, the pickpocket, the dancer and the prostitute drank rums, and listened to the fat man's mouthing and sobbing, and watched Queely Sheill soothe him.

"I ain't jealous hof the skinny dad. Queely's 'Ester's *friend*."

"Oh, yes! Oh, *yes*!" Her eyes looped in shadows looked earnestly over the surface of the drink.

"You know I'm 'er friend. 'Ester must go to 'er mam because 'er mam his sick and solitary. 'Ester will come again, but now she must go."

Presently, after the others had filled and emptied their glasses several times, and Pretty Dick had been decorated by the head-dress of plumes, and Polidorio Smith had sat on the chair with Pretty Dick on his knee, and Hester Kitchener had proudly put on her bonnet with its false and faded and scentless violets, and the harpmaker was singing dirty songs older than any of them in a voice like desert wind, John Death Sheill was soothed.

Just as the dance had slackened to its end and dried from the air, so the drizzle of drunken tears ran to their end and dried in the dimples, and John Death Sheill roared for rum, and gave Hester Kitchener her body's fee, and berated her for not sooner departing to her bed-ridden mother, and demanded that the harpmaker see her through the streets, and said farewell in harmonic and involved periods, and fell asleep.

"Come, Poli," said Queely Sheill, "snuff out the candles and leave 'im to snore. Don't take nothing, Pretty Dick, don't take nothing, I himplores. I'm haway to crib; Queely's tired."

"Pretty Dee," said Polidorio Smith, sniffing at the head-dress, "*smells* like a *bird*. He has given me a pictorial *bible*, but has *lost* his *curls*. Ah, *curls*! You must *not*, Pretty Dee, have a *jealousy*, for I shall presently *sing* to you . . . to you *alone* . . . but *curls*, Apollo. . . !"

"Oh, *quick*, Poli, I'm tired. Hupstairs, Poli. 'E'll rouse again hand weep, and Queely's *tired*."

"I shall *leave*, *ungrateful* Apollo, in a *moment*. I was *speaking* softly as a muffin. Alack, I have *forgotten*. I am losing *consciousness*!"

"*Curls*, Poli. Quick."

"Today, *today*, a yobbie *noir* with curls like *snails* came to me with a lady *black* as an *umbrella*. . . ."

"Oh, *Poli*. Queely's tired, tired. Tired. *Tired*."

"Off my *knee*, feathery *Dee*," said Polidorio Smith. "Apollo's to *bed*, and so are *we*! Poesy! Poesy!" he squealed. "Oh, diddle, diddle, *dee*!"

The eyeless shadows of heads, and shadows of plumes, and shadows of murmuring men upon the walls had been almost static for a time; the candles were shorter and their leaves of flame longer and the tears of tallow thicker. The shadows moved violently again for a moment, rose and fell and struck into each other. Then, one shadow blew away the flames, and blew away the shadows. As the men who were left climbed the stairs they heard the watchman crying an hour nearer to death than they thought.

Judas Griffin Vaneleigh heard the watchman crying the hour, and closed the magazine, and blew out his candles. He could not blow out his thoughts:

My memories . . . my memories . . . my memories . . . they pour along, pour along in bland silence, they are penetrable to no star . . . oh, smooth, spiritless repetitions now . . . are they to be relied on? . . . I must beware of dreaming errors into them. . . .

Why am I standing on the hill, why am I staring from the hill, from the old walled city of Boulogne towards the green sea . . . over the green sea . . . to England . . . green England . . . .?

Love is combating self-hood . . . leave the wind-courting pines of Boulogne . . . go! . . . do not go! . . . bask like a grasshopper in France . . . do not go! . . . go!

There is my sweetly simple, delightful village. There is Trunham Grove. There is my pillared house; and Neptune the Newfoundland dog with webbed paws. He rolls with awkward joy on my smooth-shaven elastic lawns smothered in lilacs and laburnum. Nednil House! The odorous pheasant-haunted groves, the birch-covered steeps . . . high hedges thick with hazel . . . white-barked ash . . . the wood-strawberry runs luxuriantly over the bank . . . The churchyard! The churchyard is one of the prettiest of its kind . . . I am *quite* in love with its irregular little paths paved with flags and red brick . . . the herbage long and thick without rankness, not a nettle in it to alarm ladies' silk-covered ankles . . . my wife's ankles, Fidelia . . . and her half-sisters' ankles . . . Marguerite . . . and Ellen.

Beware of dreaming errors . . . What did I say of Ellen's ankles? . . . What did I say of her hair? . . . *The gentle girl who bent over the shallow page the rich curls of her amaranthine hair* . . . And her ankles, what of her ankles? . . . I said to the vile questioner . . . what did I say? . . . I said, "*Upon my soul, I don't know why I murdered Ellen Abernethy, unless it was because she had such thick ankles!*"

Did I say it? Or did someone say I said it? . . . Beware of dreaming errors. . . .

The churchyard . . . the churchyard. . . .

It looks as if it were clean and neat from nature, not from art . . . the few yews are dark, but not dismal . . . the circling hedge of laurel the brightest green I ever beheld . . . its whole appearance is as domestic, cheerful, and snug, as if it were kept in such apple-pie order for the better seducing folks to come and be buried . . . Oh, very come-in-able . . . I have a delicate and sentimental gusto to be nested for ever in that cool greenery . . .

I shall never lie there . . . never lie there . . . I shall lie where? . . . nowhere or thereabouts. . . .

What did I write? . . . *Imogène et Almanzor*. . . .

Almanzor : *Hélas!*

Imogène : *Quoi!*
Almanzor : *J'expire!*
Imogène : *Oh, malheur!*
Le Choeur : *Chantons, dansons, montrons notre douleur!* . . . come, the work warms, much is done, but more remains to do. . . .

From the walls of old Boulogne, I hear Fidelia calling in Trunham Grove.

She comes out on the stone steps of Nednil House and calls me with hard sobriety from wherever I am . . . sitting lazily on an eminence . . . by the clear trout stream winding along like a snake . . . on the cool grass . . . in the old churchyard where I shall never lie. . . .

She calls, and it is autumn . . . oh, she is original and racy, and hard—and hard, *hard*. Her half-sisters, Marguerite . . . and . . . and Ellen . . . stand dimly behind her. . . .

"To London!" she says, "To London! Money for Nednil House lies in London! Money for the coal dealer, and the baker, and the grocer, for the tradesmen of Trunham Grove, lies in London!"

She calls, she beckons. Her eyes, hard with an inimical dignity, fix me with an intense *willing*. . . .

She beckons at the glass door, and it is winter, it is December, and her half-sisters stand behind her, behind the glass, Marguerite . . . and Ellen, with amaranthine hair and thick ankles.

Fidelia says, feelingly and scientifically, "London! To London!" She is pleasant and sprightly, and hard.

"He who never sets out", she says, "will never arrive at his journey's end! To London!"

From my bed in Campbell Street, the oysters eaten, and the porter drunk, I see myself on the French hilltop staring over the green Channel to watch myself leave Nednil House and the green village. . . .

Imogène et Almanzor, les deux: *Peuples, chantez, dansez, montrez notre allégresse!*

Le Choeur: *Chantons, dansons, montrons notre allégresse!*

Behind us stand the doubting tradesmen of Trunham Grove.

Before us lies the apartment over a tailor's in Conduit Street . . . it rains December rains, and feet will get wet, and oysters and porter be taken for supper . . . Before us lies the crockery-dealer of Cockspur Street, the crockery-dealer-and-money-lender we owe six hundred and ten pounds to. . . .

Before us lie the theatres in the rain; the orchestra leader taps the mahogany three times with trenchant fiddlestick; away thunder gongs and kettledrums; broad blares the spreading note of the trumpet; the tortured viola groans; and the violins shriek, and the little drums crash, as when, in forests, the lightnings rend a thousand oaks. In momentary breaches of the storm the wail of the horn arises. Then again the cloud of harmony grows thicker; the gong redoubles its thunders dread. The cut-glass chandelier quivers each particular pendant . . . rain . . . rain on the streets of London . . . while distinctly, in the midst of this furious tempest, is heard the bow of the leader rising triumphantly over the roaring wild ocean of sounds . . . who can tame the leader. . . ?

Oh, beware of dreaming errors . . . who can tame Death?

True as a Toledo to the appointed day, Death comes.

I see from Campbell Street, Hobart Town, that I stand in Boulogne, France, and look to Conduit Street, London. I read, across the green waters, over the white shoulder of Dover, the *London Times*. . . .

Harriet Foothen, servant to Mr Vaneleigh. Cross-examined by the Attorney-General, she said: Mr Vaneleigh and his wife came to Conduit Street with the two Misses Abernethy. They went to the theatre two nights following. They walked home. The weather was wet and very cold. They took supper both nights—oysters and porter. Miss Ellen complained in the morning of having taken cold. She got up to dinner. Could not tell when Dr High was first sent for. Miss Ellen died on the twenty-first of December. In the morning of that day she was considered better. Mr and Mrs Vaneleigh went out, after Mrs Vaneleigh had given Ellen a black draught. After Dr High had been, witness came into the room and found her lying quiet. Miss Ellen said she thought she heard a little boy coming along the room, and she burst into tears, and convulsions came on. No boy had been in the room. Witness called in apothecaries. The convulsions got better, and they went away. Soon after they were gone the convulsions came on again, and she died. She lay ill seven days. Witness had not received all her wages.

Montrons notre douleur . . . Ellen bends over the shallow page the rich curls of her amaranthine hair . . . Ellen walks the mud and rain of London . . . Ellen drinks a black draught, . . .

I read, over the world, over the night, over the shoulder of the years, the *London Times*. . . .

Dr High said:

Was called on Thursday, the sixteenth of December. Had seen Miss Ellen Abernethy before, when she came for a certificate that she might ensure her life. When he was called in he found her sitting in her bedroom, complaining of great headache, a weight over her eyes, and partial blindness. On Monday, she had gone to the play, and supped on oysters and bottled porter. On Tuesday, she went again to the play and got wet feet with which she sat during the evening. On her return she had supped heartily again on oysters and bottled porter. That night she was violently sick. Mrs Vaneleigh gave her a black draught from the chemist.

Fidelia gives Ellen a black draught . . . oh, beware of dreaming errors. . . .

"Doctor," says Ellen of the amaranthine curls, "I was gone to heaven but you have brought me back to earth."

"Harriet," says Ellen, "I hear a little boy coming along the room. He ought not to be there. . . ."

"Doctor," says Ellen of the thick ankles, "I am dying; I feel I am—I am sure so."

"Doctor," says Ellen, "may I have some meat."

"Ellen," says Fidelia, hard and calm and kind, "drink your black draught."

Dr High said:

Calomel was prescribed, followed by senna, until the bowels should freely act. Next morning the head was not relieved;

he ordered cupping. The pulse became feverish. He ordered tartar emetic to relieve the feverish action. It produced violent vomiting. On Sunday the feverish symptom abated. He allowed her broth. On Tuesday morning she was considerably better, though easily excited. Her pulse was agitated. She asked if she might have some meat. She asked for a cup of coffee. He went away, and was sent for between two and three. She was in convulsions and hysterical. She said she was sure she would die, and went off into convulsions. He suggested alterations in the apothecary's medicines, and then went away and returned at four, and she was then just dead. He met Mr Vaneleigh returning from the street as he was going out, and told him. Mr Vaneleigh appeared much shocked, as he had left her much better than the night before, and asked the cause of death. He told Mr Vaneleigh, "Mischief in the brain."

I see Fidelia; she firmly weeps.

Behind her the shape of Marguerite appears . . . pale . . . faded . . . dishevelled hair . . . the living half-sister in excessive grief.

Before her the shape of Ellen lies . . . her form stiffened . . . her eyeballs turned upward . . . the dead half-sister blind to the lustre of beauty . . . deaf to the charm of eloquence. . . .

Between the living and the dead, Fidelia stands.

In a mode difficult to define, Fidelia stands . . . between . . . the living . . . and . . . the dead.

My memories . . . pouring along in bland silence . . . penetrable to no star . . . to be relied on? . . . beware of dreaming errors . . . dreaming . . . dreaming. . . .

Mr Vaneleigh, Judas Griffin Vaneleigh, did not hear the watchman call the hour. He and his cat were asleep.

8

The watchman called hour by hour the hours of the night, and the hours, darkening and then lightening, precipitated themselves hour by hour over the felloe of the horizon. They took with them shadows that danced with a shadow, and shadowed memories that shuffled between the living and the dead, and the sheen of hoofs and whirling wheels, and tears, and lips moving in expression of numberless coloured and uncoloured emotions. The hours took all, drained away with the used-up backbitings, blessings, martyrdoms and mischiefs of the time called Sunday.

On Monday, Rose Knight, whose last words spoken to her husband had received the answer of a blow in the face, addressed him again.

Her tone was that of a woman resurrected; mechanical powers of finest spring-wheels and clockwork of most golden gold produced a facsimile of charm. As springs unwound, and wheel turned wheel, neither venom nor indifference showed in her manner which had a sustained, oiled and disembodied gaiety. Her manner excluded consciousness of a past; it was of the whirring present. Saturday and Sunday had not, it said, existed.

Her entire behaviour to Sir Sydney and Asnetha Sleep had the seeming fragility and exquisite arrangement of colours of a landscape in the solid glass bun of a paperweight; it could be viewed from every possible angle as brilliantly beautiful, and untouchable.

Neither Sir Sydney, with a black eye, nor the cripple, with her nose like a coarse antenna upon the atmosphere, dared make any move nearer the crystal bun lest their breaths mist its surface with their guilt, and a typhoon ravage the enchanting landscape and explode its shell in their faces. Rose Knight's engineered indulgence of manner transformed them into evil-doers guilty of plotted malignancies; *she* had been guilty only of retaliatory, though outrageous and inconsiderate, temper.

Moreover, her assaults upon them, had in other ways altered their vision, less of her than of themselves.

Sir Sydney, as a suitor years ago, and a happy *fiancé*, had not known he was not to be the husband her fervid nature required. That she herself had not realized the dangers of her heat was negligible; man, whom woman allows conceive himself the hunter, is judged unforgivable when he denies that act of grace and disappoints by being a different quarry to the one she, the subtly pretending quarry, really hunted. He had forgotten, in a man's world of abstractions and febrile ambitions, that he was not a man to her; he had forgotten too that the acquired tartness of his behaviour was no more than vinegar in porridge.

Asnetha Sleep was more steeled. She had been enraged by the pettiness of truth and the strength of feeling in its statement. She had always known that Rose Knight hated her, but had not foreseen that hatred being displayed any more than as an exercise of feminine asperity, needle-shaped endearments and feline persecutions. The attack, startling as it was, had not deeply marked. An error in fact had blunted it. Asnetha Sleep had certainly come to Van Diemen's Land hoping for a husband, but had deliberately let opportunities slip: she had learned to expect fortune-hunters, but also to assess them. She had not found a fortune-hunter, even in that island of the dispossessed and fortune-hunting, who fulfilled her requirements.

Although she had whipped, fondled and been spasmodically pleasant to Teapot, his sense of imminent calamity and of an accelerating derangement of pattern did not decrease. His uncertainty of Queely Sheill had increased. The purity of his plan in offering the bribe of the gold chain had been repaid by impurity on bewildering impurity. His jealousy remained at a constant; he had neither the brains, years, power nor information to use it. He had said nothing to Asnetha Sleep of the visit to Playhouse Cottage although the note, so mysteriously obtained and treated, still swam about on the muddled and shallow broth of his mind.

Each night when he was given his one glass of port as a sleeping-draught, he felt safe enough to sleep, but each night he found himself sneaking to listen for a little while at the cripple's door, though no warnings of intrusion came from the inanimate, no galvanic fluxes enlivened the air; whatever messages the night-birds spoke, or the frost on the roof-slates scribbled, or the moths carried in the dust of their wings, were not yet for Teapot. He waited.

He did not know that he waited for what the two women knew they waited for:

. . . thursday will be happy to oblidge . . . and will come to the window at nine so no more for now. . . .

At *Cindermead*, Monday and Tuesday and Wednesday ascended, and sank, and went to death like days. Sir Sydney's black eye was to begin fading. Lady Knight's delicate motor of graciousness ran slippery with golden oil. Miss Asnetha Sleep drank port wine, had a bath, and read William Wordsworth. Teapot was whipped twice. Thursday appeared . . . *thursday will be happy to oblidge. . . .*

The Thursday sun was about to rise.

At five o'clock, along the waterfront, from behind the crates of New Market, from the great coils of rope in Whelk Yard, from the arches of Customs House and the doorways of Salamanca Place, emerged what might have been scraps torn from the very fabric of midnight and forced to infest the daylight they had been thrown down in. Costumed in the rags of the slopshop Jews, the vagabonds who had not slept made the motions of those who were waking up, unhinging their limbs, grating their blue palms together, setting themselves into angled and jerky motion like humans of metal, like cracked engines emitting a sour steam of effort.

At five-thirty, the population of animals that live by night snatched last tidbits from outlying fields, and vanished, slyly concealing the glint of their eyes. There was a moment of no movement except the faulty and negligible staggering by fits and starts of the metal spectres of the waterfront: the population of animals that live by daylight was not yet ready to stir.

The moment came; there was a sound like the rising of a curtain; the sun lifted its flat and deadly eye.

There arose next the seeming innocent but organized clamour of birds—a composition of isolated courtesies, praise like a boiling of blood, idiot flutings, malicious squeaks, and fervent and daggerlike notes. Cocks then crowed needlessly, and dogs unnecessarily barked. In the pound, a dun bull with snail horns sonorously moaned. The slaughter-men began slashing the throats of sheep from which frothed blood *couleur de rose*.

At six, the prison porter opened the gates of the Penitentiary. In single file, the hobbled beasts of the iron gangs debouched on to the frosted ruts of Campbell Street. The overseer sliced his cane upon the air. Everywhere, milkmaids, their marks of crime branded in their hands, squatted to the milking-stools and the udders of steaming cows.

At seven, servants were breaking the ice in water-butts, and lighting fires. The medical students began Livy.

At eight, the medical students began Herodotus.

At nine, the tripe-man set up his jars of pickled tripe; the shutters of the chair-makers, of basket-makers, chandlers, grocers and butchers were taken down—all over Hobart Town shutters were taken down, and doorsteps brushed of frozen spittle and shavings of mud.

Thus Hobart Town was awake and erect and articulate and busied. Footsteps passed and were passed by footsteps in every direction and for every possible reason. To reach its sleep and its dreams and nightmares, Hobart Town must walk and stop walking, and continue walking, and stop walking again to sit or stand, talk and fall silent, ask and be refused, question and be answered, beg and be begged from, beg off in white lies or accept with reluctant lies, lie and be lied to, eat and defecate, make and undo, laugh and be laughed with and at, build and destroy, move in sumless differing ways to noon and afternoon and night.

. . . thursday will be happy to oblidge . . . and will come to the window at nine so no more for now. . . .

Night down, at *Cindermead*, at dinner, which Rose Knight had ordered for earlier than usual, she and Asnetha Sleep, in presumption of nine o'clock, were already gay before they drank more wine at table than they usually did, and became gayer. Sir Sydney and his black eye were not with them. He had played Royal Tennis with the Governor's aide in the late afternoon, and had gone on to his club to meet Dr Wake, a lauded new arrival in the colony.

Neither of the two women, trebly stimulated by expectation, wine and Sir Sydney's absence, could control or attempted to control what they were saying. Both of them could easily control what they had absolutely no intention of saying.

All who, as Asnetha Sleep was, are in love (by this euphemism lust is so often so graced) are capable of dissimulation without tell-tale ostentation only so far . . . love must somehow display itself. Dinner-table effervescence was her display.

All who, as Rose Knight did, hate deeply and purely, are capable of dissimulation until the sentence of destruction they would read on their victim is wholly drawn up. Dinner-table animation was not difficult to present and sustain.

Nine o'clock and Queely Sheill were two hours off.

Each woman ticked the seconds exactly into minutes and the minutes to quarter-hours as perfectly as wound-up timepieces embellished with hilarious and delightful ornament. Their sallies, their endearments, their maidenly gigglings and trills, their womanly laughters and decorated mockeries of Hobart Town acquaintances, sprayed with the carelessness and sparkle of fireworks under the chandelier, over the Coleport and the cut-glass. Dinner was as merry as a marriage-bell, and it seemed, when the clocks announced eight, that it had only a moment ago been seven. They both said so to each other.

Rose Knight had promised herself the pleasure, she had designedly said, even before the soup, of a novel in bed. Rising from the table at eight, she repeated her intention of retirement for this purpose. Then, throwing her table-napkin under the table to give Romney exercise for his rheumatic back, and having seen, before dinner, that Asnetha Sleep was ringless and her fingers more horrible without rings than with them, she said:

"Asnetha, honey, I've just observed that you do not wear your beautiful, beautiful rings. But—" She took care to keep her own exquisite fingers out of sight. "—you had no need of them this evening: you were yourself so brilliant. Such gems of expression!"

"My fingers..." began Asnetha Sleep, who had performed her crooked ballet and stood behind her chair, wriggling her fingers about.

"So slender!" said Rose Knight. "Honey, I declare I almost said shlender."

The rise and fall of their laughter was judiciously executed, prolonged just enough; it faded by meticulous degrees to the proper finish, and perfectly concealed that they were about to begin getting tired of each other.

"My poor, darling, poor, poor fingers, I declare, Rose, they were *aching*!"

Once again, they dangerously performed a duet of laughter. At its termination, Rose Knight decided on a finalizing remark, and the proper sequential motions of departure.

"I once heard," she said, "oh, somewhere, a man say that his *hair* was aching!"

It was a silly note, perfection on which to quit, and pleased Rose Knight with its undertone, of which the cripple would never know. They laughed together again. Rose Knight laughed, that ultimate time a shade longer, and they moved off in their opposite directions. Asnetha Sleep thought, over her shoulder, that she too would attempt a book . . . John Keats, perhaps. Parting at the exactly right moment they could have kissed each other like two enraptured sisters about to commit a delightful murder.

Rose Knight went upstairs.

Asnetha Sleep, who found that she was being more affected by wine than she had expected, reached her room where the maidservant was busy at the fire.

"Megan," she said, "to the dining-room on flat Welsh feet. Ask Romney for the decanter of port wine. Mine, I see, is nearly empty."

When Megan returned with the decanter which she was told to put with two glasses on a tabouret near one of the fireside chairs, Asnetha Sleep bade her goodnight. As the woman reached the door:

"Megan, you Taffy," she called, "a fan. The French fan with sequins. I pant. I burn. And tell my treasure, when he is ready for bed, to put on his dressing-gown. His slippers. Come here for his night-drink."

Behind the fan measled with stars of reflected flame she gave a long eructation as the door closed, but too soon for Megan not to hear it, and poke out her sharp triangular tongue.

As Teapot came to the curtains hanging heavily at the arch of the passage leading to Asnetha Sleep's room, he could hear her humming so richly and vibrantly that the closed door did not diminish the contentment which inspired and larded the sound. Its character put him instantly on useless guard; his inanimate surroundings began their warning innuendoes to his nerves. The humming was not wool-gathering; it was not flung off in idle and shredded mood; it was the humming of the very and all the zither-wires of her being. It was, for him, the threatening melody from the abyss at the bottom of the abyss.

His lips drew outward in a grimace that, had it composed noise, would have been the sour and ungentle growling of the famished. Then the lips drew inward, and combined in indigo pulpiness, and he came to the door, and tapped, and was called in.

Seated by the fire, the tabouret at hand, she fanned her mottled cheeks and nose.

"Teapot, treasure! Come, have your sleeping draught! Sit on thine own stool, treasure mine!"

He approached; he sat.

"Debased and tipsy Teapot, you have odd slippers on your big black feet! Your . . . your trotter-cases are diverse trotter-cases! Isn't your Miss Sleepy gay? And, provoking creature, straighten your night-cap. You seem as tipsy as a jockey."

She seemed to grow a little angry at that; her eyes got closer together, flared like the sequins on her fan.

He knew, not only from her demeanour, that she had been drinking unusually, because he had heard Romney, bringing up another bottle of hock for the dining-room, say to Megan in his squeezed and finicky accent:

"Meddlesome Metty *end* Leddy Paula Pry will be drunk as pipers, if *this* goes hon."

Her too unnecessarily direct and sun-blinded stare Teapot did not generally find disturbing; it led often to delights for him. But the extravagantly engraved current of her voice, her retreat into an upholstered cavern of satisfaction from which she spoke to him as to someone out in the wind, were an agony. His face grew smaller as he watched her hand streak for a glass of the port she had already poured, and extend it towards him less like handing a carnation than presenting a pistol. He saw his own fingers take the stem of the glass into whose treacherous circle of night he regretfully stared.

"Drink, treasure," she said, "your glass of dreams! Oh, immeasurably kind Miss Sleepy!" She sipped at her own glass.

"I am to drink my glass of dreams," he said, sipping as mingily as she.

"Oh, more quickly! You are slow as Billy Boots!" she said, and she cracked her fan shut and struck him on the knee, harder than she thought, for the ebony was hard as ebony.

"See!" She emptied her glass with a toper's flourish.

"I am to drink more quickly. I am slow as Billy Boots," said Teapot, and drained his glass of dreams.

"Teapot, treasure," she said, "tonight we are wanton! We *shall* be more wanton."

She lifted the decanter.

"You are peckish. Hold out your glass!"

"I am peckish. I must hold out my glass."

With horror, he saw the hand freckled as a tiger-lily tilt the decanter, and fill his glass. Yet, in horror as he was, his face remained bland except for a muscle which hopped up and down like a flea under the skin beneath one eye.

"Shall I be sick? I shall be sick," he said, unsuccessfully attempting the ominous, for his voice had got six years thinner.

"Wicked dog! Brute beast! *Shall I be sick?*"

She mimicked him in falsetto; falsely falsely and lop-sidedly smiling.

"On Sir Sydney's best port! Ingrate! 'Tis elixir, opiate, mild as milk!"

Her head suddenly lashed her ringlets this and that way.

"Drink!"

And she tapped with the closed fan again, not so carelessly hard, but merely with a decision not to be denied.

"You will sleep," she said sonorously, and increased the intensity of her unabating gaze.

"I must drink. I shall sleep."

He drank.

Wordlessly then, and beginning to hum her wordless and shameless tune, she pointed her fan at his glass, she filled it as he held it out, she tapped his knee, she stared, and droned her melody, as he drank his third glass.

His lips varnished with wine, Teapot grinned. Warmer, his eyes swimming, "Shall you whip me?" whispered Teapot.

"Perhaps yes, perhaps yes, perhaps yes. . . . Hold out your glass with black hand," she said but, as she poured, the deeply buzzing tune began again as of its own accord. Adrift on her own quickening wine and her own imaginings, she let the glass run over.

"La, la, la, *la*!" she said. "Bend like a puppy-dog! Sip carefully, Teapot, till the brimming be gone. Then, heigh-ho, down the little red lane where the chicken broke his instep!"

"Must . . . sip . . . care-ful-ly," said Teapot, all teeth and eyes, but drank quickly, spilling wine on chin and night-shirt, and sure that he was loved. Asnetha Sleep's legs buffeted each the other.

"I *shall* be whipped," said Teapot loudly as a spoiled heir, and put the wine-glass on the tabouret, and stood, and started towards the wardrobe where hung the whip. The clock struck the half-hour.

"Half-past eight!" cried the cripple. " 'Tis too late, Teapot! Go and go, and quickly go! To bed. I have a headache . . . oh, oh, oh."

Holding her forehead, she rocked about.

"Go, Teapot! Go, treasure! Softly as a ghost. Sleep and dream."

"Must go," said Teapot, undone by wine and time. "Softly . . . as . . . goats. Sleep . . . and . . . dream."

Stupidly, unsurely, confused beyond disappointment and jealousy and anger, Teapot strolled to the door, opened it, left the room, forgetting to close the door.

"He's drunk," she said, asprawl in the chair, and stared at the open door for some time, more fatigued and much drunker than she had proposed being.

"Teapot eye-ess dee-ah-you-en-kay. And I ay-em tee-double-oh."

She struggled to rise. She rose, she whirled and flapped and nearly fell, and thumped to the door to lock it.

It slammed to very loudly.

Teapot on his night-stool heard it, and began to consider and wrestle with his condition, to rouse up his drugged enmity, his subdued jealousy, his mislaid cunning. He fixed his teeth about his wrist and kept them there.

Rose Knight heard it from her writing-room. She held a novel; she had even been reading in a novel, oh, a silly, for it told of people who were not people, of events beyond reality . . . of renunciations, noble sacrifices, sweetnesses florid and scentless as dahlias . . . murders recurred like dinners but with less trouble; there was a wife like a paper rose; a husband like a sirloin; a hero with a brow and brain of ivory; a heroine whom the villain never ravished after a hundred opportunities. There was not a sour privy, or a privy at all, no bum bore a boil, no tooth decayed, no stays creaked, at a time of sacred silence, like a red-coat's boots.

She had sniffed at the words as though the unseen face flattened on the skylight of heaven might conceivably have been examining the validity of the reason she had tossed Asnetha Sleep for keeping the coast clear.

After the door slammed shut, she made her own ironic echo and slammed the book shut.

Presently she drifted to her dressing-room, and began to brush her hair as though she were a lady, a wife and a moral woman. She was waiting without appearing to do so; waiting with no plan of action except waiting without precise knowledge of what she waited for. She knew what was to happen in Asnetha Sleep's bedroom unless *happy to oblidge* meant a sewing-lesson: why then, she stopped herself from allowing herself to think, wait? In the looking-glass, her face, like the gestures of hair-brushing, had a docility, a placidity, a stringent docility and measured placidity.

At nine o'clock, punctual as the tide, Queely Sheill bloomed at the window behind which the three candles burned as before and as if before the simplest of altars. Asnetha Sleep sat, idol or goddess, dross or woman, as before, on the edge of the bed. As before she pressed herself up from the altar, grotesquely revolved, and danced to open the entrance to the temple, to let in the worshipper or sacrifice, the goth or god who came from the night.

Ah, the night!

The night, a living thing, eternally breaking from underground, moved like a river drained from the black brains of sleepers, a river so thick with blackness that nothing lay between its atoms. The night was a river that had no name, but had had always the same no-name—though sometimes harmless and balm, though sometimes flooded with dense heart-drowning rheums, though sometimes freaked and arteried with gall.

In the house, which to Teapot flickered and palpitated like the dark core of a guttering dark flame, he had himself guttered and shuddered, his teeth set on his wrists, one or the other, or in his biceps, to frustrate the wine.

Thus self-gnawed awake, he had stolen to Asnetha Sleep's door and, egged on by the suggestions of all things about him, had listened to the muted sounds which he was unable to explain to himself. Yet he was certain someone else was with her, and equally certain who the someone was. It took a long time for him to arrive at the idea that the man had entered by the window. In terror at his decision to do so, he went quietly through the half-darkened house, and, by a side door, into the blind night. He could do nothing but feel his way on the walls and their projections and hazards, nothing but obey their frightening encouragements to keep advancing inch by inch to the corner near the window where he could best discover, by what means he did not know and never was to know, the truth. As he turned the corner, his fingers, his body, touched silent cloth and a living silent body. He and this body drew in shocked breaths to the innermost doors of their hearts. Before he could yell, or fall to the ground, Lady Knight spoke.

"Who is that?" she said, and could also have fallen. It might have been night's own protruding resemblance of a hand that had touched her coverings, or someone's hand from a novel.

Then, still in shock, "Black boy!" she said. She could smell him for he had his inherited odour.

For a few moments, the two spies stood panting, unseen to each other, until she, at least, had regained enough of her routed forces, and knew what to do.

"Come with me, black spying thing," she said. "I shall go first. Do not dare to touch me again."

They felt their way back into the house where she became taller, her hair over her shoulders and, imperiously holding her petticoats and the folds of her wrapper, with a splendour of smooth motion, led him upstairs, where he had never before been permitted, to her writing-room.

In the warmth, the fire glowing, the lamp turned low and murmuring, she sat. She left him standing. On the table lay the novel, slammed shut. She looked at the page she had just opened in the vaster novel of the night outside Asnetha Sleep's window, and scanned its wretched and pathetic illustration.

He had gone a steely colour, his chin rhythmically treadled up and down, the whites of his eyes showed, his overlong fingers were stiff at his thighs.

"What were you doing?" she said, and he felt her tintless eyes range far beyond the shell of his useless body to the desert of his mind in which he conceived himself minute, naked, peeled to the nerves, bowed beneath a sky that was not there, on a surface without an horizon.

He could not speak, his functions were locked; his chin alone persisted in its noiseless treadling.

She spoke again, harder in tone yet more seductively:

"Black boy, you seem not old enough to match slippers, but you're old enough to speak. What were you doing in the dark near Miss Sleep's window?"

She had to wait until the jaw quietened, and its jerkings and idiot vibratings lessened, and it could give attention to the construction of words.

"What . . . was . . . I . . . doing . . . in . . . the . . . dark . . ."

She could have struck him but she compelled herself to bear with the unsound churning.

" . . . near . . . Miss . . . Sleep's . . ." The churning stuck.

His eyes tried madly, surging this way, that way, to snap their leashes, burst from their purses to roll away to where nothing was to be seen. His cheeks cockled up; his hands clenched and then uncurled flat and rigid. He shot them and their unpleasing palms towards her in a manner at once vicious and supplicating. Some scalding juice suffused the desiccated fibres of speech.

"The man," he said with sudden unlovely clearness, the boy traitor buying his freedom, "is in Miss Sleepy's . . . in Miss Sleep's room."

"Which man?"

"The man who is big. The man with yellow hair who ate the bread-and-cheese."

"How did you know the man was there?"

It was impossible for him to explain what whirlpools in the grain of door-panels had told him, what the pattern of mortar, the private mouths of the wallpaper flowers, the flashing stars on a fan black as night, had told. He licked his lips.

"She gave me wine, and said, 'Dream!' and said, 'Sleep!' "

"But she gives you a glass of wine every night to make you sleep."

He flapped his hands; he wrung them.

"She gave me lots of wine. Hundreds of glasses of wine. See. . .!"

He touched the stain on his night-shirt. He began, as he talked, uncorrected, of the cat's mother, to gesticulate heavily. Malice and despair accelerated. Words spurted at her on breaths tainted with souring wine.

"She gives hundreds and hundreds of wine when the man comes through the window. She says 'Sleep' and hits with the fan—*smack*! I am sick, poor boy, when the man comes. I chunder in the night-stool."

He imitated spewing for her quite wonderfully. He was a good mimic. She watched distastefully, and listened, listened.

"The man is a bad man, a monster. He tells lies, and takes my money in big pink hand, and then comes to her bedroom . . . ."

"Takes your money? Come, tell me what you mean?"

"I am to tell you what I mean. He takes my lady-mama's money on a chain. He tells lies."

"*You* are telling lies. When could he take your money? Tell me the truth."

Once again he flapped his hands in despair; once again there were difficulties of explanation . . . his bribe taken and pocketed and undervalued, his child's faith and hope denied, his simplicity challenged, his cunning outridden.

"You are a black, lying spy! Tell the truth or Sir Sydney will have you in gaol."

"I am a black lying spy! I must tell the truth or Sir Sydney. . . ."

"Stop! *Stop* that, this instant. Tell the truth."

"I gave the man my lady-mama's money."

He was beginning to swallow sobs that wanted to rise; tears began to overflow. But she pursued him.

"Why did you? Why?"

"He . . . he said he would not come . . . in the window . . . if I gave him money."

"Liar! Black snivelling liar! Tell the truth!"

Teapot could bridle his sobs no longer; they galloped repulsively out. He tossed noisily from side to side on his vertical rack.

She gave him no quarter; she merely impatiently waited to choose a trough in the waves of sorrow, and would have used a thumb-screw without giving its use a second thought.

"Stop your din. You gave the man the money?"

"I gave the man the money."

"Why, black boy?"

"So that . . . so that the man would not talk to her in the Chinese room."

"When was the man talking to her in the Chinese room?"

She was ceaselessly implacable; he could die, he felt, and she would push aside the coffin-lid, and be heard questioning still.

Alive, he was desperate, but could not hide his stupidity in tears, or in his bed, or the house, or the black night, or the last alley in the world, for she paced him a goad's length away with her lit and ruthless eyes.

At last, the fire sinking, the lamp still murmuring the beauty and peace of impercipience, she came to understand enough of what had gone on and of what he had done, and to abandon her persecution with a sense of gain, of additional power.

He prayed to himself that he would be discarded; his face muzzled in the remains of tears, snot blistering his upper lip, overtasked and dizzy, he wanted no more of *Cindermead* and its adults than his bedroom and bed, no more of the world and the night and what they presented to *Cindermead* than sleep.

But she said, for her eyes still required information no denial could melt the casing of, "Come with me, black boy."

Once more, they left the house, she moving intemperately but directly as a fever, he shambling behind her and tripping on the tussocks and boulders of the glassy floors, the jagged lumps of who-knew-what that protruded from the planished paths and drive. She glided along the drive to where the whale-oil lamps on each of the two gate-posts lit their area inside and outside the wall.

She stood, beyond the funnels of light, in a place from which she could direct her eyes towards Asnetha Sleep's window. Teapot shivered near her, and fell into misery-riddled half-dozes. She was so motionless that she might have taken root in the black earth, a superior shrub in the windless night.

Finally, composed of furtive subtleties and making no more disturbance than a swirling of atoms, came the sound she waited for . . . the departure of Queely Sheill. Since her eyes saw nothing, her mind composed pictures of that departure . . . the windows swinging outwards, Queely Sheill climbing through, the windows closing, he advancing, she thought, dangerously among shrubs and by the dead fountain, towards the drive.

"Quiet, black boy," she breathed, "or I shall kill you."

Her whisper stilled his trembling; she stilled herself more thoroughly, substracting the core of her person; her breathing was as minimized as that of any vegetable or leaf.

But he did not come as she had thought.

Suddenly, she guessed he had left the grounds by the wicket-gate at the end of the wall. At the moment of guessing, a whistling began from the direction of the gate, and she heard soles shamelessly and malely crunching and striking Sandy Bay Road—anyone's road—lecher's road, governess's road, artist's, cripple's, official profiteer's, cow-hand's, saint's, simpleton's.

Computing to the finest degree the speed of the advancing footsteps, using every sense faultlessly, she knew when the oncomer would reach the field of light sown by the gate-lamps. At a moment her senses correctly chose as the right one, she grasped Teapot with revulsion by the elbow, flung back her head to slide her long hair from her shoulders, and walked on to the drive, saying, clearly, so strikingly and maternally, that the mountain ridge could have received unsmudged those brilliant and rounded sounds:

"Do you feel less faint in the air, black boy? Does your head still ache? . . . oh!"

For Lady Knight, sympathetically trying to comfort a distressed fellow-creature by a breath of cooling air, it was startling, so late at night, so remote from the busy town, to be observed, so half-dressed, in a Christian mood.

"Oh, you quite startled us!"

Queely Sheill—it was unmistakably he and his hair and perfect profile—was unmistakably putting on his cap preparatory to striding or even loping.

"Is that you, Mr Pennyback?"

She had made her hand swing up to her breast, and was pretending confusion in front of a Mr Pennyback, but when Queely Sheill took off his cap again and stopped, his face turned towards them, she replaced her confusion with hauteur due to the manifest companion of a sickly artist who was certainly a convicted forger, and maybe, an unconvicted murderer.

"Oh!" she said. "*Oh!* I am *indeed* mistaken. Come, black boy! It was unwise of us," and turned, elated, and walked back along the drive towards the house.

"You will need to bathe completely tomorrow, black boy. Go directly to your bed. You get no sherry wine from me," she said as they reached the portico.

Teapot began vomiting in a bed of auriculas.

She left him there, and entered the house, and went upstairs.

Queely Sheill had replaced his cap, and was walking in the blackness as a man might at any funeral, even his own, nevertheless he again whistled. It was a thinner, clearer whistling, too piercing in its sweetness for the senses. It was the whistling of a disturbed mind.

9

The season, which should have been spring weeks before, had persisted throughout those weeks, that year, in eternizing winter, despite an uprising of snowdrops, daffodils and some primroses, all of wincing sorts and unable to indicate fully what they might have indicated, even in gardens that had a gardener, let alone in gardens no bigger than Brummagem tea-boards in front of the cottages in the streets climbing steeply up from Salamanca Place.

"How provokingly short their stems!" the women had said informatively to each other and, having thus reminded themselves by the shortness of stems of the length of winter, huffily rustled their petticoats, and pined yet again to wear black stockings which were bad form in winter, and to put off velvet which could scarcely with propriety, and certainly not with the approval of the discerning, be worn beyond winter. Those women who were wilder ladies—for such considerations were only for ladies—had insisted to themselves that spring was rather a numeral on a calendar than a lessening of sleet, and had boldly and somewhat raffishly contracted quite modish chills in silks and crêpes. Women who were corroborated ladies, or women who had supposed themselves so despite the oppugn evidence that their husbands sold Turkey raisins and sperm candles, or japanned water-jugs and slop-jars, or union shirting and nankeen, abided by what their persistent chilblains indicated, and saw the jonquils as demented.

However, Friday announced clearly, and ratified, what Wednesday and Thursday had already mumbled: that spring had arrived. There were, they all said to each other, evidences of the season, on *every* hand. Acne was brighter; there were seven-at-one-blow cases of gaol distemper; new carpet-beaters were bought and extra supplies of mottled soap, to thrash out and scour out the last of winter; at the Apothecaries' Hall the sale of fresh and active leeches and purgatives increased.

At *Cindermead*, Ferris, the groom, borrowed Turner's Letter Writer from Romney, the butler; Rose Knight and Asnetha Sleep slept late and dirty, and were seasonably languid, muddy of eye and glue-tongued; Teapot was considered by the servants to be in some sort of ungenial fever.

The sun shone in a most tonic fashion on the auricula bed where Teapot had been sick; the peacocks exulted artificially and vulgarly; one sow and ten piglets teetered on high heels in the remoter paddocks; another sow, gravid yet, added branches patiently to her childbed nest; the gardener was heard singing like a seal among the cauliflowers; four perfectly upright pikes of smoke ran towards the blue sky from *Cindermead* chimneys.

The servants dared not wake Lady Knight more fully: a slow, coldly chaste voice had already driven the petal-footed maid from the bedroom . . . it was the voice they could not ever forget having heard warn hare-lipped Cathleen of the House of Correction and the treadmill. It was the voice of one whose warning was execution. Opinion among the servants was that, even if Teapot were at the operation of dying, she would do nothing except arise, strangle him to feverless death, commit them all to the cat-o'-nine-tails, and return to her bed. They knew she could not bear him. But his demise without her assistance or condonement, for Sir Sydney had gone to his office in Government House, was unthinkable and dangerous; information of Teapot's state would have to be conveyed by the black boy's mistress to the mistress of the house.

Three times Megan had attempted to bring the news to Miss Sleep's attention but three times was cut down by savage groans from beneath the bed-clothes, or vixenish screams of, "Away, Taffy! Away, flat-foot! Away, or I shoot to kill!"

Romney, at length, girded himself, fussily brushed no crumbs from and straightened his waistcoat, came to Miss Sleep's door, and tapped. There was no answer. There was a defiant quality in the silence behind the door, a mutinous quality. He nibbled his cracked and flaking lips meanly, licked them, straightened his vest crooked, and tapped again, more times, more loudly. That done, licking again, he spoke severely, but with professional gentility:

"Medem, poo-er little Teapot is hailing. We are enxious."

"Who is that? Who *is* that? It cannot be that vile wine-bibbing Romney . . . can it? A vile wine-bibbing monster!" shrieked the voice of Miss Asnetha Sleep.

" 'Tis Romney, medem. We are enxious about poo-er Teapot."

"Oh, oh, oh! I am not allowed to die! My head! My heart! Who is *there*?"

"Teapot is hailing."

"Send him to me. Send him. We shall die together."

"Medem, he's in his bed and talking peculiar . . . cook thinks a low fever. . . ."

"Go, Romney!" she screamed. "Go away to hell!"

He went, smug and relieved, in the knowledge that she was fully awake, and would come.

Presently, they heard her bell, and the more melodious and carrying voice:

"Megan! Flat-foot Taffy! Romney! Bring my chair! Fools and wine-bibbers, come and get me!"

Without her stays, she lolled in the bath-chair in wrapper and shawls, a great night-cap of lace and ribbons hiding whatever hair and whichever ringlets were her own. She had swiftly taken two glasses of port wine, and put on all her rings, in an attempt at restoration. Romney wheeling, they came, in a thick nimbus of scent, to Teapot's bedroom.

Still in his dressing-gown, Teapot lay beneath the bed-clothes, as flat and straight and dead-centre of the bed as a corpse. He stared at the ceiling with a black fixity as though his sight made it a pane on some landscape beyond even that blue umbrella of spring through which the source of light lit up the welts of the foothills, the ten-catty boxes of souchong on New Wharf, the holy-stoned window-sills, the garments spread on bleaching greens, the mother-of-pearl surface of the Estuary, the medallions of snow plastered on Organ-pipe.

"Home," Teapot was saying with unassuming distinctness, and had long been saying, and intended to keep on saying, "home, home, home, home. . . ."

"He keeps on et it, medem," said Romney in a choosy way, nipping his vowels. "Since before breakfest, poo-er child, end too hailing to teek none."

". . . home, home, home, home . . ." persisted Teapot.

"Away, all of you! Such a crush!" said Asnetha Sleep. "To your duties! Back to the kitchen, cook! Barley water!"

They withdrew, somewhat sulky, for they wished to tarry, with their clay-red hands folded piously under their aprons, to observe the working-out of the sum.

". . . home, home, home, home. . . ."

Since they were being ejected, they wished calamity on Miss Sleep although not on Teapot whom they all loved as fools love a pet lamb which they will eat when it is less engaging.

When they had all gone away to murmur against her, she listened to him for twenty *homes*, then said, fairly gently:

"Teapot, treasure. 'Tis your much kindlier than kindly Miss Sleepy. With a migraine *beyond* imagination. But *here* at her treasure's side. Cease, Teapot, and tell me what ails you."

". . . home, home, home, home, home, home. . . ."

She placed her hand on his forehead. He jerked his head sideways from under, without ceasing to utter:

". . . home, home, home. . . ."

Her eyes narrowed at his rebuff. Her body had one of its spasms.

"Teapot," she said, "you are up to mischief. Be quiet."

". . . home, home, home. . . ."

"Quiet, sauce-box!" she shrilled so loudly that her headache stopped, and he stopped.

"I am a sauce-box. I must be quiet."

"Indeed, you *must*. I've a headache. I too am sick."

"The wine," began Teapot, still stiffly supine, and attracted by a new idea, "the wine, wine, wine. . . ."

"Yes, the wine."

"I was sick in a garden-plot."

"Very *well*, aggravating beast, I allowed you too much port wine. Ungrateful boy! Wine-bibber!"

"I . . . want . . . to . . . go . . . home."

"You're home. This is . . ." She jibbed. That was *not* home.

"I want to go to your home. I want lady-mama."

"Teapot, treasure, you know she is in heaven."

"Home," said Teapot, "home, home, home. . . ."

She did not attempt to stop him. She found that she too wished to leave *Cindermead*, Hobart Town, Van Diemen's Land, and return home. Slumped in her bath-chair, she had a strong vision of Brighton. She perceived that she yearned to see the carriages spanking along the Parade, the plumed bonnets nodding up the terraced streets, the naked bathers, the stony beach and fashionable waves, the donkeys, the Pavilion. . . .

"Stop!" she cried, as much to herself as to the chanting black boy. "Stop, oh, stop!"

"I must stop."

"Teapot, treasure," she said, all her silly limbs tugging about, and her jewelled hands clutching at her shawls, "we shall *go* home," and Teapot turned from the ceiling, and sat up in bed. The large glossy eyes, all pupil it seemed, stared in the large close-set grey ones with their pink whites.

"Oh, la, la, *la*! I shall set about finding a good ship . . . the *first* ship. To think of home . . . oh, cleverest of Teapots! We shall bathe this *very* morning. I shall have the Welsh one bring warm water for you and for me. We shall dress. This afternoon you shall drive me in the gig."

"I shall bathe. I shall dress. I shall drive you in the gig. Black Boy?"

"Vain monster! Black Boy . . . any horse my treasure wishes. O, my head, my head!"

"Where shall I drive?"

"Wherever thou wishest. The ships . . . the ships with white sails! The signal hill, the soldiers, the shot tower. . . wherever my Teapot wishes . . . but positively the *ships*!"

"Not where I went with ma'am."

"We shall call on Madam Bush a moment . . . she must come with her pins and tapes next week. I am in rags! Brighton would scorn me. And to Mr Tegg's library!"

"Not where I went with ma'am," said Teapot, not to be denied a reciprocal kindness.

"Wherever you . . . my head! Where did you go with ma'am, you vexing naughty?"

"A long way to get the paper from the man."

And before disinterested Asnetha Sleep could change her colours, screech, take away her alleged headache and attention from him, Teapot offered her quickly:

"The blue paper from the man with yellow hair."

Asnetha Sleep's headache returned; she became very still, jaded and blotched. Her nose slowly moved.

"You must tell Miss Sleepy of the man with yellow hair," she said. He must tell, or otherwise be tortured.

"I must tell you of the man with yellow hair. Ma'am got a blue paper from him. She threw it on the road."

He superbly mimicked Rose Knight throwing down the scorpion.

"She said, 'I have dropped my blue paper. Climb out, and pick it up, black boy.' She put it in her glove."

Once more he portrayed Rose Knight. She was seen to conceal a razor in her glove.

"Speak on, treasure," said Asnetha Sleep whose mottlings had died all to pallor.

"I must speak on. She was angry. She drove and drove. I was perfectly terrified, poor little black boy. Common people and white children called out at us. We came home."

"*We* shall go home," said Asnetha Sleep. "Ring your bell, Teapot. Ring loudly."

As the bell rang, she began to call forcefully, "Megan! Megan! Fool of a Taffy! Megan!"

When the maidservant arrived, Miss Sleep of Brighton did not scant her instructions: since Teapot was perfectly *recovered* he was to have a light *breakfast;* she herself would have the barley water she'd *told* Cook to brew; baths were to be brought to Teapot's room and *hers;* Teapot was to dress suitably for gig-driving; as soon as he was ready he was to come for her; *before luncheon* he was to wheel her in the grounds.

Before luncheon he wheeled her in the grounds. She directed him first to wheel her to a spot near the stables where she saw the groom at work.

"Tell Ferris to come here, Teapot my love. And while I talk with him, you go and talk with Black Boy."

Ferris came to her, pigeon-toed, brisk, with his yellow uneasy eyes, his foxy virility. He knew from her posture, from the fact that she had stationed herself where no ear but a passing bee's could catch what she had to say, that he walked on eggs.

"Ferris," she said, five equal and burnished ringlets hanging straight down on each side of her face, "you brought me a note the other day."

"Yuz, miss." Too much scent she used, her.

"You were taking the air on Sandy Bay Road on Sunday afternoon, you said. Come, answer me. You've said so once. La! The truth bears repetition. Taking the air. . . ?"

"Yuz, miss."

"You had a permission from Lady Knight?"

"Yuz, miss."

"You *must* take a pastille, Ferris. Your voice is fogged. A raw throat?"

"No, miss."

"You have perhaps over-used your voice—somehow *misused* it. Aggravating! If I try you *too* much you need merely nod. Or shake. *Dio mio*, I am a flibbertigibbet . . . this exquisite sunlight quite makes me forget why I am keeping you from your work. Ah, I recall, I recall, I recall. I should like the gig ready at two. Teapot will drive. Black Boy, I *think*. Let Teapot choose. But advise him. Your *honest* advice, Ferris."

"Yuz, miss."

"What *was* it, Ferris, you stole in England?"

His colour changed; he stared dumbly at her with his little earnest eyes.

"Two pencil-cases, miss." For a moment, he considered that the situation warranted no more; but dared not risk it. "A coral necklace as well, miss."

His misery charmed her. She became gracious, full of vivacity.

"Coral, Ferris! Such a *tasteful* choice. I abhor it myself... oh, a mere crotchet of mine! But how becoming to certain females. Costing—as you know—well, nothing! But I must not waste the sunlight on coral. In Sandy Bay Road you met a gentleman . . . or someone . . . who gave you a note?"

"Yuz, miss."

"Ah, pastilles, Ferris! A blue note? Folded?"

"Yuz, miss."

"Still, you have told me this before, I recall."

She touched her ringlets, each side, to each side the middle and forefinger of a hand, and smiled faintly, and jammed the white-hot torch in his face.

"He tells me he did not meet you, nor give you the note."

Ferris could not answer.

"La, la, *la*!" she said, the confused country maid. "Who tells me the falsehood? You do not answer. Your *poor* voice! Really, one meets with no relief to one's anxieties. Whom *am* I to believe?"

As he stood, his virility debased, his security threatened, his need for Turner's Letter Writer less cogent, his humiliation perfected, she exchanged confusion for melodious resolution:

"Oh, do not agonize, Ferris: I don't care to trepan you into confession. You may remain stubborn. The person positively made oath that the note was not given you by *him*. I am forced by your silence to . . . come, Teapot, treasure! . . . believe him and leave you the liar."

Teapot ran up on feet flat as bloaters.

"Come, Teapot, a turn in the sunlight, and then . . . heigh ho! to luncheon. The gig will be ready at two, Ferris?"

"Yuz, miss."

"Can I believe *that*?"

Ferris bowed his head, in assent and submission and bitter desolation.

"Push, Teapot," said the cripple, "I cannot bear the sunlight longer. We shall be in it this afternoon. To luncheon! Push, Teapot."

"I must push," said Teapot, happy as an adder.

At luncheon, Lady Knight and Miss Asnetha Sleep conversed with exquisitely proportioned light dullness and practised pointlessness.

When two women have found each other guilty of the crime of outraging, however knowingly, however much in ignorance, however deliberately, however indirectly, the privacy or hopes of the other, a space of time is needed to decide and prepare the sentence. Whether annihilation be ultimately imposed or the eternal insult of forgiveness, a preparatory disconnection from the facts of the crime is needed. An abnormal skill is brought into play to serve the purpose, and is so powerful that the pretence of no crime having been committed and therefore of no punishment being intended becomes convincing to both criminal and judge.

At luncheon, they admitted, with nice ruefulness but no complaints, too much wine at dinner the night before. Spring was discussed like a successful ballet dancer. Rose recommended the brawn as if it had been made from her own child. Asnetha was kind about the pickles, and repolished an old dream she had had success with twice in Brighton, once in Bath, and once in London, and presented it as a vision of the night before. No, dear Rose, did not want the gig for she expected visitors at four so dreadful that they would quite revivify her. Asnetha, honey, was not at all positive she would really go but her physician had recommended drives in sunlight. Rose dear, felt that Asnetha, honey, *should* go . . . perhaps she would return the boring novel to Mr Tegg, and throw it at him? Was there something different about Asnetha, honey's, rings . . . the arrangement perhaps? Rose dear, was *so* observant . . . Asnetha, honey, *had* arranged them differently now that her darling fingers had stopped *aching*.

The two actresses were able to look directly into each other's eyes as blankly and safely as dear, dear friends.

Each was abundantly alive to the skill of the other in keeping the conversation to the level of fatuity. In not displaying that consciousness they most displayed it. Yet, skilful and knowledgeable as both were, there was inadequate apprehension of all the circumstances: each utterly misunderstood the reason for the other's foolproof performance. Each one's possible plea of *Not Guilty* was already shop-soiled: Asnetha Sleep did not know that Queely Sheill had been seen leaving her room; Rose Knight did not know that her visit to Campbell Street, and chicanery with Ferris, were no longer secret. Details of the processes by which their misdemeanours had come to light were of little moment to either. Guilt was proven. Their luncheon demeanours did not reveal that there was to be a thought-out aftermath, an announcement of revengeful punishment. If nothing else, the dulling effect of too much wine, emotion and exercise the night before, restricted their conceptions of themselves, and lent the tints of truth to the social truce they both needed in which to whet their revenges.

The truce remained one for the rest of Friday; and Friday went tired to early beds.

Saturday was to be the day on which Asnetha Sleep was to sit for Mr Vaneleigh, Miss Sleep for Judas Griffin Vaneleigh.

It was, moreover, to be the day of judgement.

10

Judas Griffin Vaneleigh had recovered enough to insist on keeping his appointment at *Cindermead.*

Queely Sheill's care, and treatment from St. Mary's Hospital for the Indigent which was a convenient block away from the lodging house, had hastened recovery. Recovery gave, as recovery from physical mishap does give, a sense of relative re-invigoration. But his inmost mind knew that many more wires than ever before were missing, and for ever, from the instrument of his being. The tunes yet to be played, he knew, would be among the last; depleted tunes, briefer, eroded, waning.

He had sat, he and his cat, like two neat, grave and unsoliciting beggars, in the Friday sunlight . . . his illusion of vigour became stronger, his pride replenished itself, he slept that night as dreamlessly as the dead man he knew he soon would be. His left hand remained paralysed from the stroke he had suffered in Sandy Bay Road, a visible signal of Death's intention of fidelity and punctuality.

It hung white; it had hung, as he sat alive in the sun, white and dead. He had watched it.

On Saturday, in Saturday's sun, it hung as dead and white.

Lo, there it is, he thought, it hangs as the hand of Ellen Abernethy hung over the edge of the bed in Conduit Street . . . Fidelia standing, solemn, grand, *bewildering* . . . in a manner difficult to define . . . between the shapes of the living and the dead.

In these polished times, he thought, real character is seldom to be got at from the general tenor of conduct. The laws of the land, and the laws of society, have, together, the effect of rubbing down smooth nearly all those prominent points of the disposition, those landmarks of the mind, which separate one individual from another.

A slight word, a look, he thought, an exclamation, will often let the seemingly careless auditor deeply into the secret . . . Fidelia . . . Fidelia. . . .

Imogène: *Ah, quel moment!*

Almanzor: *Où suis-je?*

Où suis-je?

I and my dead hand sit in the spring sunshine . . . a tame and suburban swine . . . clinging to the lees of a vapid life . . . oh, base . . . unmanly . . . an action arguing a plebeian rather than a liberal and gentle descent . . . thrilled to the very marrow by the sun . . . by these raw patent yellows, Antwerp blues, cold purples, violent rose-pinks, verdigris greens . . . thrilled to the very marrow . . . and yet running riot and awry again, tormented by memory. . . .

'Tis spring . . . I had once my winter-likings . . . Fidelia, that chaste and too accurate work, polished, rubbed down smooth, avoiding calmly on jealousy-stung foot the foot-tripping roots. . . .

I must be careful how I condemn . . . though I am quite assured of an intention . . . and, besides that, pretty clear of a meaning. . . .

Où suis-je?

I read, over the arc of sunlight, the dark words of the *London Times*. . . .

On the day Miss Ellen died, Mrs Vaneleigh gave her medicine. That was about twelve o'clock. Mrs Vaneleigh went out immediately after. At two o'clock Miss Ellen was taken violently ill with convulsions. . . .

Insurance of Miss Ellen Abernethy in various offices to the amount of sixteen thousand pounds was proved, and also that Mrs Vaneleigh accompanied Miss Abernethy to the offices. . . .

James Sparrow, an attorney, deposed that on the thirteenth of December, Mrs Vaneleigh and Miss Abernethy came to him. Mrs Vaneleigh said she had a little job for him, and produced a form of assignment from an insurance office she wished him to fill up. He filled up the instrument at the dictation of Mrs Vaneleigh. Miss Abernethy took no part in the proceedings, merely signed her name. . . .

By the assignments and wills made by Miss Ellen Abernethy, Mrs Vaneleigh was placed in a situation in which the law will not allow any person to stand . . . namely that of having an interest in procuring the death of a fellow-creature by unlawful means. . . .

My wife . . . Fidelia . . . she . . . though I must pass sentence, my heart weeps while I pronounce it . . . she, Fidelia . . . of a medley fry of monsters, she the true offspring of legitimate terror. . . . A plan begun in avarice in Trunham Grove, continued in guile in the insurance offices of London, terminated in death in Conduit Street . . . the thick ankles moveless, the hand hanging still. . . .

Or . . . oh, God! . . . guess-stuff? the product of ardent imagination and mental flight? A subject for the mind to madden on? a portentous misconception not worth a Jew's eye?

No!

No, he thought, there's not an unnecessary or extraneous particle about this conception. . . . Fast and faster comes the tingling impetus, and this, running like quicksilver from my sensorium, says . . . Fidelia. One might wager a corn of salt to the continent of lost Greenland . . . Fidelia.

No friend I could trust with my condition . . . that hot coal in the hand . . . knowledge of the actual committer. . . .

Such were our relative positions, he thought, that to have disclosed this knowledge would have made me infamous where any human feeling is manifest. . . .

What to do?

I flee Fidelia . . . I stand on Boulogne Hill and see Ellen on the bed in Conduit Street. . . .

Oh, memory quick to wound and quick to heal, I see her still . . . she lies eternally . . . all hung about with rotten cobweb valances and fringes . . . richly powdered with dust and smoke-blacks . . . her hand, dead, hanging down through eternity. . . .

Already dead, my hand hangs down. . . .

You furies pouring hot upon the chase, thought Judas Griffin Vaneleigh in the sunlight, let me alone a little . . . I swore that the world which scouted me should see that I would be revenged . . . let me alone a little, thought Judas Griffin Vaneleigh fondling the cat with the hand that was not dead, let me alone a little, and I shall have finished my task. *Où suis-je?*

He heard the gulls crying over the Estuary; he saw on the Treasury walls the austere shadows of those vegetable weeds England had exported to Van Diemen's Land with the animal ones; he felt that it was almost noon and that afternoon would follow.

The afternoon weather remained superb.

Several allotments of dazzling clouds set themselves up in the manner of landscapes with uplands, wolds, steppes, gulches, isthmuses, lakes and forests. In a thousand shades of white, those landscapes offered their perspectives openly to the inhabitants of Hobart Town who, seeing on those blinding and haunting waters no lag-ship, on those slopes no prison, on those strands no warehouses, hoped for ethereal figures in perfections of robes to begin strolling there as they themselves hopelessly hoped to stroll. But no one came. The Estuary acted looking-glass to unsullied continents of vapour.

Judas Griffin Vaneleigh and Queely Sheill moved slowly towards *Cindermead* through the stairlike streets and alleys that led from torment and squalor and raffishness and guile and crudity, to more elevated points from which these elements could be looked down on and reviewed . . . mollified by distance and the sunlight to calm and beauty and quiescence and probity and mellowness. But, resting at their usual place on the summit of Barracks Hill, they had their backs to the false effect. Before them spread *Cindermead* . . . mellow too, quiescent, calm, and as beautiful as riches could make it.

"Sir," said Queely Sheill, and scratched at his chest with two hands in the manner of one who has harassed himself to an unusual decision, and was firmly skinning himself to reveal it. "Sir, with your pardon, I'll go no nearer this day. Queely'll set 'imself down by the wall 'ere, hand wait. I'll watch like a heagle; I'll race hif you stumble. But I'll wait for you *'ere*."

Mr Vaneleigh, whose sickness had refined his outline, and honed the intensity of his gaze, and slackened his perceptions, paused a little before answering:

"'Twill not be necessary for you to wait. You have already been kind."

"I wishes to wait. I can see hand watch you hall the way. Ho, 'ave no fear—like a heagle."

Mr Vaneleigh would not wrangle, and would equally, never have considered enquiry. It had never been his nature; it was less so with each departing second; the physical world infinitesimally but inexorably was sliding backward from him. He willed himself to see Queely Sheill among the transparent shades returned from the past to encompass him, he willed himself to hear him speak from among the other subtle voices:

"'Tis that I wants to sit to thinking. I been thinking, since last night, hof little black Teapot. Wanted to think this *morning* but the dad was stamping like Walking Stewart. Queely's a feeling hin 'is fugo habout the black. Queely *knows* . . . but 'e *don't* know neither, this time."

Briskly I walked, thought Judas Griffin Vaneleigh, down the Haymarket, swinging my cane with a kind of insolent confidence, singing my old favourite air *Non Piu Andrai*. . . .

"I shall," said Mr Vaneleigh, lisping and slow, "have recovered all my powers in a moment."

I whirled open the glass door of Colnaghi's, thought Judas Griffin Vaneleigh, yelling, 'There is something rotten in the State of Denmark!'

"I have seen," said Mr Vaneleigh, and Colnaghi's door slammed behind him long ago, "Walking Stewart shuffling down Garlic Hill. Shuffling as I now shuffle."

He held out his living hand which shook in the sunshine beneath the pure unexplored shires of cloud.

Queely Sheill stared at it, a beautiful fool.

"My portfolio, if you please," said Mr Vaneleigh.

"Ho, no!" shouted Queely Sheill, and a sparrow flew off the barracks' wall. "Ho, no, no, *no*! Queely never thinks when 'e's trying to think. I was thinking of the black. Queely's a bad boy; 'e must be larruped. Hof *course*, I'll come carrying. I'll come to the gates, see. But no nearer nor the gates."

"I should be in a fit of horror," said Mr Vaneleigh, "were I to mar your thinking."

"Queely's got no more gumption than . . ." He pushed back his cap, out gushed some gold, ". . . than bubble-'n'-squeak! Thinking in this sun wouldn't be worth a yennup. I'd sleep. Ho, *no*, I'll come to the gates. Then I'll brush and lope, hand stick pins in meself, hand watch, *hand* wait."

And he did not forbid himself to shout into the sunshine, in Mr Vaneleigh's direction.

"Sir, Queely was with Conky hagain, night before last. *Ho, dear!* When 'e left, there near the gates was 'er ladyship hin 'er knocking-jacket hor what-all. 'Air 'anging down. She 'ad the little black with 'er. Ho, late hit was! Mad 'as a 'atter she looked. Waiting for *Queely*. Queely knows! I knows a kill-cow look too. But I don't know *why*, not this 'ouse, I don't. Poor dear 'eart, poor little black yob . . . Queely's 'uman feelings! *Hup* again!"

Mr Vaneleigh had heard, as from another room in a house foundered in a tarn of light.

He began slowly, slowly to descend the slope.

Où suis-je?

I clapped on, he thought, I clapped on my hat furiously, the hinder part before, forced ruthlessly through the crowd—trampling on lap-dogs, and carrying away canes, parasols and umbrellas, while my spurs clanked dreadful—and rushed into the street howling, thought Judas Griffin Vaneleigh, 'There is something rotten in the State of Denmark.'

"There is something rotten in the State of Denmark," said Mr Vaneleigh.

"Take care, Queely begs, sir . . . don't tumble hover the ruts," said Queely Sheill.

"I shall not tumble over the ruts," said Mr Vaneleigh.

Follow me, thought Judas Griffin Vaneleigh, mind out: don't tumble over my hookah. Follow me through this carpeted passage, down the seven steps! Now, what say you to Judas's boudoir? An octagon thirteen feet in diameter, and full sixteen in height; light streams through rosy panes in the dome top—no other windows. Two doors are concealed with bright blue silk drapery, bordered with crimson velvet and barbaric fringe. The walls are covered with a very rich crimson French paper, formed into panels and compartments with gold mouldings; and the oak floor is spread with a glowing Persian carpet. An ottoman, matching the curtains in hue, offers its cushions to the voluptuary. Bless us, who's in the house? thought Judas Griffin Vaneleigh, here's a pair of gold scissors. . . ! Fidelia's gold scissors, and shreds of silk. . . .

Où suis-je?

"I dare not tumble," said Mr Vaneleigh mincing reservedly among the ruts, but with purpose, for there was little enough time left; St. Mary's Hospital for the Indigent, so conveniently a block away from his lodging-house, awaited him.

The bucklings of Sandy Bay Road had to be conquered, the gate-posts of *Cindermead* passed through before he could put down in pencil and brush what Asnetha Sleep's eyes were whispering in each other's ears through the crinkled partition of her nose.

Queely Sheill came no farther than the first gate-post and, having ceased speech some yards before they reached that gate-post, made calligraphic signs on the air to indicate faithfulness, drew a blue-headed pin from his coat to indicate wakefulness, tapped his forehead to indicate his resolve to think about Teapot, and withdrew to the other side of the roadway and concealed himself behind a tree to be faithful, awake, thoughtful, and to wait.

Not much more than two hours later, Mr Vaneleigh returned. Queely Sheill took the portfolio from him, and they set off towards Hobart Town. Ultimately, although he spoke as quietly as possible, the portfolio-carrier deemed himself safe, and said:

"Honour bright, Queely 'as thought and thought *hand* thought. Pricked 'isself more than winkles. Next time, I'll bring back the little black's chain. Ho, *yes*. Next time, bring the chain. *Hand* a nice knob of suck to make the poor little black 'eart 'appy."

"We shall not, I think, come this way again," said Mr Vaneleigh, pale and faint, but steadily moving.

"Ho!" said Queely Sheill, his thinking gone for nothing.

"Miss Sleep sat well, saving some spasms resulting from her unfortunate ailment. She has so original a countenance that I was able to complete the portrait."

"*Ho!*" said Queely Sheill. "Then Queely'll 'ave to think *hagain*. But I'll find a way to make Teapot 'appy *some'ow*. Was't a good likeness of Conky?"

"If hung in London 'twould make me all the rage. It is", said Mr Vaneleigh of the last portrait he was ever to do, "the best thing I have ever done."

"La, la, la! One positively does not know *what* to say," said Asnetha Sleep, holding the portrait at arm's length. She sat yet in the chair she had been drawn in.

Sir Sydney was seeing the artist to the door, and paying him.

Rose Knight had appeared in the drawing-room.

She wore something which had hitherto, until that moment, been charming, apt to the day and season, and a fit adornment of her person, but which was too frivolous, too young, too light, too striped, for what her demeanour at that moment showed she was. She should have worn, not Pekin silk cut and stitched for springtime and wit, but a downpouring burden of dark folds, and a cuirass of jet.

She appeared, stood there. She awaited Sir Sydney. She regarded the woman on whom she had come to impose her sentence.

Asnetha Sleep continued examining the portrait.

"One *does* not know," she said, "what to *think*! My ringlets are certainly there, and wonderfully glossy. One would think macassar! Oh, he has caught the *gloss* to a nicety. And that nose is undoubtedly my nose."

She laughed, and quite happily, as if she were someone else laughing at someone else.

"Even a less accomplished artist than he," she said, "could scarcely not give value to my *nose*. It is, indeed, a well-caught likeness. One wonders only about the *expression* . . . one wonders if one *has* that expression. Tell me, Rose dear. The expression. Has one?"

Rose Knight advanced. Beneath the flutter and susurration of silk were secreted the dark robes of obnoxious justice, composed and inflexible as iron—the black hems ready to flash from beneath the ruched silk.

She took the proffered drawing. She held it out, and appeared to be analysing it. She was still acting dispassionate deliberation when Sir Sydney returned.

"A charming fellow, quite," he said. "Is his portrait equally charming?"

Rose Knight extended the paper towards him, her arm as rigid and unmistakable as her voice saying:

" 'Tis an excellent portrait of a harlot."

Before Sir Sydney or Asnetha Sleep could say anything or remain silent long enough to show that either or both proposed uttering nothing, she no longer pretended silk, but clanked her metal folds, and shone like a weapon:

"You are aware, Asnetha, of my reason for speaking so? You admit that this is the representation of a harlot? You understand what I mean?"

Asnetha Sleep was ready. She wore her new and more controlling stays, and her own information about Rose Knight, hidden both, but was strengthened by them.

"Were I *able* to do so, I expect I should walk straight from this room. You are odious, Rose, but I understand what you mean."

"I do not, Asnetha," said Sir Sydney, at a loss from, and irritated by, lack of information. "*I* do not understand what you mean, Rose."

"I have accused your cousin of harlotry."

"Do not luxuriate in your coarseness, Rose. I understand what you've said of her. . . ."

She interrupted, in an ambushing manner:

"Such women . . . ach! . . . such *trollops* would be beyond your experience."

Sir Sydney put down the portrait, and looked distinguished:

"You err, madam. When I was younger they were not outside my experience. I have too perfectly understood your accusation. I wish to know your reason."

"Your cousin . . . she there, who *can* not walk straight from the room . . . will tell you."

Asnetha Sleep looked cryptically out between her ringlets, an unfortunate six-each-side:

"Dear Rose, I shall be mute on this. I shall certainly tell nothing."

"I must, then, speak for you." And she faced the cripple; she smiled scissors: "You do, dear Asnetha, understand that, for you yourself, I have no anxieties. I have never considered myself your keeper. You are old enough to designate your vices; to choose your partners in them from whichever gutter or rookery whim suggests. As mistress of this house, however, I regret . . . I grieve . . . I'll not *tolerate* . . . that you use *Cindermead* for your entertaining. There are the servants than whom you are no better. There is your pet negro boy . . . a child whatever else. There is . . ."

"Pray, be quiet, Rose," said Sir Sydney, and the bruised skin encircling his eye gave him a useful air of piratical potency. "Since your detraction is plainly for *my* ears, pray be quiet until you can accuse directly. Have you any proof of what you call a partner?"

"Asnetha will surely inform you. She can no longer gammon judicious reticence. She has already been shameless beyond imagination."

"Rose is as well able to tell you," said Miss Sleep of Brighton, she and her jewels at rest and quite aglow. "I should *never*, you realize, Sydney, have taken up your time with accusations against myself. La! it does you no harm to know. Equally, you derive no good from this knowledge. La, la, la! How stupid I have been! I blame myself, for it is useless to pretend I'm blameless. I blame myself, not for my indiscretion, about which I could hardly have been more discreet, but for my bucolic belief that Rose would never meet my partner."

Asnetha Sleep then smiled.

Sir Sydney, misunderstanding, said sharply enough:

"We shall, I hope, let the matter rest there. *I* shall have something to say, but *you've* both said too much. You have both exposed enough of the privacies of this house."

Rose Knight looked at him with paler eyes.

"You are your own fool," she said. "Privacies! They are already exposed *far* beyond this house."

She ceased there, and knew that his imagination had already sped as far as broadsheets, and footmen whispering to footmen.

"Beyond?" he said, and stroked his whiskers as though the question was long-headedness and not fear.

"Beyond," she said. "Her love is a Campbell Street lout who comes to her after she has said her prayers. His imprints are probably all over the tulip bed and hers."

"Campbell Street!" A lover from hell would not have horrified him; hell was another country.

Both women smiled, equally archaically and to themselves, for differing unmerciful reasons. He perceived that he was masculine and alone. He spoke next very softly:

"I have already been most aware of your vulgarity, Rose. You need not attempt it further in inferior epigram. Since, Asnetha, you've made no denial, this tale of a lover I assume to be true. The fact of a lover I am indifferent to. I have a wife. The kind of lover is, however, a concern of mine. Campbell Street! But no one lives there. It is not . . ." He hoped he had hit it. ". . . one of the medical students."

"A medical student," said Rose Knight, before the cripple could speak, "would be apter; love and a medical opinion at one blow. La! 'Tis no medical student pursuing the study of disjointed anatomy. 'Tis your charming Mr Vaneleigh's shadow. The cockney oaf!"

He moved to the cripple, and stood over her:

"Asnetha! Asnetha, have you lost all care for propriety?"

" 'Twas late at night," said Asnetha Sleep. "My door was locked. The curtains were most carefully drawn."

"You are crazed!" He did not raise his voice. "You are

also cynical, insolent and ungrateful. Of your immodesty I say nothing, but shall certainly oversee your consumption of port wine. Crazed! This is a small and backbiting community; the fellow is no gentleman—God knows how long and foul his tongue is!"

"He would say nothing," cried Asnetha Sleep, and on behalf of Queely Sheill. Then she said, and she was bitter, "If he were. A one to talk. To have been. In *my* bed would hardly. Be a subject. For vainglory."

"Those sorts talk of nothing else. Of any conquest. Of you or any woman. Indeed, of imagined women! A success in your room, locked or unlocked, will not be kept a secret. Foul befall him! You are crazed, crazed, crazed. You might as well have received your fancy man on the lawns of Government House in a marquee open to the public!"

"He will say nothing," she said, and all her limbs revolted and jerked about. When she was still again:

"Sydney," she said, "I speak truth, and this is no consequence of this scene, but yesterday I decided that I wish to take the next ship for England. I regret I have stayed just long enough to leave my loss of reputation in the gutters of Campbell Street."

"The gutters! You will leave it in the drawing-rooms of Hobart Town, unless steps are taken. The gutters alone I should not mind. But the gutters of Campbell Street can flow uphill. Through back-doors. Into parlours. Into inkwells. To London! You are both aware that I have every hope from His Excellency of an advancement. 'Tis the one I've for years set my heart on. This is exactly not the moment to have a scandal. Great God, you recall what the tongues of Hobart Town can do—a governor himself recalled by Mr Gladstone earlier this year."

"He will say *nothing*. He is an honest man."

Perceiving the cripple's conviction, Rose Knight said:

"Asnetha, honey, you are positively mistaken. Ah, love's blindness! He is a thief."

Asnetha Sleep found this too amusing:

"Your knowledge of him—dear Rose—is perfectly extraordinary. How did you know he was my lover?"

"I saw him leave your room by the window on Thursday night."

"Oh!" But she rallied. "Ah, you were. About late, Rose, my love . . . I do remember now. Your novel. Was a bore. You chose to spy."

"One is not a spy in one's own house. One needs to *inspect*, however, when one has an abnormal guest. Events have proved, surely, Asnetha, my love, that I was wise to have doubts."

" 'Twere wiser still, Rose, to have had no doubts at all . . . to know in detail the lover, the day, the place, the very hour."

Sir Sydney sharply said, "Asney, what do you imply?"

"That Rose not only reads my private correspondence, and eavesdrops at doors and windows, but is also an accomplice. She carried the note from my lover to me."

"I gave you no note."

"You would hardly be shameless enough to thus reveal your visit to Campbell Street . . . I dare not hazard a guess *why*."

"Your lover lies. I took no note from him."

"Ferris, then, also lies. He got no note from you."

"Your oaf lies. I repeat that he lies. He has your sanction to visit you. Asnetha, I could pity you. 'Tis the *house* he wishes to visit, not the crippled guest in it. Why does he trail the convict artist? To visit the house, to observe its plan, so that he may plunder in the safety of knowledge. What else has been stolen I cannot tell, but your black creature has been robbed. . . ."

"Teapot! Rose, you are. A wicked woman. You are not. To be believed."

"Enquire of your swarthy imp!"

They had become noisy. Sir Sydney silenced them with inclement softness:

"I beg you both to stop. I've listened enough and heard enough, and wish to hear no more and know no more of your mischief than I do. Let me forgo the pleasure of disentangling further luxuries of recollection. Whether the one or the two of you engaged this swashbuckler as lover leaves me indifferent. Were he a gentleman, he could only be pitied. But as he is no gentleman, he is dangerous to *my* peace. I'll not have his tongue loose in the streets of Hobart Town with the suggestion that I run a house of ill-fame. If he *has* light fingers so much the better."

Sir Sydney walked to the door. He opened it and called, "Teapot! Teapot! Teapot!" From the distance came the music of Teapot agitating his bells in reply.

Sir Sydney turned back to the women.

"I shall find out, if that be possible, whether this hanger-on of Vaneleigh's is as nimble-fingered as he is an inflammatory influence on the . . . I had been about", said Sir Sydney, whiskered like a man, and pitiless as a woman, "to say ladies."

"I foretold," said Lady Knight, "that the introduction of a murderer into the house would. . . ."

"Mr Vaneleigh has done nothing except most skilfully portray you both with a crayon. I fear he was underpaid. Mr Vaneleigh, Rose, was transported for a forgery. You are in error about him, you were in error about me, you were both in grave error about Mr Vaneleigh's fellow. When I saw him it seemed to me fit and proper to take him to the stables. It seemed fit and proper to you to take him to your beds."

At the doorway the little bells musically preceded the entrance of the black boy.

"Come in, Teapot," called Sir Sydney, and Teapot, gorgeous in his embroidered coat, his ear-rings, his bracelet of bells, entered, and instantly knew that he was at last a god and that the words were his. Beneath him, far far beneath him, were three creatures whose posture and eyes demanded something.

"Teapot, treasure, come to your. . . ."

"Be quiet, Asnetha. Stand where you are, Teapot," said Sir Sydney.

"I must stand where I am."

"Teapot, I wish you to answer a question, and you must answer truthfully."

"I must answer truthfully."

Rose Knight did not move, but her voice overrode Sir Sydney's:

"Black boy, who has your gold money on a chain?"
"The man!"
"Which man?" Sir Sydney's voice was milk.
"Ma'am knows the man. Miss Sleepy knows the man. He has my lady-mama's money on a chain."
"Oh, Teapot, treasure! Teapot tell the truth, the truth. For Miss Sleepy, tell the truth!"
Asnetha Sleep pleaded, she pleaded almost raucously, she pleaded that she had been visited for herself by the handsome man, she pleaded not to be humiliated.
"Tell the truth, Teapot. Has the man really got your chain? Treasure, the *truth*!"
Teapot's voice had never been clearer, purer in diction, more truthful, and more destructive. His bells tinkled.
"I must tell the truth. The man has really got my lady-mama's chain."
Asnetha Sleep hid her face in her jewelled hands.
"You must tell Sir Sydney," said Rose Knight, "that you saw the man through your bedroom window."
"I must tell Sir Sydney that I saw the man through my bedroom window," said Teapot. He rattled his bracelet. "With my shining black eyes."
"You saw him take it from the drawer."
"I saw him take it from the drawer."
"You asked him for it in the Chinese room."
"I asked him in the Chinese room."
"That is enough, Rose," said Sir Sydney. "I have heard *enough*. Run, Teapot, to Ferris. Tell him to saddle Pale Lady. You shall ride to Hobart Town for me."
They listened to the slapping soles, and the bells, and the door slamming far away.
"I shall go to my study," said Sir Sydney. "I shall write an information for the Police Office. You will both, I pray you, be here when I presently return. Ring for Romney, Rose. I wish for brandy. Asney should have some also . . . unless her preference is otherwise. As it will be. But remain. There are still things to be said."
Sir Sydney left the room.
Asnetha Sleep, when at last she was sure that the ugly

blood of shame had been drawn off the canton of her face, removed from before it the screen of freckled skin and gem-thickened metal circles. She could be looked at again. But neither of the two women looked at each other, nothing in each other's faces would have given refreshment; except for a sick lassitude, there was nothing to see. They said nothing for there was nothing to say. Whatever graces or artifices of communication they were in possession of, whatever compassions and allegiances, whatever of gentler honesties, had fled like girls when the more maniac honesties had lunged on to the field. Their hatreds, capriciously accoutred, had confronted, had spurred towards each other in brittle and ornate armour, and whirled their brilliant rags at each other. Neither had won nor lost. Negativized, in ostentatious exhaustion, they had reeled apart and, regardless of each other, listened to the circling eddies of wind from their *pas de deux* of conflict distantly combining to breed a blizzard that was already taking the black boy upon its crest, and would, in its time, rebound to them and whirl them and their depravities to fulfilment.

Presently, Sir Sydney came back to the silent drawing-room with the air of one consciously forbearing yet nevertheless a headmaster who has expelled the devil.

No one had rung for Romney. Uncertain whether forgetfulness or defiance were responsible, but needing brandy more than information, Sir Sydney rang. When Romney had gone, he said:

"What has occurred this afternoon need not be spoken of again, to *me* . . . what you say to each other—if, indeed you've anything further to say to each other—I care not. I shall regard the matter as dropped—at least until such time as a new consideration needs to be given to the complexity of facts. This cognac is admirable. The facts are, I am in no doubt, veritable. In your empty-headedness you have both been lucid. That is, you have both got as near lucidity as females ever do get . . . your mutual jealousy has wonderfully stimulated that lucidity. I can only repeat that, were your amorous felon a gentleman, I should commiserate with him.

"You have been unfair to me, Rose. That I have never found in you before, and should be shocked . . ." He touched the corner of his blackened eye. ". . . did I not realize that your recent lapses in ethics were a concomitant of your age. Your showy behaviour in the gig has come to my ears, and has been suitably accounted for. I know you too well to suppose that you'd care to be divorced. When my new appointment is confirmed, and we are again in London, I shall be only too happy to give you every assistance in making you a rejected woman, ageing and immoral. But I shall see, in the meantime, that you continue to appear a sane and respectable wife. I suggest that you take no lovers—even if at your age you can induce a *gentleman* to share your incontinence—until my appointment is confirmed. In fact, I forbid it. If I have failed you in bed, I have not in leniency. Pray, give that leniency its due—you formerly have. Continue to do so. Whips are not needed, nor melodramatics. A bruised eye is painful, but is nothing . . . you've long ago bruised my heart and inner being to an extent that makes a bruised eye less than negligible. Moreover, since I had struck you, the blow in return can only be quibbled about in the matter of its being public. Ferris will remain here, where his tongue is clipped."

He poured brandy. He sniffed, and sipped.

"Asney, you may return by the next ship. I hope you will not; I think you will not. A Dr Wake whom I met at the Club the other evening is to visit us within a day or two. He is gifted, quite charming, more gentlemanly than many who aspire to that quality in Hobart Town, and is well-connected. He is a bachelor, Asnetha, of Rose's age. And a cripple. You are a woman of resources . . . a control upon feverish affectation and the intake of port wine . . . who knows! He expresses a desire to meet you. From Miss Sleep to Mrs Wake . . . I find a nice symbolism in the thought. I leave it with you.

"Teapot is riding to Hobart Town, to the Police Office. I have asked for your former lover to be apprehended on suspicion."

It is most necessary, in a world too lavish of all things, to be miserly, for that is what abundance and plenty perversely advise the mind. A mean activity, says the mind, is preferable to the apathy of mere acceptance.

With prideless parsimony, that baronet and those two women, had raked the hours for sops to vanity, for carnal satisfactions, for that pinchbeck felicity and power self-pity wants for itself.

"Apprehended!" cried Asnetha Sleep. "Teapot tells lies. Oh, you can never imagine the lies he tells!" She was in anguish for Miss Asnetha Sleep lest he would tell truths of her, or lies of extraordinary and unfitting colour. "Oh, oh, *oh*, he tells such lies!"

"We all tell lies," said Sir Sydney. "We all tell lies, dear cousin. Tomorrow, we must go to church."

On the horse of diamonds and flame, the enchanted and beloved prince flew along the amber road.

On Pale Lady, Teapot galloped along Sandy Bay Road. His bells unceasingly splashed out their sparkling tune; his embroidered coat of gold and many colours fluttered and gleamed; his ear-rings shone; he had cut his hand on the dirk stuck in his sash—the blood kept running out as though from a blood-letting that was freeing him of his terrors and doubts and jealousies. Now and then he wiped his glistening hand of blood on the shining mane.

Ahead of him, Mr Vaneleigh and Queely Sheill had moved slowly along the road, had crossed Sandy Bay Bridge, and were half-way up the bank of Barracks Hill, when the tattoo of hoofs on the bridge-planks made Queely Sheill turn.

As he turned, Teapot, who had expected to see him last of any mortals at that moment, perceived who he was and, without thought, dismayed and alarmed, reined in the horse.

To Queely Sheill that seemed a gesture of salutation. He was holding his cap in his hand; he waved it, and ran into the middle of the road and capered about.

"Oh, sir, 'tis the black come to talk! Dear black 'eart!"

Teapot set his horse in motion again, struck it to galloping, and advanced towards Queely Sheill. He snatched the dagger from his sash and brandished it aloft, and rode straight at the elated man, who would have been run down had not Mr Vaneleigh cried, "Back! Oh, stand back!" so loudly that Queely Sheill swiftly moved, and the horse shattered the space he had a moment before filled.

Thus Teapot galloped barbarically by in the declining sunlight, his teeth bared like a warrior's, his eyes wide and maddish, the dirk held high above the ceaseless bells, the coat badged with flourishes of gold, the mane streaked with blood.

Queely Sheill was aghast. His lips had withdrawn their colour.

"Queely thought . . ." he said, biting at his knuckles. "Queely thought . . . Oh, they 'ave been bad to Teapot."

He struck at his forehead.

"They 'ave done 'im some 'arm. I thought to see blood."

The horse and rider reached the top of the hill, and seemed stuck there, curvetting mysteriously as for ever against the sky, objectified denunciation scarring the luminosity beyond, before tipping out of sight like a runaway rocking-horse.

"And I looked," said Mr Vaneleigh, "and behold a pale horse! And his name that sat on him was Death, and Hell followed him."

"I don't com-pre-'end."

"The bible," said Mr Vaneleigh. "The fourth seal was broken . . . and behold a pale horse!"

"Queely's hignorant," said Queely Sheill, and the horse with its blood-blotted mane and the rider with his bloodless snarl having sunk from sight, the hoofbeats and bells ran out of the air, and the two men, for the last time, climbed to the top of the hill.

"I do not," said Mr Vaneleigh, after a little, as they looked down on Hobart Town which a powdery saffron haze gave the appearance of a suburb of a holy city. "I do not, for a fraction, infer that your little . . . *protégé* is Death, or that Hell follows with him. However, the bible does continue . . . 'And power was given unto them over the fourth part of the earth, to kill with the sword, and with hunger, and with death . . .' Beneath that mist of splendour. . . ."

He indicated with his living hand the town beneath.

". . . might lie a very compact of the fourth part of the earth."

"Queely's hignorant. 'E don't need no bible. Poli's got a bible with pictures. But Queely don't need none. 'E's a good boy."

They descended the hill, the one with agonizing circumspection and dignity, and laden with doom, the other radiant and seemingly immortal with his unruly appetite for a clemency that was for ever beyond his powers.

Queely Sheill plunged towards his future.

Mr Vaneleigh trailed his past; his future too short to be contemplated; his forces at the lowest ebb.

I sneaked home, thought Judas Griffin Vaneleigh, to Great Marlborough Street; poked in the top of my hollow fire which spouted out a myriad of flames; exchanged my smart, tight-wasted, stiff-collared coat from an easy chintz gown; and established myself cosily on a Grecian couch. Having first placed on the table a genuine flask of rich Montepulciano, the maid-servant, a good-natured, Venetian-shaped girl, closed the door, carefully rendered air-tight by a gilt-leather binding. I instinctively filled a cut-glass of the liquor, meanwhile stroking into a sonorous purr my favourite tortoiseshell cat. . . .

" 'Ere's puss awaiting," said Queely Sheill at the doorstep of No. 8 Campbell Street, Hobart Town, that sunset, that day, that year, and he gave Mr Vaneleigh the portfolio, and they parted, and never saw each other again.

With the last of the sun in his eyes, for it was about to subside behind Organ-pipe Mountain, Queely Sheill walked dreamily towards Playhouse Cottage.

Already the shadow of the mountain had seeped downhill, from the graveyards and chapels and hospitals and the Penitentiary, and over the cottage. Queely Sheill, in the yet unshadowed lower of the street, halted, soaked and glowing with sunset's spilling, to stare at the extravagant billows of fire, and the islands of gilt that sailed the writhing currents above the mountain.

His face was a rose. His hair was gilt. It was as though to a man of flame, breathing in rations of coloured air blandly and without savouring on them the acrid seasoning of danger, that Polidorio Smith burst from the cottage, tottering, and screaming:

"Fly, Apollo, fly! A stag! Oh, mind your eye—a stag!"

His long shadow poured down towards Queely Sheill, his huge ears shone transparently, his face was a berserk clown's, he was disaster itself.

Dazzled by light and amazement, greeting destiny in a blaze of beauty, Queely Sheill stood still as the distraught frame stumbled nearer.

The sun snatched back its final shafts of light; Polidorio Smith tripped on the shadows, and fell in them. Crashing from the cottage in pursuit, a police officer reached the fallen actor, and struck him with the flat of his cutlass. The contagion of disaster, like the shadow of Organ-pipe, reached and broke over Queely Sheill.

"Fly! Double-quick! A stag! A stag!" Polidorio Smith screamed desperately.

"You snot! You bloody snot! I'll stag you!" cried the officer striking again and again, while the other continued to scream, "They've come for you! Fly!"

As Queely Sheill ran towards them, the officer straightened up from his belabouring, his cutlass ready for the newcomer, his eyes conscious of forms emerging all about, from the walls, the ground, the shadows.

Years of being under the influence of a disorderly imagination had made Polidorio Smith cowardly, but his love for Queely Sheill was strong enough to fortify his spirit. He entangled his long monkey-weak arms about the officer's knees, and brought him heavily down, and grappled with him.

Pistol drawn, another officer ran from the cottage towards the group where Queely Sheill had dragged Polidorio Smith away from his opponent and kneeled beside him and his bloody face.

From the walls and the dust and the shadow, it seemed; from the quagmire under the Palladio, it seemed; and from the weeds below the hospital cliff, it seemed; and the rat-warrens in the sandstone, it seemed; an effusion of beings had silently floated, and silently encircled the central four.

They watched.

They waited on Queely Sheill.

They watched from eyes veined like leaves and as hooded as their servilities were; they watched from faces in which scars of bygone desires branched among the scars of smallpox and the scars of hunger; they watched from under hair hanging like grasses withered on the banks of despair. Blemished, smelling of torment and the decay of peace, they watched an officer hold a chain weighted with coins towards Queely Sheill, they watched lips moving, and the head of golden hair nodding acquiescence.

The teeth missing from their gums were already bared in their snarling hearts . . . a gesture, a whisper, from Queely Sheill, and they would swiftly and silently have shredded the officers to bones, ground the bones to pulp, and returned like shadows to the shadows.

They heard, ears and lopped ears, John Death Sheill give a vibrant and beautifully sustained note of sorrow at the cottage door where he reeled as Queely Sheill was arrested. They heard Polidorio Smith give a scale of screams like a milliner in a man-trap, screams of which the loftiest slashed the absurd curdlings of fire and gold above the mountain with a blade of terror and truth, and set flowing the dark blood of night. They heard the waters of the Rivulet pillaging its rims of their muck with a murmur of content, of smugness, as though pillage itself had a voice and a philosophy. They heard the gold sliding, crying, falling from the sky behind the mountain, and a god falling, falling, falling from his plinth.

Their shadowed bodies, their shadowed faces, their shadowed eyes, their shadowed mouths, grew darker, and from the hedge of shadows came the murmurous stir that follows on great and unbelievable disaster.

11

The Court being duly constituted, the indictment against the prisoner, Queely Sheill, charging him with the theft of a gold chain on which were strung seven gold coins, was read over.

Mr Creamly (the young, the suave, the earnestly suave, the young and earnestly suave) opened the case by saying that the crime of which the prisoner stood charged was, undoubtedly, one of greater—of far greater—magnitude than it might first appear to be; its perpetration had, in fact, been attended with no common heartlessness.

(Mr Creamly looked into four of his wonderful fingernails —left hand, fingers curled towards palm—fingernails that had surely never scratched itchy anus. He looked into his fingernails as into looking-glasses in which he practised looking into fingernails as into looking-glasses.)

He did not mean to ask them however, to pronounce a verdict of guilty on the evidence of heartlessness, nor indeed on the evidence of the impudence with which the theft was committed, but merely on the evidence of the theft itself.

Of the heartlessness (Mr Creamly's fingernails floated towards where, beneath a velveret waistcoat and a hairless chest, his heart glowed like the eye of God) he had merely to say that the victim was an innocent child, (Mr Creamly skilfully gave no masonic hint that fathers knew—even young fathers such as he—that innocence was itself lies and liar), an innocent black of tender years who had but recently arrived in the colony, and whose acquaintance with the prisoner had begun—but, alas, not ended—when the kindly boy brought him food.

(Mr Creamly's voice suggested, and his vellum-coloured hand sensitively sketched on the air, a naked and prettily pot-bellied black with a cornucopia—grapes of three sorts, melons, strawberries big as turnips, a gush of wine).

Of the audacity he had this, and only this, to say: it was an emphatic certitude that crimes—and this was important—*most*!—that crimes, especially those committed by newcomers to iniquity, were penetrated in darkness—by *stealth*, in *darkness*.

(Mr Creamly, with sonorous clouds and a night-wind of obloquy darkened the room already dark enough with the emanation from, the sinister attention given by, those who packed the court.)

If the evidence he had to adduce were substantiated and believed, the prisoner would be shown to have committed his thievery in mid-afternoon, in *full daylight*, with a brazen disregard of the possibility of intrusion by members of the household, a household composed of the family, and numerous domestic servants of Sir Sydney Knight, who were all nearby and quite constantly passing to and fro about their affairs. This singular effrontery, he suggested, was that of a man lost to all sense of shame or fear . . . who but a person so brutalized would have dared display, he might even say flaunt, his criminal art?

Whether the prisoner at the bar was, by reputation, the best or least estimable individual in society was no part of their present consideration; as false an impression of a person's hidden character could be created by the indiscriminate praise of misguided, or hoodwinked, or immoral people, as by unfounded slander.

The prisoner at the bar, Queely Sheill, whose father was an actor (Mr Creamly's exacting mouth crinkled its lips as though *actor* were *quinine*) and whose employment with his father was of a haphazard nature, leaving the son—who had been put at the bar as the unfortunate result of it—too much time in which to develop and foster dubious inclinations.

He had taken up with a ticket-of-leave man whose ability

as a portrait artist had gained him an *entrée* to the houses of eminent citizens and cultured families (Mr Creamly's mien revealed him as the darling of cultured families, although he had three children, one with scurvy), families whose nobler qualities did not lack that of pity (Mr Creamly did not visit under this stigma). These philanthropists, he needed scarcely to point out, were performing a commendable charity in encouraging the talent of, and reimbursing, this ex-convict for the products of that talent . . . a *momentary* and *commercial* acquaintance only.

Sheill had passed months, many months, in habits of acquaintance, if not of deeper intimacy, with this gifted bearer of a conditional pardon after eight years in the Penitentiary. It would seem that the prisoner at the bar, as an intimate of this recently freed man, went with him to the houses of those benevolent enough to offer him their patronage.

It was in this manner that Sheill, as hanger-on to the more gifted man . . . an unfortunate whose education and background were immeasurably superior to that of the prisoner, but whose judgement was perhaps confused and impaired by the flattery and apparent frankness of Sheill's manner . . . it was in this manner, he suggested, that Sheill had gained admittance to Sir Sydney's household.

While Lady Knight was sitting for her portrait in the drawing-room, Sheill was sent, under the charge of the child, to be made comfortable by a fire, and to be given a repast.

(Mr Creamly seemed to present, in lieu of cornucopia, a game pie, an oyster *pâté*, Moselle.)

The boy, after serving the prisoner with his own hands for the servants were occupied with other affairs at the time, left Sheill to himself, and ran off to play in the garden.

Presently, in the course of his games, he found that he was outside his own bedroom window, and perceived, through the window, some movement within the room. He imagined this movement to be made by a servant, and the frolicsome notion entered his head to steal up and, boylike, appear suddenly, and tap on the pane to startle whoever was inside. He stole along the wall to the window, and was on the very point of putting his prank into action when, to his absolute amazement, he perceived not a servant in his room but—the prisoner!

(Mr Creamly's voice rang. Many observed by the inward look in his eyes, and the delicious glaze on them, that he, with satisfaction, heard it ring, and was commending its timbre to himself.)

He watched the prisoner search through his childish possessions, and finally lift the chain of coins from a drawer. The boy immediately ran to the nearest door, and entered the house, and ultimately came to his room. But the house was large and spread-out: by the time he reached his bed-chamber, its recent visitor had vacated it. In distress the child hastened to the room in which he had left the prisoner who was again sitting there as though he had never left it, and calmly—nay, boldly, *unblushingly*—regaling himself with ale and bread-and-cheese which his victim had, a short time before, brought him.

He courageously accused the prisoner of the theft and requested—entreated rather, *pleaded*, poor child—(Mr Creamly clasped his hands, but loosely not to bruise their texture, and uplifted his eyes as in a Roman Catholic holy painting, probably Italian) for the return of his treasure which had for him a value in sentiment infinitely greater than the value in gold and, as such, was as irreplaceable as if his heart had been stolen.

The prisoner strenuously denied the theft that the boy said, and insisted stoutly on reiterating, he had seen with his own eyes, the chain actually in Sheill's hands.

With tears in his eyes (Mr Creamly hid those tears, as if they were his own, by lashes longer than a woman's and almost as long as a man's) the boy implored the return of his precious memento, promising to say naught of what he had witnessed if this were done.

At this the prisoner made a threat, vile enough if said even to the most debased and degenerate of grown humans, vile beyond all imagination when hurled at a defenceless and susceptible boy. This monstrous threat he promised in the most alarming manner to carry out if anything were said.

(Mr Creamly's features brilliantly acted classic revulsion.)

Such was the nature of his threat that the boy was too terrified for days, for weeks, to reveal that he had been robbed. This terror, so long sustained, brought on a fever and consequent nightmares, and, finally, so disrupted the balance of nature that an involuntary sleep-walking was the result. He concealed his terrors long enough for them to weaken at last his powers of further concealment, so that Lady Knight was able to penetrate his fear by her own anxiety and loving care, and the boy confessed what he had seen.

(Mr Creamly was not old enough to stop. He regarded his looking-glass fingernails, while feeding his voice with a final unconfused thought.)

They were not trying the prisoner's good character, much less his bad character—and God forbid that the laws of the country should be swayed by any such circumstances!—they were not to try whether he had been a bad man (if bad he had been) but whether he had stolen. Conversely, if he were *otherwise* as pure as an angel, it would be their duty, in justice to their fellow-creatures, to pronounce their verdict accordingly.

Orfée Maka was examined.

Orfée Maka was his name.

He must tell the truth.

Yes, he always told the truth or he would not see his lady-mama in heaven.

When? He last saw the man when he was riding Pale Lady into Hobart Town.

Where? The man was half-way up the hill above Sandy Bay Bridge.

The bad man stood out in the road, and tried to stop Pale Lady with a dirk.

By making Pale Lady gallop faster and faster he escaped the bad man and the dirk.

Yes, that was the bad man standing over there.

He had seen the bad man at *Cindermead*.

Where? In the Chinese room eating bread-and-cheese.

Yes, he had spoken to the man.

What else? He had spoken, and cried, and cried.

He was asking the man for his lady-mama's chain.

He asked for the chain because he had seen the bad man in the bedroom taking it from a drawer. The man was a very bad man.

When he cried, and cried, and asked for his chain in the Chinese room, the man was angry, and went. . . .

(The witness retracted his lips to show his excellent teeth in a vicious snarl.)

What else? He said 'I will do something to you if you say anything to anyone.'

He said he would do something common.

He must tell all. He must tell the truth, and tell all. The man said, 'If you say anything I shall come through your window at night, and blow out the lamp, and cut pieces from you with my dirk.'

He must tell all. Yes, the man said, 'I shall be watching every night. And the wind will blow and blow, and will tell me if you have told, and I'll get my dirk, and stick it in your throat, and chop pieces, and cut off your black candle.'

Yes, that was his chain that his lady-mama had pressed into his little hand before she went to heaven.

Orfée Maka was cross-examined.

Yes, he knew he must tell the truth.

Yes, he always told the truth or he would not see his lady-mama in heaven.

He was not making up tales.

Yes, he had dreams.

He had dreamt of the bad man.

He dreamt the man was outside in the dark.

He had not dreamt the bad man was inside.

He could tell the difference between dreams and real things.

Because he was in bed for dreams, and it was night.

He did not ever go to bed in the daytime.

He did not dream that the bad man took his chain, because it was daytime and he was in the garden.

He did not give the man the chain. The man took it with his big pink hand.

He did not like the bad man.

No one had told him the man was a bad man. He knew because he saw him take the chain from the drawer.

Yes, he was frightened of the man.

He did not give the chain because he was frightened. He was frightened because the man took the chain.

He was frightened to tell ma'am and Miss Sleep because the man said common things.

He did not dream that the man said them.

The bad man said them in the Chinese room.

He did not call out, because he thought the man would hurt him.

He was not frightened of ma'am or anyone at *Cindermead*.

They were not angry with him. Ma'am let him drive the gig, and he had an embroidered coat, and his own elegant room.

Yes, they told him to tell the truth.

He did not know he was walking about until ma'am woke him up.

Yes, he had been dreaming that night.

That he had been walking about the house.

He did not dream what he had told ma'am.

He went to bed after a restoring glass of sherry wine.

No, ma'am had never given him sherry wine before.

He had never had sherry wine in the daytime because it made him go to sleep.

He knew, because he went to sleep after ma'am gave him a restoring glass of sherry wine.

Yes, that was his chain,

He was perfectly positive.

How many coins? Hundreds of coins.

No, he had not lost his chain. He put it in his trunk in Brighton.

He did not carry it about.

He did not leave it anywhere. It was always in his drawer until the bad man took it.

He did not know why the bad man tried to stop the horse. To cut him up, he thought.

Yes, Pale Lady was galloping fast.

He could see the dirk because the man held it up.

He did not dream that, because he was not in bed, and it was daytime.

Yes, he wanted to go to his lady-mama in heaven.

He was not saying things because he was frightened of anyone.

He did not know why the man said he had given him the chain.

Lady Knight was examined.

(Lady Knight's dress was most passively sentimental; it had pocket holes but no pockets. A muff trimmed with grebe concealed her gloves which concealed her hands. Her hair concealed her ears. A bonnet almost concealed all her hair, and was almost concealed by divinely curled and disposed ostrich plumes. A sorrowing indisturbance concealed her face. Whether on the black boy's behalf or to intimate her attitude to dark-skinned servants, she had attached at her waist by a chain a dress-clip in the form of a negro head. Beneath her bodice, that day, she was wearing breasts that could have belonged to no one but a mother. Her posture, apparently indifferent, made this, proudly yet modestly, most carefully clear.)

Yes, she was the wife of Sir Sydney Knight of *Cindermead.*

Cindermead was about three miles, she thought, by Sandy Bay Road, from Hobart Town.

Mr Vaneleigh had come to sketch her portrait.

Her husband had engaged him.

Mr Vaneleigh arrived in mid-afternoon, about four o'clock she thought.

He had someone with him.

She had presumed the other person to be a friend or some sort of hired assistant.

She saw this person only through the french windows of the drawing-room.

Yes, she was able to recognize the prisoner.

They were one and the same person.

She recognized him largely by his height, and his shabby pea-jacket—its colour was crude and unmistakable.

She would also be able to recognize him, even if blindfolded, by his harsh and common voice.

She asked Orfée Maka, who happened to be in the drawing-room at the time, to direct the prisoner to a room they called the Chinese Room where there was a fire, and to order something for him from the servants.

She did this because it was a chilly day. It was also a *Cindermead* custom to give vagabonds and beggars something at the kitchen door.

No, never *in* the house—but the circumstances were a little unusual.

She had not for a moment considered it imprudent. She had, indeed, not given the matter thought at all at the time. Had she considered Mr Vaneleigh's former imprisonment, and therefore the possible field of his acquaintance, she would perfectly possibly have been far less offhand.

She began to notice a certain strain, she might say unhappiness, in Orfée Maka soon after this visit.

Oh, their feelings for him were of the tenderest.

She had—*naturally*—been a little anxious but decided, after several conversations with Miss Sleep, that it was merely an upset occasioned by a change of the blood as is usual at the turn of the seasons. In their conversations they also attributed his mood to his age.

She became aware of the sleepwalking when she found Orfée wandering about the house one night.

She led him to her writing-room and, when he was fully awake, gave him a restoring glass of sherry wine. She then implored him to tell her what was troubling him as she felt from his manner that something was.

His manner was perfectly *distrait* and somewhat incoherent.

She finally persuaded him to confess his anxieties. He told her of the theft, and that he had been in too great a terror to inform anyone in the house because of a terrible threat that had been made by the prisoner. She was horrified, and he was in quite dreadful distress.

Her husband sent to the Police Office near Government House for constables to search the prisoner's lodging where the chain was found.

David Frost, Police Officer, was examined.

David Frost, Police Officer of Hobart Town.

Yes, he and another officer was sent to Playhouse Cottage.

The Police Office had received a message of information from Sir Sydney Knight.

They went to the cottage about half past five in the afternoon.

Tidswell Green was the other officer.

He was not present in court because he was sick.

He was sick of . . . of . . . Jerry-go-nimble.

Oh. He thought the *proper* thing to say was: Tidswell Green could not come because he was sick of the diarrhoea.

A gentleman of full habit who said he was the prisoner's father was in the cottage drinking.

He was drinking with a very tall gentleman, a lodger, he thought.

They was both roaring drunk, or seemingly.

They was surprised but said nothing to object to the search. They laughed, and offered drinks, and went on laughing and drinking.

Yes, they told them where was the prisoner's room.

They found the chain almost immediately hanging on a nail on the wall.

They came out of the room, and told the other two, and asked them where was the prisoner.

The father started up weeping, and the tall man went running crazy, and crying out into the street. He was trying to warn off the prisoner who was coming up the street.

He was squealing, 'Mind your eye! A stag!'

That meant, 'Watch out! Police!'

Tidswell Green went chasing, and caught the tall man, and they wrastled.

The prisoner run up where they was, and stopped the wrastling.

No, the prisoner didn't wrastle or fight when they arrested him.

He seemed taken aback but brazen, and no spunk left from shock. But calm and pretty brazen.

The prisoner said several times something about a little black heart.

He took the prisoner to mean he was in a rage because the black had told of him, but he said no more, and come along with them, and was locked up.

Yes, that was the chain they had taken from the prisoner's room.

Miss Asnetha Sleep was examined.

(Miss Sleep was in her Byron brown velvet; Miss Sleep was all in brown; brown gloves, brown bonnet, brown reticule, brown shadows under her eyes. Dr Wake, who limped, nevertheless wheeled her bath-chair quite nimbly into position.)

She was visiting Van Diemen's Land as the guest of her cousin Sir Sydney Knight.

She had lived at *Cindermead* for nearly a year.

Orfée Maka had come from England with her.

He could be said to be employed by her as a page-boy.

He was, alas, an orphan child whose mother and father had been esteemed servants in the family house in Brighton. They had been well-bred, *perfectly* well-bred West Indians. When they had both died of a consumption within a short time of each other she had, as it were, inherited the child who became by habit, and finally by decision, her personal boy.

He had been a favourite of her family and, until the age of ten or eleven, had been taught by the same governess as her two younger brothers. Indeed, he had been given the same sedulous attention and care as her brothers.

She recollected that—how diligent soever he had been—he had not been a proficient in writing and arithmetic. Especially the latter.

She had never known him to lie. La! never *ever*! Not *once*! 'Twas distasteful to his nature and Christian training.

She could *not*, she positively declared, recall having seen the chain at *Cindermead*, but had known it constantly in his possession at Brighton. But she needed not to have seen the chain to *know*, to be perfectly assured, that it would be with him. Orfée had been allowed, before leaving England, to pack a trunk of his private treasures. No doubt the contents would have been amended by the housekeeper where they were deficient. Yet she would swear the chain to have been the first object boxed by the child. He had the deepest regard for it. It had been the last thing pressed into his little hand by a dying mother. . . .

He had been distressed to delirium by its loss. Sorrow must have been cruelly aggravated by the wicked, wicked threats of the prisoner.

Yes, she had observed the prisoner at *Cindermead*.

Once, maybe twice, in passing. She felt he had cold, cruel eyes.

She did not realize that she was not to give an opinion on his eyes, however cruel.

She thought him Mr Vaneleigh's servant. She now realized that this assumption was a careless one for, although Mr Vaneleigh had once been a gentleman . . . and still retained some of the *je ne sais quoi* of a person of breeding . . . he could hardly have been in a position to afford a man.

Yes, that was the very image of the chain she had seen Orfée's dying mother give him.

She had noticed Orfée's strange behaviour after Lady Knight's first portrait-sitting.

She put it down to a seasonal *malaise*.

Lady Knight had told her the horrifying truth. She had fainted. The enormity of the crime. Peculiar and inhuman disregard. Susceptibilities of. Innocent boy. So *sweetly* innocent. Carefully protected from unpleasant. Contact. Guarded from. Evil. She begged forgiveness. For the extreme. Anxiety of mind. Under. Which she laboured. Orfée. Close quarters. Evil itself. Evil.

(The agitation of the witness, Miss Asnetha Sleep, in

Byron brown, became so excessive, and her nose so active, that she was unable to attend further questions. She made sobbing ejaculations, and Dr Wake, who had limped to her chair, finally wheeled her a little aside where the two cripples scrabbled in the reticule for the vinaigrette, even though the one was not yet wearing the other's engagement ring.)

The prisoner, a hanger-on, a threatener, a snarler, a bad man, a very bad man, in a shabby pea-jacket of unmistakable and crude colour, in defence of his audacity, brazenness, uncommon heartlessness and thievery, of evil itself, looked with his cold, cruel eyes at his accusers, and said in his harsh, common voice, and said no more and would say no more:

"The little black give Queely the chain. Queely is hinnocent."

Mr Jennings then led proofs of the prisoner's character.

Mr Polidorio John Angelo Smith, actor, had *known* Mr Sheill for eight . . . no, no, *nine* . . . no *eight*, yes, eight years; a golden *head*, a golden *heart*, what need had this *paragon* for a golden *chain*? He was temperate as a *dove*. Drank no *strong* waters—not even *rum*, not even a *harmless nostrum* of rum. Circumspect as a *dove*. Not a goodly *apple* rotten at the core. A perfect *dove*. *Benign*. The *Apollo* of Campbell Street, of *Hobart Town*, of Van Diemen's Land! Oh, the *kindest* of kind *sons* to *his papa*, and a good *cook*, and *would* not harm, could *not* harm, had never *proposed* harming, and had never harmed *any* of God's creatures. Not a *tittle*! An *aversion* to *blood* stronger than a dove's. God was *surely* sitting on his chair in *Paradise watching* like a *pigeon* with horror, and listening to *calumnies* most cruel. . . .

(The witness, whose weak voice had weakened to inaudibility, and who had been flourishing, and dropping, and picking up, a large muslin handkerchief, suddenly applied it to his streaming eyes, and was incapable of further speech.)

Mrs Fauntleroy, actress, had been acquainted with the prisoner for six years, both in England and in the colony, and could only fervently, and, she hoped, to his dear advantage, say that of all the many, many young men she had met—and ladies in her profession met many—he was the pink, the trump, the admirable Crichton. He was obliging, straightforward, upright, and had as high and penetrating a standard as any man she had ever known.

Matilda Ozier, slop-woman at the Ragged School, had known the prisoner for two years. He had brought her ointment for her inflamed hands. He had often bought toys for the children, and twelve plum puddings at last Christmas. He was a good, *good* man, and the orphans esteemed him.

Hester Kitchener, out of employment, said that in the last year, after she had lost her post as a hat-binder, the prisoner had on many occasions given her several shillings to buy her sick mother physic. She had not asked him. He had asked her nothing in return as many gentlemen did.

Dove Burn, out of employment, and with no sick mother, but often hungry himself, said much the same as Hester Kitchener.

James Dew, rat-catcher, Mr Timothy Nathaniel Yatman, harp-maker, Mr Gamaliel Hunt, patten-maker, Haviland le Mesurier, pot-boy, had never known a kinder-hearted or more benevolent young gentleman. At times when they had been out of employment, and cold and hungry, he had shared his fire with them, and bought them mutton-pies and ale.

Mrs Boshnel, actress, Caroline Williams, servant, Cambridge Collington, wire-walker, Mr William Duncalf, toll-gate-keeper, Robert Church, out of employment, said that the prisoner was a *man*, was manly, was frank, the kindest mortal alive, would not harm a fly, would not steal a pin, would not steal a crust, coveted nothing, was the very prince of Good Samaritans, had never had an enemy in the world until now, and was the victim of a dreadful mistake or some scandalous plot.

The penny-bundle people in the court, those set one pinch above the pinch of want, and one wall's breadth from prison, and one emotion more, one instinct less, above the brutes, nodded and sometimes smiled at the naming of qualities they knew were possessed by the prisoner at the bar. The men with the stripes of the cat still on their backs, the women with the stripes of the cat still on their backs, emaciated ex-beaux with a farthing, gully-rakers, prostitutes, dungaree men, currency men too proud to be shepherds, Johnny Raws, wastrels, cadgers, resurrectionists and tinkers' women, nodded with their heads and their hearts.

Yes, yes, yes, they nodded gently as wise dukes and sweetly as clever princesses, gently, sweetly, sagely and dreamily, lulled and warmed by their nearness to each other, enclosed in a mist of their own reeking breaths and exudations, yes, yes, yes, they nodded and sometimes smiled, yes, yes, yes, he is not guilty.

There, before them, beyond them, riding the scud of the world, was the human being they had not the fibre to be or imitate, or the luck to look like. There was the saint at those feet they had all, at one time or other, displayed their pettinesses of want or monstrosities of fault, there was the man who had given them the unique smile and the half-guinea they knew he knew they lied a need for, who had shouted their contemplated cruelties or transgressions over the horizon.

At that moment, there was nothing, they lied in thought to themselves, that they would not do for him even though it meant deprivation of their meagre possessions or their debilitated faculties or their sense of safety in being alive enough to draw yet another fetid mouthful of air.

Deprivation and torture would be nothing, and death by inches would be nothing.

Knowing that they lied in thought to themselves, they cherished the lie for its purity and unreality. They felt themselves ennobled by it, angelically beautified in soul and appearance and health and costume. It was silk from a celestial worm, trousers from the looms of heaven, that clothed their flawless bodies: they were stately, sinless, gifted to genius, and dexterous as magicians; uncountable guineas bulged their pockets and purses. It was inconceivable that their golden-haired knight should be in bonds. The testaments of their representatives had broken those bonds before they were welded.

Stinking, lice-ridden, scab-speckled, shifty and cowering,

draped in shoddy in which were set tattered pockets, hung with rags of skirts and shawls, their bone fingers poking from split gloves, out-at-elbows, they waited and nodded and sometimes smiled and did not spit or fart, patient and sure of the words that would set them dancing from the Court House to Campbell Street crying out what they nodded—yes, yes, yes, he is not guilty.

"How say you," said the clerk of arraigns, after calling over the names of the jury, "are you agreed upon your verdict, is the prisoner at the bar guilty or not guilty?"

The foreman said, "Guilty."

Lady Knight, Miss Asnetha Sleep, Master Orfée Maka, Mr Creamly said nothing.

The prisoner at the bar, guilty, a hanger-on, a threatener, a snarler, a bad man, a very bad man, in a shabby pea-jacket of unmistakable and crude colour, audacious, brazen, uncommonly heartless, a thief and evil itself, looked with his cold, cruel eyes at his accusers and said nothing.

The prisoner at the bar, guilty, golden head, golden heart, paragon, temperate, benign, benevolent, shilling- and toy- and plum-pudding-giver, mutton-pie sharer, Apollo, kind-hearted, kindest of kind sons, kindest mortal alive, who would neither harm flies nor steal pins nor crusts, good *good* man, *man*, victim of a dreadful mistake or a scandalous plot, looked at his accusers and said nothing.

Lady Knight not moved and not closed her eyes, not showed by any sign that anything pleasant and necessary, or unpleasant and unnecessary, had happened. Her demeanour was perfectly unchanged. The faintest—the so very *faintest*—and only and momentary flicker came from the muff that concealed the gloves that concealed hands, and was, perhaps, indicative of the tiniest relaxing of control over a justifiable restlessness to leave as quickly as possible the discord and defects of the Court House for the concord and felicity of *Cindermead*.

Miss Asnetha Sleep exhaled a trembling female sigh, closed and opened and closed again her eyes, and swooned or seemed to do so, and her legs opened and shut like violent scissors under the Byron brown velvet and the brown shawls.

Orfée Maka grinned a wider, longer sustained, more deadly, more brainless, more enchanting grin than he had even grinned even as a molly-coddled plaything in Brighton.

Mr Creamly, without opening his mouth, smiled a partial and solitary smile, regretful and autumnal for one so young and sound and suave and black-and-white. It was a smile that scarcely forgave himself.

The others, mortised together in court, ignorant and wily and verminous as monkeys, swayed backwards together as though the cry of "Guilty!" were a gust thrusting back a wrack of flame, and all together sucked their tainted breaths between their dreadful teeth into their fifth-rate bodies and then, in a mass, the unseen flame flopping forward from its retreat, pressed towards Queely Sheill. Once again, as in Campbell Street in the shadows of sunset, their shadowed and fuming hearts slid forward, coals sliding forward under the shadowing ash and smoke, and a long-draw-out moan whose depth and persistence whitened even their own tallow faces, escaped their souls as though they had witnessed a calamity greater than any of their own.

Queely Sheill then received sentence.

He was to be transported to Port Arthur Prison for the term of seven years.

Until such time as the new prisoner's quarters at Port Arthur were ready, and the next movement of prisoners from Hobart Town to Port Arthur took place, he was to be returned to his cell in Hobart Town Gaol.

At this laconic announcement, a customarily mild one, a quite ordinary and to-be-expected cruel and illiberal one, there was an extraordinary uproar and surging about and seeming multiplication of the number of regrettable beings in the body of the court. It was a brief and bitter manifestation. The voices of those who had experienced Port Arthur, or knew the remnants of men who had, supplied a muffled harshness, a drumfire of doom and omen. Other voices neighed and rang with horror.

This instance of unrehearsed, and uncalled-for, and worse than savage ferocity, began and ceased so immediately that the voice of a clerk was heard quacking for silence in a silence so shocking that it seemed coarse and bloody.

12

Day by day, the cameos of snow hung on the scarps of Organ-pipe became more blunted in contour, their hauteur loosened, the profiles so aristocratically averted from the errors, ardours, rectitudes and mendacities of Hobart Town thawed to profiles of idiots looking nowhere, to profiles of skulls, of ghosts, of nullity. The ladders of snow slipped away under the unforbiddable feet of spring clambering more and more hotly towards summer. The gallows and crucifixes packed like salt in deeper clefts endured longer before decomposing to icy gruel, and then to an unsullied and downpouring sweat. The moss-fostering brooks, descending the mountain and Knocklofty, fattened for a time, and ran swifter and talkative as in a gross sleep.

At night, the houseless, in their cradles of trash, or peeping like foxes from their dust-holes, could see that the constellations had moved. In secret, behind the clouds of winter, planets had been filched, or scraped off by the machicolated upper of the mountain while the Zodiac ground over as relentlessly as the days and the weeks and the sleep-walking movements of the starved.

Below, in the streets and alleys and *cul-de-sacs* of Hobart Town, deliverance moved. Its sunnier soles were listened to as one listens to a hymn of lies in a dream.

Sailing ships freighted with banister brushes, Caledonia jugs, Malmsey sack, brass hooks and eyes, muskets, psalters and handkerchief-thieves came to berth at nightmare.

Judas Griffin Vaneleigh, his last portrait executed, his will and its engine undone, his sparsity of vigour and time and money diminishing, left his room rarely. But its four walls, keeping out Hobart Town, did not keep in his mind. Chronology, he thought, is nothing to genius, and smiled thinly beneath his moustache, and, too weak and aloof for movement on Campbell Street and the Palladio, moved in Nednil House, in Trunham Grove, Great Marlborough Street, Conduit Street, in Paris and Boulogne and Howland Street, in Mansion House, in Newgate Prison.

He opened the door to his cat; it twined its way among the visitors from the past, and might have been his London tortoiseshell; it purred with remembered sobriety and tolerance as though it were that bygone cat, and he the host to actualities rather than visions . . . Charles Lamb, Hazlitt, Macready the actor, Fuseli, Flaxman, Sir Thomas Lawrence, John Clare the poet, Ellen Abernethy, Daniel Forrester the Bow Street runner, Fidelia Vaneleigh. . . .

I used once, he thought, to affirm myself a Sir Oracle. I was the invincible *Ah ha*! fit for everything, prepared for all accidents: ready to pass from grave to gay, from lively to severe, from praise to revilement. I admired purity, was enviable in my friends, pitied sensitiveness, gave way before passionate forces. I trilled a love-song or played the devil. I used to pronounce myself, he thought, to be, not one, but all mankind's epitome.

Now and again, each time frailer, he crept to St. Mary's Hospital for his opium-tinctured medicine, and crept away again, his back turned upon the world, to his phantoms and his cat. Each time he returned was one time less. One day he would creep under the brownstone door-arch of St. Mary's Hospital, and not return.

Streets away from Campbell Street, in the Hobart Town Gaol, Queely Sheill had shaken off perjury as dewdrops are shaken from a lion's mane, and was content. He lived in his enclosure, occupying a space of time in which all progression had ceased, all ardour abated. There was a session of rich stagnation, a seasonless season, a time in which to waste time.

He ate, he slept, he shaved, he bore costiveness patiently, he emptied his slops, he mended his boots, he sewed, he carved toys for the gaol-porter's children, he waited—without a sense of waiting, and with no fears or hatreds or disillusions—to be transported to Port Arthur. His visitors, having decided to find him downcast, misliked finding him buoyant, as handsome as if at liberty. He warned them not to be unhappy. His innocence, doubly nourishing as an innocence of purpose also, was enough for his spirit to feed on eternally. Since memory dotes on such pickings from eternity, his eyes were dazzling. He had lived so long behind the iron grille of unorthodox simplifications that he had grown eyes that saw no grille. He had the perfected and adamant vanity of a clever animal. To have been gaoled for others' lies had not startled him—he had always known that others told lies. He was a good boy. Punishment could not make him bad.

He wondered about the others—Lady Knight, Miss Sleep, Teapot—and was impressed by their acting, their angers and malices and lusts. He felt a responsibility in that his angerlessness, mercy, and animal purity had stirred up opposite emotions. Since he, he thought, had intended nothing but salvation, and had failed, there was nothing possible for them to do but act being what he had hoped them to be.

Recalling Mr Vaneleigh's warnings, he was pleased that the artist had spoken truths. He thought tenderly of Mr Vaneleigh, as of a gifted son, one having the extra wisdom an articulate, though sickly, gentleman should have. Mr Vaneleigh had learned, as he was learning, the duties of innocence. He also thought tenderly that, as Mr Vaneleigh himself had, how long ago soever, been of the quality it was natural he should know the commonplace tricks of the quality which Queely Sheill had only guessed at. Imagining their evil to have a different taste, he felt justly enough punished for insolent misconception, for his undervaluation. He could not forgive them more. Their lies were merely their lies. He was sorry about the colour of his pea-jacket, about his voice and his cold, cruel eyes. He wished they would visit so that he could ask pardon for these offences. But he expected no visit—from them, or God, or a future more novel than the well-organized present.

He expected no visit from Mr Vaneleigh. Not only was Mr

Vaneleigh too proud, poor, clever and sick to be making such a trip without protection, but why, thought Queely Sheill, should he who had already had his fill of prisons and prisoners visit a prisoner in a prison? Mr Vaneleigh, he recalled, had unemotionally but with conviction expressed a dislike of prison.

Queely Sheill listened to the cathedral bells across the street calling successfully the population to prayer, among them Sir Sydney Knight who had received news of his advancement, his stately and gracious Lady Knight, Miss Asnetha Sleep and the attentive Dr Wake, and a number of other persons equally Christian. Queely Sheill listened also to doors and fetters and cries inside the walls, and to cries outside. He scratched dandruff from his golden head, wished occasionally for a mutton-pie from the Scotch Pie House, and itched sometimes to see what Port Arthur was like. He waited happily, without plans or dreams.

However, dreams and plans for him scurried about whispering, wearing the masks of fantasy and zeal and spite and mania, up and down Campbell Street, under the beams of *The Shades*, on the Palladio, in the lanes behind Salamanca Place, at the Hiring Depôts, in attic and basement and rumshack and brothel.

A hundred schemes for his escape from the gaol were proposed, argued about and talked down; fields of suggestions were sown, and watered with vows of martyrdom . . . how rock-cluttered already the fields! how touched by immediate frost! how quickly the bracken of common sense overtopped and destroyed with shade the flowerless seeding of conspiracy!

John Death Sheill harangued an audience of wicked world, of millions stacked behind evil millions from horizon to horizon. Or he lay drunken on his bed, soliloquising behind the dune of his belly, "Oh, my son Absolawm! Oh, Absolawm, my son, my son!" and kissing his dead wife's miniature in a pinchbeck locket. Or drank more rum, and sobbed grandiloquently on Hester Kitchener's bosom, or any woman's bosom.

But Polidorio Smith, with boils on his nape, his ebony-rimmed uncut fingernails growing more uncut, his dark tooth never hidden in brilliant grimacings of terror and fatigue, scudded from cabal to cabal, salvaging one notion of a broken scheme here and another there, scavenging under the bracken, among the rocks and frost-wounded schemes, to gather particles for the fitting together of a disaster-proof formula of escape.

As the weeks passed, Polidorio Smith learned to see that, in their garrulous fervour, in their grease and rags and delusions, the other conspirators were whispering themselves dry of action. Queely Sheill was becoming to them no more than a ballad prisoner in a romantic Newgate sharing Ludgate Hill and a view of London with St. Paul's, and subject of a moonstruck game. Legend was building its jewelled barnacles on Queely Sheill. For the actor those passing weeks which scooped cavities in his miller-white face, and dilated his anguishes and insomnias and nightmares, brought hurtling breakneck nearer the wagon to take Queely Sheill beyond the chimera of escape.

Obsessed and inelegant as an apostle, squeaking oaths as vile as dockers', he raked and re-raked the leavings of cast-out discussions and abandoned dreams and, near collapse but exultant, finally presented his project to Queely Sheill.

The care with which the contented prisoner and his quaking outline of a visitor were left alone was accidental so strikingly that Queely Sheill scarcely bothered until the gaoler was out of earshot:

"Poli," he said, "whatever you and 'im is hup to, there's no hescaping to be done. You've 'eard that a 'undred times. Queely's got no rights to hescape."

Polidorio Smith's face fitted his skull like a wet dish-rag; his ears seemed thinner, and raggedly torn by cyclones. He smelt sour, and could whisper only.

"But you are *innocent*, my child. You are *guiltless* as a sucking-dove. You are a *sacrifice*."

"I don't know habout guiltless and sacrifice and what-all. But I knows you ain't been sleeping, *hor* heating proper, *hor* 'aving a wash . . . Queely knows."

"Queely *knows*! Queely *doesn't* know! What *is* this talk, what is it? Do not *distract*. You are not *meek*: you do know you didn't *steal* the negro's chain, and that you're locked *up* like *salt-cellars* for stealing it. *That's* not playing at skittles."

The tall man was desperate; he trembled constantly; he became hare-brained with distress:

"I declare I'll *never* play at *skittles* again," he said querulously, scratching in confusion at some horrid stain on his vest. "*Never*! *Blackamoors*, my love, are deceitful *wretches*! Coquetting! Eyes *rolling* at me like skittles. *Certainly* of the *Romish* persuasion. Your humble was perfectly *unmoved*. 'Ethiop,' I said cold as *seltzer*, 'you are *black* as *sin*!' Oh, no, no, *no*, Apollo," he cried hoarsely, coming to himself, and frantic with grief. "Oh, *no*! I am distracted. I know why I am here. You must *listen* to your friend who loves you."

"Listening, Poli," said Queely Sheill. "Listening, but don't want to 'ear hescape. Queely's hin the snooze. 'Appy! Ho, yes! Heasy as an old shoe hin the snooze."

"That's without *rhyme* or *reason*. You're a demmed *ungrateful* Apollo. I'm *quite* out of spirits. Always on the *gad* to find a *way*. Ungrateful, *ungrateful*. I have *suffered*. *Deathie* has suffered . . . cupshot *every day* . . . he'll die of *rum* and *tears* . . . Oh, Apollo, my love! . . ."

" 'E won't die, Poli. 'Ave no fears. Queely'll be back to you hall in seven years."

"Oh, oh, my head will drop *off*! But I'll not *falter*, no not for Ethiops or *cutlasses*, *reptiles* or volcanics. I'll perish on *pavements* ere I deviate from my labours of *freeing* you. I'll . . . I'll see you genteely *demmed* first. . . ."

Tears overflowed, streamed down, kept on overflowing and streaming so that they splashed on the stone floor.

"I declare I'll *kill* myself. I shall . . . cut my *throat* . . . like jam *roly-poly*. I . . . shall *jump* . . . into something *deep*. . . ."

He hooked and twisted his fingers into Queely Sheill's yellow jacket, and approached sobbing collapse.

"Your devoted . . . has *laboured*, Apollo . . . has *laboured* . . . They will blame me if I *fail*. I shall . . . be *stoned* . . . in Campbell Street . . . stoned like a *street-lamp*, and dropped . . . in the Rivulet . . . in my new *coat*. . . ."

Queely Sheill saw, in the sunken and bloody eyes of the distraught man before him, a gentle and terrified scarecrow stalking the days and nights, beating at its own fears, stumbling through and retracing steps back through the maze of its own irrelevancies and bewilderments, and the intricacies of others' plottings and lapses, but convinced of the value of its travail, and alone single in purpose. The others had schemed in a confusion of motives . . . defiance of law, hatred of prisons, revolt against the quality, love of intrigue and anarchy, love of Queely Sheill. Polidorio Smith had one motive. It was love.

" 'Ere," said Queely Sheill, taking in his hands the talons trapped in the material of his jacket, " 'Ere you'll 'ave *Queely's* new coat hin strips. 'Er Majesty wouldn't go to like that. Stop tearing canary's coats, and grizzling, and tell what you're hup to. Listening there'll be, but no promising. Tell me hof your new coat."

With a hoarse and foul-smelling cry of relief Polidorio Smith began, and continued then for an hour. The escape was to be attempted during the cathedral bell-ringers' practice on the evening of the next day, and while alterations to the gaol bakehouse were still at a stage which made the gaol walls momentarily less invulnerable. Hester Kitchener's body had played a large part in the scheme: it had satisfied the carpenter of a ship sailing north in two days, it had more than satisfied Queely Sheill's gaoler. Next evening, during the bell-ringing, the gaoler hoped to make it possible for the prisoner to be near the bakehouse section of the wall—this necessary contribution to the scheme the gaoler prayed could be managed without danger to himself. Polidorio Smith and Pretty Dick were to be outside the wall with ropes and a rope ladder. A change of clothing, and a ship at anchor, and the hazards of lawless freedom lay beyond the walls which lawfully enclosed Queely Sheill's liberty of resignation.

He found it impossible, on consideration, to refuse stubbornly to satisfy Polidorio Smith's entreaties. He gave his promise, and told the actor to return to the cottage, and bathe, and eat, and go early to bed.

"I shall," said Polidorio Smith in a whisper so faint as to

be hardly heard, "*surprise* and *ravish* you with my new coat and a new *coiffure*, Apollo, my love. You will scarcely *sleep* this night from *curiosity*. 'Twill be", he said, as the gaoler indicated that he *must* go, "*repayment* for the *climb*. Bye-bye!"

Left to thought of forward-looking and striking rather than retrospective and soothing kind, Queely Sheill began to see that illegal and liberal movement to unknown places could be as exciting, perhaps more, than legal and illiberal transportation to one unknown place. He had little more to do than climb ropes. The gaoler said nothing to him but, although slightly cross-eyed, his look had been that of someone from a novel by Sir Walter Scott and privy to a design.

Night came.

Prison usage, by daylight, was as a pruned tree, ever leafless, undeniably man's planting. Darkness, like a midsummer, like an equatorial cloud-burst, like soil charged with miraculous nourishment, excited the sap, galvanized the branches. The tree put on elaborations of bud and leaf, fruit and flower. Uncouth parasitic growths swung down their lively viciousnesses. Bodies and minds moved, grew pulpy; perverse fruits exuded their bitter-sweet juices; nightmare flew into the foliage to drawl and bibble-babble.

Queely Sheill slept under that canopy, snoring pleasantly and dreamlessly as a virgin.

Daylight showed the tree bare and neat. He saddened to consider himself doing for the last time on that day what he had been doing for weeks. No visitors came except clouds, and a late afternoon downpour that, in a windlessness, fell utterly vertical with the simplicity and intention of persistence of a plague.

All day he felt the mind of the gaoler dubiously circling nearer him; it dodged through the comings and goings and fashionable curses and obscenities, reserving its expression until the choice second, retaining itself until that second in a condition of vacuity so that it would have as little as possible connection with even a prisoner as amiable, uncomplaining and satisfying to the aesthetic sense as Queely Sheill. Once only, a passing glance and an upturning of the gaoler's squint showed Queely Sheill that rain was an unforeseen but acceptable ally. It drove eyes indoors.

At twilight, the rain had long softened Hobart Town, had chastened it, and cleared the precipitous streets where the gutters chanted like delirious priests, and the low-lying lanes along which cobbles protruded from overflow like rats' backs or oily crania.

At twilight, the bell-ringers began to practise in the cathedral.

At twilight, Polidorio Smith, wearing his new coat, and in relief from two burst boils, and further encouraged by freshly dyed hair, left Campbell Street with Pretty Dick who carried two portmanteaux.

At twilight, those chain-gang prisoners who had been working outside during the day returned from the stone-quarry to the gaol.

Those bipeds, grotesque when they had left in cloudiness and the twilight of morning, were more grotesque in the rain and the twilight of night. Man's animality is not so brought to the senses by his gait in his more animal movements . . . in unencumbered walking, in skipping, dancing or running. But, hobbled by a long chain that was manacled at each end to the ankles like a wasteful and weighty piece of *bijouterie*, and was held up from the nasty ground, as it were fastidiously, by a ladylike sling of twine, man employed a gait that recalled that of animals—a waddling, a shambling, a dragging.

To the assured clashing of cathedral bells, and the dull sonata of the links swaying in suspension, in a single file that the oil-lamps deformed to a frieze of impossibilities, the monsters returning home conventionally entered.

Two of them were to be flogged. The squirting and cascading rain in the quarry had infected the tongues of those two to muttering behind the back of the overseer whose ears the rain had given such an irritated clarity of perception that he had been able to hear insolence in muttering.

Queely Sheill's gaoler who had begun, as twilight began, to have fears, and to spit too often, threw aside his fears on hearing of the floggings to be given, and returned to spitting at customary intervals; the parading of all other convicts to watch the floggings would make a diversion useful to the scheme of escape. As he unlocked Queely Sheill's cell he whispered, "You skedaddle vhere 'e said v'en I vinks."

He said no more than what he thus appeared not to say but, as the convicts were let from their cells and mustered at the flogging-post, he prodded the golden-haired prisoner to an outskirt position nearest the bakehouse building.

The flames in the gaolers' lanterns tossed and undulated as the lanterns, held high or swung low, themselves undulated, so that the prisoners and their shadows tossed about in a sombre choppiness. Shadows of distended heads, elongated ears and vast noses, slid up the saturated walls, like torn combers, to break high over the roofs and through the wall spikes into the drenching and thickening night that the bells sledge-hammered at, fractured, and violently dominated. A surf of eyes, the lids scraped back from the polished balls, reflected the pitching lantern-flames. At the top of the flogging-post the flame of that lamp alone was moveless above activity.

The two mutterers of insolence were stripped to the waist.

Nudity, in the midst of the clothed, gave an impression of birth or some like outrage.

The first to be flogged, Crazy Ralph, was a massy block of muscles, a giant with a skin white as lard. When his huge arms were stretched up above his head, and strapped to the post the black nests of hair in his armpits seemed an exhibit of shame: wailing could have burst from their sooty turf, a lament that such secrets of guardlessness and dark should be on brutal display. A tartan of old wounds, an heraldic device of scars, was embossed on his back and, under this less immodest and more ornamental layer, knobs and welts of muscle nosed and punted at each other. Over the white, and over the ornate, an additional skin of water glistened.

The second mutterer was stooped, a thing of bones over the basket-work of which an inferior skin was stingily stretched. His back was an unfurrowed field of most meagre soil. Whatever mean muscles he had, twitched with terror as he watched from under horizontally protruding eyebrows Crazy Ralph's useless lustihood arrayed for correction.

As the cat-o'-nine-tails struck for the first time on the enamelled back, the second flogee, alone of them all, closed his eyes; all the others drawn up in the dwindling rain and the dwindling year avidly watched. As the cat was uprooted from its plot of flesh, and wrenched back to descend again, *One*! they all recorded, for an inner system of counting had begun in the senses of the sightseers. They were more soothed and delighted than they could express . . . cock-fighting, bear-baiting, wrestling, boxing, fox-hunting were noise-inducing pleasures with sordid implications of gambling. To condone, it seemed, that purer performance of skill, the bell-ringers rehearsing Christmas exulted in metal.

Queely Sheill watched his cross-eyed gaoler who had stationed himself nearby.

At the fourteenth stroke of the cat, Crazy Ralph, who had allowed himself to emit nothing except sizzling exhalations no one else could hear, and who had, with a regrettable disregard of the watcher's feelings, made no interesting movement to betray the fact that he was trapped, began to struggle. Blood had been drawn; nearer and clearer-sighted spectators observed worms of it dissolving in the skin of rain. For the first time the flame of the flogging-post lamp jumped about. In a voice shriller than the solidity of his body suggested, Crazy Ralph began to curse with old-fashioned turns of obscene phrase. Someone laughed, and all the faces turned like pages of *Isaiah*. The cat, re-invigorated, tossed its tresses, and prepared for the fifteenth plunge.

The gaoler near Queely Sheill loudly cleared his throat, loudly spat, raised the lantern to illuminate his face, miraculously uncrossed his eyes, looked directly, and winked. Queely Sheill winked back, and warned his own muscles that movement was under consideration.

Crazy Ralph, still shrilly vilifying, jolted and ducked and dipped in his bonds. The second skinamalink was hiccoughing with panic.

Queely Sheill moved quickly. He passed unseen into the shadow of the bakehouse. Even the gaoler did not see him go; having given a wink at the appointed moment he immediately subtracted himself from the scheme, relieved that circumstances had made his promise to Hester Kitchener easier to fulfil than it could have been, and thinking that he might buy her a petticoat.

Crazy Ralph, with the gesture of a colossus, and the screech of a matron who snatches her baby from the fangs of doom, tore one hand free, and grabbed at, and caught the descending thongs of the cat. There was a male uproar, as at a bull-baiting. That devil-may-care din of civilization, unseemly in that place, was accompanied by an extra hullabaloo—not at all planned—from the cathedral bells. There was a jostling and bumping to and fro without direction, considered intention or much feeling. Someone had dropped a lantern. The shadows, immense, crazy and vehement, were the most violent members.

Queely Sheill had reached the corner between the bakehouse and the wall, and, though thinking the noise from the flogging-quadrangle was the result of his absence, whistled as he had been told to. From above, from behind the half-demolished bakehouse chimney, Pretty Dick's voice was heard:

"Oi'll unroll ladder. 'Tis fixed to two ropes around chimley. Oi'll go down ropes to Polly. Pull ladder up after you."

As the ladder unrolled to Queely Sheill's feet he heard Pretty Dick scraping his way down outside. Queely Sheill had his hands on the ladder.

Someone ran around the corner of the bakehouse, and was upon him before his foot could find the first rung.

His arms enfolded a bare and bony body, active and clawing in a mania of shock and funk. It was the second flogee who, as the gaolers and guards strove with Crazy Ralph, and roared at the frolicsome mob and its caricature of menace, had fled the hurly-burly unnoticed. It would have been flight to nowhere, a hopeless shift, had not Queely Sheill squeezed and shook him like a lay-figure, and thrust him to the ladder.

"Hup the ladder!" said Queely Sheill, "Hup the ladder, quick, quick, quick."

In his silly nightmare the distraught skeleton climbed

whimpering up, and Queely Sheill followed when the other had reached the top to cling in panic to the half-demolished chimney.

"Quick, quick. Down the ropes houtside. Ho, quick, quick, bugger-boy. *Quick*!"

As the other descended outside, Queely Sheill reached the top, embraced the chimney and, standing on the projecting brick-width of foothold, drew up the rope ladder.

Holding the folds of the ladder hooked over one arm, he began to giggle at the thought of Polidorio Smith's amazement below as he received the toothless and bare-bones guest. He moved to make the descent and, thought he heard Polidorio Smith keening below, and called rashly down to those he could not see,

"Don't be hafraid. 'Ere's Queely. 'Ere 'e is!"

He slipped.

He fell.

He fell back into the gaol-yard. The ladder, tangled about his arm, and attached to the ropes passing outside, tore them from the hands of his rescuers so that those long tails followed him, and fell with him.

He fell through the blasphemies of Crazy Ralph, and the maelstrom of noise in the quadrangle, and the last of the December rain, and the bells rehearsing the Christmas that was fourteen days away.

He felt the bones of his leg smash like a branch on the stone ground; he felt the bridge of his nose smash on the stone wall, and his teeth smash like glass on the stone wall; he felt all the world he had so far known smash in every direction and into every shape, and he himself, already stopped falling, and prone on the wet slabs, nevertheless keep on falling through the smashed ceilings of world after world after world.

He heard, or imagined he heard, wild voices outside imploring through the inferno of chimes, Polidorio Smith's raised to shave the rain from the sky, to scythe through the clouds and the night, to shrill like a wheel of sickles across the floor of Heaven, and hurl God like an Aunt Sally from His throne of mercy.

He could cry no answer of peace to his friend uselessly skirling outside the prison and yet imprisoned in the cellar of the world for, from behind his mask, nothing came except a bubbling and gobbling.

When he was found, the rain, having performed its various tasks, had finally retracted itself; the carnival at the flogging-post was over; the bells held their hard tongues stiff and silent in their gaping mouths. The tree of prison life throbbed with its own unheard and unmentionable nocturnal flourishing.

Into all this silence, he was able, when the gaolers moved him from under his creepers of rope, to project a number of appalling screams, for the bones of his smashed leg had stabbed through muscle and flesh into the air, and movement caused inconvenience.

The next day, the hideous Queely Sheill was taken by wagon to the Convict Hospital which was situated on a low sandstone cliff, and overlooked the Palladio in Campbell Street, Hobart Town, Van Diemen's Land, that season, that summer, that year.

13

The newly-appointed Colonial Assistant Surgeon always, as his predecessors had, corrected compound fractures by amputation.

He ordered preparations to be made at the Criminal Hospital for an amputation, at nine o'clock in the morning, of the upper thigh of a convict who had been injured, two days before, while attempting to escape from the Hobart Town Gaol. Those preparations were made with official regard for the teachings of the authority most in vogue.

If the assistants, said the authority, are not habituated, let the surgeon be careful to appoint them their places and their duties, for nothing tends more to the right performance of an operation of magnitude than the composure and quietness that results from such arrangements.

The assistants were pass-holding convicts or tickets-of-leave employed at sixpence a day and a full diet. One had been a poacher, one an area-thief, one had stolen a hat, and one a doll. They were habituated to amputations, knew their places and duties, and had become more skilled in their cruel mercies than they had been as four maladroit thieves.

Let the surgeon reflect, said the authority, that everything, even the meanest article, is dignified by an occasion when the life of a fellow-creature is at stake.

Let the instruments be a large amputating knife, one of second size and a smaller *ditto*; an amputation saw, and bone nippers to grip the bone while the saw is employed; two tourniquets, and a compress for the large artery.

Let a strong table be placed in a good light, a blanket upon it and pillows, a dish of sand beneath.

A massive pine table stood on the first-floor landing of the two-storey Criminal Hospital. From that landing, wards led off; on that table all surgical work necessary to save the lives of criminals was done.

On a side table, said the authority, we affect to see:

One—A large cushion with needles, pins, forceps, and instruments finely hooked for seizing and drawing out blood-vessels from the face of the wound for the purpose of tying them off.

Two—Ligatures of waxed thread, well arranged.

Three—Adhesive straps, well made and not requiring heating. If they should, let a chafing-dish be at hand.

Four—Lint compresses, tow, waxed lint, broad roller bandages of calico, split cloth for retractions. Let there be no want of sponges, so that when the surgeon calls for a sponge, you have not to seek for it among the patient's clothes; and when a sponge falls among the sand let it not be necessary to touch of the face of the wound with it.

Five—Brandy wine. Water and hartshorn.

Six—A kettle of hot water, a stoup of cold water, basins, buckets, towels, apron and sleeves.

These various preparations, said the authority, should be concealed from the patient who should then be brought in in a loose dress proper to the nature of the operation.

His legs bare beneath a short hospital night-shirt, the patient was carried in by the poacher and the hat-stealer. He had been made to drink brandy in large quantities, and drams of tincture of opium so that he was stupefied. Above his appalling smashed face his golden hair held the neat flutings of a comb. One leg had the perfect form and ivory whiteness of a carven classic hero's; the other had not, and was fly-blown.

Let the assistants, said the authority, look next to the position of the patient; seat him near the edge of the table with a folded blanket under him.

"Ho, Queely's Martin-drunk," said the patient so thickly

that no one knew what he said. He was seated, and a medical student and the poacher fixed the tourniquets on his imperfect leg.

" 'Tis aggravatin', the drone of flies," said the medical student, straight from Homer, and already sweating. " 'Tis aggravatin', the heat."

Let him, said the authority, recline in the arms of an attendant; place a dresser on a low stool before him.

Two thieves, one each side, area-thief and doll-stealer, grasped the arms of the patient and supported him against the pillows. The medical student, as dresser, sat on a low stool before the fly-blown leg that dangled over the table-edge, ready to grasp the unsavoury thing. The poacher stood by to control the tourniquets until the dresser's first simple task was over. Already, the hat-stealer had grasped the perfect leg, tensed to restrict frivolous movement of that member by his own weight and zeal.

From the surgeon's vest-pocket, his watch (it had suspended from its chain a *breloque* in the form of a heart not broken) chimed . . . slow, delicate, silvery, and nearly louder than the blowflies . . . *one*, *two*, *three*, *four*. . . .

"Ho, pretty!" said the patient to ears not understanding.

. . . *seven*, *eight*, *nine*.

The surgeon had taken up the large amputating knife.

"Pray," he said, to the hat-stealer, "pray you part the legs more. A little more yet, if you please. So! Hold firmly, all. 'Tis nine o'clock."

The patient being held firmly, said the authority, the surgeon, with the large amputating knife, makes the wide semicircular sweep of the blade, from the inside of the thigh, beginning beneath, and cutting up and around to meet the point of commencement.

It was useless for the patient to strive with the thieves, for they were mercy; it was useless for his voice to cry for succour against mercy. He had not cried out against blind justice; his ruined functions could make no reasonable utterance against open-eyed mercy.

The strap tourniquet and compress, said the authority,

previously applied over the femoral artery, controls haemorrhage. If this does not fully serve, digital pressure on the artery must be used.

When the skin, and the muscle sheaths, and the muscles have been divided, said the authority, they are all drawn back towards the groin by a retracting cloth.

The medical student had left his stool, and the tray of crimsoning sand, and drew back with crimsoning bands of split cloth and towards the groin the hindering and weeping mass of flesh.

In this way, said the authority, the bone is exposed to the saw. By the use of the saw the limb is separated from the body.

The surgeon dropped the limb in a bucket.

It was three minutes past nine.

The medical student poured hot water from the kettle into a basin and cold water from the stoup, and took up sponges and returned to his stool.

At each short interval of the operation, said the authority, be ready to clear the face of the wound from blood with a sponge well squeezed out in tepid water.

With a finely hooked instrument, one by one in their turn, and taking care that the great nerve be not mistaken for an artery, draw down each of the large blood vessels, and securely tie them off with waxed thread. Let the ends of these ligatures be long so that they hang well beyond the surface of the stump.

" 'E's in a swound," said the area-thief, and, dismayed at himself, gave a sneeze, though one of much restraint.

"Bless you," said the poacher whose manners had always been good, and his mother's pride.

"Hartshorn, if you please," said the surgeon, tying away, and the hartshorn mixture was held at the mutilated and swollen nose. "Give him the brandy when he has a little sense, and the measure of opium. There, 'tis finished. Do you, Mr Trotter,"—the medical student's name was Piggin—"clean the wound while I am away for a moment. I shall return to watch you strap the flaps over the end of the bone." He took off his apron, and twinkled, for he was one who did so at proper times. "The adhesive tapes will require no chafing-dish *this* morning."

It was eleven minutes past nine.

"No, 'tis a crackin' hot mornin', sir," said Mr Piggin, but the surgeon had limped briskly away.

What the prisoner in the midst of thieves, the one-legged ugly man, was saying, they could not tell and cared not, in their mercy, to interrupt or to know; moreover, brandy, tincture of opium, a tongue and lips bloated, and festering in the lacerations made by jagged teeth, all those, combined with the debilitation consequent upon his recent and crowded experiences did not favour an articulation specific enough for any ears, let alone ears inured to the irresponsibilities and pitiful tritenesses of those attempting to express the inexpressible.

The flaps of flesh skilfully left by the knife's semicircular sweep were of perfect shape for the thigh had been of perfect shape, and the surgeon a gifted one. They were folded over the bone, and adhesive strappings applied to hold them. Under the surgeon's eye, Mr Piggin, with nervous dexterity, and sweat dripping from the point of his nose, applied the straps and dressings and bandages. Beneath all neat that, the ligatures were left to slough off, and infection to breed.

By the morning of Christmas Eve, eleven days later, gangrene was well-established, and added its stench to the stench of other gangrenes and other stenches.

Queely mustn't go screaming, Queely mustn't go screaming, he thought, lying on his bed in the Criminal Hospital. Daylight had gone. Already the windows were shut to keep out pollutions of Christmas twilight, and the ward lamps were lit. The shadows of those who moved, and came and went, came and went among the beds. Sounds and voices came and went. Shadows of voices came and went, those of the past flexuously winding among those of the present, as the dying currents of life wound and twined among the swelling currents of death.

He heard the pus from the stump of his amputated leg detaching itself in rich globules and plunging into the brimming tray set below the gangrenous fag-end of his body. These drops struck the surface of the reeking skilly with notes of much sweetness . . . sweet . . . sweet . . . a harp in the shadows. . . .

Timothy the harpmaker, beaked and gimcrack, plucking in the shadows on the unseen strings of air. . . .

A wardsman moved about pouring a stink-minifying mixture of ammonia and vinegar on the bandages, in the folds of which maggots glistened like mobile ivory. Queely Sheill heard the tray of pus being emptied into a pail, and heard the wardsman speak. What did the wardsman say in his lisping voice . . . far-off, purling. . . ?

"The slop-boy of the blasphemous and filthy . . . I've carried pails enough of the dung of felons to build a muck-heap high as Knocklofty. I've poured away enough porringers of blood cupped from the veins of highwaymen and rapers to flood the Rivulet until it washed over the Palladio. Blood!"

"Queely 'ates blood," the man with black and pustulous lips thought his gigantic tongue was saying.

"Don't you go to start a-screaming again," said the wardsman. " 'Tis Christmas, and there's ten of you in 'ere to mind, and all stinking."

"You smell it?" lisped the shadow. "I am freed today from the hospital at your very elbow. You smell it? You hear the reel of pain the fiddler tortures from the strings?"

I smells it; I smells me, thought the foul shape, I 'ears Timothy the 'arpmaker . . . pluck . . . pluck . . . pluck . . . Queely mustn't go screaming. . . .

"I am freed," the shadows lisped, "to listen to the rats in the ooze under the arch. . . ."

Pretty Dick lolled in the sediment of shadows, melting and rotting in the currents of muddier light, and the cross-currents of muddier shadows.

"I am freed to watch the pretty son of an actor write his name. . . ."

The scarred and distended tongue moved to say, to try to say, "Queely thirsts."

The wardsman had gone into the shadows, into his own

tiers of shadows of cupping scarificators, bolus knives, urethra syringes and pewter blood-porringers.

"I thirst," Queely Sheill thought he said, thought he might have screamed. Were the others screaming? He turned what used to be his head. In the shadows, in shadow night-shirt and night-cap, stockings and list slippers, another shadow patient sat on his far-off shadowy bed. . . .

Asnetha Sleep was seated on the bed . . . the shadows of firelight imitated fire in movement . . . fingers interfitted so that her two hands manufactured an orb from which the bluebird or weasel of future had gone to freedom. She . . . he . . . he on the bed . . . he lisping . . . those shadows opened their toothless mouths. . . .

"I thirst," they screamed, and Timothy fingered wildly at the harp of pus, and shadows fell and blew like enormous leaves.

"I thirst. I thirst."

Shadows came running.

"Awh, dawnce my goddess of rum, awh dawnce! Dawnce, *de*vine being, dawnce!" said a shadow.

Polidorio Smith danced. Grave and grotesque, his arms rising to the restless ceiling, he tangled the foggy skein of years gone with years to come and go. He and the mingling shadows were useless spectres that may have been dancing unknowingly for Time itself, or for Life, to halt its accumulations of ever-blackening blood, or for the undying god who grants all—Death.

While the mutilated fragment of Queely Sheill, rotting and grisly, lay screaming, it heard from time past, as it ran praying, "I prays for you: sleep hor die!", as it ran through the wind and under the constellations, under the empty Cup, The Crown that fitted no head, The Cross tilted to fall, the screaming it knew it could never make itself rising and falling with exquisite regularity. It heard too, as it ran under its halo of golden hair, that the flawless screaming was accompanied by many voices cursing in impure and irregular pattern, and several crude voices attempting in harsh song to snarl the signal of agony. Queely mustn't go on screaming and stinking and screaming at Christmas, he thought as he screamed, and as the shadows fell across him, and rebuked him, and prayed for him to die.

Presently, the screaming stopped, and all sound that he could make stopped, and twilight deepened to night, and the pile of putrescence was taken from the bed to the dead-house, and the warder told the bandy gate-porter, and he ran across Campbell Street to the Playhouse Cottage, and told Polidorio Smith, who had last heard beauty calling rashly and with merriment from the wall-top of the gaol, what it would no more call:

"Don't be hafraid. 'Ere's Queely. 'Ere 'e is!"

Although Queely Sheill died completely, five minutes before the first guest arrived at *Cindermead*, the party was a success: on that Sir Sydney Knight, Bart., had insisted, and so gently distinctly, that it could not have been otherwise. Despite success, it was enjoyed by members of the family, and some of the servants, including the gardener who was not, of course, at the party, but whose covert consumption, owing to a minor carelessness of supervision, of the best wines and spirits in Van Diemen's Land, so delightfully confused his senses that he fell asleep in a back paddock until awakened at dawn by one of the piglets eating off the lobe of his left ear.

Miss Asnetha Sleep who, from an overlapping of particular circumstances, had reasons rather than one reason for enjoying the party, proportionately enjoyed it more.

Miss Sleep, who had been born on Christmas Eve thirty years before, was celebrating her twenty-fourth birthday, for which Sir Sydney Knight gave her a miracle of a French parasol. That celebration, with the celebration of the coincidental birthday of Jesus Christ, and the celebration of the announcing of her engagement to Dr Wake made her, she said, at proper intervals and with the proper ecstatic inhalations and exhalations of peppermint, the happiest young female alive. 'Twas all—and how could't be otherwise!—she said, the most positively *perfect* ending . . . as in a nice, nice, *nice* novel . . . to the *happiest* year of her *life*! She was persuaded by naughtier teases among the ladies, because of the threefold nature of her happiness, against her will and with tinkling modulations of the gayest protests, to drink a third glass of claret punch which was, admittedly, and rightly, a mild beverage. It was, she declared, sipping like a finch, quite *wickedly* strong. In a circle of scented ladies, who sparklingly declared themselves *positively* also so, she declared she was—la, la, la!—tipsy as a jockey, and quite a *toperess*. She re-polished an old dream she had had success with twice in Brighton, once in Bath, once in London, and once, privately, in *Cindermead*, and presented it as a vision of the night before. Lady Knight, overhearing in graciously passing, said that Asnetha honey was a provoking puss not to have told her immediately on waking that morning. The circle of ladies in satin shoes . . . Sir Sydney had been much more than careful about the composition of that circle . . . sparkled more at the dream, and squealed stylishly not too much, and were utterly helpless in their visible new gloves and unseen, frayed but still potent garters. Each agitated her fan which was more exquisite than anyone else's more gracefully than anyone else, and told each other loudly enough for Miss Sleep to hear that dear Asney was the *wittiest* woman in Hobart Town, in the *world*. Her hideous gown with vulgar and outdated Donna Maria sleeves excited their attention for it was of Sylvestrine a horrid artificial silk made from wood and, they said, perfectly *ravishing*. It *maddened* them all, they all said to her, to frenzies of *jealousy*. Thrice in the course of the evening she had ostentatious muscular spasms, just as though she were not in company, but not even the startled Mrs Creamly, who had no *right* to drop her fan, noticed those active antics.

Just as Sir Sydney Knight's *breloque* remained plumb and an ornament of tasteful design among more skittish and less suitable *breloques*, so he remained plumb along the more skittish gentlemen. Since he had never looked, sounded or been elevated to be more distinguished, he was firmly deprecating about the fact that he was celebrating his advancement which had, his manner intimated, come to him as a surprise. During a quadrille, he looking virile, the Governor's lady, in her French accent which became more roguishly broken as the party proceeded, complimented him on his pomade and teased him until he confessed its name so that she could surprise Ees Excellency and Ees Excellency's wheeskers by a geeft of some which, everyone who overheard understood, between the lines, would be provided, one dozen pots, by Sir Sydney.

Lady Knight or Rose or dear Rose looked younger than even the few ladies who liked rather than esteemed her cared to think she was. Chandeliers suited her; she persisted in glittering like one under one or other of them. The ladies were, since they expected themselves to be, agog about the newest invitable arrival in the colony who was handsome beyond imagination, and a bachelor young enough for mothers to pinch the elbows of old enough eligible daughters in warning to continue sparkling and to keep their mouths in tinier pouts than possible. Lady Knight, the ladies discovered, did not think him *quite* as handsome as they did . . . she had, they assumed, less reason to. She agreed with those ladies who thought his curls natural rather than with those who *wondered*, though she inclined to think that she did not head-over-heels admire a man with curls. Although he was tallish, she announced, her fan aiding her, a preference for taller men. It went without saying that Sir Sydney was taller in a maturely considered modest way. She was not, however, less gracious to an insufficiency of two inches when her bracelet of linked Wedgwood plaques, actually bought in Charles Street, Mayfair, tiresomely undid itself, and he, handsome and curly, who happened to be nearest her and her ejaculated vexation, was able to do it up in the most charming long-winded way while several sparkling daughters with tiny pouts were pinched by gloved fingertips on their gloved arms for not having thought to feign the accident Lady Knight had had. He was taller than she, bending his curls towards her under the largest central chandelier.

On the requests of several more volatile ladies, Orfée Maka was permitted an appearance of just a few seconds for fifteen minutes. Those requests had been wisely foreseen, perhaps willed diplomatically, by Sir Sydney who had asked his cousin, the future Mrs Wake, the day before the party, to see that the boy was bathed, combed . . . or whatever it was was done to his flocculence, dressed, and ready on demand. Since fame had come to the boy under his baptismal name he, Teapot, had indicated detestation of his nickname and was found ravishing under the chandeliers as Orfée, and Orfée's coat was ravishing, and Orfée's ear-rings were ravishing, and all the ladies said they were desolated that evening turbans were no longer in, for Orfée's was ravishing, and Orfée was a very brave boy. He said he was a very brave boy with shining black eyes. Before he was lovingly dismissed by Lady Knight he said that Dr Wake was a good man, and had given him a horse for Christmas. When he had gone everyone said he was very brave and perfectly intelligent, and superior to the unclothed, degraded and ferocious cannibals who had been cleared from the island.

Miss Sleep's maidservant Megan had been found, several days before, to be most inconveniently and selfishly half-way through a pregnancy but would admit of no lover by name. That made her condition more reprehensible: when the turmoil of Christmas and picnics and race-meetings and New Year was over she would naturally be dismissed.

Ferris the groom was suspected of being the Welsh hussy's Holy Ghost, but unjustly, for he was too experienced a man, and had fornicated with too many women, to be so carelessly immoral. In any case, guilty or not of impregnation, he was not pregnant, and was too good a groom to lose.

Romney, than whom only Sir Sydney was more dignified in posture that night, suffered the rheumatic back, which stiffened that posture, with the aplomb of a bishop, for he was a snob than whom only Sir Sydney, that night, was more snobbish.

The younger spinsters wore pearls, the married females wore emeralds, amethysts or gold snake bracelets. Most wore aigrettes of diamonds, or apparent diamonds, to one side of the head, and in the form of barley ears, corn or feathers, from which ascended real feathers, all ostrich and curled, except the Governor's Lady's. Hers were peacock which her hostess declared her first love, and, behind her fan, would wear except that Sir Sydney was *un petit peu* superstitious. The Governor's Lady complimented her reciprocally on her French accent.

Nothing was spilled, nothing alarming said or done, nothing was broken and no surface scratched, no jewel slipped its claws, no truth its fetters. Lady Knight's Wedgwood bracelet alone undid itself and once only, for once was enough.

Dr Wake limped about, as twinkling and witty and manly and captivating and beautifully dressed as only a well-to-do and cold-blooded fortune-hunter needs be. He had sawed off Queely Sheill's leg nearly a fortnight before in the Criminal Hospital.

Too big to burn in the incinerator, the leg had been heaved over the hospital wall so that it bounced down the low sandstone cliff and splashed into the Rivulet. It had moved slowly to the Palladio arch, and had caught there.

It had been a hot hot day. The night was cooler, but still hot, even at *Cindermead*.

A harpist played sadly and badly as he customarily did at Government House, smiling secretly and plumply the while, and gave the party, to which no one with the most hair-line taint had received an invitation, its final *cachet*.

The gate-porter who had run bandy-legged across Campbell Street from the Criminal Hospital to Playhouse Cottage with the news of Queely Sheill's death had brought, it seemed, among the keys that clashed at his belt, a key to unlock cries of extraordinary power and quality, the first from Polidorio Smith, next from John Death Sheill when he was aroused from a stupor of rum.

But there is always an end to cries, and to tears, the more the sooner.

The mind must give over its delicious dream of eternal grief as of eternal love or eternal youth or eternal innocence. The body, that mind's wretched victim, does not care a whit for grief or love or youth or innocence. Eternity is not for it. Stop draining my reservoir of tears, says the body, and fill my belly with lamb chops; stop watching the door for one you know will not come, and sleep to refresh the burning eyes for one who will come; stop calling harshly to who cannot hear, and softly address the anxious pedlar, the next lover, the gin-palace barmaid. Bathe me, warm me, fill me, empty me, keep me alive! If you have married grief, and the rumpus of consummation is by, you must take your wife decently walking.

When the two bereaved men at last came out, silently, exhausted, they moved through the thick dust across Campbell Street, and stood for a little while on the Palladio before going to *The Shades*. A voice they had once heard might have spoken but did not:

"Never a tear, never a tear, poor 'earts, poor darling 'earts. Be roaring and reeling! Buy grog for hevery ligby and ganymede and gutter-blood from Jericho to June. Be 'appy! Never a tear! I don't judge no-one! The little birds and whatall don't fret habout tomorrow, nor shall I. Sleep hor die! You mustn't fret over Queely. Them who're frightened of nettles don't piss in meadows. I ain't frightened."

From every gin-crib, rum-shack and grog-shop in Hobart Town gushed the bawlings and whinnyings of the celebration of Christmas. From Nature, eternally at her lewd balance sheet, could have come nothing but a smirk of approval. From heaven came nothing but what its ears had tasted and rejected: the echoes of glory of ribaldry.

It was a hot night.

It stank of the slaughter-house and its moaning plume of blowflies, it stank of the Rivulet and its simmering rafts of maggots, it stank most of Queely Sheill's leg six feet beneath their noses.

The fat man and the tall man could bear the sickening smell and each other's reeking silence no longer. How boring, selfish and fatiguing is another's grief!

They left the parapet, and walked across to *The Shades*; turned their backs on the scent of death, and opened the door on the stench of life.

The Shades, like a world's mouth gaping to show the rum-swollen tongue and dripping molars and song-raked purple gullet, belched thunderingly, once. Immediately, as though gulping back its own drunken horror, the mouth shut, and Campbell Street was empty.

Campbell Street was empty for a moment.

A shadow ran in the dust. It had left a room, it had descended stairs, it had passed through the open door of No. 8 Campbell Street.

The shadow disregarded the cockchafers and moths, and leapt on shadowed paws to the parapet, and watched with its cat's eyes the door it had escaped through. It had fled without fuss or any gesture of recrimination the other living being who had become distasteful to it, and, it knew, was no longer of use to it.

Inch by inch, Judas Griffin Vaneleigh left the cat's room; breath by shallow breath, descended the cat's stairs for the last time; left No. 8 Campbell Street that hot Christmas Eve, that year, for ever; second by second, crept along walls and fences towards St. Mary's Hospital, and the cat on the Palladio coping watched dispassionately in the lamp-light the bowed-over shade.

"*Sir! Sir, are you—are you wretched?*"

I who creep and creep, thought Judas Griffin Vaneleigh, my fermenting brain oppressed as yet by its own riches, I who creep through under these cataracts of incoherent sounds, this iniquitous joviality, was once of a giddy, flighty disposition ever wiled away by new and flashing gauds. Wise, frolicsome, temperate, furious, tragical, comical, helter-skelter—one thing down and another come on—the every-place-with-gusto-enjoying Judas! I held my rushlights to the sun! Now, the last movement of the last quadrille, and I am tired. I was long ago tired to death of skipping from one thing to another . . . tired . . . to . . . death. . . .

"*Ain't you un'appy, sir? Ain't you wretched?*"

I creep away from this age of vulgarity, from the festering whispers, the smiling deliberate cruelty. I creep away from those with their veins filled with mud, those with the microscopic vision of the fly for filth, those crowding and squeezing and riding upon each other's backs, those cutting each other to pieces with squeamish bigotry.

You must forgive them. They don't know what they say. They're 'appy. They mean no 'arm.

Oh, dark condition of blind humanity!

No! No 'arm comes of 'uman feeling, no matter what!

My soul entertains no affection for it . . . how can it?

Queely hassures you no 'arm. No 'arm, no 'arm!

Does the farmer love the unseen wind that overturns his barns, devastates his granaries?

No 'arm! I sees your 'eart, sir.

Once I swore that the world which scouted me should see that I would be revenged. Then, let it see to that; let it see!

You 'ave a 'eart, sir. It 'ides.

I've done with the odious task of finding fault—it curses doubly finder and findee—I creep away. I am nothing.

You 'ave a 'eart, sir.

To where do I creep?

Ah! A very queer thing how materially terror is increased by obscurity, the instincts snuff like a horse the coming terrors, the longer one looks the deeper the terrors grow . . . muddled lights . . . opaque shadows . . . grief-telling waters . . . Or is this vision from a mood of mental atrocity, a fearful exhalation of the brain, creating another atmosphere of sooty portentous darkness through which one's past images throng in hideous dumbness like phantoms doing unearthly deeds . . . ?

Queely 'ates blood . . . 'ates blood . . . 'ates blood. . . .

I feel my personal identity annihilated . . . I am nothing . . . and the world has abated to less than a musical snuff-box playing half its measure of pigmy sweetness. . . .

Yet, even fire and water have sympathetic particles, and lie open to a sort of reconcilement . . . Can it be that . . . excepting the body . . . nothing, however subtle, evaporates during the transfusion and that, ere another hour, another week, another month, whenever I die, Judas Griffin Vaneleigh will have mingled with the past eternity and be flying on the swift wings of a new reputation to the north, the east, the south and the west?

From the north and the east and the south and the west, unpredictably, and for an unpredictable brevity of time, the dramships blotting with outspilt ruddiness the dark of the town were merely grumbling in their scalded and ruptured throats.

He reached the door of St. Mary's Hospital.

Before he could knock, before he could fall, the door opened, swung silently in as though those within, who had not expected him, were nevertheless ready for him.

Something not tangible in the body, thought Judas Griffin Vaneleigh, something only to be approached in the spirit.

Queely tells 'is 'eart what 'is 'eart tells 'im.

I am nothing.

Do we really individually exist? he thought, as he retreated beneath the lintel.

Are we?

Or is matter nothing but an idea? This life a swoon of the spirit and the grave a waking?

The door closed behind his body and his thoughts.

No human being moved on the slope of Campbell Street for that moment, that night, that summer, that year.

June–August, 1960,
Hedley, Vic., Australia.